TEMPEST

A.G. Karine

ISBN: 978-1-7377591-3-3

*For my husband
and his unwavering love*

Chapter One

THE FIRE CRACKLED and popped, spitting embers onto the hearth. Lord Frederick Tours shifted his feet to the rug, staring into the flames as they danced hypnotically. There was a log in the back that looked as if it might collapse—it was nearly burned through and perched precariously on top of another. He waited in eager anticipation, swirling the glass of wine in his hand.

It was past midnight, in the early hours of the morning. The night was dead and quiet, and the fire was the only sound in the room.

Tours was tired—his body was growing old and did not appreciate the lack of sleep. It had been a long day filled with endless meetings, appointments, and parties. The king's health had rapidly deteriorated and it was only a matter of time before he would pass. The king's son—the only surviving heir—would be too young to rule, and so Tours was charged with his upbringing and protection. He was the only one who knew where the boy was hidden.

It would be so easy to remove him, but that was treason. Treason was a risky game to play without everything in order. There was still so much to do—still so much that was taking his time.

Aedin's disappearance had created more administrative troubles than he had anticipated. Trade deals on Lailan had temporarily ceased without the approval of their lord, and the backlog was becoming a regular annoyance. His replacement—the newly minted Lord Cabot—was a headache, taking forever to get up to speed and continually hounding Tours for favor appointments for his friends.

It was a constant struggle. With a frustrated grin, Tours silently wished for Aedin—it had been so much easier. But no.

The pigeon had arrived on Lailan as planned, and the Rhidge had set off to the fortress a day later. Although he'd wished with all of his heart to join them, Tours had reluctantly returned to Radiance. Duty called, and his skills were needed elsewhere.

He waited each day with bated breath—counting down the minutes until the Rhidge should return.

Since becoming the Director of the Rhidge, Tours felt as though the hours and days flew by. He thought back to his youth when he'd felt invincible, when he could go for days without sleep, enduring endless hours of training, and still manage to defeat his opponents. Time had moved slowly then. Now, he felt as though there was never enough of it to accomplish what he wished. Perhaps this was the worst part of age—not the slow deterioration of the body but the sudden quickening of time.

Tours felt a presence outside and heard the door open and shut quietly. He exhaled in relief but didn't move from his chair. "Please tell me some good news," he grumbled as Bela moved in front of the fire to bow respectfully.

"My lord." The Rhidge clasped her hands behind her back and stared down at him with pitiless eyes. "I'm afraid… that I do not."

Tours steeled himself as he drained the wine and set aside the glass. He pulled out the dagger at his hip and twirled it softly in his hands. That helped him feel a bit better. In the bated silence, she watched him carefully—with a slightly crinkling of the brows. An almost imperceptible fear.

"Well?" he said gruffly, meeting her gaze.

"We lost two. A third is gravely wounded and being attended by the medicators. Aedin and Gwyneth escaped. We were… attacked."

"An older *former* Rhidge and an untrained Gifted *killed* two of you and gravely wounded another?" Tours repeated with a look of incredulity. He coughed a scathing laugh. "*You* should know better—"

"My lord, there were others," Bela whispered, her eyes growing wide. "There were other Gifted we didn't know."

The dagger was suddenly still in his hands. "Who?"

"I… don't know. They appeared suddenly—only minutes after we broke through the fortress doors. They must have known. They were dressed in an unfamiliar cloth."

His heart pounded as he scanned her face. Unknown Gifted—it was impossible. Unless…

"They took Gwyneth and drugged her. I was locked in combat, but I saw them take Aedin's body as well. We watched a boat with silver sails leave the shore—heading east."

Tours digested this with a grimace. "And what of Jon and Rebecca?"

"We searched the fortress twice over but could not find Rebecca. Jon surrendered and pleaded to stay at the fortress. We drugged him with flussidik and brought him back with us."

Jon.

A sudden shot of energy brightened his eyes. He began twirling the dagger again. "Good work," Tours murmured, watching the firelight dance on the hard angles of her face. At least he would have one thing to celebrate.

But the escape of Aedin and Gwyneth was concerning. Tours wondered if they were aided, but then why drug her? It sounded more like they were captured—but by those on the eighth island? He recalled the stories with a shiver. Perhaps the island had finally risen from their great slumber.

"Anything else?" he asked quietly, watching her shift onto the balls of her feet. She was like a wound coil about to spring—eager to leave his presence.

"No, my lord."

The log in the fireplace fell with a satisfying crunch. Sparks exploded upwards as Tours rose with a sigh, sheathing his dagger. "Lead me to him."

They exited his rooms without making a sound. The halls were still and empty.

Walking quickly to the left, Bela pushed at a section of the ornately carved wood of the wall. Mounted with a silver sconce, the wall swung inwards to reveal a dark passage. She lit a flame in the palm of her hand, stepping aside respectfully to allow Tours inside, before shutting the door behind them with a soft click.

With the room illuminated, Tours removed his doublet and rolled up the sleeves of his black shirt. He pulled on a pair of gloves—the leather had once been soft but was now hardened with dark stains from use. Flexing his fingers with a delighted shiver, he thought of what was to come.

Tours tightened his fist and motioned for Bela to continue.

A deadly and indiscriminate cold seeped into his skin. Their footsteps were soundless against the stone floors. It was pitch-black inside the Rhidge—there were no windows to allow sunlight or prying eyes. Torches lining the wall sprang to life as they advanced, extinguishing when they passed. The hallway doors were closed, and the air was thick and stale. There was the sound of a sudden scream from somewhere on their left—they continued unperturbed as it was quickly silenced.

Bela stopped at the end of the hall and put her hand on the door handle. She paused and then pushed inwards to reveal a black room. A torch on the opposite wall crackled to illuminate the scene.

A large body was curled in the corner, face shielded with his bound hands. Tours crinkled his nose at the smell of urine and blood. Another Rhidge sat motionless in the corner, watching them. Bela nodded to him—he stood and quietly left the room, closing the door.

Tours walked towards the body on the floor and crouched just above. There was slight movement—he was still breathing. That was a good sign.

"It's been a long time," he crooned softly. Tours couldn't resist the grin that spread across his face.

The body shifted, waking from sleep or unconsciousness, and tightened into a ball.

"Did you miss me?" Tours whispered as Bela settled into the chair by the door.

There was no response.

Tours counted to five and then touched the hilt of his dagger, drawing it slowly from its sheath. The sound lingered painfully in the small room.

There was a sudden movement as Jon threw out his hands. Tours stepped back, deflecting the blow with a wave and easily regaining his balance. "Jon," he murmured silkily. "You should know better."

Jon's blue eyes were bright in the dim light of the torch. His face was bloodied and bruised, but his jaw was firmly set. Shifting his weight to a seated position, Jon winced in pain. Testing his mouth carefully, he finally whispered, "I thought I knew."

Tours gave a smug smile. "And yet—fate would bring us here again," he said simply, fingering the tip of his dagger in his gloved hands. "I heard you had a lovely visit with your friends. It must have been so heartwarming to be *reunited*."

"It was." Jon's voice was hoarse as he assumed an expression of casualness. His lips cracked with the movement. "If only we'd had a barrel of ale to accompany the visit."

"*Well*," Tours said with relish. "You did your part and alerted us, which was very kind of you. However—the small fact that they *escaped* does not make this an ideal situation."

Jon shrugged. "I had no control over that."

"Did you not?" Tours frowned, flipping the dagger thoughtfully. "Because it sounds as if it was too easy for them to escape. And—to make *your* situation worse—I lost two Rhidge."

"I may have fought, but I didn't kill. You trained Aedin—you know what he's capable of."

"All I hear are excuses." Tours shook his head. "Where did they go?"

"How should I know?" Jon said carelessly, itching the side of his face with the back of his hands. The action smeared more dirt across his already filthy skin.

"There were other Gifted. How did they get there?"

"They flew across the sea," Jon offered with a wry grin.

Tours hit Jon with a wave of air. His head knocked back against the stones with a sickening thud. Jon's lips spread into a cringing smile at the sudden pain. He paused, swallowing and clearing his throat. "That hurt," he croaked.

"Good," Tours replied sweetly. "Did Aedin ever discuss the eighth island?"

Jon rolled his shoulders, adjusting his position. "Not to my knowledge, but he knew about it."

"Did they have contact with the other Gifted previously?"

"No," he answered with confidence. "They had no further plans after escaping to the fortress."

Tours wasn't sure whether this answer was good or bad news. He eyed Jon carefully. "And what of your… *wife*? Where is she?"

Jon stared at Tours evenly. "I don't know."

Tours knew he was lying, but he didn't have time to pursue this line of inquiry. Rebecca was the least of their worries. "Well then," he sighed dramatically. "We should get this over with."

Jon's eyes shifted to the dagger in Tours' hand. "Will you please kill me then? If not, I should like to go home."

"Home?" Tours laughed. "How sweet."

Jon's body visibly eased away from Tours as he advanced. He shakily rose to his feet, stepping backwards. "You know"—the words rushed desperately from his mouth—"Aedin's wife has incredible power. Did you know that?"

"I did," Tours said softly, without stopping.

Jon backpedaled around the room, desperate to avoid the steady advance. "She can push down a grown man as if he's a leaf—multiple times! She even overpowered Aedin—"

"How interesting," Tours said indifferently. He held out his hand, "Give me your arm."

"Isn't that more of a formality?" Jon shot him a teasing smile. "I'm just here for a short visit."

Bela rose from her chair and walked over to Jon. He felt her coming and shot his arm backwards. She struggled and fought against the wall of air.

"Jon." Tours smirked. "It will be *so* good to have you back."

Jon raised a long leg in a kick, but Tours sidestepped the blow and lifted his dagger to Jon's chin. Jon stiffened in response, his Gift growing weaker by the second. The wall of air became a soft breeze that Bela easily broke through, pulling down his chained hands.

His prisoner was tired—Tours eyed the circles under Jon's eyes with patient pleasure. There was no rush.

Tours brought his dagger down to the sleeve of Jon's right arm and cut through the fabric. He pushed it up to reveal the scar on his bicep—the "R." It stretched across the skin with a sinister gleam of silver. With a thoughtful gaze, Tours ran his hands along the metal of his dagger—the blade flickered to life in the dim light of the room.

With relish, he pressed the tip of the blade against the soft skin of the scar. It opened in response, blood gathering quickly at the site of the incision. Jon hissed in response, his jaw tight and eyes closed.

"Oh come now," Tours cajoled. "You're quite out of practice. This won't hurt a bit."

As his blade retraced the long spine and curves of the "R," the only sounds were the breaking of skin and the flickering flame of the torch. Bela watched Tours' blade with a soft gaze, her eyes wide and unseeing. The muscles at Jon's shoulders flexed at the pain as the blood began to seep down his elbow, staining his shirt, and pooling onto the floor.

"There." Tours stepped back, appearing satisfied with his handiwork. He wiped the blade on the dark cloth of his shirt and re-sheathed the dagger.

Jon was finally quiet—he had run out of words. His head hung limply as he refused to meet Tours' gaze.

Tours smirked. "You didn't Dream this one, did you? And yet, life is full of surprises."

Jon swallowed and turned slowly as Bela stepped away, allowing him to pass. He settled in a corner against the wall, curling his knees into his chest, his chained hands clinking on the floor.

The right arm hung limp, the hand lifeless against the floor.

The "R" was bright and gleaming in the shadows.

Bela opened the door, extending her palm to light the darkness of the hallway.

"Welcome home," Tours said softly, extinguishing the torch and depriving the room of light. He left the room and shut the door.

Chapter Two

WHEN I REGAINED consciousness, the first thing I noticed was my body—or the fact that I had no control over it.

It was the strangest feeling—as though my muscles had been liquified and asking anything of them was impossible. Even my eyelids refused to flutter, and my tongue lay slack in an open jaw. Only my heart remained, miraculously, pounding in my chest.

I was sprawled over a cool, hard floor. In the darkness of my mind, thoughts began to frantically whirl, clearing away the cobwebs of oblivion and attempting to make sense of what had happened.

The Rhidge had breached the fortress.

My heart raced as I remembered the ring of metal and the shadow of feral shapes.

And then they had appeared.

Images flittered through my barely conscious mind. The green eyes of my captor. A silver sword jutting through the body of the young girl. A cloth that absorbed the colors of the night.

But they weren't from the Empire.

I had been drugged—I connected the cold prick at the base of my neck with my comatose state—and I didn't know how long I'd been unconscious. Depending on where I was, it could have been minutes, hours, or days.

I endeavored to open my eyes again—satisfied to find that they flickered open for a second—enough to make out a distant, white abyss. The firm and unyielding ground was cold, a hard slab of stone against my head.

My ears strained for any sign of noise, any lingering breath other than my own. Panic rose in my throat as I forced my eyes open wider—where was Aedin? Where was *I*?

Unsuccessfully, I tried to stand. Twisting around to lie on my stomach was hard enough and left me tearing up in frustration, gritting my teeth at my feeble muscles. I forced my fingers to flex, focusing on utilizing the minute movements in my body. A subtle tingling echoed through my nerves—I was satisfied to find I could shift my body to the side.

But I only got as far as planting my hands on the ground before the white walls spun; I shook from the effort, collapsing once more. Perhaps I would die here. The quiet pull of oblivion was beckoning.

I closed my eyes, my cheek resting on the cool floor, wishing for the dizziness to fade before it ignited nausea.

I searched for the familiar thread—the feeling of my Gift—but my blood felt muddied and dull. As if there was nothing in my veins. I was powerless.

Eyes pricking again, I exhaled angrily. Anger—yes, that would keep me alive. Breathe. Collect yourself. Relax. You won't die. I won't die. I wasn't going to die—

The sound of an opening door was an avalanche of sound that echoed through the room; and it was followed by a pair of crisp footsteps. Repeating the previous words over and over in my mind, I let my body relax, closed my eyes, and forced a complacent expression, fighting panic as I heard them draw closer.

The footsteps stopped not far from where I lay.

"She should be awake by now," a voice said in a whisper, as if not wanting to disturb me.

"She is."

I recognized the second man's curt tone from the night of my capture. As the words left his mouth, something grabbed my shoulders, pulling me from the floor.

An instinctive cry escaped my throat as my eyes flew open. I was hovering above the ground—my slack body suspended in the air. The white walls were solid, blank pieces of stone. Thick and clean and lit by torches that spiraled with flames of blue, green, red, and gold. The Gift.

The pair of men eyed me skeptically. They were both tall, their bodies lined with coiled muscle visible even beneath their tunics —one with thick golden hair and the other with bright scarlet. The latter one stepped forward, his emerald eyes narrowed in assessment.

"I thought you would be… taller," he stated coolly, cocking his head as I floated helplessly.

I searched my blood for the power once more—hoping to release myself by any means possible—but my Gift remained quiet and subdued. Panic tightened my throat; I was at his mercy. He watched me float with a mixed expression of eager anticipation and suspicion.

Testing my jaw, I found it could move, and so I said, "W-W… Where a-am… I?"

He ignored my question, folding his hands diplomatically behind his back. "Are you Gwyneth Aedin from the island of Lailan?"

"Y-Yes," I managed in a whisper. "Who are you?"

They were both older, perhaps middle-aged, but their bodies held a youthful vigor, an ancient grace marking them as worthy opponents. The cloth of their tunics glittered dimly and shimmered with a multitude of colors—one moment silver, the next a muted sage or light blue. It was exhausting to watch, so I focused instead on their faces.

The red-haired man inclined his head gracefully. "I am Rowyn, son of Reynolds. Captain of the Guard."

The blonde man remained distant and wary—one hand on the sword at his hip. His sharp jaw was fixed into a firm line of dislike. I was certain he would disapprove of whatever action I took, so I turned my gaze again to Rowyn.

"Can you please let me down?" I asked quietly, flexing my feet and preparing for the ground.

In response, my body was gently lowered until my boots touched the stone. I braced my knees and rubbed my arms—my entire body was sore from my shoulders to a particular area on my chest. I recalled his forceful push with a wince, wondering how badly my skin was bruised.

My legs were shaking but steady—no waves of nausea roiled in my gut. The stone walls remained still, and I could feel my blood begin to clear.

"You have been drugged and taken captive by the island of Iselleden," Rowyn announced, placing a hand on his buckled sword. It was a casual reminder of his place, and mine. "You will not attempt to escape, nor use your Gift to harm us."

Iselleden. My heart pounded in realization. "The eighth island?" I blurted.

"Yes," he replied as if it was obvious. "We are the last bastion of the Gifted—the land that is untouched and pure."

A shot of relief coursed through my body—we'd done it. We'd escaped—

We.

My mouth went dry. "Where is Aedin?" I whispered as the thought suddenly crashed through my mind. "Where is my husband?"

I whirled around, searching the small white room as if he would appear. Seeing the pure terror on my face, the blonde man tightened his grip on his sword.

Rowyn scowled. "You will come with us—"

"Where is he?" Panic threatened to close my throat.

"You will come with us," Rowyn repeated his words slowly, as if talking to a child. "Everything will be explained in the morning. For now, you must regain your strength—"

"Please!" A cry bubbled in my chest. "Where is he? Was he taken by the Rhidge—"

"Don't say that name!" Rowyn snapped, wincing as his body stiffened. "Your *assassin* husband has been drugged and will remain in captivity until we have decided… what to do." He pinched the bridge of his straight nose with a grimace.

"Decide *what*?" I snarled, tensing my body. "We are being hunted by the Rh—*them*. You can't send him back—"

Rowyn shot me a look that said otherwise. "He is not supposed to be here," he hissed, his green eyes glinting dangerously.

"*Supposed* to? You have to help us—"

"We did!" At my words, the blonde man sprang forward with a growl. "We fought them and lost a *life* in the process." The sound of ringing metal resounded in the room as he unsheathed his sword in one swift motion. His blue eyes were furious as he spat, "Your *husband* killed Loran—"

"Celion." Rowyn held out a hand as Celion stopped in his tracks—his knuckles were white around the sword's hilt.

I held his stare as my stomach dropped—Aedin had killed one of their own. This wasn't a good start.

"He didn't know…" I protested lowly. "I'm sure he didn't—"

Celion opened his mouth to retort when Rowyn interrupted us. "He will be punished for his crimes—*whether* or not the action was maliciously intended," he added as he saw my lips ready to hurl more vitriol.

Rowyn looked at Celion meaningfully—he lowered his sword and grudgingly re-sheathed the weapon.

Whether from the sudden panic or anger, I felt the familiar thickening and lively sensation dance in my blood. Like a lifeline, the power curled through my bones, renewing my will and strengthening my senses. I pulled forth my Gift, flexing my hands with anticipation—

Rowyn looked at me knowingly. "*Don't*," he said scathingly. "Don't push our generosity."

I reluctantly grimaced: I was outnumbered. There was no point in testing my wasted strength on the slim chance of taking them out. Even if I were to succeed, two to one, I was unlikely to find Aedin in an unfamiliar place or make it off the island. Alive.

With some regret, I let the Gift drift back into my blood. "How did you find us?" I asked hollowly, watching Celion's anger decrease to a simmer.

"The Dreams," Rowyn said softly. "But… everything will be explained in the morning. For now, you must rest. Please follow us."

He turned on his heel and opened a door, gesturing me forward. My breathing quickened as I numbly followed.

Celion stalked from behind, his hand never leaving the hilt of his sword.

I entered a hall lined with a troop of waiting guards in identical garb. There were a dozen or more. All were tall—Jon's height—with strong faces and stern eyes. They eyed me with incredulity as waves of the Gift radiated from their bodies through the small space.

I was overpowered. And still no sign of Aedin.

Wordlessly, Rowyn led the way and I followed obediently, the line of guards filing to flank my sides.

As we left the bright lights of the white stone room and entered the night-time air, I wondered how many days I'd been out. I didn't know how far Iselleden was from the fortress—it could have been at least three or four days. The thought was unsettling, and my stomach ached in hunger.

The air was crisp—a light breeze brushed my face as we walked along a darkened path illuminated by the light of the moon. But it was enough to make out the hills, the moonlit blades of grass and faraway lights in the distance.

I had never before seen such an expanse of wild beauty. We were on a hill, one of many that nestled a habitable valley. Looking down from the dirt path, I saw lakes—little puddles shining silver, reflecting the light of the full moon—surrounded by rolling hills, nestling a sprawling town in a comforting embrace.

Houses dotted the ground, some packed together in larger earthly complexes, bright and shining festively. Others sat alone in the blackness, flickering like delicate candles among the trees.

The whispering breeze and crickets were the only sounds that accompanied our progress underneath the starlit sky.

But for all the beauty before me, it was nothing compared to the power surrounding my body. It was as if I stood in a room full of Gifted and felt part of a giant swarm. It wasn't a force pressing against my body but an expanding from within. The air *filled* me—I nearly smiled as I inhaled—with a warmth that tickled my skin. It was as if the land itself were exhaling.

The hairs on my arm stood on end—I had never before felt so alive.

Nobody dared to break the silence, the grass alongside the path whispering as we passed. The guards moved around me with ease, their light tunics glistening silver and violet beneath the starry sky. From my view behind Rowyn's tall form, I could see the beginnings of a structure rise from beyond the crest of a hill.

First a tower, then a sprawling complex of low buildings, the stone walls seeming to glow silver with starlight. Easily five times the size of the villa on Lailan, they twisted and turned with the natural curves of the land. It was hauntingly beautiful.

"The Haven," Rowyn answered my wordless question, glancing back without breaking his long stride. "You'll be staying in the residence here."

I arched a brow at the name. We had sought haven here, but was it that to us?

Our feet hit paved stones that led us through a tall arch, supported by caryatids twisted with blooming flowers. We were in a terraced garden overlooking the town below—even in the night air I smelled sage, lavender, and the rich earth. The grand courtyard before the tower was empty, void of people in the late hour.

Rowyn led us through the opposite building and into a winding hall. A silver light illuminated our path—I looked up in wonder and saw that the ceiling was made of glass. Clean and unadorned, the stone walls twisted and blurred together in sameness occasionally interspersed by doors.

Rowyn stopped before a door that looked the same as the others. He opened it and beckoned me through.

It was a single room, with glass doors thrown open to the night breeze and view. A fire crackled merrily in a hearth, surrounded by a simple linen couch and chairs. Tucked away in a corner of the room was a large bed, neatly made and covered with pillows. It was a far cry from our simple straw mattress in the fortress and more similar to the villa on Lailan.

Was this my prison?

Once more, Rowyn answered my silent question. "This is where you'll be staying. Tomorrow morning, I will fetch you for the Council meeting. In the meantime, someone will bring you some food."

I swallowed self-consciously. Perhaps he'd heard my stomach on the walk.

"*Please.*" I decided to try one last time. "Where is Aedin?"

The other guards remained in the hall, but Celion stood in the doorway, his arms folded with a challenging frown. Rowyn turned his back on me and headed to the door.

"Please!"

They left the room, and the door shut with finality.

It wasn't the answer I'd wanted. Shutting out panic, I forced myself to count to ten before I tried the door. It was locked, and the knob vibrated with the Gift.

Frustrated, I walked to the open doors of the balcony and looked out. High, arching mountains soared in the distance, like sentinels guarding the nestled valley. I leaned against the railing and looked down—two guards were lounging below, watching me passively and exchanging quiet words. The railing vibrated with the Gift—I couldn't move past the edge.

There were no other exits, doors or windows. Just a simple bathroom and a bedroom—my prison.

Cursing low under my breath, I collapsed on the sofa and logically examined my possibilities. I didn't know where Aedin was being kept. Even if I tried to escape to find him, they would likely stop me before I got very far. And in my weakened state, I wasn't stupid enough to even try to fight them…

There was little I could do.

Rubbing my face, I inhaled and grimaced. I hadn't bathed in some time. I supposed there was—at least—one thing I *could* do.

Entering the small bathroom, I drew a bath and peeled off my dark shirt, pants, and boots, folding the clothes and carefully placing them aside. The uniform of the Rhidge. Despite the cruel history of the cloth, I felt oddly attached to the garments. Like they were evidence of my strength—and a lifeline to my husband.

When the bath was full, I sat in the water and scrubbed my body. It took some time for the dirt and soap to leave my skin and cloud the water. When I was finished, I dried myself with a towel and opened the door. To the smell of—my stomach grumbled again—

Food.

It was sitting on the low table in front of the couch.

Still in my towel, I crouched on the cushion and grabbed as much as I could in my hands and stuffed it in my mouth. I almost moaned at the taste, the textures, just having *something* to eat.

Forcing myself to slow, I focused on savoring each bite and almost didn't notice the pile of fabric next to me on the sofa.

It was a silver cloth, neatly folded, and shimmering in the light of the fireplace.

I touched it—and a sparkle of colors alighted where my fingers traced, sending a ripple of waves through the fabric. Immediately I pulled back my hand in terror.

The dress had *moved*.

The ripple faded, and the cloth lay dull and still again on the couch.

Heart pounding, I wiped my hands on my towel and hesitantly reached out a hand. When my fingers were an inch away, the fabric begin to flutter, gently reaching up towards my outstretched hand, eagerly responding to my movements. My mouth went dry—it was impossible.

With a wince, I placed my entire hand on the fabric, waiting for a sudden pain or reaction.

But there was no pain, only a barrage of color.

In the warm light of the fire, purples, golds, and blues spun and sparkled underneath my palm, dancing and shimmering. It was just like the guards' tunics—so this was the fashion on Iselleden. Mystified and slightly amused, I ran my hands up and down the fabric and saw the colors swirl with delight.

I held up the cloth—it was a long pair of pants and a short-sleeved shirt. Gingerly, I dropped my towel and pulled on the clothes, the cloth sliding across my clean skin. The fabric was baggy against my frame but slowly settled on my body, shrinking to fit snugly around my waist and shoulders.

"Incredible," I breathed, twisting and turning. It stretched and moved with the action, feeling similar to silk. It must have been imbued with the Gift—there was no other explanation for how the fabric seemed to have a mind of its own.

As I sat down to continue my meal, the bottom of the pants gently floated in an invisible breeze—breathing in time with my body. The motion tickled my ankles and shin—this would take some getting used to.

I reluctantly set down an unfinished apple as my stomach protested at the sudden expansion of food. The crickets echoed through the dark. I realized that this was the first time—in a long time—that I had been alone. Truly alone. Without Aedin by my side.

Loneliness stabbed in my gut as I stood and walked numbly to the bed. My clothes had become strangely still and hung limp along my frame.

Feeling small, I curled on my side, watching the wisps of clouds float past the full moon. It was too bright to sleep. I hugged a pillow and shielded my eyes, thinking of Aedin and missing him more than I ever had before.

Chapter Three

A SHARP KNOCK on the door startled me to wake into the gray light of the morning. Instinctively, I reached under my pillow for my knife—which wasn't there.

Cursing low, I threw off the blankets and rubbed my face. It had taken a long time, but I had eventually fallen asleep, although I could have used an entire week of it. My stomach was ready for food again—it ached with hunger.

More knocks followed on the door. I shouted something, grabbing an untouched apple from the previous night's tray, nearly tripping over my own sluggish feet, and opened the door.

Glittering emerald eyes stared impassively. "Good morning," Rowyn said stiffly.

I said nothing in response, my gaze shifting to the same retinue of guards—including Celion—flanking him. They nearly took up the entire hall.

"Are you ready to appear before the Council?"

I bit back a yawn—I wasn't. "Can I have something to eat first?"

Rowyn eyed the apple in my hand. "Is that not enough?"

I glared at him and took a bite of the apple, turning back to sit on the couch before the tray of leftover food. The bread had gone slightly stale, but the cured meats and fruit were perfectly acceptable. Finishing my apple, I began picking at the tray as Rowyn ambled into the room to sit in the adjacent chair.

Celion took his place, his broad shoulders and scowl filling the entire doorway.

I watched the hem of Rowyn's pants as they fluttered gently in the still air. In the morning light, they were a pale sage that shifted between silver, green, and blue.

He acknowledged my gaze with a nod. "I assume our Gifted ceremonial dress would be anathema to the Empire."

Swallowing a piece of bread, I admitted quietly, "It likely would."

Rowyn crossed his arms, his eyes roving over my body. "You don't have it."

"Have what?"

"The 'R.'"

"You mean the scar of the Rh—" I stopped as I saw his lips automatically twitch. "Of course I don't," I said brusquely. "I'm not… that."

"What a relief," Celion muttered from the doorway. I gave him a scowl that matched his own.

"I thought you might be," Rowyn admitted. "But your husband has it."

I grimaced, remembering the silver, puckered skin on his bicep. "Yes… he does."

"How long was he there for?"

"Fifteen years or so. Until he was appointed to the lordship of Lailan."

Rowyn considered this information with a tilt of his head. "A lord?"

"It's… a long story," I managed, biting off a slice of cured pork as I felt my stomach began to fill.

"Why didn't he kill you?"

I choked back a laugh seeing Rowyn's serious expression. I wondered what he knew. "Aedin married me to protect me from the Rh—that organization. We fled to the fortress when Lord Tours discovered my Gift." I paused, remembering that night at the fortress. "You saw it in a Dream? How else could you have known where we were…?"

"My Dream of the present," Rowyn clarified. "I saw you at the fortress—training. And I understood that we had to leave at once. Fate had fortunately determined the timing as we arrived alongside the assassins sent to kill you."

It *was* fortunate timing. We likely would have been killed—either by Jon *or* the Rhidge—if they hadn't intervened.

I nodded automatically, wondering whether Rebecca had survived. Where Jon was now.

"Are you done?" He looked at my still fingers.

My stomach was satiated. "Yes." I brushed my hands on my pants and rose, automatically wincing at the stiffness that still plagued my limbs.

The pale walls were streaked with a soft gray light from the morning sun. Yet even despite the early hour, we passed a few others—Gifted wearing the same ceremonial cloth. They largely ignored us, bent to the task of sweeping the spotless floors of errant dust and leaves. Rowyn bowed his head respectfully and they responded in kind; but as we passed, I didn't feel the same lively pulse of power that exuded from the guards. I briefly wondered if the social hierarchy on Iselleden was based on the power of one's Gift.

I tried to track our winding path through the halls, but the sameness of the walls made it difficult. Although my mind was clearer after the food and partial sleep, I was still groggy and not entirely myself. I blinked away a headache as we stepped out into the same open courtyard that we'd crossed the evening prior. In the night, the landscape of the Haven had been a mystical and sacred geometry of plants and stones. Fearfully beautiful under the starlight. In the daylight, it was softer, less wild and more tame.

An olive tree stood in the middle, flanked in geometric patterns by sage, lavender, thyme, and other herbs. The white stones were dotted with benches as insects buzzed and flitted from plant to plant. In the distance, the bright green valley was bordered by distant, arching purple mountains. Every inch of the land was fresh and teeming with life.

A shiver ran across my skin—as if I had been here before. As if I belonged to this earth.

We crossed the courtyard and entered the mouth of the tall tower. In the low hall, the floor and walls glowed with a multitude of colors. I looked up—hundreds of miniature glass tiles formed the ceiling. Pinks, blues, oranges, greens, purples, and reds—there were too many to count—the colors sank into our clothes, tunics, and skin.

We entered through double doors and suddenly the colors stopped.

Blinding white light came roaring through my senses—I winced at the pure, unadulterated sunlight that poured from the towering glass dome. We stood in a circular room surrounded by seven daises carved into the wall.

There was a soft hum of conversation that ceased as soon as we stepped through the portal. In the dead silence that followed, our footsteps echoed awkwardly as Rowyn led me to the center of the tower.

"Please stand here." He gestured to a space on the spotless stones.

I eyed him warily but obeyed.

Celion and one other guard—a woman—stood at my sides as Rowyn left to ascend one of the daises. He paused to exchange words briefly with an older gentleman, helping him up the steps. The other guards exited back into the hall, and I was left among the seven Gifted—staring down from their thrones with expressions of hope, fear, and bitterness.

My stomach flipped in terror. I reached into my blood, satisfied to feel the thread—the access to my power. Though I didn't have a dagger, at least I could fight.

"I now pronounce this Council open," stated a low, feminine voice.

I whipped around to see the woman who had spoken. She rested on her throne with ease and power, the fabric of her dress drifting lazily around her bare feet as her green eyes roved from each of the six thrones to finally rest on me.

Cunning, sharp, and intelligent. I flinched.

"We have had good fortune. Rowyn received his Dream of the present and—together with the guards—traveled to the fortress from the Ancient Wars to rescue Gwyneth Aedin, a Gifted woman from the Empire. However… this fortune came with a great price, as we lost one of our guards in the fight—Loran, son of Liam. Let us remain silent for a moment as we thank Fate for his life and service to Iselleden."

There was a hush as her words sank into the inhabitants of the room. Their eyes fluttered in despair and anger at the news, but I was transfixed by the woman who had spoken.

Her angelic face looked as though it had inspired the statues of the gods. From the curling cascade of strawberry-blonde locks to her long sun-kissed arms, she was the epitome of perfection.

Those eyes never left my face. That red mouth was set in a grim line. The hands resting on her throne were curled into loose, waiting fists. Alarm gripped my throat at the raw power that wafted from across the room. I knew she could have easily crushed the stones of the Council Tower and then just as easily walked away.

"Gwyneth Aedin—we have received a prophecy regarding the fate of Iselleden and the Empire. The Prophet spoke to Rowyn that you would bring to life a new empire to restore the power of the Gift across our world. We, the Council of Iselleden, call upon you to fulfill this prophecy—to depose the tyrannical kingdom which rules the Empire and to obliterate the Rhidge."

Out of the corner of my eye, I saw Rowyn automatically wince at the word, but I gave the action little thought as her words sank in.

A prophecy? Rowyn's words from yesterday resurfaced in my mind. *"He is not supposed to be here…"*

"What—?" I managed to whisper before I was cut off.

"Silence." Her voice sliced through the room. "We did not give you permission to speak." She looked down at me from her dais as if I were a heathen, unworthy of even standing on the same floor. "You will be trained by Rowyn to complete your mission and depart from Iselleden—"

"Wait!" I cried, stepping forward, ignoring the guards who tensed in response. "This is *insane*! I can't destroy the Rhidge—"

"You will depart from Iselleden in four weeks' time," she continued with a raised voice, ignoring my protests.

"No!" I bellowed, anger rising in my chest. "We can't go back! We need *your* help—"

"*You* will follow the prophecy and kill the king and end the terror of the Rhidge."

My hands prickled with the Gift as I longed to wrap them around her elegant throat. "But I've never killed before! I won't do it—it's impossible—"

"Rowyn will teach you everything you need to know." She waved a hand dismissively. "You will become as proficient as your *assassin* husband."

"Speaking of my *husband*," I growled, shooting Rowyn a scathing look. "Where is he? You have him here—where are you keeping him?"

As the final echoes of my words faded in the room, a grim expression spread across her face. She rose from the throne and slowly made her way down the steps. I flexed my fingers as her tall form proudly straightened only several feet away.

The scent of honeycomb and fresh earth wafted through my nostrils as she scanned my face and body, her eyes probing for any sign of weakness. "Will you fulfill the prophecy?"

My back was rigid as I held her stare. "I don't know what gods or prophet *you're* listening to, but they're clearly wrong. We sought your help—your protection from the Empire. And now you want us to return to the place that's *thirsting* for our blood to battle an entire *army* of Rhidge?" I nearly laughed until I saw her expression darken.

She was serious. They were serious. And they believed this— this *prophecy*.

Her eyes shifted to Celion—he nodded and walked to the double doors, gesturing to someone outside. He grabbed something and began to drag a long, dark shape into the circular chamber.

A body.

I recognized Aedin in an instant.

My mouth became dry—the horrified words of protest stuck in my throat. His chest was bare and there was dried blood almost everywhere; dark brown smears across his face, arms, and covering his hands. The "R" was nearly indistinguishable beneath the layers. His black pants were filthy and his hair matted—as if he'd been rolled through the earth in a cage of blood, dirt, and sweat.

I hardly acknowledged the flinches of alarm on the other Council members' faces. Rowyn sat erect and still with one hand on his sword—ready and waiting.

Celion dropped Aedin's body several feet away. As soon as his knees hit the floor, I rushed forward—and was stopped. A wall of air blocked my path.

The guard's face was fierce and cold.

I pulled forth my Gift and shot out my hands. A crackle—like the logs on a fire—sounded as our powers met. But the shield remained. Celion tightened his jaw with determination.

The woman gently stepped around the barrier to join Celion and stand over Aedin's unconscious body. Fear rushed through my veins as I saw the fixed set of her mouth and eyes.

"Please," I cried softly, my former confidence gone. "Give him to me."

Her eyes were the color of the valley below—but not soft and gentle. They were hard and unyielding, like unforgiving tempest waves.

"Your husband killed Loran in battle," she said softly. "We do not tolerate the crime of murder."

Aedin's body began to shift on the ground, a low hiss escaping his mouth as he struggled to move. My chest tightened at the sight of his pain. "Please—"

"Will you fulfill the prophecy?" she asked patiently, her words slow and intentional.

"No!" I blurted. "It's impossible—"

She extended a hand—Aedin's body lifted gently in the air, his knees just touching the ground. His dark eyes were vacant and dull—I heard him swallow as he looked around unseeingly. Just like me, he'd been drugged and was only now surfacing to consciousness.

I struggled against the invisible wall before me—Celion squinting in concentration—but it was unmoved.

"Consider this a preview of how you will accomplish your task." Her voice was cold and determined.

"Please," I gasped instinctively as she lay her hand on Aedin's back.

My husband's eyes widened and focused, dazed, on my face. A quiet sizzle echoed around the tower through the sounds of his rough breaths. Blood began to run down his back.

"Stop," I rasped, my throat tightening at the sight of his blood. It was fresh and bright in the early morning light, flowing in glittering lines through the dried brown stains. The muscles underneath the "R" on his right bicep contracted at the pain. Something like a knife twisted in my gut.

Her fingertips quickly became red as they descended down his back.

An acute pain gripped my throat. "*Stop*, please!"

She looked up at me, withdrawing her hand momentarily. "You will fulfill the prophecy?" she asked innocently.

"No, just *please*—"

Her hand resumed its course.

Aedin's head hung limply from his shoulders. Beads of sweat began to drop alongside the blood on the floor. I felt sick.

I pushed again and again at the blockade—but Celion's blue eyes were firm and unyielding. He grunted in response to my attacks, firmly setting his feet on the floor.

"Stop!" I thrust my body against the barrier, ignoring the pain in my shoulder. The crackling grew louder—a cry escaped Aedin's lips.

"STOP!" I screamed, unable to fight the panic rising in my chest. There was a distant ringing in my ears. With all of my might, I pushed into the air and found the barrier dissolved. I nearly fell in surprise but didn't waste a second. Throwing out a hand towards the woman, I hurled her body across the unsullied stones.

Aedin collapsed, gulping for air as the pain subsided. With each breath, the tiny rivulets of blood flexed and contracted, springing forth fresh droplets that ran down his back.

Fighting nausea, I turned to Celion. He took a step back, his hands up in a posture of defense as he prepared for an attack. Across the room, the woman gingerly stood, brushing off her dress and coming to a stand.

"I assume, then, that you will fulfill the prophecy?" Her words echoed hollowly through the room.

I looked from Rowyn, to the woman, to each member of the Council. Their faces were etched in a mixture of discomfort and disgust. As if this was painful for them.

Untouched and pure—this was no haven to us. Anger erupted in my chest.

"This is your idea of peace?" I hissed, watching her aloof, green eyes. "Inflicting pain? *Torture*? I know Iselleden has suffered, but you can't reverse the past with more blood."

She watched me quietly and I saw the arrogance in her gaze receding. The entire room held a breath as I bent with shaking hands to lift my husband.

A cry was ripped from Aedin's lips as soon as I touched his back. I cursed lowly as my palms came away bloody. Summoning that thread of power, I hovered his body until he was safely off the ground. Then, without a word, I walked out the tower doors, my husband's body hanging limply in front of me.

———

"Gods above," I breathed as I set Aedin down on the couch in my room.

The blood instantly stained the linen. Lying on his stomach, head lolled to the side, Aedin looked almost asleep.

A headache throbbed in my temples. Whether from rage or exertion in my weakened state, I wasn't sure. I allowed the Gift to drift back into my blood, assessing the damage before me.

I could barely distinguish his dark skin underneath the sea of red swirls that ran from his shoulders to his lower back. Like the flowering vines in the courtyard they twisted elegantly—mocking me.

How had I let this happen?

Biting back a cry, I lay my hands on the bottom lines, healing them partially. I was exhausted—exhausted from the drug, the little sleep, and the use of the Gift—but I managed to heal the deepest wounds. The shallow ones would have to wait until tomorrow.

With shaking hands, I wet a towel in the sink and began to wipe the excess fresh blood from his back, then the dried blood on his face. It was stuck to his eyebrows, his cheeks, and nose. I scrubbed at a spot—he suddenly flinched and turned away.

"Aedin," I whispered as he stirred and inhaled. As the muscles on his back flexed, the tiny rivers of blood cracked anew, gleaming in the muted sunlight. I stifled my tears and murmured again, "Aedin."

"Gwen," he mumbled, flickering his eyes open to search for me. They were pained, his voice sluggish.

"I'm… I'm sorry," I choked, dropping the towel and smoothing back his hair.

"Remember?" he whispered hoarsely with the ghost of a smile. "Never apologize."

"It's my fault that… that they did this to you." I clenched my fist, fighting back tears. "They're going to pay… They *used* you…"

"S'not your fault," he said, painfully clearing his throat and swallowing. His right arm moved to brush away my tears. I grabbed his hand, holding it against my cheek, and kissed it.

My breath became rhythmic as we sat in a painful silence. Through the open doors I could hear the sounds of cheerful laughter, moving carts, and the chirping of birds. The sounds of daily lives, going about their routines unbeknownst to our suffering. It was so alien to the stark pain in the room.

After I felt I could speak without crying, I asked quietly, "How did you find me?"

Aedin moved as if to shrug but stopped the movement. "As soon as you were captured… I-I dropped my weapons and begged to be taken as well. Their one request was that I was drugged too… Flussidik…" He coughed a dark chuckle. "I woke in a dark room without light. They continued drugging me until…"

"What about the Rhidge? And Jon and Rebecca?"

"I'm… not sure," Aedin paused. "I left Jon when I felt you outside."

"I saw Rebecca before I exited the fortress… She let me escape…" I swallowed the lump in my throat at the memory. "Aedin—they didn't have a choice…"

"They did, Gwen." Aedin closed his eyes with finality.

I was silent as I considered his words. Jon and Rebecca had faced an impossible choice. We had been betrayed by our friends. But their own lives had been threatened by the Rhidge —and Rebecca with her child—

"Aedin?" I turned to see his eyelids were closed, his dark brow unfurled in a peaceful expression. His breath became heavy and even.

A breeze passed gently through the room, ruffling my hair as I watched daylight bathe the floor. I felt hollow and pained, even with Aedin beside me.

I leaned against the couch stained with my husband's blood and let my eyes fill with to the brim with tears. They ran gently down my chin as I stared, unfocused, at the late morning sunlight and wondered where we went from here.

Chapter Four

EPHRAIM WOKE WITH a start.

He had been dreaming about Lailan—running through the jungle as the heat pressed mercilessly against his body. Gwen was gone. The plants tore at his clothes as he searched behind rocks and under the thick and stretching branches for his sister. There were no clues; it was as if she'd disappeared into thin air. He'd called for help, but there had been no answer.

It was then that he'd realized that she was dead.

He felt hot—his room was beginning to warm in the late morning light. What time was it? Ephraim shifted to look out of the window, frowning at the sight of the bright and distant pines. It must be late.

Hollyn moved in his arms. She frowned up at him, then burrowed her face in his chest. "What are you doing?" Her voice was soft and husky.

"Nothing," he said quickly, settling back down and rubbing her bare skin. "Go back to sleep."

Hollyn mumbled something indistinguishable in response. Ephraim smiled briefly at the feeling of her body against his and inhaling the familiar scent of her hair. They were quiet as he looked out the window, watching the few clouds pass through the sky, just the tips of the pines piercing through the bright blue.

The fire had gone out during the night and the smell of ash lingered in the room. Hollyn's heartbeat sounded loud, and her pulse thudded softly against his skin. There was something about the predictable rhythm that was calming. That reassured him she was alive.

Alive—the word sank in his stomach.

In the weeks since Gwen and Aedin's death, Ephraim had written to his father but received few letters in response. The replies felt predictable and numb. Gregory wrote of the weather, how much he had sold in the shop, and what he made for dinner. Ephraim had hoped that writing to his father would bring them closer—perhaps they could console each other through their mutual mourning. But Gregory refused to mention her name—it was as if their time in Lailan had never occurred. That his daughter had ceased to exist.

Soon, the letters to his father became more infrequent. And the length between replies became longer. Ephraim told himself it was because he was busy with meetings and social gatherings, but he couldn't stand the formulaic responses. He grew frustrated with his father, and soon withdrew to focus on palace life once again.

After his beating of Daniel, Ephraim had received a stern warning for disrupting the peace. But the rebuke had been well worth the sight of Daniel's bruised face in the weeks after. Daniel avoided his gaze at dinners and moved the other way when they passed in the hall. Ephraim watched this with silent satisfaction, enjoying the red and irritated skin on his own knuckles. As if it would solve the pain in his own heart.

But he still felt a dull ache as he caught the smirking gaze of Lord Tours. If there was anyone else Ephraim desired to inflict harm upon, Tours was next on his list. It was unfortunate that he was untouchable.

Hollyn's hand rubbed his waist, bringing him to the present.

"Yes?" Ephraim murmured playfully, kissing the top of her head as her eyelashes tickled his chest.

"Mm." Her blue eyes squinted up at him. "When is your meeting…?"

His arm under her head was growing numb, but he couldn't bear to move it.

"This afternoon." He wrapped his other arm around her shoulders. "I have to copy some more decrees for distribution this morning, but otherwise, I'm all yours."

She smiled in satisfaction, leaning forward to meet his lips. Despite the stale taste from the morning, Ephraim relished the feeling. Her hand moved lower—he stirred in response and shivered, kissing Hollyn deeply as she stroked him. Marveling in delight, Ephraim let himself forget the world, the troubles of life melting from his conscious.

————

After Hollyn left later that morning, Ephraim washed himself in the tub. Humming to himself, he dressed, combed his hair, and donned the purple doublet with the insignia of the king. Ephraim was pleased to see it was a looser fit than before. He and Hollyn had been taking walks daily—avoiding the crowds and skirting the edge of the gardens for the long way around the park. The extra miles were paying off, he thought as he cinched his belt a notch tighter than usual.

He laced his boots, grabbed his bag, and left his room. The halls were already buzzing with activity. Courtiers passed with idle chatter, bright clothes, and strong perfume. Ephraim's stomach grumbled as he passed the back door of the kitchens and smelled the roasting meat. But he was already short on time. And he would happily trade any breakfast he'd missed for time spent with Hollyn.

Remembering her touch with pleasure, Ephraim wondered when it was too early to call on her. They'd been spending most evenings together, but he didn't want to appear overeager or desperate. It was a delicate balance, and yet he couldn't keep away. He was incredibly grateful for her companionship; she was the one constant in his life now. In the absence of his blood relations, Ephraim was stranded on an island that was reluctantly becoming his home. There were few whom he could trust or count on—save Hollyn.

The walls of the palace changed from stone to stone draped in tapestries to ornately carved wood as he entered the halls of the king. He slowed his pace, matching the unhurried footsteps of others.

Whispered conversations were muted amongst the thick rugs that covered the floor. Ephraim passed through the first doors into the outer chamber where the usual crowd of courtiers waited. He saw their expressions of frustration and boredom and was glad he didn't have to wait.

Shouldering his bag, Ephraim weaved through the crowd, easing towards the doors to the private chamber. He stopped in his tracks, recognizing the sharp chin and auburn hair of a familiar figure.

Daniel met his eyes with a nod, beckoning him forward. It was the first communication Ephraim had had with him since he'd beaten his fist into his face. Ephraim noted with satisfaction that although the bruises had mostly healed, his lower lip was still swollen and cut.

Nonetheless, he frowned as he came to stand before his old friend.

"Yes?" Ephraim asked curtly.

"You're late," Daniel said haughtily, lifting his nose in the air.

Ephraim wanted to give him another black eye. Instead he pushed past him and entered the receiving room. The advisors were clustered together in packs—chatting idly amongst themselves in the unseasonably warm room. Pulling at the collar of his doublet, Ephraim set down his bag and set up his table, assembling the quills, ink, and parchment with perfunctory motions. Although his personal life had suffered through so many changes, at least he was getting used to his job.

The tall, dark shape of Tours entered the room, Daniel on his heels. He shut the door with finality. Ephraim wondered when the king would appear.

"Settle down," Tours grumbled to the room as he stood on the steps of the throne.

Kellen frowned up at him, squinting under his thick gray brows. "Where is His Majesty?"

"He is… unwell." Tours savored the word, smoothing his groomed mustache. "Now please take a seat so we can get this over with."

Greymont eased his large body into the nearest chair, folding his arms over his chest and exchanging quiet words with Kellen. Ephraim dipped his quill in the ink pot, trying to make himself as inconspicuous as possible—avoiding that sharp predatory gaze.

Tours' blue eyes scanned the room with satisfaction—as if he enjoyed causing turmoil and then seizing control. With patience he waited, savoring the muffled whispers as the room descended into a gentle simmer.

"Now then," he began, clasping his hands together with satisfaction. "Let us discuss business."

The scratching of Ephraim's quill against the parchment was the only other sound as Tours spent the new few hours running through the list of issues facing the Empire. Some topics were quick to deal with; others took much longer—the backlog from the administrative disaster on Lailan had created a mass of ships waiting outside the port of Tahuna; a failing of what crop mid-summer meant grim prospects for winter or Tente; and the king was eager to raise taxes, despite the pushback from some of the lords. It was a contentious topic amongst the advisors.

The backlog from the administrative disaster on Lailan had created a mass of ships waiting outside the port of Tahuna. A failing of wheat crop mid-summer meant grim prospects for winter on Tente. And the king was eager to raise taxes, despite the pushback from some of the lords. It was a contentious topic amongst the advisors.

"It's ridiculous to oppose the tax—the increased funds will support our efforts." Greymont scowled as he poured himself a glass of wine.

"But there's little the king *does*," piped a smaller man, appointed by Lord Tremer. "He just sits on his throne and eagerly collects whatever capital is created by the lords—"

Kellen cut him off. "The king plays a crucial role in the Empire. It's stability. And tradition."

"But it's the *lords* that actually create the wealth!"

"The king creates more wealth than you could imagine," purred Tours. "Stability and power *are* wealth. Without them, we are no better than a warmongering cluster of islands that feud amongst each other. The Empire is what makes us strong."

"Well," sniffed the man. "If he needn't be so *greedy*—"

Tours let out a loud laugh. "Greed! If you wish to talk about *greed*, I'm sure Greymont would be happy to oblige."

Greymont paused mid-sip with a snarl. "I'll have you know my family's farms have survived for *centuries* because of—"

"Yes, yes. We all know of your hard work ethic." Tours plucked a fallen hair from his black doublet with a coy smile. "What you *don't* know," he continued in a growl, "is the increased taxes will fund our forces—expand Radiance's army and intelligence operations to expel any outside threats."

"But Radiance's army is over five hundred strong!" Kellen exclaimed. "We have no enemies, no threats. The few islands that exist outside of our seven are small and insignificant. Hardly worth a second thought. No—the increase should go to improvements in the capital. New buildings, roads, and infrastructure—"

"Renovations of certain parts of the palace *are* crucial—I will not deny it," Tours admitted. "But the maintenance of our armies and the expanding of our forces will ensure peaceful stability, even if we were attacked by… unknown forces."

Greymont scoffed. "Unknown forces. What unknown forces?"

Tours eyed him coolly. "It is always good to be prepared."

Ephraim's hand ached from recording the exchange. He dully wished for someone to stab him with his quill.

Kellen shook his head. "Why put money towards events that *might* happen? We should be addressing the issues that are *currently* facing us."

"We will let the king decide." Tours closed the discussion with a wave of his hand. "He will read the notes from our dear historian and decide for himself."

The men looked as though they might object but read Tours' sharp gaze and decided against it.

The advisors all stood. Ephraim scribbled some last-minute notes as he watched the man who'd objected to the taxes immediately seek out Kellen. They gestured together wildly and exited the room in a huddle. Tours watched on, stroking his mustache and speaking lowly with Greymont. Slowly, the advisors trickled out.

Scattering sand onto the parchment, Ephraim wondered briefly if he still had time to walk with Hollyn before dinner. Fresh air sounded like the perfect tonic to relieve the stress from the meeting.

A large, firm hand placed itself on the wood of his desk.

"I hope you wrote it all correctly," a low voice murmured dangerously.

Ephraim swallowed as he looked up into the piercing blue eyes of the Lord of Radiance. "Yes, my lord," he said quickly.

"Because we wouldn't want the king to get the wrong idea," Tours continued silkily. "As his historian, it's important that you accurately represent the best options facing the Empire."

A sickening sensation dropped thickly into Ephraim's stomach. "Of course… I agree."

Tours' hand fluttered through the pages, scattering sand across the desk. Quickly scanning the last pages, he narrowed his eyes. "Perhaps you should revisit this section."

It was the debate about the tax increase. His heart lurched. "What did I misrepresent?"

"I believe it was a unanimous agreement to raise taxes to afford spending more on military improvements."

In the span of a heartbeat, Ephraim considered the two paths before him.

The first would rewrite the entire section and comply with the Tours' wishes. The most powerful man in the Empire, who'd likely executed his sister and brother-in-law "in the name of justice" with his own hands.

The second would be to resist, object, and likely be beaten into a pulp until he complied.

Ephraim chose the easier route, dashing his hopes for an afternoon in the garden.

It felt like many hours had passed. Although there were no windows in the king's reception room, Ephraim was sure it was nearing dusk. Daniel had remained for some time, conferring with his lord in a low voice, until he left to change for dinner. Tours remained the entire time—examining his spotless nails and tracking Ephraim's every movement with that glittering stare.

With an aching hand and a burning headache, Ephraim finished the rewrite. He cast the sand on the fresh ink and waited patiently as Tours unfurled from the chair and grabbed the new pages.

"Good." A smile curved his lips. "See you at dinner."

In response, Ephraim rolled up the pages, gathered his things, and left.

———

"Cheer up—it could have been worse."

Hollyn clinked her goblet against Ephraim's as they sat in the dining room with the rest of court. As the king's historian, he could have pushed his way to the main table where the advisors sat on either side of the king, but Ephraim preferred to keep his distance. He fumed over his cup of wine, staring daggers at Lord Tours as he whispered his lies into the king's ear.

"You're right," Ephraim muttered, flexing his wrist. "I wouldn't have been surprised if he'd cut off my hand."

Hollyn winced. "That's a bit extreme."

"I wouldn't put it past him."

She didn't disagree, taking a sip of her wine with an impartial expression. "Well, my day wasn't much better."

"Yes," Ephraim said quickly. "I'm sorry, I should have asked."

Hollyn shrugged. "I will admit, being threatened is slightly worse than having to deal with vomit *and* excrement all day long."

Ephraim made a face. "That sounds miserable as well."

"It *was*. Thankfully we have servants to actually handle the soiled towels, but the *smell*..." Hollyn made a face as Ephraim couldn't resist a grin.

"So he really was ill."

"The king?"

"Yes."

"Of course—why wouldn't he be?"

Ephraim shrugged. "I thought it might have been an excuse or something. Part of Tours' plan or whatever he's scheming."

Hollyn considered this. "What do you think he wants?"

"I... don't know." Ephraim watched Tours' dark blonde hair dip as he turned to Kellen on his other side.

"The Lord of Radiance is the most powerful position next to the king. What would he want that he hasn't already got?" Hollyn mused.

"*More* power?" Ephraim suggested bitterly.

"Maybe he killed Lord Aedin and... well, because he was becoming too powerful?"

Ephraim flinched at the name, a sharp pain ripping through his gut as his sister's face rose in his mind. "Let's talk about something else."

A soft, warm hand gripped his own. Reminding him that he wasn't alone to face the demons of his past. And the demons that still thrived in their midst. "Yes," Hollyn agreed. "Let's."

The dinner plates were beginning to be cleared and people rose to begin their dancing.

Hollyn's blonde curls were a burnished bronze in the candlelight. "Dance with me?" She held out her hand.

"Isn't is the man that usually asks?" Ephraim teased.

"I couldn't care less"—Hollyn pulled him to his feet—"as long as it's with you."

Chapter Five

WHEN AEDIN WOKE later that day, I drew a bath and helped him ease into the tub. As the water submerged his back, his lips thinned into a tight line, but he made no sound. The water in the bath turned a soft pink.

I used a cloth to gently wash any remaining dried blood from his hair, his face, and—very gently—his back.

Aedin took the cloth and quietly scrubbed at his hands—those hands that had killed. I wondered if the crusted blood was that of Loran or a Rhidge—I doubted it was his own. I remembered the sickening thud of a body hitting the floor in the fortress, the lightning-fast blows. The scent of fresh blood—metallic and thick in my nostrils.

The reality of his past had never felt so near the present.

Once again, the "R" was fresh and clean and gleamed silver in the thin light of the bathroom.

It felt odd to care for him like this—when he was vulnerable and weak. Our entire relationship so far, he had been the strong one; the one to protect, or care for, me. Watching him bathe, I mused on the changes in our life. We were stuck in a foreign world with the threat of an impossible task hanging over our heads.

The prophecy. I couldn't resist a grimace or put the thought out of my mind.

A matching pair of shirts and pants hung lifeless in the closet —as if they'd known. I helped to dry his body, pull his legs in the pants, and guide him to the bed. The fabric was limp and dull—mimicking the actions of his own body.

Aedin lay shirtless on his stomach, his head propped to the side. The glittering vines on his skin were red and tender from the water.

And soon enough, he fell asleep again.

Sitting on the couch—the linen now stained brown with dried blood—I watched the light shift from late afternoon to early evening. I played with the dancing hem of my pants, practiced moving things around the room with my Gift, and half dozed as if in a trance. I had never had such a lack of activity or quiet. It was unnerving—I felt listless without a purpose. The sounds of the world moved outside of our window as the light turned from a warm gold to a soft purple.

I wondered if they would come for us. Or when.

But no one came.

When the stars were bright in the sky, I crawled into bed next to Aedin. His heavy breath was a comforting rhythm that slowly guided my body into sleep.

In the morning, a tray of food had appeared on the low table before the couch.

I started at the sight, blinking the sleep from my eyes, fearful that someone had entered the room without my knowing. I should have set a barrier.

Cursing my lack of discipline, I slowly eased from the bed to grab the tray and brought it back with me. I ate quietly, and when Aedin awoke, I gave him some food as well. Checking his back, I was pleased to see that the shallow wounds were healing of their own accord. But the vines were still an angry red that tightened my throat at the sight.

Soon enough, exhaustion overtook him again, and he fell back asleep.

I dozed on the bed—my body mostly recovered but my mind uneasy. The sun rose high, illuminating the sharp angles of mountains in the distance. The lower parts were covered in a thick forest of trees, until the high, arching stone shot out of the base to tower magnificently over the valley. I smiled briefly at the snow dusting their tops—I hadn't seen snow since Berge.

Projecting out past the walls of our prison, I still felt the presence of two guards outside the balcony, and another pair just outside the door. And then—

A soft knock echoed through the room.

I froze, glancing automatically at my husband's sleeping form. He didn't move. I quietly stood and opened the door a crack.

Rowyn's green eyes were soft. "How is he?"

A flurry of harsh words caught in my throat. I whispered coldly, "Why do *you* care?"

He swallowed, as if expecting my anger, and held up a tray. "I brought you some more food."

The sweet smell of roasted meat wafted towards me. I hesitated—torn between my growing dislike for Iselleden and my hunger. Common sense won—I carefully pulled open the door to admit him, my stomach grumbling audibly.

Rowyn stepped through the door frame and placed the tray on the table. He eyed the bloodstains on the couch with distaste, muttering, "I'll have someone take care of that…" before his eyes were drawn to the bare skin of Aedin's back.

Relieved to not see Celion trailing behind, I closed the door and asked with a rough voice, "Is your bloodlust now satiated?"

He was silent, gazing at the red vines that covered my husband's skin. "I didn't know she would do that…" he protested quietly. "But he had to be punished for his crime…"

"Punished?" I scoffed. "It was a *battle*—how could he have known?"

"We are not like them," he whispered with wide eyes. "We do not *look* like them—you saw me, even in the dark of the night, and understood."

I remembered that moment of panic when I had realized they weren't Rhidge. When I had understood that it was our only way out—and dropped my defenses to accept the blow.

Instinctively I rubbed at my chest; it was still sore.

"It doesn't matter now," I muttered, waving my hand at Aedin's incoherent form. "The damage has been done."

Rowyn was silent, his arms folded solemnly. I watched his long red hair sway gently in the afternoon breeze as a sudden thought occurred.

"Are you related to her?"

"Who?"

"The woman who did this?"

Rowyn shifted uncomfortably. "Her name is Raine. She is… my sister."

I looked at him accusingly. "And you didn't know."

"Raine is…" He struggled to find the words. "Different. *We* are not accustomed to such activities…"

"But she is?" I finished for him.

He didn't respond. I saw his fingers twitch as he stepped forward towards the sleeping form of my husband.

"Don't touch him," I hissed, fighting to keep my voice low.

Rowyn ignored me and placed his hands on my husband's back, following each line of blood there, knitting the flesh back together. I stood mute and resolute—ready to push him away at any hint of harm. But there was none. Perhaps Rowyn felt obligated to repair the damage his sister had wrought.

As his hands passed over them, the scarlet vines faded into a dull silver.

Like the silver vines on his ceremonial doublet on Lailan.

I swallowed back tears at the memory—it felt like a lifetime ago.

"Thank you," I forced myself to say quietly when he finished.

Rowyn turned his head in surprise and spoke gruffly, "Don't thank me."

But despite the terror we'd seen since coming to Iselleden, I still owed him my life.

"You saved me." I paused as the memory flooded back. "That night at the fortress… you saved me from the Rhidge."

Recognition sparked in his eyes as he smiled humorlessly. "If they'd killed you, we would have had a greater problem on our hands."

I thinned my lips, looking down at my bare feet. "Do you really believe… all this?" I whispered.

Rowyn studied me, stepping away from Aedin's sleeping form. "Why would I not?"

"It's absurd." I shook my head. "A prophecy that says that *I* will end the wars of the Gifted…?"

"I, myself, thought it was impossible when I received word from the Prophet," Rowyn admitted slowly. "But Iselleden has trusted Fate this long—there is no reason for deception."

I struggled to understand. "But… who is this Prophet?" I demanded.

"The Prophet is… the form of Fate itself."

"Fate?" I furrowed my brow.

"A great force that controls us… our world."

"What about the gods?" I objected, remembering the stories of the Empire. I had rarely attended services at our local temple. The belief had often felt insignificant and forced.

"The gods," Rowyn scoffed, shaking his head. "Your gods are lovely figments of imagination. Nothing more."

"I used to believe that the gods controlled us all," I admitted, shifting my weight. "I used to believe that everything happened for a reason and everything would work out for the best… But I'm quite sure I was wrong… Our actions are the only forces that bend the future to our will."

Rowyn was quiet and didn't respond. His emerald eyes were thoughtful as the breeze ruffled his ruby hair.

"So you are… to train me?" I asked.

"Yes."

"When?"

"Tomorrow morning—at dawn."

Mutely, I nodded and stepped back, allowing him to walk past. He exited the room, and the door clicked shut.

Chapter Six

WHEN THE ROOM fell silent again, I heard Aedin's voice echo dimly from the bed. "What training?"

I bit back a smile—of course he'd heard everything.

"Aedin," I said his name softly, sitting on the edge of the bed as he rolled gingerly onto his side. "How are you feeling?" I asked, tracing his brow.

"What training?" he repeated, ignoring my question. His dark eyes were insistent and probing—they scanned my face as I struggled to find the right words. I wasn't sure what he'd heard or if he even remembered what had happened in the Council Tower.

I hesitated. "They—the Council—want to train me to kill the king… end the Rhidge and 'depose' the Empire… whatever that means." I tried to half-joke the last part, but it fell flat.

Aedin looked at me blankly. "You…" he said slowly, his shoulders tightening—stretching the "R" across the bicep.

"It's according to a prophecy that Rowyn received… I don't understand how or why, but they sound intent on it happening…" My stomach turned as I remembered the flash of Raine's eyes as she placed her hands on Aedin's back. *Consider this a preview of how you will accomplish your task…*

Aedin shifted his body to sit up against the pillows. Instinctively, I reached out a hand to help, but he dismissed it and completed the action himself. I was satisfied to see that he could lean against the headboard without a sign of pain and silently thanked Rowyn for what he'd done.

Finally, Aedin looked at me squarely. "Do you want to do this?" he asked quietly, his voice sounding clearer than I'd heard in days.

"Want?" I clarified with a bitter smile. "I didn't *want* any of this…"

"You have a choice. You always have a choice."

"I… don't think I do," I faltered. Did I? "What other choice is there?" I wondered aloud.

"We can leave," Aedin said simply, folding his hands. "Either by force… or otherwise. We can live quietly on an island—there are wild areas on Acedes for one to simply disappear—"

"Until we get caught again," I interjected.

"*You* can't know that," Aedin pointed out sharply. "You haven't Dreamed of the future—"

"I don't want to live in fear," I growled. He must have been feeling better—his mahogany eyes were clear and persistent, matching the forcefulness of his words.

"Neither do I. But I also don't want my *wife* to be trained as an assassin, attempt to dismantle the Rhidge, murder the king and get *killed* in the process.

I paused. So this was what it was about.

"What if I want to?" I asked quietly.

Aedin watched me carefully. "That's why I asked—what *do* you want? If it's your choice, then I won't persuade you otherwise… despite what I think."

His words hit me in the gut.

For so long, I had obeyed Aedin's wishes—worried about what *he* thought, what *he* was going to do. We'd spent our entire marriage so far living under his directive.

And now we were thousands of miles away from our home and confronted with a decision facing *me*.

What did I want?

Exhaling, I scooted further onto the bed and sat cross-legged facing him. I solemnly met his eyes. "I don't seek out pain or suffering any more than you… but I don't see how this will end without trying. And so I want to try."

Aedin inclined his head in understanding. "There will be more pain and suffering. Much more."

I stared down at my fingers, picking the dirt from beneath my nails. "Perhaps they're right," I offered in a low voice.

Aedin exhaled shortly, slowly moving his arm to rub his neck. I watched the firm lines of his torso flex with the action. "They *may* be right… but we can't know that for sure."

"Not now," I said.

"What do you mean?"

"I mean, if this is all part of a greater plan of *prophecy*"—I said the word with distaste—"then perhaps we will know for certain, or there may be a sign. You're right—I haven't Dreamed of the future. I don't know what will come—*yet*. But *they* know something."

My husband looked down at his hands, considering this. "It's a possibility…" he offered, but his face became strained. "I fought *so* hard to protect you from all of this… I don't want you to suffer… like I did."

I considered his words. "Will you hate me?" I breathed, fearing the answer. "If I want to do this?"

Aedin's eyes softened—the familiar mahogany flecked with dark sage and deep cerulean. "Gwen… I would never hate you."

"You can't know that," I objected.

"I can be furious at you. Exasperated, angry, and even tired of you. But I will *never* hate you… Because I love you."

I froze, realizing he'd never said that before.

Eyes burning, my chest expanded with fullness. "I love you too," I said in reply. And it was the truth.

As the words left my mouth, Aedin's face softened. I crawled across the bed to tuck my shoulders under his outstretched arm. He kissed me gently as my chest stirred in excitement. His lips were warm—I smiled as the hair on his cheeks scratched mine.

I touched his jaw with a giggle. "I think you have a proper beard."

He rubbed his chin with a wry grin. "I suppose I do." And then he paused, looking at the wall—lost in thought.

"What is it?"

"This was… my Dream," he said hoarsely, blinking and looking around the room. "My Dream of the future… We were here. On the eighth island…"

I entwined his fingers with mine. "Iselleden…" I clarified. "It's not such a bad place to be."

"No," he said slowly and then looked at me with a gentle gaze. "Not at all."

Aedin cupped my face in his hands and our lips met. I moved against him, reveling in the response from my body. I kissed the tightly coiled hair on his cheeks, the soft skin of his neck, and the taut muscles of his shoulder.

"I love you, Ciaran," I murmured against his hot skin.

He rolled on top of me as I pulled down his head to greet him. Spreading my legs, I welcomed his weight and wandered my hands gently down the vines on his back. My head was spinning with desire, every inch of my body aching for him.

Aedin kissed my neck, his hands running up my sides and pushing up my shirt. The fabric freed itself with ease, as if it knew what we wanted.

What I wanted.

He was my closest companion—my confidante and partner. My equal in mind and body.

As our bodies joined together, I felt a lightness ease the weights of doubt and sorrow. We were meant to be here—together—and nothing could stop us now.

Chapter Seven

AEDIN SAT IN the early morning air and stared at the flame in his hand.

With his wounds healed and Gwen naked at his side, he'd slept through the night. It was a deep and unbroken sleep, where he had no dreams and reveled in the black abyss of rest. His body had woken with the morning birdsong and for a fleeting moment he'd thought he was in the villa. But his eyes had opened to unfamiliar windows and distant hills as everything came flooding back.

His wife's long curls—tangled notes of chocolate, amber, and earth—were stark against the white sheets.

Aedin pulled on his pants and shirt, frowning as the unfamiliar fabric fluttered gently at his ankles and cinched itself around his waist. Devouring an apple from yesterday's tray, he situated himself on the balcony, reveling in the fresh air of this new foreign world. A world where everything was changing and nothing made sense.

And yet—they had escaped the Rhidge. They had escaped their greatest fear. But at what cost?

A dark, hollow hole resided in his chest, like an empty cavern threatening to collapse. It was a mass of dichotomies—feeling simultaneously numb and full of grief; wanting to scream and crawl into silence. Jon had betrayed them. Rebecca as well. They had sold them to Tours—to Aedin's greatest enemy.

And they had barely escaped with their lives.

Aedin closed his palm and extinguished the flame as Gwen opened the door to the balcony. "Rowyn's here," she said.

Standing and reentering the room, Aedin placed the apple core on the tray and wiped his hands on his pants. As Gwen moved towards the door, Aedin automatically felt into the hallway and tensed—there were four Gifted outside.

His fingers itched at his sides, wishing for his dagger. Moving closely beside her, he prepared to throw himself in front of her if necessary. Just in case…

The door opened. Aedin recognized the red-haired man from the day prior and his muddled memory from the Council.

Rowyn stood in the doorway, regarding them carefully. "Good morning."

"Good morning," Gwen responded stiffly, waiting.

A golden-haired man scowled behind Rowyn, next to a pair of female guards.

Rowyn's pale tunic shone silver and gold in the morning light. He looked over Gwen's shoulder, briefly meeting Aedin's steady gaze. "May we come in?"

Gwen inclined her head, opening the door further to allow them entry.

Aedin stood tall and silent. An impassive mask covered his face as he watched the two men stride into the room.

The golden one placed himself just behind Rowyn, one hand resting on the hilt of his sword with an expression of distaste as he assessed Aedin. As if he was disappointed to see him alive and well—no longer drugged and weak.

"I see you're recovered," Rowyn began quietly, his eyes fixed on Aedin's face.

Aedin didn't respond—only straightened his back, holding Rowyn's stare. His tunic glistened a deep violet and blue, so close to black, as if it knew the color of his previous uniform.

"I don't believe we were formally introduced. My name is Rowyn, son of Reynolds, and I am the Captain of the Guard on

Iselleden," Rowyn offered, before gesturing towards his comrade. "And this is Celion, son of Caraway."

There was no avoiding the pleasantries, and to go along with it was better for Gwen's sake. "Ciaran Aedin," his voice rasped in response.

Celion made no response; his body steeled with every ounce of willpower to prevent himself from lunging at Aedin's throat. They assessed each other mutely as waves of the Gift ricocheted through the room. Gwen winced.

Rowyn pushed through the discomfort, addressing Aedin. "You were punished for the crime of murdering one of our own at the fortress—"

"It wasn't murder," Gwen objected.

"—which is a reprehensible action on Iselleden," Rowyn continued without breaking Aedin's stare. "Do you regret your actions?"

There was a brief pause as Aedin tilted his head.

"No," he whispered, his voice starved of emotion. "I don't regret anything. I was challenged, fighting to stay alive, and saw you capture my wife… I did what I felt was necessary at the time—"

A swelling tension tightened the grip on Celion's sword. "You *bastard*," he seethed through gritted teeth.

"My only regret"—Aedin shifted his eyes from Rowyn to bravely meet Celion's—"was that your comrade did not lower his guard and chose to fight me."

The ring of steel reverberated through the small room as Celion brandished his weapon. "I have never had a desire to kill. To end a life," he snarled. "Not until *now*."

Aedin didn't flinch with the point close to his chest. "I understand your anger," he said evenly. "I do… But you can't tell me that you wouldn't have done the same."

The blade flickered. Celion's eyes were the color of the ocean —deep blue and crashing with the power of a storm.

Rowyn stepped forward, placing his hand on Celion's naked blade. A mute conversation passed between them—strained and tired. As if they'd been through this before.

The sword dropped and dangled at his side.

"No one can say what they would have done in battle," Rowyn muttered wearily. "We have faced more pain and suffering in the past months than we have seen in this entire century."

"I'm sorry my actions have caused you pain." Aedin's voice was strained yet firm. Remorse was etched on his brow. "And I'm sorry for the loss of a life. But I do not regret my actions."

Rowyn appraised him with his emerald eyes. "It was a difficult decision, you know. We considered leaving you on that spit of land. I only saw Gwyneth in my Dream of the present—we didn't know you would be there."

Aedin acknowledged his words with a bowing of his head. "I'm grateful that you didn't leave me—"

"Only because you *begged* on your knees and dropped your weapons," Celion growled. "It's fortunate that *our* captain has a conscience."

"Your existence here brings… complications." Rowyn gestured towards Aedin's arm, where the bottom of the "R" was peeking out from beneath his sleeve. "Most of our people are unaware of the… Rh… your *kind*, and many of them distrustful of the Empire. We have not yet decided what… to do with you. Which is why we ask that you remain in your room and under guard—"

"You can't be serious," Gwen snapped.

Celion's eyes flashed in response as Rowyn reluctantly addressed her. "I can't put my island at risk by allowing him free rein of the land—"

"What do you think will happen? That he'll wreak havoc on the town?"

Celion prickled in response. "He has killed one of our own—what's to stop him from doing it again?"

Aedin could see Gwen resist the urge to roll her eyes but also saw the true fear on their faces. They *were* frightened of him.

Gwen continued her insistence, lowering her voice to reply. "My husband can be *trusted*."

"We don't know that for certain," Rowyn responded carefully. "In the meantime, while you and I train, we must leave him under guard."

There was a finality to Rowyn's expression that closed the argument. Aedin's shoulders sagged in response.

"Where will we go?" Gwen asked Rowyn.

"To the guards' quarters—to assess your skills."

"And no harm will come to Aedin?" she clarified, watching Celion.

Celion sneered. "Do you think so little of me?"

"I'm not sure entirely what I think of you," Gwen replied contemptuously. "Especially knowing your leader—and Rowyn's sister—hungers for blood."

Rowyn winced, objecting, "Raine does not *hunger* for blood."

"It certainly seemed that way the other day."

"Regardless"—Rowyn shifted restlessly, giving her a significant look—"we need to go."

Aedin stepped back, accepting the outcome of the discussion. His wife shot a final glare at Celion before stepping forward for a kiss. "I'm sorry," she whispered under her breath.

"Remember?" Aedin replied with the ghost of a smile. "Never apologize."

Gwen offered a half-smile as she pulled away and followed Rowyn out the door. Celion gave Aedin a warning look—one hand still on the hilt of his sword—as he exited as well and shut the door.

The room descended into a sudden silence. Aedin felt Rowyn, Celion and Gwen move further and further away—out of the periphery of his mind—until the only presence that remained was that of the two guards. A buzz of conversation outside the door was an annoying murmur. Aedin blocked out the sounds as he sat on the floor and once again lit a flame in his palm.

The emptiness swelled again in his chest.

Time passed.

The blues, greens, and golds swirled and danced in his open hand, reflecting off the pale walls of the room. His knees ached from sitting cross-legged on the floor. Wincing, he stretched out his limbs.

Leaning against the foot of the couch, he wondered if he should burn the fabric. Burn the entire room to the ground. Perhaps he should do exactly what Celion thought he would do —murder, plunder, and wreak havoc on their island.

But it wouldn't change their reality. All actions felt futile. There was little he *could* do, save to recover his strength.

It was like his early years in the Rhidge—a constant dull, aching pain that riddled the body. It had been a long time since he'd been badly wounded. Earlier, he'd examined the scars in the bathroom mirror—the thin vines that wove up and down his back—with a dull impartiality. There was no fresh pain at the sight—it was as if they had magically appeared.

Granted, his memory was fuzzy, having been drugged with flussidik. The hazy, tired feeling could linger for days. And though his mind was feeling sharper, his back was sore, and his muscles were heavy and tired.

Although the sun was high in the sky, the call of sleep had never been so alluring. An oblivion that darkened his senses, quieted his thoughts.

Aedin closed his hand and the flame disappeared.

He held his breath for ten seconds, as if cutting off his air supply would erase the busyness of his mind. But nothing changed.

Leaning forward over straight legs, he tried to touch his feet. The taut skin of the healed scars seized, and his hamstrings twinged in protest. Frowning, he tried to inhale and exhale, stretching his body closer. It didn't work.

How far he had fallen.

Wincing, Aedin curled his legs beneath him and slowly stood. Small bright stars flickered briefly in his vision as his head felt light. Blindly grasping the arm of the couch, he steadied himself, slowly counted to three, and then opened his eyes. The world was unmoved.

He opened the door to the balcony, and a wall of sound washed over the quiet of the room. There were voices, wheels creaking against the dust, feet moving along the road. He blinked in the bright sun, shielding his eyes with a hand. The air was fresh and cool.

He stepped forward but this time he found his foot couldn't cross the threshold of the door frame. Reaching out a hand, he found the entire frame was a wall of air, pressing him back into the room.

He couldn't see the people below—and they couldn't see him. Perhaps this was what they wanted.

Leaving the door ajar, Aedin turned back to the bed and let his body fall onto the mattress. The sheets were welcoming, warmed by the sun, and smelled faintly of his wife.

He crawled onto his side and faced the wall. The sun heated his back, temporarily soothing the dull ache of his muscles and skin. He closed his eyes, inhaling the scent of the clean linen and lavender.

Minutes later, he was asleep.

———

The sound of a door opening and closing stirred something in his memory. Aedin swallowed and blinked. His vision blurred, until Gwen's familiar blue-gray eyes came into focus. They were assessing and hesitant.

"Hello," she said, offering a small smile.

Aedin grumbled in response, pressing his face further into the pillow and shaking the sleep from his mind. He felt a hand on his shoulder, briefly, before it left. Opening his eyes, he watched her walk into the bathroom and heard the sound of running water.

The light on the wall was a bright orange—it was early evening. His stomach grumbled as he flexed his fingers and toes. Raising his head, he saw a tray of food on the low table by the couch. He sensed this was becoming a routine.

Slowly setting his feet on the floor, Aedin walked unsteadily to the bathroom. His wife sat in the broad tub, staring at the flow of water from the tap.

Gwen looked up at him. Her dark hair flowed down her back, and the tips were wet from the water. Her naked shoulders were losing the tan from Lailan. From their home.

Wordlessly, Aedin pulled off his shirt and shrugged out of his pants. The fabric fluttered to the ground as Gwen shifted to one side of the tub to make room.

Aedin eased into the warmth, curling himself into a ball as the water rose in response to his weight. Leaning back, he turned off the tap until the only sound was of the distant road and the dripping of water. Aedin's eyes flickered towards her bare, pale breasts and then back up at her face. She was quiet, staring at him.

"How was it?" he asked softly, clearing his throat. He realized his voice had been unused since the morning.

"Straightforward." Gwen trailed her fingers along the side of the tub. "Celion challenged my skill with the sword, we sparred for a bit, and then Rowyn and I walked along the path that encircles the Haven… then came back here."

Aedin rubbed his chin. "Did you beat him?"

"Celion?"

"Yes."

A spark of delight flickered across her face. "Several times, yes."

Pride swelled in his chest. He wished he could have been there to see it. "Good."

"He accused me of having been trained by the Rhidge and I agreed quite wholeheartedly." Gwen reached for his fingers, entwining them together. "They seem to be a bit more… predictable with their swordplay."

"They never received a proper challenge until now," Aedin grumbled, placing a kiss on her fingertip.

She agreed with a low sound. "When we were walking, Rowyn told me about Iselleden… their history…"

"To gain your sympathy?" Aedin offered.

"Perhaps," Gwen offered impartially. "I just don't know how… I'll do it."

The word hung between them. He was afraid to say it out loud. *Kill.*

Aedin looked at her significantly. "You said you wanted to last night."

"I want to try," she admitted, "I want to end the terror of the Rhidge and make this world a better place, but I fear the unknown. I fear failure… and death."

Aedin watched her restless gaze with resolute calm. "Death is inescapable. We can only delay it for as long as we try," he said quietly.

Gwen bit her lip and looked away. "Do you think they're all dead?" she whispered. "The guards, the servants, Mary…"

"I don't know," Aedin replied truthfully. His voice echoed hollowly through the small room. Gently, he leaned forward to kiss her knuckles.

Gwen met his eyes with a sad smile, running her hand along his jaw. "Today, when we were walking along the cliffs, I saw the ocean and smelled the salty air… and I realized I miss Lailan."

He ducked his head. "I miss it as well. It… was our home."

She nodded jerkily, blinking and looking away. Aedin cupped the water in his hands and splashed his face, rubbing the short hair of his beard and blinking away the burning sensation in his eyes—the beginning of tears. He cleared his throat and rubbed his face.

"What did you do today?" Gwen asked suddenly, watching him.

"Nothing," he admitted, looking away.

She was quiet, as if knowing his struggle. "You have to heal," she said softly after a moment's pause.

Aedin pressed his lips together in annoyance. She was right, but it didn't take away the shame of helplessness. He changed the subject. "Will you train every day?"

"That's what Rowyn says," Gwen replied evenly.

Aedin rubbed his biceps, feeling the familiar "R" against his left hand. "I should start training again," he announced quietly.

"You don't have to…"

"I do." He gave her a meaningful look. "We don't know what they're planning."

"Rowyn said we'll train for some weeks before returning to the Empire—"

"He could be lying."

"I don't think he's lying."

Aedin shrugged. "Regardless, I need to be ready."

"For what?" Gwen waved her hand around. "Look at this place—this is the safest we've ever been."

"We don't know that," Aedin whispered fiercely. "And we can't become complacent. They are holding us here against our will."

"Aedin." Gwen looked at him in amazement. "There's nowhere else to go."

He fell silent, looking away from his wife in frustration. "*I* am held prisoner. *You* are free to do as you please."

Gwen eyed him and said humorlessly, "How the tides have turned."

Her words hit him like a hammer.

For months, she had been captive in the villa—held to his rules and regulations. And borne the restraints with a graceful determination to end them.

Aedin winced, seeing her wry grin and admitted gruffly, "It does seem that way…"

She gave a low chuckle and slowly wrapped her legs around his waist. "Now *you* understand."

Aedin grabbed her waist, pulling her close. He inhaled her familiar scent and the dust from the road in her hair. "I do," he said simply and kissed her lips. The fatigue from the day seemed to disappear as a thrill washed through him at her touch.

Humming in contentment, Gwen rested her chin against his shoulder as Aedin's hands rubbed her back. The light began to fade from gold into a soft purple and light gray. Aedin suddenly became aware of the lukewarm water and the press of her breasts against his chest.

Gwen pressed her lips to his cheek and slowly stood, exiting the bath. "Are you hungry?" she asked.

"Famished," Aedin said and ducked under the water for a final plunge.

They feasted on the couch, eating a cold meal of meats, fruit, and bread. Little was said, but it was comforting to have Gwen again in his presence. Aedin found himself relishing in every look and touch, and the feel of her familiar Gift wafting through the room. As if a part of him had finally returned to his body.

When they were full, they lay in bed. Aedin tucked his arm beneath her head, her back against his chest, and they watched the sky grow dark.

Stars were beginning to dot the horizon. Aedin felt his wife's warm breath grow steady and long, and he realized that she was asleep. He followed soon after.

———

Aedin woke in the morning when he felt Gwen stir. His eyelids were heavy, and they refused to open as she moved from his side and he heard her feet touch the ground.

Pulling the sheets higher around his shoulders, he situated himself deeper into the bed and the haze of his mind. He dozed, relishing the heavy weight of sleep, as he listened to her move around the room. After some time, the door clicked open, then closed, and then he knew he was alone.

A dull aching echoed through the vines in his back.

It was another day.

He didn't rush to move from his position, waiting until the morning light was full and forcing itself through the room, Aedin finally blinked open his eyes. Breathing slow, he willed himself to move. It took several attempts before he was able to convince his body to obey.

There was a new tray of food on the table. Aedin sat on the couch and idly picked at the fruit, forcing it into his mouth. Some energy returned, though his mind still felt groggy and his limbs were tight. He wondered if he would ever regain the ruthless vigor that he'd always prided himself in. Even the smallest actions felt ambitious and forced.

Aedin itched for the dagger he'd relinquished at the fortress. It was a shame—it had been his favorite that he'd brought from Lailan. But it was a price to pay for being here, in Iselleden, with Gwen.

He would have given his arm, if Rowyn had required it.

That night was a blur—he hardly remembered it. As soon as the fortress doors had blasted open, his body had thrown itself into a mindless fury of action. Aedin didn't remember the first Rhidge he killed, nor the second. He hardly even remembered the Iselleden guard, Loran, who had challenged him in the forest. He hadn't registered the blood coating his hands, splattering onto his face and neck. His only focus had been survival—survive the Rhidge, get Gwen to the boat. And then they had appeared…

He bitterly bit into a grape, hating his helplessness. It had been his choice to surrender, and yet he could have never foreseen what had happened next. Being here—with a prophecy hanging over their heads. Crippled by exhaustion, a drug, and *torture* or punishment for his crimes. It was one in the same.

The distant smell of smoke wafted through the room.

Rising from the couch, he peered out the open glass doors. A column of silvery air rose from the crowd of buildings in the village. There were no sounds, no screaming. The smoke was neat and orderly and so Aedin understood—it came from a pyre.

A funeral pyre for Loran.

Heaviness hung in his chest.

Backing away from the door, Aedin collapsed on the bed, wearily rubbing his face. His hands shook—as if the man's blood still coated his skin. Crawling under the covers, Aedin let himself be sucked back into the oblivion of sleep.

But it was not a restful sleep. A thick, lively pounding echoed in his blood as images flashed behind his closed lids.

It was a Dream.

The shapes arose from a puddle of muddled colors—tightening, clarifying, and becoming sharp. They sucked in his body and spat him out into a place he knew well; a place he had never wanted to return. The king's private room.

The air inside the chamber was stuffy. A small group was gathered around the four-poster bed, shadowed in the dim candlelight. The acrid stench of urine and waste stifled his throat—Aedin choked back a gag.

A familiar pale face, sitting reluctantly at a table in a dark room. And another standing—a mop of dark brown hair combed back fashionably. And then—

His pulse quickened intuitively as he recognized Tours. The stone around his neck shone as thick as blood in the candlelight. Intuitively, Aedin tensed and reached for his dagger—

It was a Dream, he had to remind himself. Just a Dream. But the familiar sharp profile set his stomach into a spiral of hate. And the sight of the smug Daniel standing near the door and Ephraim, shoulders hunched at the table... Aedin felt nothing but pity for his brother-in-law. Ephraim looked as if he wished he were anywhere else.

A medicator was leaning over the bed, prodding the king's arm with a steel instrument. There was a hoarse sound that might have been the king's voice, but the words were indistinguishable. Tours bent towards the bed, whispering something in response.

Kellen—Aedin recognized him from his years at the palace—and a priest from the temple stood in the corner, shifting uneasily at the sight of the sinister dark tools in the medicator's bag.

It was an awkward silence interspersed with fits of coughing, muttered words, and painful breathing. Aedin felt as if he might choke on the thickness of the air. Minutes stretched into more minutes, and Aedin wondered when it would finally end. It was a Dream of the present—he knew that. But what was the purpose? Was it simply to show the king's illness?

Ephraim shifted in his chair, which squeaked painfully in protest. Aside from his evident discomfort, Aedin was relieved to see him looking well. The roundness from drinking was lost and color bloomed in his cheeks. He looked almost happy—almost. With heavy eyes, Ephraim cowed from the others in the room. He played with the latch on his satchel, fingering the lock and strap, anxious for any form of distraction.

Daniel moved from the door to stand alongside Tours as he towered over the bed. Whispering something into his ear.

There was a moment when the shuddered breathing came faster and the medicator moved closer to the bedside. "Your Majesty," he whispered as a gurgled cry emerged from the bedside.

Ephraim looked up, startled at the sudden noise. Limbs thrashed the sheets. Aedin saw the profile of Tours—stern and cold—assessing the scene with an aloof gaze.

In the following seconds, the sound stopped.

And all became still.

Aedin held his breath. The medicator murmured something under his breath, moving his hands along the body. A dense silence fell on the room as Tours exhaled loudly.

"The king is dead," Tours announced promptly, looking at Kellen. "Do not leave this room."

"My lord…" Kellen's brow furrowed.

"No one leaves this room," Tours said in a low voice. "Daniel." He gestured to his assistant. Daniel moved confidently to stand in front of the door and turned the latch on the lock.

Aedin's stomached dropped. He knew what would come next. He felt helpless, wishing to stop it somehow, but there was nothing he could do.

It was then that he understood the purpose of the Dream.

"Now then." A soft smile broke across Tours' face. He smoothed his mustache with grace and turned to Ephraim. "We finally have use for you."

Ephraim swallowed uncomfortably. "Yes, my lord?"

Tours waited expectantly, raising his eyebrows. "Will you write something for me?"

"Yes…" Flustered, Ephraim grabbed his bag and pulled out a sheet of parchment, a quill, and a bottle of ink. He set them on a table, carefully uncorking the ink, and dipped the quill inside the bottle. Hesitantly, he looked up at Tours.

"I, King Serge the Ninth of the Empire of the Seven Islands, hereby break with tradition and decree that Lord Frederick Tours succeed my position on the throne—"

"Wait! This is absurd!" Kellen exclaimed, his eyes wide. "This is *treason!*"

Ephraim's quill paused midair as he winced, his shoulders hunching even further upwards.

"My good sir," Tours simpered. "*Kellen*—it must be so." He folded his arms, watching Kellen sputter with a knowing smile.

"You *cannot* do this." He gestured forcefully towards Tours. Even in the dim light of the room, Aedin could see his face growing red. "No one will let you get away with this—"

"The question is not who is going to let me? It's who is going to stop me?" Tours grinned wolfishly. "*I* alone have run this empire for quite some time. It is only a natural progression— think of it as a *ceremonial* position—"

Kellen was shaking his head. "No! The king's son succeeds him on the throne. That is the way of the kingship."

"Ah." Tours made a face. "Yes… that." He sighed dramatically. "Well, not to worry—I've taken care of it."

"What do you mean?" Kellen scoffed. "Taken care of it?"

"I have removed the obstacle that was in my way."

"What?" Kellen was aghast. "You *what?*"

Aedin watched Ephraim trying to make himself as small and unnoticeable as possible amidst the brewing tension in the room. He prayed to whatever gods were listening—to whatever out there *existed*—that Ephraim's blood would not be spilled.

"You were supposed to *protect* him!" Kellen shouted. "For *generations*, no—*centuries*, the Lord of Radiance has ensured the survival of the bloodline of the king—"

Tours slowly drew out the dagger that was sheathed at his side. "I thought it was time for a change," he said softly.

"This is *madness!*" Kellen cried, his hands balling into fists at his sides. "*No one*—no advisor will back you—"

"You will." Tours looked at him with a deadly stare.

The blade of the dagger was fully exposed. Tours gripped the hilt lightly, running a finger along the naked steel with precision.

"I will *not*," Kellen objected, ignoring the dagger.

"You *will*." Tours stepped towards Kellen, twirling the dagger in his fingers. His blue eyes were thirsty and unwavering.

Kellen visibly swallowed, his eyes finally moving to the weapon. "You cannot…"

"Oh, but the game is already set." Tours grinned. "The pieces are in motion. And you will do your part."

Kellen summoned a burst of courage, stiffening his wiry frame in protest. "You will be *executed* for this!"

Tours extended the dagger towards Kellen, lips curling in satisfaction. "I think *I* will be the one doing the executing."

There was a bated silence as the audience watched Kellen struggle to swallow. His soft face scrunched and tensed, his mouth opening and closing as if to evoke some passionate words of protest. But none came forth.

Daniel surveyed the scene without surprise, his handsome face a mask of grim acceptance. Aedin wondered how long he'd been an accomplice to this plan.

"Now…" Tours announced brightly, "there are two ways forward. One is that I can kill you here and now. The second option is that you sign this declaration, wrangle in the advisors outside that door, and be rewarded for your service to your new *king*…" The word hung in the air between them. "The choice is yours."

The dagger was steady in Tours' hand.

Kellen's eyes were bright and bewildered. "They will not follow me," he objected quietly.

"Oh, I think they will." Tours smirked. "Don't pretend otherwise."

Kellen licked his lips, his shoulders dropping in resignation. "I… will sign," he admitted after a brief pause.

"Good man." Tours flipped his dagger, and Kellen flinched at the sudden action.

Tours grabbed the hilt, replacing it at his belt, eying the medicator and priest standing awkwardly beside the dead body. They bowed their heads, murmuring, "Your Majesty."

Daniel offered a quick bow, muttering the words as well.

Tours' eyes roved over the crowd to finally settle on Kellen. His advisor bowed briefly with a tight, "Your Majesty."

"I would like to hear some more enthusiasm," Tours crooned, his hand once again grazing the hilt of his dagger.

Kellen fixed his jaw, his face reddening as he inclined his body forward again, deeper. "Your Majesty." Kellen let the words linger in his mouth.

"Good start." Tours watched Kellen straighten with unapologetic relish. He graciously waved his hand and turned back to Ephraim, "Now then, let's continue."

Ephraim dipped his quill in fresh ink. A scream caught in Aedin's throat at the madness of it all.

And then the words were put to page.

"Aedin... *Aedin!*"

He awoke in a sweat to Gwen's pale blue-gray eyes. It must had been hours later—the light was dim and his shoulders were sore. Shaking, he forced himself to the present, hearing his wife's soft and consoling words as he sat upright. The smell of smoke lingered alongside the damp dew of the early evening.

Gwen curled herself on the side of the bed, wrapping her arms around his shoulders. "Aedin... You were shaking—what happened?"

Struggling to control his racing heartbeat, he saw the scene unfold again and again in his mind. "I... Dreamed," he said hoarsely. "I was in the palace... Your brother was there and Daniel. The king is dead... and Tours is now king."

Chapter Eight

MY MIND STRUGGLED the comprehend the words.

"Tours is king," I repeated in a whisper. Fear washed through my body—the words sounded unbelievable.

Aedin was silent as his shaking body began to ease into a deadly calm. The deadly, calculating calm of my husband. He folded his hands beneath his chin and stared unseeingly at the floor. "Yes… I'm sure of it."

"H-How could this happen?" I stuttered. "There must be things in place to prevent this from happening—"

"The king mistakenly entrusted Lord Tours with the location and identity of his only son. Tours removed him and threatened Kellen to bring the other advisors to agreement. He already has a stranglehold on the palace—I imagine there will be some resistance, but it's not impossible that he will succeed."

I shook my head. "But *why.*"

"Power?" Aedin mused with a faint smile, his dark eyes flickering to mine.

"He knows about Iselleden," I pointed out in a whisper.

"He knows there's an eighth island… other than that? I'm not sure."

"Do you think he was planning to do this before we escaped?"

"Very likely, yes." Aedin rubbed his shoulders. "I don't think many factors would have deterred him."

We fell silent. I considered this new information, unable to make sense of it. What did Tours want? Other than power over the Empire, did he want to invade Iselleden? And for what purpose?

Aedin vocalized my thoughts. "I don't foresee war coming to Iselleden anytime soon… but it could happen in the near future."

I uttered a low curse under my breath, brushing back my hair. A brief smile flickered over my husband's face at my choice of language.

"We need to tell Rowyn… and the Council," I said slowly. "This could affect their plans."

Aedin nodded mutely in agreement.

I stretched my legs, coming to a stand. My stomach grumbled at the sight of food on the low table, and I began to pick at the platter. Aedin remained on the couch, thoughtfully watching me.

"How are you feeling?" I asked, watching his furrowed brow.

"Hm? Oh… fine," he said absently.

"Did you do anything today?"

"I stretched and then slept," he said in a clipped voice. I saw the glimmer of frustration behind the words.

I changed the subject, offering as I tore off a piece of bread, "Well, Rowyn and I went into the valley."

"What did you do?" Aedin winced as he stretched his legs.

"Walked… talked… His training is more pleasant than Jon's," I tried to joke with a smile. It fell flat as Aedin didn't respond.

I looked up. "Are you going to eat?"

"Yes…" Aedin said and unthinkingly grabbed something from the platter. I watched his actions carefully, seeing the distant and detached look in his eyes.

We were quiet as we ate, and I wasn't sure what else to say. When we were full, we curled in bed together and watched the sky shift from sunset into stars. Aedin's brow eased and I watched him fall asleep. I wrapped my hand in his and considered the possibilities.

———

I woke to a threatening gray sky and Aedin's steady breath. Pushing back the sheets, I rubbed my face and stared out the window. The mountains were shadowed in blues and purples, not yet lit by the sun. A pressing wind, ready to exhale all of its force, pushed lightly at the curtains. A summer storm was brewing.

Tours' hungry eyes flashed in my mind. I had to find Rowyn—this was too important to withhold from the Council.

Exiting into the shadowed hall of the Haven, I nodded to the two guards standing upright against the wall. They were unconcerned with my presence and obviously relieved to not see the dark shadow of my husband.

My boots padded softly against the stones, and I saw no one else in the early morning. A gust of sharp wind slapped my face as I stepped out into the courtyard garden. The olive branches jerked awkwardly in the haphazard gusts. Picking my way through the garden, I looked for Rowyn, but there was no sight of his stern, familiar figure.

I picked absently at a stem of rosemary, smelling the leaf and feeling the oil on my finger. Wandering to the cliff, I stood and gazed out at the town. Without the protective walls of the Haven, the wind rushed through my clothes as they flapped wildly in response. Dark clouds were building on the horizon, about to crest the tops of the mountains. A bright color caught my eye, and I saw an upright figure battling against the currents of air further down the path.

A spine as straight as steel.

Flaming red-gold hair streaming in the wind.

She was watching me.

My stomach flipped as Raine studied me from a distance. Even through the wind, I could feel her power radiating steadily from her body. Hitting me with soft, probing tendrils—like ripples of water reaching the sand.

Slowly, I moved down the path, swallowing back any fear. I dropped the rosemary and it tumbled drunkenly across the stones.

I came before her, standing with folded arms. Her emerald eyes appraised me mockingly.

We were silent—the only noise the growing howl of the coming wind—until I finally asked, "Have you seen Rowyn?"

"No." She turned towards the expanding clouds over the mountains. "It looks to be a storm."

I ignored her comment. "I need to speak with him. It's urgent."

"You may speak with me," she offered lightly, watching my guarded expression with amusement. "I am the Speaker of the Council, you know."

I fixed my mouth in a tight line, considering this. "I don't particularly like you," I confessed, studying the thick ringlets that flowed over her shoulders.

Her laughter was like the rush of a summer stream. "Every individual has their own battles—I suppose mine is that I'm unlikeable."

She was right. Even Rowyn held more warmth in his reluctant amicability.

"Have you enjoyed my brother's company?" Raine continued, watching me with her calculating eyes.

I shrugged. "I wasn't given the choice to spend time with him or not."

"He is honorable and disciplined—perhaps too much for his own good."

"How so?"

Raine shifted her gaze to the walls of the Haven. They were gray and shadowed without the sun. "The nobility of one small action does not determine the outcome of the world. Fate has given us much room for error—more than we think."

I frowned at her words. "And you are not honorable?" I surmised.

"No one is without sin," Raine said lightly. "It would be naïve to think so." Her lips stretched into a beautiful smile.

I let the growing howl of the wind drown out the awkward pause. Raine took a seat, perching elegantly on the edge of the terrace wall. She patted the space next to her, looking down at the darkening road to the town. I hesitated and then joined her, leaving plenty of room between us. The power of her Gift was simultaneously repellent and intoxicating.

The wind painfully whipped my hair against my face. I squinted at the view, feeling small, erratic drops of rain on my bare arms. Shivering, I watched her absent gaze at the darkening valley before us. There were few people on the road. Tiny windows of the homes in the valley glowed with warm light.

"The Director of the Rhidge—Lord Tours—has become king of the Empire," I said, projecting my voice through the growing wail of wind.

Her brow creased in concern. "How was this revealed to you?"

"My husband saw it in a Dream late yesterday."

She was silent as she considered this new information. "Who is this Lord Tours?"

"He is—" I paused as a large gust of wind howled, pressing against our bodies. Stiffening against the impact, I steadied myself on the wall. "We should go inside," I shouted.

Almost reluctantly, she nodded, casting one final glance at the swelling clouds. The raindrops were growing larger and more persistent. I rubbed my arms, folding them against my chest for warmth as a cold wind descended. Raine stood—her tall form towered over me—and led the way through the courtyard back into the Haven.

My ears rang—suddenly devoid of noise—as we entered the near-silence of the residence. Droplets of rain tapped on the glass ceiling above as the wind fought its way into the halls. We walked past the guards at my door—they stiffened at the sight of Raine—and continued deeper into the halls. She finally opened a door, identical to the rest, and ushered me inside.

It was a simple and small room, unlike what I would have imagined for one with such a high position. A bed was furnished in the corner, next to a table, some chairs, and a fireplace. Plain, comfortable, and lived in.

Raine bent before the pile of wood, extending her hand and projecting a blue flame. The wood glowed and sparked to life. Withdrawing her hand, she pulled two chairs from the table and situated them before the fire. I sat obediently, grateful for the sudden warmth of the crackling fire. The echoing howls of wind sounded distantly through the window. I wondered if Aedin was awake yet.

Resting gracefully in her chair, Raine folded her hands and watched me silently. I felt uneasy under her gaze and especially in such close proximity.

"Who is Lord Tours?" she repeated herself.

"The Director of the Rhidge… and the Lord of Radiance. The capital island in the Empire where the King resides."

"Is he Rhidge?" She didn't repeat the word with the same fear and loathing as Rowyn.

"Yes, he is."

Raine paused, scanning my face. "Are you Rhidge?"

"No!" I objected quickly. "I… I didn't even know of my Gift until recently…"

"But you have been trained."

"I know some things," I admitted. "But hardly enough to end someone's life."

"But you will likely have to end a life," Raine pointed out. "You are called to destroy the Empire."

I wavered, until I considered. "What does the prophecy say exactly?"

Raine shifted her green eyes to the fire. "The Prophet spoke to Rowyn—only he knows."

"Why don't you ask the Prophet yourself?"

A brief smile passed over her full lips. "I have only spoken with the Prophet once before—when I was Called to lead the Council… One does not ask the Prophet for themselves. The Prophet seeks out whomever they wish to reveal themselves to."

I frowned at the mysteriousness of it all. "Well, where does...
he live?"

Raine shook her head at my pronoun. "The Prophet is neither
a man, nor a woman."

"How is that possible?"

"They are not bound by the materiality of our world."

I still didn't understand. "Does... Do *they* reside in Iselleden?"

"Yes... Everywhere—and nowhere," she offered evenly.

I wondered if she knew and just wasn't telling me, or if she
was truly ignorant.

"Well." I shifted in the chair. "Unless we get more clarity
regarding the situation, it seems impossible to move forward."

"Why?" Raine lifted her eyes to mine.

I opened up hands in question. "How do you expect me to *end*
the Rhidge's hold on the Empire? And now with Tours as *king*?"
I gave a short laugh.

"Fate will ensure that you are prepared for your task."

"Fate," I muttered bitterly, shaking my head at the burning
logs in the fireplace.

"There are some things beyond our comprehension," Raine
said sagely.

"You've given me no concrete information or assistance." The
words fell bitterly from my lips. "Even Rowyn's 'training' is
hardly preparing me to assassinate a group of *assassins*. Do you
expect me to die?"

Raine didn't respond. She just stared thoughtfully at my face
until I looked away, uncomfortable.

"Why did you torture my husband?" I whispered, exchanging
my fears for a sudden and rising anger.

Raine blinked at me. "He had to atone for the death of Loran
—"

"You did it as a threat. To threaten me to complete your stupid
prophecy."

"It was a thought that had crossed my mind," she admitted
blandly, crossing her legs and leaning back in her chair. "The
action served dual motives."

My fingers curled around the wood of the chair as I watched her indifferent expression. "You hurt him," I said in quiet fury. The wood began to vibrate beneath my fingers.

Raine must have felt the shift and changed her tone. "It was nothing irreversible," she pointed out plainly. "He is healing."

"He is still hurting." My voice was hoarse. I forced myself to breath and calm, despite the pain in my chest.

"I understand."

I looked at her sharply. "Are you married?"

"No," she said simply.

"Then you cannot understand," I replied scathingly.

"There are other forms of love," she said quietly.

I shook my head, unwilling to agree with her at that moment. The wood ceased moving beneath my fingers as my anger shifted to a dull sadness. Distantly, I heard the wind continue to howl—a high-pitched whine that echoed through the walls.

Raine looked up seconds before a polite knock echoed through the room. She cleared her throat and ordered, "Come in."

I knew it was Rowyn—from whatever sense of mine that had identified him. Something had been heightened since my training with Jon and Aedin, since my arrival here on Iselleden. It was like a distinct smell or small tug in the back of my mind that recognized the feel of his Gift. The way the power wafted from his blood and mingled with his everyday musk. I could even detect another lingering note on the back of my tongue—Celion—but Rowyn entered alone and shut the door, looking at me accusingly. "I was waiting for you."

"I was looking for *you*," I retorted without hesitation. "I need to tell you something." And so I relayed exactly what I'd told Raine. She remained silent as I retold the incident, thoughtfully picking her manicured nails as the fire curled lazily in the hearth.

When I'd finished, Rowyn exhaled with an expression of pain and pushed back his hair. "This is not good news," he stated obviously.

I didn't even bother to verbalize my agreement. "We need to come up with a plan," I insisted. "The only way I can be successful is if *we* find the best way forward. You want me to succeed, don't you?"

I looked at Rowyn—I wasn't sure if Raine actually wanted me to succeed or not. She watched her brother impassively, as if she was wondering what to have for lunch.

"Yes," Rowyn replied. "*We* do want you to succeed," he clarified, shooting a meaningful look at his sister. "But we don't know the Empire. I have faith that the Prophet will reveal—"

"Just—stop it!" I sputtered. "No more Prophet or prophecy—we need an actual *plan*."

Rowyn grimaced at the words that were about to leave his mouth. "We can't know—"

"Do you have a plan?" Raine spoke softly, her gaze returning to rest upon me.

"Our *plan*"—I ground my teeth—"was to seek haven on Iselleden. To live here in peace under *your* protection."

"And our *plan*," Raine purred, "was to have you end the wars of the Gifted and destroy the Empire while we remain in peace on our island."

"Well as it seems that neither of our plans will likely manifest as we thought, we need to continue with one together," I stated with finality.

Her eyes fluttered with distant agreement, though she remained silent.

Rowyn looked down at his crossed fingers, his brow creased in concentration as if he could manifest a plan right that minute. I wondered if he'd even tried. Raine was curling a long lock of her hair around her finger, eying me thoughtfully. We heard and felt Celion as he passed through the hall and stopped at our door.

"Well isn't this a party," Raine growled, waving her hand. The door opened on an invisible wind as Celion ducked through the doorway, his eyes roaming over the three of us. The room suddenly felt too small for all of its inhabitants.

Celion squeezed into a place next to Rowyn, standing by the mantel. "We have a situation," he muttered to him.

Rowyn wearily looked up. "What is it now?"

The golden jaw was fixed. "It's the guards," he grumbled, shooting a look in my direction. "There's some… discontent."

"Is it anything the Council can assist with?" Raine asked archly, assuming the full power of her position.

Celion looked uncomfortable. "No—no," he said quickly.

"Is it Selena?" Rowyn rubbed his chin with a wince.

"Er—yes."

"Who is Selena?" I asked.

Rowyn looked reluctant to elaborate, but he answered, "One of our guards. She has been adamant that we continue training."

"Continue? Why did you stop?"

Celion and Rowyn shared a look, before Rowyn sighed bitterly and crossed his legs. "Months ago—before we found you—a merchant ship from the Empire became shipwrecked on our shores. We… killed them out of fear they might be Rhidge. Since then… it just hasn't felt right to pick up the sword."

Raine's bitter hardened gaze became soft and empathetic as she watched her brother. "You did what you had to do. And however painful it is, you must continue that work."

"I suppose," Rowyn admitted reluctantly as Celion placed a hand on his shoulder. "But what if training isn't necessary as we already have a solution…?" He trailed off, his gaze falling to me.

I resisted a groan. "We need a plan," I said for what felt like the hundredth time that morning. "I can't do this alone."

"What of the Rhidge that resides already in our residence?" Raine waved her hand at me. "He can train them while you and Gwen continue to work.

"Absolutely not," Celion snarled, momentarily forgetting his fear of Raine. "Out of the question."

Rowyn was silent as he considered this. "Our people are unused to… their methods."

"It might be time for them to learn," I pointed out. "War may come to your shores. Tours knows about the eighth island."

His reluctance was palpable as he shied away from us. "I don't feel comfortable—"

I was ready to launch into a tirade about doing hard and uncomfortable things when Raine spoke up. "Let him do it, Rowyn. Your burden lies elsewhere. Celion will be there to oversee and intervene if necessary, but it is crucial that you keep up their training. We don't know if or when they will need it."

Her last words dripped from her lips, and she turned to me. "I'm assuming your husband wouldn't mind."

"On the contrary." I shrugged, ignoring Celion's tight expression. "He would thoroughly enjoy it."

Chapter Nine

THE RAIN HAD stopped by the time I returned to our rooms. My mind was aching, swimming with possibilities, filtering through scenarios for the best way to proceed. I knew I was right—we did need a plan—it was just a matter of coming up with one.

And I suspected I'd found an unlikely ally in Raine. Although she had a proven capacity for violence, at least she understood the necessity of a plan. She was more open-minded than her brother, and though she held a soft spot for Rowyn, I now knew she was able to direct him as she saw fit.

As I'd anticipated, Aedin was more than willing to help train the Iselleden guards. He quickly dressed, stretched, and was ready by the time Celion met us at the door.

We followed the same path I'd walked the night I'd arrived, but in reverse. It twisted along the courtyard, stretching to the outer edge of the Haven, leading to a collection of low, square buildings nestled among the grassy hills behind the Council Tower.

We were silent through the walk—I suspected that Celion had no words to express his displeasure, and Aedin didn't want to push his luck.

I trekked carefully through the muddied path but soon realized my efforts were useless. My boots and pants were quickly damp with mud and water clinging to the blades of grass. When we reached the guards' quarters and stepped across the pale stone threshold, I winced at the footsteps that quickly dirtied the spotless stone. Glancing back across the field from where we came, the Tower of the Council looked small and fragile against the puffy gray clouds.

Voices echoed as we ventured deeper into the hall. Various doorways and adjacent halls broke away, leading to living areas or personal rooms. We continued until the corridor turned and opened into a large and airy room. Lit by torches with dancing blue and gold flames, the room fell silent at our arrival.

Rowyn stood among thirteen other guards—some I recognized from our time here so far. He clasped his hands behind his back as they fell into a straight line, standing tall and proud. Celion left us to join the line as Rowyn nodded towards the rack of weapons against the far wall.

"There is everything you need," he told Aedin.

My husband was silent, his eyes scanning everything—the room, the weapons, the way the guards stood with fearful anticipation. "Where are the others?" he asked quietly.

Rowyn frowned. "Others?"

"You only have fourteen. Where are the others?"

"There are no others," Rowyn clarified. "We have fourteen guards to protect the Haven and Iselleden."

Aedin and I exchanged looks—I wasn't trained in battle tactics, and even I knew it was insanity. Iselleden had existed on an island of its own—protected by its own folklore and the Empire's ignorance—and had lost the memory of true battle. If we were to be attacked at this very moment, no matter if the soldiers were Gifted or not, we would likely lose.

I was proud that he swallowed any comment or admonition and instead stepped forward to assess the guards. There were seven men and seven women—nearly all tall with long hair braided down their backs and clad in the same Gifted fabric that fluttered in the invisible breeze. Their eyes tracked Aedin's every move as he slowly walked to the weapons rack and pulled out a sword.

Celion tensed, his hand automatically flinching to the hilt of his own as Aedin inspected the blade.

"Good," Aedin announced to no one in particular as he returned to stand with Rowyn in front of the guards. "What would you like me to start with?"

Rowyn opened his hands in a gesture of impartiality. "Whatever you suggest."

Aedin let the point of the sword relax to the ground as he faced the guards. "My name is Ciaran Aedin," he said to the quiet room. "Although... I suspect you all already know who I am. I was captured by the Rhidge at a young age and tortured, brainwashed to serve the Empire and its interests. For fifteen years I served the king and Director of the Rhidge until we... left." My husband's eyes shifted to hold mine; I found an aching sadness and resolute determination in their depths.

"We will begin with basic sword training to assess your skills and move on from there. Any questions?"

A woman with olive skin and thick, dark hair spoke up. "We have already been trained with the sword."

"What is your name?" Aedin asked.

"Selena," she replied.

I watched Rowyn's brow furrow almost imperceptibly—she was the one who'd started this entire affair. Although shorter than the others, her stance was lithe and her arms strong. She looked like a fighter.

"Selena, I want to see where you and the others stand in regards to the basics before we begin sparring or advanced movements."

She didn't seem entirely convinced of Aedin's answer but nodded in a short jerky movement. Aedin turned to Rowyn. "How long do we have?"

"Several hours with the entire troupe. Moving forward, you'll work together in units of seven—half training while the others guard the posts."

Aedin inclined his head in agreement and began organizing them into pairs, including Celion, to run through basic drills. Rowyn and I stepped back against the wall, watching the scene as Aedin took charge. I could sense a note of relief in his voice as he said lowly to me, "He was born to do this."

"Yes," I agreed, watching as Aedin effortlessly cut the sword through the air, demonstrating with that infectious confidence and authority. "He was."

We were silent as we watched them fall into drills. Despite being small in numbers, the guards were skilled and fit. I understood how they had given Aedin a fair fight at the fortress, the night of the attack. Even Celion's large, sturdy frame was quick and agile as he moved through the motions.

After a while, seeming satisfied with the way things were progressing, Rowyn gestured out into the hall. "Walk with me?"

I shot one last look at Aedin—correcting Selena's grip on the blade—and decided he could handle himself. We left the clanging of swords behind and entered the sharp brightness of a cloudless sky.

The sudden sunlight hurt my eyes as we stepped onto the dirt and grass. We left the guards' quarters and walked along the path back towards the Haven. But instead of entering the residence or Council Tower, we passed through the courtyard and followed the road as it grew wider and descended into the valley.

"Where are we going?" I asked as we began to weave in between the buildings.

"You'll see," he replied evasively, continuing along the route.

The passing Gifted became more frequent as we continued to descend. Some acknowledged Rowyn with a courteous smile and bow of their head, but most ignored us. I felt foreign and was startled when I was greeted with the same civility but then realized that I blended into the crowd. Although a bit formal, my ceremonial garb wasn't uncommon. The same waves of power—some more grand, others subdued—washed over us as we passed each one.

"Does everyone have the Gift on Iselleden?"

Rowyn looked surprised. "Yes. Why do you ask?"

"The men and women sweeping the halls in the Haven," I recalled, "I didn't feel the same power from them as I've felt from others—like you."

"They are called the Wardens. They conserve and maintain the property. It is an honored position, to which only a few are Called. The Gift resides in every individual on Iselleden," Rowyn stated. "That power can be stronger—or weaker— depending on the individual. But that is irrelevant—each individual is Called according to their strengths and the needs of Iselleden."

"Called?" I furrowed my brow.

"What Fate requires from them."

"How does Fate… Call them?" I asked slowly.

He looked up at the sky, pondering my question as we sidestepped a cart lugging vegetables and goods. "It's a feeling," he began, "that you have a place in our world and can contribute to the betterment of our society."

I mulled over his words. "And you were Called to be the Captain of the Guard?"

A bitter smile crossed Rowyn's face. "Yes, I was."

"When?"

"About ten years ago."

I watched his face, suddenly realizing his age. Although each step was graceful and nimble, his face was etched with a weariness that betrayed his years. He was handsome—less so than Raine—and yet carried himself with a heavy posture—as if there was a weight on his shoulders.

"What training should I expect today?" I asked quietly, preparing myself.

"Knowledge," Rowyn responded. His brow crinkled as he looked down at the stones while we descended.

The snow-tipped mountains were bright and colorful in the afternoon light. I looked back to see the Haven grow small as we continued to descend, its pale walls warm and inviting. My stomach dropped as we moved further and further away from Aedin. I was in an unfamiliar country and an unlikely prisoner forced to trust strangers.

And yet, for the pain and confusion from our first arrival, I didn't believe Rowyn wished me any ill. Though we saw the situation differently, we both wanted the same end.

The town was called Farist, as Rowyn informed me, and it was nestled at the foot of the main route, with homes dotting the hills beyond. Simple wood and stone structures were clean and organized. The air was cool down in the valley, the dusty road traded for cobbled stones. Rowyn continued unhurried through the town; his long strides easy.

I watched children play in the fountain of a large square. Families milled about in the buildings, washing clothes in the water, and chatting amongst themselves. A fresh breeze swept through the buildings as we headed down an alley that opened up onto the edge of the town. The buildings grew less compact, and more spread out, as the path curved in multiple directions. We continued straight ahead, nearing some fields where cows and goats were milling about in their pens.

"Does everyone know of the Empire?" I asked, the thought suddenly occurring to me.

"For the most part—yes." Rowyn shrugged. "The Wars of the Ancient Days are part of our native folklore. That the Empire exists is commonly known, but it is a damned and feared place."

I thought of Lailan with a sad smile. "It isn't so bad…"

"Yes," Rowyn said shortly, with a severe gaze, "it is."

I scoffed. "Have *you* been there?"

"No." Rowyn clasped his hands behind his back. "I haven't."

"Then how can you make that judgement?" I raised my eyebrows.

"Because the Empire corrupted the Gift." Rowyn lowered his voice as we moved aside to allow for a cart to pass. "They believed they could control the Gift and harness its power to instill a reign of terror."

"You mean the Rhidge."

Rowyn winced at the word. "Don't say that word so lightly."

"Sorry," I muttered, looking down at my dusty feet. Tall grass emerged on either side of the path and bathed the hills in a soft green.

"But it's only the… that group," I protested. "There are still good people there—my father and brother, for example. Our friends back on Lailan."

Rowyn shook his head, looking at the ground. "There may be innocents, yes. But your world is still plagued with the same fear and despair. The greed, avarice, lust for power…"

"That may define certain individuals, but it doesn't condemn an entire population," I objected.

"These things don't exist in Iselleden." Rowyn looked at me carefully. "We follow the ways of Fate."

"Oh." I eyed him with an incredulous laugh. "So you're saying that *no one* here is ever envious? Or takes advantage of others?"

"On a small scale, yes," Rowyn admitted. "But as part of the fabric of our identity? No."

I wasn't sure if I believed him. I watched his tanned, crinkled brow with suspicion. "If you say so," I granted evasively, watching the cows in the field. The trees lining the path provided periodic shade as we walked through the countryside, leaving the town behind. Large houses lay unobtrusively amongst the trees on the sides of the path. I turned briefly for a glimpse of the village and the bright spot of stone that was the Haven in the distance.

The road turned back into dirt as we left the town for the gentle slopes of the hills. My legs burned from the exercise and I wondered if Aedin had finished training. "They must be done by now," I commented.

"Yes." Rowyn squinted at the sun. "I hope it was productive."

We passed an older woman who took note of our dress and gave a courteous nod of her head. She hardly gave me a second glance, shouldering a bag full of produce as she passed. "Do they not know that I'm from the Empire?" I asked Rowyn.

Rowyn angled his head slightly. "We haven't exactly publicized it."

"Why are you hiding me? Us?"

"I'm not hiding you," Rowyn protested, gesturing to the surrounding countryside.

I looked at him with impatience. "But other people—they don't know I'm from the Empire. They think I'm just another Gifted."

"You are," Rowyn said slowly.

"You know what I mean," I snapped.

Rowyn smiled briefly at the game. "The Council plans to hold an open meeting next week to inform all of Iselleden of the prophecy and your presence. I'm sure already a few know— such is the way of life—and the word may spread by that time."

I considered this. "So how will it work? How do you expect me to dismantle the Empire and destroy the Rh—?"

Rowyn's gazed was turned to the hills in the distance. "I don't know," he admitted. "But I'm confident that Fate will reveal this to us," he added quickly.

"What were the words that the Prophet spoke to you?" I asked suddenly, remembering my earlier conversation with Raine.

Rowyn's face twisted at the thought. "I have not told… anyone what was said."

"I believe that you're acting in the best interest of your island, the Council, and your family. But I have a right to know what was said."

Mutely he nodded in agreement, brushing away a buzzing insect.

I didn't push him. I waited in silence for several minutes, watching the wheat wave in a gentle breeze, until I was rewarded for my patience.

"'Through the sea and waves of time,
A woman comes with gray eyes
To restore destruction of the past,
Ensure the Gift will live and last.'"

As the words faded in the wind, I started and looked at Rowyn with suspicion. "That's it?"

"Yes," Rowyn admitted, avoiding my glance.

I crossed my arms, shaking my head. "There are no… instructions? Advice?"

"No," he sighed, and I saw he was equally frustrated.

Pressing my lips into a thin line, I looked out at the wave of crops. "It doesn't even mention the Empire," I said finally. "*Or Iselleden.*"

"No," Rowyn conceded. "But the meaning can be inferred."

"It can be mistakenly inferred just as easily as it can be interpreted correctly. Perhaps it's less likely to be correctly interpreted."

Rowyn shrugged evasively. "Perhaps. But Fate will show us the way. I Dreamed of the present and saw you at the fortress, which is how we knew to rescue you that night. Your name echoed in my mind. Even if there were some… surprises, it was still correct."

He paused, looking at me. "You have Dreamed?"

"Only once, when I was on Lailan." I inhaled the scent of rich earth and was reminded of home. "I Dreamed of the past and saw my husband training when he was in the Rhidge."

"So the present and future—"

"Remain to be revealed, yes."

Rowyn turned at the last house on the right. The trees shadowed a broad porch that wrapped around the solid wood beams. It looked as if it had stood there for ages. The steps creaked as we walked up them, and Rowyn pulled on the handle of the door without knocking. High voices echoed from inside and grew louder as the door swung open.

"Rowyn!" A small boy stood eagerly, his shoes half untied.

"Darien," a woman warned, shooting a glare at the boy as she laced the shoes of a grinning, short girl with a halo of red hair. "Finish what you started."

He quickly bent back down, clumsily finishing his laces, and then ran to Rowyn and wrapped his skinny arms around his waist. Beaming devilishly, he looked up at him. "Did you come to bring my sword? Can I practice?"

I saw the woman shake her head as she eased herself to stand. Her scarlet hair was coiled into a bun, though stray pieces fell into her face, and she smiled at Rowyn with an easy grin. "I'm sorry you came at such a chaotic time—they've just returned from school." Her gaze rested on me. "Have we met?"

"No," I said hesitantly, watching as the toddler eyed me skeptically. "We haven't."

"This is my sister, Rea." Rowyn gestured towards the woman. "And her son, Darien, and daughter, Demi. Rea, this is Gwyneth."

"Hello," I said softly, watching Darien's small fingers fiddle with the laces. He crowed in delight when they were finally untied, kicking off the shoes with glee.

"Go play outside," Rea instructed her children.

Darien leaped up, grabbing a nearby toy and his sister's hand and hurtling himself through the nearest door.

"Where is Darra?" Rowyn asked, watching them leave.

"She left earlier with some friends," Rea sighed. "I'm glad they're growing up so fast… It gives *me* more time.

I heard their steps on the porch and then Demi's cheerful chatter echo in the lane outside. It was such a simple and joyful sound.

"Tea?" Rowyn asked, striding into the kitchen.

"Yes!" Rea called after him. "There might still be some hot water in the kettle."

Unsure of my purpose here, I followed Rowyn, easing around the maze of chairs and discarded toys. The doorway opened into a room still warmed from the residual heat of the fire. Rowyn stoked the flames and poured more water into an iron kettle. Hesitantly, I sat in a chair and watched him.

"So you have two sisters," I remarked softly.

Rowyn didn't turn to me as he worked, placing the kettle onto the fire. "Rea and Raine are as different as the sunrise and sunset."

"Is it confusing to track the names?" I mused. "Rea, Rowyn, Raine…"

"It's tradition that the children adopt the first letter of their father's name. Rea and Darius, for example, have Darien, Darra, and—" He suddenly fell quiet, and seconds later I heard Rea enter the room.

"Where is Celion?" she asked her brother. "And what brings you to the valley?" Rea eased herself into the chair across from me.

"Celion is training the guards," Rowyn lied casually. "And so Gwyneth and I decided to go for a walk."

The fire began to crackle. I shifted awkwardly under their gaze. Was there something I was supposed to do? Or say?

In the pause, Rea's green eyes flitted back and forth between Rowyn and myself. "How is the Haven?"

"Good." Rowyn nodded, clasping his hands together. "We'll be holding a public meeting next week."

"Oh?" Rea said lightly, watching the kettle as steam began to slowly curl into chimney.

"I never told you this…" He paused, taking a seat at our table. "Some time ago, I was visited by the Prophet and told of a prophecy that would end the Wars of the Gifted. We now know of whom the prophecy spoke."

At his words, Rea's eyes snapped to his face. "Rowyn," she breathed with a bewildered expression. "Are you serious…?"

His face was grim. "Yes," he said plainly.

"When did this happen?" Rea shook her head. "That you should bear this burden…"

"Many months ago. Raine and the Council were the only ones who knew. I'm sorry I had to keep it from you."

"Don't apologize," Rea said quickly, brushing a lock of hair behind her ear. She reached forward to grab his hand. "This is… Do you truly *believe* this?" A broad grin spread across her face as her eyes crinkled.

"Yes." Rowyn looked at me.

I held his gaze and lifted my chin.

A whistle from the kettle echoed through the warm room.

Rea removed her hand and stood, grabbing the handle of the kettle with a towel. She poured the water into three mugs, replaced the kettle onto the fire, then handed us the mugs before dousing the coals in water. They let out a loud hiss.

Grabbing the mug in both hands, I looked down into the murky water, avoiding Rea's curious eyes.

"Is she—Gwyneth—concerned with…?" Rea began hesitantly.

"Yes." Rowyn took a sip from his mug. "She is from the Empire."

A cold silence followed. I looked up at Rea's suddenly pale expression. "The Empire…" she repeatedly dubiously. "But how —?"

"We found her on a small island just west of Iselleden. She was fleeing from the Empire… alone… and sought refuge in Iselleden. My Dream of the present disclosed to me their location, and we rescued them."

I smiled humorlessly, remembering the taste of blood in my mouth as Rowyn's tall shadow had bent to drug me. So this was the narrative he was propagating.

"It's a miracle that you're here." Rea smiled at me. "For centuries we've feared the Empire…" She trailed off, shaking her head. "Who else knows about this?" she whispered, turning to her brother.

"The Council, the guards… and yourself." Rowyn inclined his head generously towards his sister. "I wanted you to know before the meeting next week."

Rea smiled, reaching for his hand, "Thank you for trusting me." She paused. "And you." She extended her hand in my direction. I looked at it cautiously before resting my fingers in her grasp.

"We're so glad to have you." Her severe brow softened as she looked at me. "And *anything* we can do to help, please let us know."

There was nothing Rea could have done to save me from the haunting finality of my situation. Nonetheless, I offered a tight smile in return and said, "Thank you." My skin vibrated with the familiar sensation of the Gift in her grasp.

Over her shoulders, I saw into an open backyard where trees arched above a meadow of grass and flowers.

"Excuse me." I took back my hand and stood, then moved around Rowyn, ignoring his stare, and opened the door. The hinges creaked as it opened and closed, and I walked down the steps to a coarse path that wove through the grass.

My steps whispered against the crushed grass and dirt. The chorus of the birds was quieting in the late afternoon breeze. I looked up and saw the stretching branches of trees that reminded me of my childhood on Berge. They fluttered in the gentle wind, the sunlight flickering through the shades of green.

There was no gate—nothing to stop me from continuing into the hills and the mountains bordering the valley. I briefly thought of running, of trying to escape from Rowyn's watchful eyes and Rea's empathetic gaze. A lump formed in my throat as I suddenly felt a longing for Lailan. I missed the halls of the villa, Andrea and Catherine, the guards, and Mary—

I grimaced as my eyes pricked with tears. I wondered where they were—if they were even alive. A shiver ran through my body as the possibility of death became very real. All of those lives suddenly extinguished by the darkness of the Rhidge.

Rowyn and Rea's whispers trailed from the house; the sound was mingled with a rush of air through the trees. Even though Aedin was only miles away, I suddenly felt very alone in this new and foreign world.

Chapter Ten

"YOUR MAJESTY."

It was days later, and those two words had still not lost their luster. Tours smiled silkily, opening his eyes to the canopy of rich fabric above his head. Candles were lit and the room was cast in a warm glow. Stretching his limbs, Tours eased out of bed and wrapped a robe around his body. A servant set down a tray on a table and bowed before exiting.

After relieving himself in the bathroom, Tours splashed water on his face and head, pushing back his damp hair. It was growing long and he wondered if he should get it cut.

He brushed his mustache, clipping a stray hair that had grown out of line. Satisfied by the symmetry of the composition, he sat down at the table to eat his breakfast.

A quiet knock echoed through the room.

"Enter," Tours called out, sipping his tea.

A tall dark shadow slipped into the room and bowed before him. She left a pile of papers next to the food. "Your Majesty," Bela murmured.

"Thank you." Tours set down his cup on the saucer and began thumbing through the papers and scanning the words on the page. "Any sign of Mary?"

"No, my lor—Your Majesty," Bela fumbled. "But Kitra Devereux boarded a ship for Radiance several days ago. She should be arriving soon."

Tours smirked—she was always the first to arrive at the scene of the crime. Even before the Lord of Lailan himself would make the journey to visit their new king.

"Anything else?"

"Nothing you don't already know."

"Indeed." He grabbed a piece of toast. "Thank you."

"Your Majesty." She bowed again, moving towards the door.

"Oh—" Tours looked up from the papers. "And how is our newest recruit getting along?"

Bela's face darkened. "He still needs some work."

"Of course." He waved his hand. "Please see to it."

She inclined her head and left the room without a sound.

Tours read through the papers as he finished his meal. It was the usual gossip of the palace and reports from the other islands. Lord Cabot was getting a handle on his work in Lailan; he'd improved the situation in the port, and the backlog of ships was decreasing. Berge was facing a shortage of game for their fall hunting season—Lord Tremer had requested to purchase some elk from Radiance to aide their dwindling population.

Tours had expected some tediousness in the actual governing part of being king, and yet he found the reality to be quite the opposite. He relished knowing every little issue within the Empire, no matter how insignificant or grand. It meant he was the most informed and could utilize the information for his advantage. Knowledge was power—and he wanted to hold the most of it.

Yet for all the enjoyment he received through reading the papers, Tours was still frustrated by the inconclusive nature of the Aedin situation. There had been no word—the fortress was empty. No ships on the horizon. Nothing. It was likely they were in the hands of the eighth island—but he didn't even know if they were dead or alive.

It was frustrating to not have control.

Sighing, Tours shuffled the papers and aligned their edges parallel to the table. He bit into a slice of meat, enjoying the smoky flesh. Indeed, there were many benefits to being king. Food was chief among them.

A knock echoed for the second time. "Enter," Tours called again.

Daniel and Ephraim entered the room, bowing low before taking their seats at the table. Ephraim sat at the end, avoiding his gaze, while Daniel took the closest seat. The thick stone of Radiance hung around his neck.

"My Lord Terrace," Tours said with relish, noting the smug look pinching Daniels' nose. "And Mr. Doyle," he added off-handedly.

Ephraim said nothing in response, pulling out his bag and quietly assembling a parchment and quill on the desk.

"Your Majesty." Daniel grinned at him. "I wanted to run through our schedule for the day."

"Go ahead."

"We have the advisor meeting in fifteen minutes, where we'll review the accounting ledger for this past year. Lady Hollande of Avellian sent a letter noting her undying fealty to your reign and wishes you every health and happiness."

"How kind." Tours cut another slice of meat with relish.

"After the advisors, you'll have a private meeting with Greymont. I suspect he wants to suggest his daughter as a potential match. In exchange, he would like his orchards to be the primary supplier of fruit in the palace."

"Is she pretty?"

"Calinda Greymont?" Daniel considered this with a shrug. "Not bad."

Tours nodded thoughtfully as Daniel continued. "We did have several other meetings lined up after Greymont, but I received a request for an audience from Kitra Devereux. I thought that might take precedence," he added hesitantly.

"Yes." Tours nodded, sipping water from his goblet. "After Greymont."

"Yes, Your Majesty. There are several parties you might wish to attend later this afternoon and then dinner in the evening."

"Fine." Tours waved his hand. "But I'll need time in my schedule tomorrow morning to go over some business. Please do not book me until mid-afternoon."

"Yes, Your Majesty." Daniel made a note on his paper. "Anything I can help with?"

"No." Tours looked down at the papers on the table, shifting one that was out of place and pressing it back into line. He thought of the dark halls of the Rhidge with a thoughtful smile.

"Mr. Doyle," Tours pronounced as Ephraim looked up with a start. "Did you receive any conflict regarding our proclamation regarding the succession?"

"None in Radiance, my lord. And I've not heard otherwise from elsewhere."

"Good." Tours smiled in satisfaction.

Ephraim ducked his head again and scribbled on his parchment. Tours saw Daniel shoot a look of exasperation in his direction.

"Well, my men of Berge." Tours stood as they hurried to their feet in response. "Let us begin our day."

———

The advisor meeting was uneventful and abstract. The men were silent—likely still struggling to tread water in this new political environment. At least Kellen kept his mouth shut and Greymont simpered in agreement throughout the hour. There was little profit from last year's taxes, but the increase in taxes was set to pass next week. Though it would be a while until the gold was in his pocket, Tours looked forward to putting that money to good use; an expansion of the Rhidge, new weapons, and trainees.

After the meeting was adjourned, Tours beckoned Greymont to his private rooms. Goblets of wine were poured and they chatted idly before Greymont brought up his daughter. Tours offered a noncommittal answer, unwilling to publicly associate himself so soon with a potential match.

There were many other factors to consider. For one—did he even want to establish a succession through blood? And if so, would it be through the same structure? Or a traditional marriage? It was thrilling to consider the possibility of starting afresh. That he could bring to life a *new* Empire. One built on ruthless efficiency, powerful and strong.

Tours poured himself another glass of wine as he grew bored listening to Greymont describe the superior quality of fruit from his orchards. It was a painfully parochial subject. He was grateful when a knock echoed through the room.

"Your Majesty." His valet, Fray, poked his head through the doorway.

"Yes?" Tours looked at him in anticipation.

"Your next guest is here."

"Thank you." He stood extending his hand. "Greymont, I shall consider this."

"Please do, my lord," he said gruffly, smoothing his graying beard. He bowed low and exited through the door.

Seconds later, a familiar figure entered and ducked into a low curtsy.

"Miss Devereux." Tours held out his hand.

"Your *Majesty*." Kitra placed her lips on his knuckles, rising with a smile.

She looked as beautiful as when he'd last seen her a month ago at the reception on Lailan. Her thick blonde hair was pulled back into a low style, and her emerald gown was tight. He knew it had cost her a fortune to have that one made, and that she'd saved it especially for this meeting.

"I came as soon as I heard," she said breathlessly as Tours gestured towards the table, pouring her a fresh glass of wine. "I could hardly believe it."

"And yet, it is true." Tours lifted his goblet in a salute as she joined him. Their goblets clinked together and Tours savored the taste of wine.

"It was long overdue," Kitra continued, her voice low and soft. "Serge was growing old and incapable of ruling to the full extent of what was required."

Tours inclined his head in agreement. "Your political acumen is one of your many charms."

Her full red lips stretched into a modest smile. "I owe it all to my many teachers—yourself included." She smoothed her dress, taking another sip of wine. "And is there any assistance that I can offer you? How is Kellen adjusting to the change?"

"Kellen is already taken care of." Tours waved his hand dismissively. "But I'm sure if you find the time in your busy schedule, he would appreciate a *reaffirmation* of faith and loyalty."

"Of course." Kitra inclined her head demurely. "And I was quite surprised to hear our new Lord of Radiance was so… young."

Tours chuckled in spite of himself. "I *love* a good success story… Nearly a year ago, our young friend Daniel was merely a guard for the Lord of Berge. Now, he is *Lord* of Radiance." He gestured towards her. "He'll be needing a wife."

Kitra eyed him with a cool gaze. "I had set my sights elsewhere."

Tours met her eyes unflinchingly. "Of course you have," he said smoothly with a coy grin.

"And what of the historian? Will you keep him at his post?"

"Ephraim Doyle? Yes, I should think I still need him."

"Do you?" Kitra's tanned brow wrinkled. "His sister and Lord Aedin are dead. He has no use to you."

"Ah." Tours considered telling her the truth but decided against it. "But you see, he's not very fond of me. And I would rather surround myself with those who detest me than those who love me. I like to know what they're doing and keep a close eye on them."

"I understand completely." Kitra sipped her wine. "Then I shall have to board the next ship back to Lailan." She emitted a heavy sigh, her chest rising and falling in the action.

Tours gave a wolfish grin. "Oh but, my dear, I do thoroughly enjoy our games together."

Kitra smiled smugly, leaning forward in anticipation. "Then what shall we play?"

Tours let his hand wander to touch the tight skin of her knuckles. "I had something in mind," he growled, watching her full lips pull into a wide grin.

———

Kitra left when Tours was spent. He lay on the sheets of his bed staring at the closed door, feeling thoroughly satisfied and tired. His back ached—he wondered if it was the penalty of age.

Nevertheless, he forced himself to rise and pull on his pants. It was pertinent to remain on schedule, despite the small diversions he allowed himself.

When he exited his private rooms, Fray leaped to attention. "Your Majesty, there is a gathering in the garden to celebrate your kingship that you should attend."

Tours nodded brusquely. "Of course. Is the Lord of Radiance there?"

"Yes, Your Majesty." He bobbed his head, swallowing conspicuously. Fray had always feared him—even when he'd been the Lord of Radiance. Perhaps this change had only increased his fear.

"Your Majesty." A soft voice echoed from his side. Tours turned to see a young, blonde woman holding out a thick ceremonial robe he'd often seen the king wear. He stared at her in mute frustration—what was her name again?

"You remember Hollyn Litany." Fray coughed in the pause.

"Yes," Tours lied easily, holding out his arm as Hollyn helped him into the robe. "You were assisting Priscilla before she was sent back to Acedes." It all came back to him. She had then transferred to the king's household. And now his.

"Yes, Your Majesty." Hollyn brushed off some lint from the shoulders of the robe. Her round face was sweet, plain, and utterly professional as she addressed him. "And it is a pleasure to serve you." She stepped back with a curtsy.

Tours looked in the mirror, trying not to grimace at the weight of the thick robe. His hands itched towards the dagger hidden at his calf to ensure he was still able to reach it, but he restrained himself. Nonetheless, he thought he looked quite regal and straightened his shoulders intuitively.

"And this." Hollyn held out a thick diamond resting on a chain. It was the stone of the king and the Empire—far superior than the other stones worn by the lords. Tours ducked his head as she stood on her tiptoes to gently place the chain around his neck.

It was heavy against his chest. Tours watched Hollyn step back and look to Fray for direction. Fray cleared his throat and waved his hand towards the door. "This way," he said with a bow.

Tours inclined his head to Hollyn, and she curtsied in response. She was direct, quiet, and aloof; exactly what a servant should be. But could she be trusted?

Ignoring the bows of the waiting courtiers outside the door, Tours strode through the halls. Some followed him as they progressed—Tours in the lead and Fray following shortly behind. They exited the thickly carpeted halls of the king and entered the main hallway, descending among the flow of people. Many stopped to the side, bowing and whispering as he passed.

Tours watched them with pleasure, relishing the thought that he was now king. From within these stone walls, he'd been shaped and molded into a man of strength and power. He'd risen from a youth of pain and suffering. He'd survived the Rhidge by embracing it and vanquishing his enemies; by being the strongest and superseding the weak. It had been the natural choice to select him as the Director of the Rhidge and the Lord of Radiance, but *he* had chosen his own path to the kingship.

He projected his Gift as a habit—searching for any possible threats that might had been overlooked. The tendrils of power seeped through the crowd, but there was nothing in response. All was secure.

As they exited from the main halls into the garden, the fresh breeze was intoxicating. Tours looked back at the looming stone structure of the palace and the trail of people who followed. They were all sheep—following his every whim as he pleased. He grinned predatorily watching the expanse of courtiers on the lawn. Tents were erected over long tables laden with food and wine. A server came forward with a bow, extending a tray of wine. Tours took a glass, rolling the liquid over his tongue to detect any poisons. Nothing unusual.

He swallowed with satisfaction, catching sight of the Lord of Radiance through the crowd. Daniel was speaking with a woman who was clearing enjoying the conversation. At the rustle through the crowd, he caught sight of Tours and left the woman to come by his side.

"Your Majesty." Daniel bowed low. His brown hair was freshly washed and combed fashionably. Taking a glass from the server, Daniel fell into step with his king.

"Are all of the advisors here?" Tours asked gruffly.

"Yes, Your Majesty," he said lowly, gesturing towards the tents.

Tours scanned the crowd, spotting Greymont and the rest of the group. He frowned suddenly. "Where is Kellen?"

"Kellen?"

"Yes."

Daniel squinted as he studied the lawn. "He was here earlier…"

Tours waved a hand in dismissal. "Perhaps he went to go piss in the bushes."

"Yes, Your Majesty." The corners of Daniel's lips quirked into a smile.

Tours sipped his wine, spotting Kitra in the crowd. She was chatting gaily with the elder son of Greymont, laughing suddenly at something he'd said. Tours watched hungrily as she placed a hand against her breast, a wave of desire rising in his own. But there was time.

He tore his eyes away, catching sight of another familiar figure at the edge of the crowd. Ephraim Doyle sulked by himself with a cup of wine as he watched the scene morosely. Suddenly, his expression melted into one of excitement as Hollyn Litany strolled to his side, offering him a kiss on the check.

As Ephraim straightened and brightened, Tours placed the puzzle pieces together, grinning at his luck. He would indeed have to keep Ephraim around. Or, he supposed, Hollyn's presence kept him at the palace regardless. He didn't even have to lift a finger.

Tours motioned to Fray, who in turn gestured to an adjacent trumpeter. He let out a series of notes as the crowd gathered together expectantly and grew silent.

"The King of the Empire," the trumpeter announced loudly, his voice resounding through the grounds. Tours straightened his shoulders, breathing in to project loudly.

"It is with great pleasure that we join together on this lovely afternoon in a show of unity and strength," Tours said, his words thundering through the crowd. "These have been trying times, and they indeed test our will to persevere when circumstances become hard. The death of King Serge and his last will for succession was entirely unexpected, and yet I rise to the challenge to guide this Empire into a new age of glory.

"Our seven islands are bastions for the wealth of production, the seeking of knowledge, and stand as a testament to the perseverance of the human spirit. We—the people—are defenders of all that is good and worthy despite the threats to undermine our power and authority. Do not fear the spirits of the past—shackled by tradition and rituals—let us look forward to spread the powerful might to those who need to hear our sweet words of freedom."

Through the sea of faces, Kellen weaved into the crowd to join the other advisors at the back of the tent. Whispered words were exchanged as they bent their heads together. Tours ignored them, focusing on the enunciation of his words as they reverberated across the field.

"Therefore, we join together as blood from a long line of hardworking men and women who built the greatness of this empire. It will require more sacrifice and more pain, but all good things require patience accompanied by great efforts."

There was a movement out of the corner of his right eye. An unknown man was shifting towards where Tours stood.

"So we raise a glass." Tours raised his goblet in the air. "And salute those who came before us and those who stand beside us at this very moment. To the king and Empire."

The crowd echoed his last words as Tours took a sip of his wine. The man drew closer, easing through the growing crowd that encircled Tours, coming to kneel before him. His long brown hair was tied, and his clothes looked slightly too large for his thin frame.

"Your Majesty," he murmured, his eyes cast to the ground.

"Rise," Tours commanded.

As he stood, Tours caught the glint of light reflecting against the blade of a dagger.

His instincts kicked in.

Dropping the wine on the grass, Tours pushed the man's arm aside as the approaching blade glided towards his waist then grabbed it, thrusting a knee into his stomach and a fist into his face. A loud cracking sound echoed, and the dagger dropped uselessly to the grass.

Shouts and cries began to reverberate through the crowd. Tours ignored them, picking up the dagger and slamming it into the man's shoulder. He cried out, and Tours forced him to the ground.

By now the nearby soldiers were beginning to react.

Tours looked up and saw them running towards him as the man lay groaning on the grass.

He stepped back, pulling out the dagger from the flesh and tossing it onto the ground. Brushing back his hair, he watched them bind the man's hands and pull him to a stand.

"Take him for interrogation," Tours ordered brusquely. "And get me another glass of wine."

"Your Majesty." The soldiers nodded respectfully, their eyes wide and slightly panicked. They dragged the man across the grass as the crowd parted, their cries fading into murmurs.

Fray appeared by his side, holding out a glass of wine with shaking hands. Tours took it, finishing the liquid quickly with a satisfied sound.

He handed it back to Fray with an amused look. "Why so frightened, Mr. Fray? You weren't the one who was attacked."

Daniel pushed through the crowd with an urgent expression, not even bothering to bow before Tours. "Your Majesty," he gasped. "Are you well?"

"Indeed," Tours said casually. He nudged the bloody dagger on the grass with his foot. "Give this to the solders, Mr. Fray, will you?"

Daniel shook his head in admiration. "It all happened so fast—you reacted so quickly."

Tours' gaze swept over the field as he saw the party begin to resume and the looks of shock dissipate into whispers and laughter. His advisors were still huddled together, exchanging forceful words and looks of concern.

Tours met the eyes of Kellen as he looked away quickly. Too quickly.

"Years of training, my lord." Tours smirked, addressing the crowd loudly. "It will take more than a rogue assassin with a blunt blade to kill me."

Chapter Eleven

"ARE YOU READY?" Rowyn's voice echoed through the door.

"Coming," I called back, running a brush through my hair.

Aedin was chewing on a piece of bread, patiently watching me. I frowned in pain as I detangled the knots, attempting to appear somewhat decent for the day.

"Maybe I should just cut it all off," I grumbled at my husband as he sat watching me with a quiet smirk. He didn't comment and instead picked up some grapes from the tray.

Satisfied that I finally was able to run my hands through my hair without any snags, I stepped to the mirror and assessed myself. The traditional fabric of the Haven danced above my tanned feet, the short sleeves of my shirt fluttering just above my biceps. Pale blue like the morning sky with a hint of verdant green, the colors shifted and swirled just above my skin. I intuitively looked to smooth the creases, but there were none.

Shrugging, I walked to the door and pulled it open. "*Now* we're ready," I said sweetly, seeing Rowyn's impatient gaze.

Aedin rose from the couch, tearing off a final chunk of bread. Perhaps having him train the guards was helping him heal more than I'd thought. The past week had given us both a sense of rhythm, a feeling of normalcy although our position here remained plagued with the impossible task hanging over my head.

Though the skin on Aedin's back was completely healed, the swirling vines remained, along with residual phantom pain from the torture. But Aedin's dark skin had returned to its bronzed and healthy glow, filled with life and energy.

We left the room and entered the hall, Selena and Celion trailing behind Aedin. They too appeared freshly bathed and somewhat neater than normal. Celion's golden jaw was a bit more relaxed; he gave us a curt nod instead of a scowl. It was certainly an improvement.

As we wound through the halls, an unfamiliar sound drifted in through the courtyard—a multitude of voices. When the bright sun hit our faces, I blinked at the crowd gathered among the olive trees and benches. There were many unfamiliar faces— as if I would recognize any at all. Few wore the matching traditional dress of the Haven—most were wearing their everyday clothes. People from Farist, and perhaps beyond.

Rowyn suddenly appeared at my arm, touching my elbow in a gentle command, pulling me from my frozen surprise. He'd told me about this meeting, but I hadn't expected it to be so… public. Or crowded.

There was a raised platform in the center of the courtyard where the other six members of the Council were already gathered. Raine stood tall, her wide shoulders thrown back and impassive emerald eyes glittering as we ascended the steps to join them. An elderly man smiled gently at me, but I struggled to return his kindness. I was suddenly nervous. It felt as though all of Iselleden were present—and to see *me*.

Gesturing to the side, Rowyn guided us to a spot adjacent and slightly behind Raine. I was grateful to have her be the center of attention.

I clutched at the sides of my pants as I felt Aedin's hand loosen my grip, entwining our fingers together. Turning my head slightly, I saw his small, encouraging smile and forced one in return, swallowing my nerves.

"We are grateful to have you all gathered here this morning," Raine's voice boomed across the courtyard. She waited as the final trickles of conversation ceased to flow before she continued. I watched the sunlight reflect off her red-gold curls. "And we thank Fate for a beautiful day."

The courtyard was now silent. People shifted under the warm sun, squinting at us. They stretched along the paths that extended along the crest of the cliff. Silent and waiting.

"Months ago, our Captain of the Guard, Rowyn, son of Reynolds, was visited by the Prophet and told of a prophecy. The prophecy spoke of a way to end the terrible reign of the Empire and restore the power of the Gift and the ways of Fate across the land. The Prophet spoke of a woman who would come from across the sea to aide us in our struggles. She is here now."

Raine looked at me, along with the hundreds of other eyes in the crowd. I stiffened, tightening my grip on Aedin's hand.

"Gwyneth Aedin—will you fulfill the Prophet's words and endeavor to abolish the horrible deeds of the Empire?"

There was a pause as I realized she wanted me to speak. My heart thundered, and in the seconds-long pause I considered what to say. The structure of her phrasing didn't escape me and I was grateful that she didn't force another yes or no question regarding the prophecy. It was easy enough to endeavor to do something and she had said nothing about killing.

"I will." I attempted to project my voice and was glad it didn't shake. Rowyn's emerald gaze was steadily watching me.

"Then we will celebrate as today is the first step—among many—to ending the systematic genocide of our people in the Empire."

As the last of her words echoed through the courtyard, there grew a resounding sea of noise. Claps and cheers reverberated through the Haven, and I saw the faces of joy and hope that stood in front of us. Even Raine's face stretched a grin as her hands joined in the clapping. She looked at me and gestured off the stage in the opposite direction.

I descended the steps and was immediately drawn into the midst of the crowd. I felt Aedin's sudden anxiety at their proximity, and his hand met the small of my back to propel me forward. Hands reached out from expectant faces. There were young women, old men, even children gazing up at us curiously as we slowly moved through the throng. I realized we were headed towards the Tower and saw Raine, Rowyn, and the rest of the Council follow behind us.

"Matr, matr," I heard the word echo around me.

A small girl stepped in front of my path holding up a broken flower with a shy smile. I reached down and accepted the gift as she scurried back to the shelter of her mother's cloak.

I gripped the stem gently and tried not to crush it.

We reached the edge of the crowd and the guards beckoned us through the doors to the Tower. I released the breath I was unconsciously holding as our bodies were bathed in the kaleidoscope of colors.

Aedin's brow finally smoothed and he dropped his hand from my back, though it remained close. As the rest of the Council filed into the hallway, watching me curiously, Raine resumed her control. She lengthened her strides, and we followed her to the Tower as the rainbow of colors was traded for a blinding white light.

Seeing the familiar seven daises rising from the spotless floor made my stomach churn. They'd managed to remove the stains from Aedin's blood, as if they could erase our memories as well. Aedin was also uneasy, his steps deliberate and slow as he watched Raine slowly ascend to her throne. I saw his fingers twitch towards his waist, wishing for his dagger. Although he'd been allowed to train the guards, they still denied him the luxury of a weapon.

Rowyn helped an elder man up the steps before taking his seat as well. We stood awkwardly in the center watching them settle until the noises faded into silence.

"Rowyn." Raine's voice floated through the room. "Where are we with her training?"

Rowyn cleared his throat before responding. "She's familiar with the art of sword fighting, and her Gift is strong but needs more direction."

A woman with short black hair spoke. "And what of her husband?"

"He is already fully trained in combat—both with swords and the Gift."

"By the Rhidge," Raine added quietly.

Rowyn hesitated, a look of disgust briefly crossing his face. "Yes."

"How much longer do you need?" Raine continued, looking at Rowyn.

"Several weeks I believe."

I frowned at his words. "Several weeks?" I repeated dubiously, glaring at Rowyn. "That's hardly enough time."

"The Prophet hasn't revealed any further instructions aside from the original prophecy." Rowyn opened his hands helplessly. "We must proceed as we see best."

"We've already discussed that your plan is impossible." I scowled at Raine, which she easily ignored. "But I have another idea."

This time, Raine didn't ignore me. Her eyes turned to me, narrowed in suspicion. "Do you?"

"Yes. We need more time to train everyone."

"Everyone?" the older man croaked from his dais.

"Yes," I said impatiently. "I can't do this alone. We need to train the guards and recruit others to create a force of Gifted that will overcome the Empire *together*."

Muttered words began to echo throughout the walls of the Council Room—they drowned out my voice.

Rowyn's face became red, his hands tightening into fists. "I will not let Iselleden blood be spilled for this," he hissed. "*You* were called through the prophecy—"

"I can't do it alone," I objected. "It's madness."

"Fate will guide—"

"We do need to raise an army," a deep voice echoed in agreement as a burly man spoke. "We should have invaded the Empire long ago!"

"They will be slaughtered by the Rhidge," a woman said with exasperation. "We can't confront them in direct combat."

"Iselleden is *pure* and will remain as such," Rowyn continued, his hands gripping the arms of his seat.

"How else do you expect me to do this?" My voice rose and ricocheted off the walls. "You *yourself* admitted the obscurity of the Prophet's words. There is no direction, no suggestion that it has to be me alone—"

"*Silence.*" Aedin's voice echoed powerfully, ceasing the activity in the room.

I took a deep breath, calming myself as my fingers itched to push Rowyn off his dais. The expression on his face suggested that he wouldn't have minded shoving me off the Council Tower.

Aedin stepped forward, scanning the room with his dark eyes. "Ending the life of the king or slaughtering the Rhidge will not bring peace." His voice was hollow. "It's like cutting off a branch on a tree and expecting the tree to die. The tree will grow another branch. We need to begin from the roots."

Raine shifted in her seat, her shoulders tensing in anticipation. "And what do you propose?"

"As Gwen has said—we train the guards and anyone else in Iselleden who wishes to join, and bring a force to the island of Lailan. There are Gifted there—many in hiding from the Rhidge —who will help our cause. We will draw out the Rhidge to Lailan and attack them there."

Silence filled the space where his words ended.

Rowyn watched the scene unfold with a look of horror. "A battle?" he choked.

Aedin was unperturbed, folding his arms across his chest. "How else? We could attempt a singular assassination of Tours, but the rest of the Rhidge would be intact. We need a large-scale confrontation, and one that is *public.*"

Raine considered the words with an elegant tilt of her head. "You think you can persuade Lailan to follow you," she surmised.

"It's our best hope. The strength of the Rhidge lies in its secrecy."

"But the Gift…" I hesitated. "No one in the Empire knows of the Gift."

"It's time that they understood," Aedin said with finality.

"We will *not*," Rowyn hissed, "give the lives of our people for *your* cause."

"But this is *our* cause, isn't it?" Aedin looked around the room. "Our lives are joined together."

Raine inclined her head in a halfway nod as the black-haired woman spoke up again. "How do you propose to train our people? They are unfamiliar with… your ways."

"We train them to use their Gift offensively and in basic sword combat." Aedin folded his arms across his chest. "It will take several months—perhaps longer—depending on their skill."

Rowyn's face was tight and red, his hands still clutching the arms of his throne.

"And how will we get to the Empire?" the older man croaked. "We do not have the warships of your Empire."

"How many ships do you have?" Aedin looked at Raine.

She tilted her head towards the burly man. "Berius?"

"We have dozens used for fishing, but there are several larger ones that could ferry a hundred or so each."

"We can outfit them for the journey," Aedin said simply, as if it was done every day.

"It can be done." Berius inclined his head with a look of respect. "Though it will take some time."

"We don't have the luxury of time," Aedin added quickly. "The Rhidge could be headed here today. We need to start tomorrow."

Rowyn stood with a sudden movement. "I *will not* allow this," he hissed.

Several other Council members murmured their assent in the brief silence.

"You aren't supposed to even *be* here." Rowyn pointed his finger at my husband. "This prophecy involves only *her*"—his finger aimed towards me—"and the Empire. You are an unfortunate accident."

Aedin's dark brows were lowered. "My Dream of the future was being *here*," he growled. "My *wife* was brought here without her consent. I have every *right* to be here."

Rowyn shook his head. "No, this will not happen this way."

"Then what do you propose?" Aedin folded his arms and glared up at Rowyn.

"Gwyneth returns to the Empire to assassinate your king in secret and uses the power of her Gift to assassinate the rest of the Rhidge."

"There are nearly a hundred young assassins cloistered within the walls of the palace," Aedin stated. "They are eager to kill and prove themselves. How will she kill them *all*?"

"By using the power of her Gift."

This was getting out of hand. "*Stop*," I projected my voice through the room, pointing my hand at Rowyn. "Sit down," I ordered.

He struggled against the force of my Gift but finally assented.

The temperature in the room decreased to a simmer. "I can't do it alone," I began slowly.

"We have only *just* begun your training—"

"Regardless," I said, raising my voice to cut him off. "The chances of success are exponentially greater should we bring our forces together to obliterate the Empire."

My words rang in the sudden silence of the Council Tower. The Council members shifted in their seats, exchanging concerned glances.

"We will consider these options," Raine said. "And return with a solution. We have much to discuss." Her eyes drifted towards her brother as he fumed silently at the floor.

Aedin looked pained at this decision but kept his mouth shut. I was glad to see that Rowyn was silent as well.

"Good." I clasped my hands together. "Then we'll leave you." I turned towards the door with Aedin's footsteps echoing behind.

Chapter Twelve

THE CROWDS HAD long gone when we emerged from the Council Tower, the stone courtyard empty but for a few Gifted talking quietly among the benches. We were still flanked by a pair of guards, though at a distance, as if it was more of a tradition, rather than a threat.

I aimed for an open spot along the low wall spanning the cliff, Aedin following silently at my side. The wind ruffled his hair as he scratched his beard, thoughtfully gazing out at the valley.

"Well that went well," I began humorlessly.

A tight grin flitted across Aedin's face. "We received more support than anticipated. That counts as a successful attempt."

"I'm glad we spoke." I ran my hands along the warm stones beneath me, basking in the afternoon sun. "Although I hope it didn't destroy what I've built with Rowyn since coming here."

Aedin angled his head, his mahogany eyes scanning my face. "Rowyn has good intentions, but they are misguided. Have you received *anything*—any Dreams, any direction, any visits from their Prophet since you've been here?"

Biting my lip, I looked out at the expanse of the valley. "No," I admitted lowly. "But we need to give them time to consider. *They* need to come to this decision collectively."

"Raine will do whatever Rowyn thinks is best," he grumbled.

"I wouldn't be so sure," I said slowly. "She's open to whatever will work best for Iselleden. And Rowyn told me of the Prophet's words. They're… quite obscure."

"Really?"

I nodded mutely, unwilling to reveal more. His hand touched mine as it rested against the stones, and I entwined our fingers together. This was how it should be—us together, fighting against whatever forces we faced. I pressed my lips against the tight, hazel skin of his cheek and saw his lips curve into a smile. He sighed and turned away from the valley.

"I want to go for a walk," I announced. "Do you wish to join?"

"No." He shook his head. "I think I'll retire."

Aedin leaned down and kissed me. I grinned as his beard tickled my skin and wrapped my arms around his waist, pressing my face against his shirt. "We will survive this," I mumbled into the fabric.

"As long as we're together," Aedin finished.

———

Following the path along the cliffs, I let my feet guide me. They walked over the stones—warmed from the afternoon heat —as the valley shimmered in the colors of summer. Green, gold, and brown—the trees waved in the breeze, and the rich dirt shone in the sun.

The entire world of Iselleden vibrated with the power of the Gift. Attuning myself to its wavelength, the feeling grew gradually and swelled through me. My chest felt like a sail—full of wind and speeding across the high seas.

The path turned to dirt, and I crossed to the right, away from the Haven and towards the cliffs overlooking the sea.

As I turned away from the town and towards the open expanse of grass, I wondered if Rowyn was right. Perhaps this should be my task—and mine alone.

My hands were open and the tips of my fingers brushed against the tall grass. It would be painless to die—and noble to die fighting for a worthy cause. And it was an abstract terror that no emotions roiled my gut or griped my stomach as I considered the possibility of my life ending. I would die anyway someday—wouldn't it be best to have choice and motive in the event?

The sea emerged through the grass and greeted me with its endless horizon. White caps crested the blue void—countless and consistent. A thrill echoed through my body as the sight halted my steps. I became conscious of every breath and smelled the fresh and potent salt in the breeze.

Squinting through the sunlight, I saw a flicker out of the corner of my eye. It was a distant form—silver and gold—reflecting against the sun further along the path as it climbed along the cliffs. I placed my hand over my forehead, peering through the light—it was something large.

Resolute to discover the cause, I continued along the path as it sharply ascended. Very quickly, I became out of breath, and my legs ached with the climb. Nearly tripping over a stone, I sidestepped another as the path grew rocky. I looked to my left and noticed I was only several feet from the edge. Intuitively, I reached for the ground, knees bent for balance.

Gripping the rocks, I dared to look ahead.

The flickering light was a tall form, hooded and cloaked. It was only twenty paces away.

I increased my pace, favoring the right side of the path that was safer to the grass. From rock to rock, I crawled, careful not to slip. The humming in my chest grew louder—my hands became numb. Flexing my fingers, I fought to retain any feeling, but it escaped me. The grass below my fingertips was beginning to curl and fold as I passed.

A voice echoed around me.

I stopped in my tracks—only several steps away—as the sound of the waves crashed through my ears. I wondered if I was imagining things. The looming shimmering form was shrouded in the colors of the sun. Spiraling echoes of gold and silver were intertwined by deep blues, bright purples, pinks, and whites. It reflected the colors of the sky with a cowl pulled down to obscure any face.

I straightened, finding my balance through the wind and the precarious height of the cliffs. The cowl turned in my direction—away from the west. There was nothing underneath.

Gwyneth.

I heard it again—this time the word was distinct and clear in my ears. I recognized my name. My mouth opened to form a word, but it never left my throat. Swallowing, I forced the word into my head and enunciated.

Prophet.

The swirling cloak of colors came closer—the wind whipped at the fabric, snapping it back and forth. I watched the changing hues with amazement, my fingers outstretched.

In a sudden movement, my finger grazed an inch of the cloak and the bright sunlight was cast into immediate darkness.

The wind ceased and everything became silent.

My eyes were wide and straining to see, but everything was dark. Lungs burning for air, I forced my chest up and down to breathe but couldn't hear a sound. I wondered if I was breathing at all. Or perhaps I'd fallen off the cliff and was dead.

A warm nothingness muffled my senses. My entire body felt numb—whether from the Gift or the void. There was no pressure beneath my feet, as if I was floating.

Without warning, an arc of light pierced the darkness and fell upon my shoulder. I felt a sudden sharp pain and cried out, blinking in surprise. The light returned and I was able to see.

It was a moonlit night. Familiar limestone columns rose above me as a balmy wind caressed my body. I looked down and saw a stream of red gathering at my clutched shoulder, the warm liquid running down my arm. A rapid heartbeat echoed in my ears, and my vision swam as the blood began to stain the stones beneath my body.

A dark shadow stood above me holding a dagger.

I felt nauseous and struggled to stand, slipping in the wetness. My body was light—so light—as if I was made of nothing more than air. The smell of rich dirt and blooming flowers entered my nostrils as I collapsed, realizing that it was futile.

Death was near—I could feel the blood continue to flow from my body. Soon I would be drained and gone.

Gwyneth.

The voice pulled me from the bright scene and back into the void. The pain was gone—I touched my shoulder and felt no wetness or hurt; just intact skin beneath the silky fabric. The blackness gradually subsided into a thin gray light, and I was able to distinguish a form standing near.

The cowl had been pulled back and the face beneath was otherworldly. Tight skin swam in a multitude of colors—whipping between light to dark and back again. The face was void of emotion, void of any expression or hair that might suggest a gender. Their eyelids snapped open and the pupils were a dizzying vacuum of white. They shimmered like an opal—churning with unknown colors.

Prophet, I repeated.

You are here. The words echoed in my head. They were soft and lilting—like the warmth of summer.

Yes.

There was a silence when I forgot to speak, mesmerized by the kaleidoscope on their skin. Reality snapped back into my mind as I realized this was my chance.

Tell me what to do, I urged.

What you must do.

Should I face this alone?

What you must do.

Should we bring Iselleden to the Empire? Even through the numbness of the void, I grew frustrated.

What you must do.

The colors spun maddeningly against the gray landscape. A distinct smell of salt became sharp as the gray began to shift into further light. I was running out of time.

Tell me what to do, I repeated in a panic.

There was no response.

Tell me! I cried.

You are the matr *of a new time.*

The form began to dissolve with the wind as the sun pierced my vision. The cloak disappeared along with the numbness in my body, replaced by thousands of sensations insistent and vying for attention. The soft tendrils of grass beneath my fingers, the sharp wind, and piercing light.

Blinking into the bright sun, I sudden awoke on the path, alone in the dirt.

Chapter Thirteen

MADAME ANDREA SPENCE sat on the balcony of her estate, fanning herself with a frown. The summer was hot and her dress stuck to her back. She watched a red-and-black speckled insect crawl on a nearby leaf, curious as to what would happen when it reached the tip. Holding a breath in suspense, she emitted a sigh of relief as it continued on the underside instead of falling to the ground.

As the chilled, pale wine passed through her lips, she thought of Gwen with a grimace. This barrel had been intended for her—until she'd been murdered like the rest of them.

"… it's just so odd." Catherine's cheery voice broke through her thoughts.

Andrea blinked, refocusing on her friend as she sat wilting in the opposite chair.

"I just don't feel the baby. Perhaps she went to sleep—or she might be dead?" Catherine eyed her with a slightly panicked expression.

"She's asleep," Andrea said impatiently. "Stop worrying yourself over every little *thing*."

"But she's due in a few months." Catherine rubbed her swollen stomach in concern. "Shouldn't she be more active than ever?"

"Perhaps she's wise enough to stay inside that stomach of yours," Andrea commented dryly, finishing her wine with a satisfied sound. "A sensible decision—considering our world is not much better."

Catherine frowned at this pessimism, thoughtfully sipping her drink.

"Besides," Andrea continued, waving at a nearby servant for more wine, "how do you even know *it* is a girl?" She bent down a hand to pet a small brown-and-white dog—Felicity looked up expectantly.

"Madame Porter said that if a baby is conceived during a full moon, it is likely to be a girl," her friend recited, brown eyes wide.

"Rubbish," Andrea snorted. "How can that be true?"

"It is!" Catherine was indignant as she placed a hand protectively over her bump.

Andrea rolled her eyes, a wave of relief washing through her as the servant refilled her glass. Her auburn curls hung limp in the heat. Even though the Spence estate was on the coast of Lailan, the summer months were still overwhelming with the added pressure of humidity and the constant beating of the sun. Dabbing some sweat with the hem of her dress, she ignored Catherine's aghast expression as she displayed her thigh.

"Andrea!" Catherine scolded.

Andrea swatted the fan in her direction. "Oh hush."

"You aren't much fun today," Catherine commented tartly.

"No?" Andrea looked at her archly.

"What's wrong?"

"Nothing." She slapped at a flying insect. "Just the heat."

"Yes, it's been difficult to sleep."

They lapsed into silence, watching the waves undulate across in the great cerulean abyss. The salty air mingled with the scent of flowers. Andrea gripped the stem of her wine glass, enjoying the cool beads of moisture that rolled down onto her fingers.

The words bubbled in her mouth until she couldn't force them back any longer. "I miss Gwen," Andrea said finally, avoiding Catherine's eyes.

For once, Catherine was quiet and didn't respond immediately. She swallowed and looked out at the ocean. "Well," she said finally. "It is what it is…"

Andrea ground her teeth. "What it *is* is cruel. They weren't like the rest…"

Catherine didn't know how to respond. "It… it is unfortunate… She was so kind…"

Kind. That was the least of it. They had been *young*. The previous Lords of Lailan had been elderly men, drunk on their newfound power. Their wives hadn't been much better—if they even had wives. Many had entertained prostitutes instead of securing domestic stability. The removal of the previous lords had been unfortunate occurrences—much like the presence of a tropical storm. Andrea hadn't taken it personally. Until now.

Her finger slid up the glass, separating the drops of moisture and tracing a fine line. The wine was tartly sweet and salty on her tongue. She suddenly wanted to be very drunk.

"Andrea."

She stiffened at the sound of her husband's voice.

"Liam," she cooed automatically, looking up at the familiar face.

He was unaffected by her words. She noted the bright sheen of sweat across his brow—dampening the brown hair on his forehead. "I am going to the port—should be back later this evening."

Andrea smiled politely. "Of course."

"Don't wait up for me." Liam ducked inside as abruptly as he had arrived.

She didn't bother to respond. Fixing her jaw, Andrea took a large mouthful of wine, glaring at the ocean in front of her.

"Does he do that often?" Catherine asked softly.

"Leave? Why yes," Andrea replied scathingly. "He enjoys gambling in the port with his friends. It's become a weekly occurrence. Perhaps even more than I know. You would think for being the accountant to Lord Cabot that he'd have a more responsible *hobby*."

Catherine pursed her lips. "Perhaps he has made money from the games…?" she ventured.

"I don't care if he loses it all." Andrea finished her glass and raised her hand for another.

"Andrea," Catherine said cautiously, watching the wine fall into her glass. "It's not good to drink *too* much… You might be with child."

"I certainly hope not." She laughed darkly, impatiently watching the servant pour the wine.

Catherine shifted in her seat. "Well, perhaps I should go…"

"No," Andrea said suddenly, guilt washing through her. "I'm sorry, Catherine… Please forgive my… ill humor."

Her friend tucked a loose lock of blonde hair back into her bun. "I don't enjoy being with you when you're like this." She gestured helplessly.

"I'm sorry," Andrea repeated, forcing sincerity into her words. "The past months have just been… hard."

"Well, let's talk about it," Catherine offered. "Why are you sad?"

"I'm not *sad*," Andrea scoffed. "I'm just annoyed."

"Very well." She folded her hands diplomatically. "And why?"

"Because…" Andrea struggled. "Because Liam is irresponsible and *dull*. He doesn't even want to have—" She paused, shooting a look at the nearby servant.

"Would you please?" Andrea smiled generously as the servant bowed, moving inside. "Wait!" He stopped. "The wine."

The servant placed the pitcher on the table between them and exited the balcony, shutting the doors.

Andrea turned back towards her friend. "He doesn't even want to *bed* me," she hissed to Catherine. "And when he does, he's *drunk*!" The irony wasn't lost on her as she took another large sip of wine.

"That is unfortunate." Catherine's lips twisted empathetically. "But perhaps you could charm or flirt with him when he's sober?"

"Believe me." Andrea shook her head. "I've tried. You know me! I'm the biggest flirt in all of Lailan!"

"But you enjoy the men you can't have," Catherine pointed out.

"Thank you for that revelation," she muttered sourly.

"It's all a matter of perspective." Catherine straightened in her chair. "You have a good life—a lovely estate and comfortable home. Not all are so lucky as you."

"Yes, but I feel so ineffective!" Andrea heaved an exasperated sigh. "I want my life to have meaning—without having to give birth to multiple children," she added quickly as Catherine's mouth opened.

"Well…" Catherine pouted. "What about starting a book club? Or—or charitable giving?" She struggled to come up with more options.

"Giving money is boring," Andrea said flippantly. "I want to be *involved* in something."

"I've heard of a new charity in Tahuna that takes in orphaned children," Catherine offered brightly, suddenly remembering. "Francesca told me about it recently. Perhaps you should see if they need help."

"I don't particularly like children," Andrea grumbled. "They're smelly and noisy."

Catherine shot her a warning look as Andrea sighed. "Well," she began, looking at the sun as it began its descent into the horizon, "I'll look into some options. And I don't want to keep you from *your* husband…"

"Thank you." Catherine stood with grace and a hand to her stomach. She leaned over to kiss her friend on the cheek. "Please cheer up," she said crisply. "I don't like you when you're sad or annoyed. It's depressing."

Andrea chuckled, watching Catherine's generous and warm expression with gratitude. "I shall try my best," she promised, summoning a smile. "Thank you… It's always good to see you."

"Next week then?" Catherine looked at her knowingly. "Francesca has offered to host a group at her home."

"Yes, it will be quite a bore. I can't wait." Andrea smirked as Catherine slowly grinned.

Catherine squeezed her hand and went indoors to call for the carriage. Felicity sat pensively in a corner, the coastal breeze playing with the soft hair of her long ears. Even she looked hot. They shared a pitiful look.

Andrea poured a generous helping of wine into her glass and stood to lean on the balcony railing. Her thighs stuck together as a fly buzzed around her head. Felicity rose to her feet, delicately sniffing Andrea's ankles and licking the salt from her calves.

Although further down the coast from Tahuna, her new home was comfortable and grand. Her father had been right—it was a good match. Despite his shortcomings, Liam was well respected, and his family was highly regarded on Lailan. The estate he'd been given was perfectly situated overlooking the outskirts of the main port and perched on a rocky cliff.

If Andrea leaned forward and looked to her right, she could just see the balcony of the villa of the Lord of Lailan—

"No," she muttered to Felicity. "I'd rather throw myself over the cliff than go there again."

A pit sank in her stomach as she let her mind wander to the tragedy of her friend's death. Although not everyone had mourned her stoic and unpopular husband, the absence of Gwen had been felt in their group. Even Francesca had been quieter than usual. It all felt so ominous and unforgiving. What had Aedin done to deserve such a dreadful end?

When the sun sank below the horizon, Andrea finished the pitcher of wine and dined alone with her dog. She ordered a bottle of red wine to be opened and didn't speak as each course was presented, chewing slowly and thoughtfully. Felicity sat obediently by her chair, eager to taste the array of food whenever her companion lowered her hand.

By the time Andrea was finished, her mind was pleasantly buzzed and absent. Banging her hip on the table, she moved clumsily from the dining room and staggered down the hall. Felicia's footsteps pattered just behind.

She squinted at the stones beneath her feet, grasping the edge of the door frame as it swam in her vision. The bed was near—she knew it.

Finally finding it, Andrea allowed herself to collapse on the mattress. Ungracefully removing her sandals and tossing them in a corner, she snuggled under the covers and bit back a yawn. After some time, she fell asleep.

But her rest was short lived.

A bang reverberated intrusively through the room; she squinted in surprise at the bright firelight from the hall. A shadowed form closed the door and mumbled words of apology. Andrea sighed as her heartbeat decelerated and turned over to feign sleep.

She felt Liam sit on the bed and a clammy hand touch her shoulder. "My love," he mumbled, moving his hand up and down her arm.

Squeezing her eyes shut, Andrea forced herself to be still. Maybe he would give up and fall asleep.

The hand left her shoulder and she heard the rustle of clothing and squeaking of the bed frame as he moved about the mattress. Minutes later, she felt a body press against her—insistent and wanting.

"Andrea." His breath was hot and stank of rum. She grimaced into her pillow as she felt him push up her nightgown. Lips descended awkwardly onto her neck as she realized there was no way around it. It would be quicker this way. Obediently, she shifted into position and was quiet.

———

A roaring headache was the first thing that woke Andrea the next morning. It pounded through her temple—her mouth was thick and dry.

Blinking with a frown, she dabbed at the crusted sand from sleep in her eyes. A soft snoring echoed beside her—Andrea shifted to locate the source. Although her husband was asleep next to her, it was the small body of Felicity that emitted the ungraceful noise.

Careful to not wake the occupants of her bed, Andrea pushed back the covers and lurched to her feet. The throbbing resurfaced. There was an unpleasant stickiness between her legs. Stifling a groan, she moved to the bathroom and turned the tap of the bath. It felt like forever to wait for the water to fill the basin. Andrea chugged a glass of water, stripped off her gown, sat awkwardly in the tub, and waited.

She eyed the freckles on her forearms with distaste. The damn sun. Soon enough, she would be old, tanned, and wrinkled like the rest of them.

The soft patter of feet—Felicity came around the corner, her tail wagging at the sight of her owner.

Andrea looked at her archly. "So *you* decided to get up."

Felicity took a seat by the tub, her scrunched face watching her wordlessly.

"Well, don't mind me," Andrea said.

Felicity tilted her head in response.

Andrea bathed—relishing in the lukewarm water as the morning air became hot once again. When she deemed herself clean, she dried and put on a casual gown as Felicity licked at the water droplets on the floor.

She peeked into the room—Liam was still asleep.

Beckoning wordlessly to her dog, Andrea tiptoed across the floor and opened the door, praying it wouldn't squeak. Her prayer was answered—Andrea and Felicity filed into the hall and shut the door.

Releasing a dramatic sigh, Andrea looked down at her dog. "*Now* it's time for breakfast."

Felicity whined in response and licked her lips.

"Yes, you've been very patient," Andrea praised.

They ate breakfast together and watched the gulls hunt to feed their nests on the cliffs. Felicity particularly enjoyed this morning ritual—barking at any who came too close to the balcony. Most stayed away, diving into the ocean in search of fish or pecking at the rocks for crabs. Andrea sipped her tea, grimacing as she drank the hot water—she was already beginning to sweat.

"I'm off." The voice of her husband made her jump.

Andrea turned with a practiced smile. "Very well," she simpered, watching him duck back inside the house, his footsteps echoing through the dining room.

"So." She glanced at her dog with an amused look. "It's you and me again."

Felicity turned her head and sat obediently.

"You're always hungry." Andrea rolled her eyes, her hands tapping the arm of her chair. The sun was already bright and beating onto the balcony. She wanted to order some wine but then chastised herself. It was too early—or was it?

"Madame." A servant opened the door and extended a slip of paper. "This came for you."

It was perfect timing, saving Andrea from the impossible urge. She took the paper, hoping it was an invitation to an event —anything to provide distraction from the endless, open sea.

Windward and Fifth—Ask for Philippa.

Andrea frowned. The writing was certainly Catherine's, but what did it mean?

"Carriage!" She stood with resolution, eager to solve the mystery. Felicity barked at the sudden excitement, wagging her tail.

"Not you." Andrea shot an apologetic look at her companion. "I'm sorry!" She rushed to grab her hat and shoes, Felicity trailing at her heels.

When the carriage came to a stop at the corner of Windward and Fifth, Andrea wrinkled her nose. The smell of the port was almost unbearable here. Spoiled fruit, fish drying in the sun, human refuse and waste from the passing workers. The nondescript building had a rotting exterior wood and hardly any windows. She wondered if Catherine had finally gathered the courage to play a prank—this had to be a jest.

Hesitantly, she descended the carriage. "Wait here," she instructed the manservant as he bowed. She felt out of place and was grateful that the passing crowd of workers, donkeys pulling carts, and servants largely ignored her. Picking up her skirts and avoiding a nasty-looking puddle, she made her way to the building and pushed open the door.

Inside, the walls were whitewashed and brightly lit by lamps on the wall—a stark contrast to the ominous exterior. There were sounds of pleasant chatter, some crying, and yelling of instructions. She frowned, looking around for any person, until a small figure turned the corner.

A child.

"Oh!" she exclaimed, suddenly tense. She eyed the young girl hesitantly. "How are you…?"

The small girl gazed at her with large blue eyes, wiping her nose with the back of her hand. She was silent—an undecided frown on her face.

"Er." Andrea paused. "Is there an *adult* here?"

"Tabitha, come!" a voice commanded as the girl wiped her nose a final time before running back down the hall.

Andrea sighed in relief as she left, self-consciously drying her palms on her dress. "Hello?" she called.

An elderly woman entered the hall, eying her carefully. "Yes?" she asked abruptly, her keen eyes watching her from underneath a dark and wrinkled brow. Something triggered a memory in the back of Andrea's mind and she struggled to place her face.

"Yes, hello." Andrea brightened at the prospect of addressing an adult. "My name is Andrea Spence and I was…er… *sent* here by a friend. I was told to ask for Philippa?"

"Ah, yes. I am Philippa." She beckoned with a hand. "Come— we need your help."

"Very well." Andrea watched warily as another small child emerged to clutch at Philippa's skirts. "Is this… an orphanage?" she ventured.

Philippa looked at her impatiently. "How did you guess?"

"I—" Andrea stuttered, swallowing nervously as three more children joined them in the hall.

Perhaps she should return to her pitcher of wine on the balcony and the quiet comfort of her dog. "I'm sorry." She grimaced. "I think I was mistaken. I was looking for—"

"Nonsense. Madame Dagny informed us of your arrival. Come with me," she ordered, turning in the opposite direction of the front door.

Andrea was trapped. She chided herself for her words yesterday—perhaps she should have donated five gold pieces instead. Cursing Catherine under her breath, she reluctantly followed Philippa, keeping a wide distance from the curious children.

They entered a large playroom and Andrea stiffened at the wall of noise. Children were everywhere. Hanging off the chairs, playing on the ground, crying in the corner, giggling on the couch. It was chaos. Andrea gritted her teeth—she would need a *large* pitcher of wine later this evening.

"We are one of the few places in Tahuna that welcomes children from all backgrounds," Philippa announced, gently prying a set of small fingers from her skirts. "That hurts, Ryan. Please don't grab hard… Some have lost their families, others have unstable parents. We keep them for as long as necessary and provide for their needs. And here is where the children are free to play." She serenely waved her hand towards the mayhem in the room.

Andrea winced as children screamed in laughter. "Er— lovely," she said, wishing for Felicity and the peace of her home. "And what do you need my help with?"

"A very important task," Philippa replied, turning on her heel and continuing down the hall. She opened a door to a strong waft of urine, feces, and lye. Andrea stifled a choke and held her breath. The room was small and filled with baskets upon baskets of soiled linens and clothes. An adjacent doorway was open to a small yard, where clean, miniature cotton shirts hung like flags of surrender on a line.

"Washing," the old woman announced, looking up at her expectantly. "Unless you would prefer to help with the children…"

"No," Andrea said quickly, dreading the thought of returning to the room. At least washing would be quiet. "This will do."

"Good." Philippa smiled. "Now let's begin."

Chapter Fourteen

I DIDN'T KNOW how long I lay there in the dirt, letting the cry of the gulls and the fresh salty air bring me back to reality. From wherever I had been. It took me hours to crawl, slip, and hike down the cliff, my head in a daze. And when I arrived back in our room at the Haven, I found Aedin in our room, lounging on the bed with a book.

He looked up at me. "Did you know that the Empire and Iselleden share the same written language?"

I shook my head, joining him on the bed. His hair was ruffled as if he'd just woken from a nap.

"What are you reading?" I asked, glancing at the spine.

"Just some poetry," he said offhandedly. "Whatever was in the bookshelf." Aedin studied me, slowly closing the book. "Where did you go?"

"I walked along the cliffs," I began hesitantly then paused, unsure how to continue.

His dark eyes searched my face and body, catching the stray dirt I'd tried to brush out of my clothes and skin. Putting away the book, he reached out a hand and cautiously touched my arm. I frowned at the formality of his gesture. "What are you—"

Aedin's voice was low and intense. "What happened?"

"What do you mean?" Suddenly self-conscious, I brushed off his hand.

"You…" Aedin's brow furrowed as he again scanned my person. "You're… different."

"No," I replied indignantly. "No, I'm not."

"Your Gift is… stronger. More obvious." Aedin sat up as he studied me. "What happened?" he repeated.

"I met… the Prophet," I confessed quietly. "On the hills along the cliffs."

A cautious hope arose in his eyes. "And?"

"And…" I said slowly, remembering the feeling of blood dripping down my arm. "And I heard my name in my head. I asked what we should do, but there was no response…"

My husband frowned in disappointment. "No response?"

"All I heard was 'what I must do'." I shrugged. "And I think I Dreamed… of the future."

"Really?" Hope lightened Aedin's face again. "What did you see?"

Summoning the memory sent chills down my arms. In those painful seconds, I didn't know what to say to my husband. Should I tell him that I saw myself lying on the floor of the villa, bleeding to death? Or withhold the knowledge from him entirely?

"I… can't say." I avoided his gaze.

Aedin looked surprised. "Why won't you tell me?"

"The Prophet said so," I lied, staring down at the minuscule threads in the cotton sheets. They were suddenly so evident, I was surprised I had never noticed them before. Neat and tiny as a pin, I traced my hand over the pattern. Through the closed window, I caught muted voices chatting about the weather. I felt Aedin's Gift soft and pulsating beside me. A distant pressure revealed another brewing summer storm. Perhaps I was different.

In the momentary pause, Aedin was silent. I met his frown with an awkward hesitation, praying he wouldn't ask again.

"It's nothing, Aedin," I stumbled over my words.

"Why won't you tell me?" His voice was low and quiet.

"Because…" I fought for the words. "I just… can't."

Because I feared of what he would do if he knew the truth. I feared that we would never return to Lailan if he knew I would die.

But I had never withheld a secret from him before.

As if deciding what to say, he looked out the windows behind me and then again at my fingers playing with the sheets. Frustration pinched at his face. "Though you have every right to keep a secret… I would hope that you trust me enough to share your knowledge," he continued, his words spilling out in force. "I have trusted you with all of *my* knowledge, and I would expect you to do the same."

Swinging his legs off the bed, Aedin stood with a harried look.

"Aedin!" I scrambled to my feet. "Please, you have to understand—"

"Then tell me." He opened his arms, watching me expectantly. "Enlighten me."

My mouth moved, but I couldn't force out the words. I was afraid to tell him—afraid of what he might do if he were to learn the truth.

In the gaping pause, Aedin dropped his arms and shook his head. "How you've changed," he mused darkly.

"Please," I gasped, reaching for his arm. He turned away, brushing off my attempts, and pulled open the door.

"Aedin—" I stopped, suddenly self-conscious as I saw Ophelia and Selena's surprised looks. I wondered what they'd heard.

Aedin didn't wait for the guards as he strolled out the door. They leaped into action, following him down the hall. I stood awkwardly in the doorway, watching them until they disappeared into the maze of halls. Even without the power of the Gift, I knew they would go and train.

———

The door clicked shut with an ominous sound, and the room was quiet.

The book of poetry lay forgotten on the bed. Picking it up, I leafed through the pages as my mind struggled to grasp the words. It had been a long time since I'd read. I considered sitting down and applying myself to the task but felt restless. Replacing the book on the shelf, I wiped my palms on my pants and looked around for a distraction. The room was still and lifeless without Aedin's presence.

And yet in the gaping absence, I could hear the echoes of words through the walls. Dozens of conversations—like the buzzing of bees in a garden—humming at the periphery of my attention. They fought for my attention, and I found it hard to ignore. Rubbing my face, I released a long, long breath.

Unable to sit still, I pulled open the door and left my room. The voices continued to echo in the empty hall. I touched the cold stones of the wall and closed my eyes, gritting my teeth. They were still there. Focusing on the lines of sunlight on the floor, I flipped through the voices. There were many I didn't recognize, until I heard two I did. *Raine. Rowyn.*

Instinctively, I felt for them—like a bloodhound scenting its prey. I followed the hall as it wound through the Haven. When I was close, I heard their conversation stop and pulled open a door that looked just like the others.

The siblings looked up at me in surprise, stiffening in their chairs next to the fire.

Shutting the door, I wrung my hands and looked at them. "I heard you talking…" I began slowly.

Rowyn's tanned forehead wrinkled into a frown as Raine thoughtfully brushed a lock of hair from her face. "You've changed," she commented.

"So it would seem," I muttered, dragging an empty chair from the corner of the room and seating myself between them so we formed a half circle.

They were silent as they watched me fall into the chair. Heaving a sigh, I avoided their gazes and studied the fire, impatiently scratching at the arm of the chair.

"You encountered the Prophet," Raine said, her voice soft and lilting.

"Yes." My breast felt heavy with sorrow as the vision flashed again and again before my open eyes. A bad dream—a memory —that I was unable to erase.

Rowyn leaned forward eagerly. "And?"

I shook my head at him. "Nothing."

"Nothing," he repeated dubiously.

"I asked the Prophet what I should do, and the only response I received was 'what you must do'. And then I heard 'you are the *matr* of a new time'." I opened my hands in frustration. "What does that mean?"

Rowyn and Raine exchanged a look. Rowyn's lips were pressed into a thin line as he rested back in his chair and remarked, "The Prophet's words are not intended to tell us what to do but to guide us to the will of Fate."

"That doesn't make any sense." I could feel the frustration building again in my chest. "How can we follow Fate's 'will' if we don't know what to do. Simple inaction is an action in itself."

The firelight was soft on Raine's angelic face, even in the light of the afternoon. "It's our choice that ultimately becomes the right path—even the mistakes we've made can lead us to the greater good."

"Then if it's our responsibility to choose," I began slowly, "we should decide on a course of action."

Raine looked at her brother. "We were discussing that—"

"I know," I cut her off. "I heard you… in the halls."

She inclined her head demurely. "Rowyn is *open* to the idea of assembling the guards—"

"And only sending a select group to the Empire," he finished quickly. "Not civilians."

"So you would give us fourteen guards, myself, and Aedin to defeat the Rhidge." I counted. "That's sixteen Gifted."

"Your power has grown." Rowyn waved his hand at me. "You may be capable of challenging an army *alone*. Perhaps this is what the Prophet intended."

I laughed darkly at the thought and then sobered, remembering the sight of blood in my Dream. "I… When I touched the cloak of the Prophet… I Dreamed of my future."

Rowyn's eyes widened. "You touched the cloak?"

"Yes." I shifted my gaze to the brilliant colors of the fire. "And I saw… my death."

The fire crackled in the silence between us. I didn't know why I told them, how it came out so naturally. Perhaps it was because they saw me as a tool, not as a person they loved. For all of their language about peace and kindness, our relationship was a business transaction. I knew they would see my death as an unfortunate result of a predetermined path, not the preventable loss of a wife.

A tightness gripped my throat, and I struggled to force out the words. "And I was on Lailan… at the villa where Aedin and I lived," I said. "I'm sure of it."

Raine's emerald eyes were piercing yet empathetic. "Death is an unfortunate reality in our situation—"

"You mean *my* situation," I corrected with a glare, looking at Rowyn. He was silent, awkwardly avoiding my gaze.

"The will of Fate encompasses all of us," Raine said wisely, shifting her eyes to her brother. "And how did your husband react to this?"

"I… couldn't tell him," I said quickly, sinking further into my seat as guilt washed over me. "I'm afraid of what he might do, should he find out."

Raine nodded slowly in understanding. "That was wise."

"Was it?" I muttered darkly, rubbing my face. I certainly didn't feel wise. "Please don't tell him," I continued quietly, watching their identical eyes. "I can't bear for him to know."

Raine inclined her head in assent as Rowyn spoke, "But it may instill in him the ownership of *your* mission if he were to understand that it would result in your death."

"No," I said. "Aedin would force us to remain in Iselleden indefinitely and renege on the prophecy. He cares more about protecting me than the fate of Iselleden or the Gifted."

"Then he is short-sighted." Rowyn crossed his arms.

"He is in love," Raine added softly. "Would you not do the same?"

Rowyn looked away, visibly uncomfortable. "Well, it doesn't change the reality," he said quickly. "We must continue training, and then you must leave for the Empire."

"Rowyn," Raine said quietly. "We need to consider our path—the path of Iselleden—"

"Our lives are already at stake," Rowyn said gruffly. "What more could we sacrifice?"

"Losing our *only* chance to change the course of history," Raine pointed out. "Perhaps Ciaran Aedin is right—perhaps we should amass an army of Gifted to return to the Empire—"

"No!" Rowyn exclaimed, rubbing his face. "We cannot risk more lives for this."

"Just allow us to spread the word," I pleaded. "Give your people the option to fight. They should have the right to choose."

"*No.*" Rowyn stood with resolution, his mouth twisted bitterly. "What the Prophet spoke to *me* did not include Iselleden lives—"

"Nor did it say I should do this alone," I pointed out, recalling his words.

"That doesn't matter," he said impatiently. "This is what I think is best, and *I* am the Captain of the Guard."

"And *I* am the Speaker of the Council of Iselleden." There was a sharp note to Raine's voice as she looked up at her brother. "It is *my* decision that will be final."

The shadows on her face seemed to deepen, catching my breath and making me wonder what power prowled just below the surface of her skin.

Rowyn felt it too. He stiffened towards the door, as if a great energy was pressing him out of the room. But it soon passed and Rowyn gave a bitter shake of his head, pushing back his hair. "You know, I never understood why the Prophet chose *you.*" He looked at her with incredulity. "You, who constantly question and challenge the decisions of Fate."

"Do not think I accepted this Calling willingly," Raine growled, the nails of her fingers biting into her chair.

"It should have been Josiah. It should have been Pria. Even *me*! *I* would have served the will of Fate more faithfully than you."

"*I* was Called—*not* you nor anyone else!" Raine's anger was visible through the lines marring her angelic face.

I watched them with wide eyes as I felt the Gift ricochet through the room.

"You were a mistake! You weren't even supposed to be born!" Rowyn spat.

"I think you should leave," Raine said coldly.

Rowyn stopped, regarding his younger sister with outrage and disbelief. He turned to leave but stopped and said, "Don't you *dare* destroy this island."

Raine's eyes didn't move from the fire. The golden flames reflected the pain and sorrow in her bright green eyes. I held my breath until Rowyn shut the door and we were left alone.

Chapter Fifteen

I SAT IN silence with Raine for some time, waiting for her to speak. I could almost imagine Rowyn's words spinning in her mind, their bitterness poisoning the room. When she didn't say a word—and almost half an hour had passed—I left and went back to my room to wait for Aedin.

Sitting on the balcony, I watched as the colors of the sunset flew over the mountains and heard the crickets begin their nightly song. Aedin's footsteps echoed on the floor when the air became cool and the sky turned a dark gray. The warm light from our lamps spilled onto the stone floor outside.

I heard the door open and prepared myself, looking up into his shadowed face. "Hello," I offered diplomatically.

Wordless, he took the seat beside me and leaned forward, resting his forearms on his legs. "Hello."

I wasn't sure what to say next, but thankfully he saved me from having to decide. "I don't condemn secrecy," he said slowly. "But I don't like knowing that you're hiding something from me intentionally."

"Perhaps I shouldn't have told you that I Dreamed."

Aedin's full lips pressed into a line. "No… I'm glad that you told me, but I want you to know"—he reached out to grasp my hand—"that you can trust me. I mean it."

In the depths of his irises, I saw swirls of mahogany, inky black, and cerulean. If I studied closely, I could even distinguish faint lines and freckles across the tight skin of his face. A whiff of sweat and dirt nearly clouded the faint scent of soap on his skin. The information presented to my senses was overwhelming. I really *had* changed.

Gripping his hand, I pressed his knuckles to my lips. "I know," I said truthfully. "And I *do* trust you… But what I saw with the Prophet… I feel that knowledge has to remain within myself."

Reluctance crossed his expression before it turned to resignation. Aedin released a sigh. "Then I can't force you to do otherwise."

I shouldered closer as he wrapped his arms around my body and I threw my legs over his lap. "No," I admitted. "You can't force me. Just as I couldn't force *you* to tell *me* anything."

Aedin allowed a demure smile as I kissed the side of his face. "This is what I deserve then," he admitted ruefully.

"I can think of some appropriate punishments," I murmured, touching the bridge of his nose playfully. I was satisfied to see his lips curl into a grin.

Aedin bent his head to kiss me and I felt a shiver run through my body. His hands grasped my back, pulling me closer as our lips moved together. A thrill beat in my chest—I clutched his arm feeling the tightly wound muscles underneath his shirt.

An overwhelming power drifted through my body, intoxicating and heavy. It was as if every fiber of my being was pulsating in time with his heart, his skin, his blood.

We paused as I opened my eyes, my heart swelling at the sight of his familiar face. The face I'd come to know intimately and trust with my life.

In an instant, the memories of past loves flickered through my mind; suddenly pale and empty in comparison. There was nothing that could separate us—we had chosen each other. He had my heart, and I his. It was a mutual understanding; driven not by the passion of desire but the consciousness of choice. I nuzzled my face against his and whispered, "I love you."

"I love you," Aedin replied with his quiet smile. In the sky above, the stars burned as he pressed his lips once again to mine.

———

I sat in silence with Raine for some time, waiting for her to speak. I could almost imagine Rowyn's words spinning in her mind, their bitterness poisoning the room. When she didn't say a word—and almost half an hour had passed—I left and went back to my room to wait for Aedin.

Sitting on the balcony, I watched as the colors of the sunset flew over the mountains and heard the crickets begin their nightly song. Aedin's footsteps echoed on the floor when the air became cool and the sky turned a dark gray. The warm light from our lamps spilled onto the stone floor outside.

I heard the door open and prepared myself, looking up into his shadowed face. "Hello," I offered diplomatically.

Wordless, he took the seat beside me and leaned forward, resting his forearms on his legs. "Hello."

I wasn't sure what to say next, but thankfully he saved me from having to decide. "I don't condemn secrecy," he said slowly. "But I don't like knowing that you're hiding something from me intentionally."

"Perhaps I shouldn't have told you that I Dreamed."

Aedin's full lips pressed into a line. "No… I'm glad that you told me, but I want you to know"—he reached out to grasp my hand—"that you can trust me. I mean it."

In the depths of his irises, I saw swirls of mahogany, inky black, and cerulean. If I studied closely, I could even distinguish faint lines and freckles across the tight skin of his face. A whiff of sweat and dirt nearly clouded the faint scent of soap on his skin. The information presented to my senses was overwhelming. I really *had* changed.

Gripping his hand, I pressed his knuckles to my lips. "I know," I said truthfully. "And I *do* trust you… But what I saw with the Prophet… I feel that knowledge has to remain within myself."

Reluctance crossed his expression before it turned to resignation. Aedin released a sigh. "Then I can't force you to do otherwise."

I shouldered closer as he wrapped his arms around my body and I threw my legs over his lap. "No," I admitted. "You can't force me. Just as I couldn't force *you* to tell *me* anything."

Aedin allowed a demure smile as I kissed the side of his face. "This is what I deserve then," he admitted ruefully.

"I can think of some appropriate punishments," I murmured, touching the bridge of his nose playfully. I was satisfied to see his lips curl into a grin.

Aedin bent his head to kiss me and I felt a shiver run through my body. His hands grasped my back, pulling me closer as our lips moved together. A thrill beat in my chest—I clutched his arm feeling the tightly wound muscles underneath his shirt.

An overwhelming power drifted through my body, intoxicating and heavy. It was as if every fiber of my being was pulsating in time with his heart, his skin, his blood.

We paused as I opened my eyes, my heart swelling at the sight of his familiar face. The face I'd come to know intimately and trust with my life.

In an instant, the memories of past loves flickered through my mind; suddenly pale and empty in comparison. There was nothing that could separate us—we had chosen each other. He had my heart, and I his. It was a mutual understanding; driven not by the passion of desire but the consciousness of choice. I nuzzled my face against his and whispered, "I love you."

"I love you," Aedin replied with his quiet smile. In the sky above, the stars burned as he pressed his lips once again to mine.

———

Raine and the Council entered into their deliberations—an anxious and bureaucratic deliberation—for a week.

We weren't asked to attend the Council sessions, and I was secretly grateful to spend time training rather than arguing. In between sparring sessions, Aedin and I took walks through the endless green hills of Iselleden. Although I desperately wanted to know what was happening, I was rather glad to not be stuck inside the white walls of the Council Tower.

Rowyn joined us most days, though occasionally slipping into the tower for an hour here or there. I sensed that he felt his presence was futile—Raine would do whatever she felt was best. He had voiced his opinion and she knew it. There was little he could do, and so he threw himself into training.

Rowyn commandeered my time with lessons on the Gift and more sword training. It was satisfying to fall back into a routine, like the one we'd established with Jon at the fortress. Breakfast, training, midday meal, training, dinner, and sleep. The lines of muscle on my body continued to expand and grow. I felt quicker in my actions, sharper and more aware of the fine details of combat.

Aedin even appeared satisfied with my progress. One morning, he paused in his sparring with Selena to watch me disarm Rowyn within three moves. I didn't miss the tilt of his head and mocking smile as he saw Rowyn bend to pick up his sword.

Thankfully, I had no further run-ins with the Prophet, though the opalescent eyes and swirling cloak of nauseating colors haunted my dreams. I would wake—often in the early hours of the morning—expecting an endless void of black pierced by a flashing arch of light. My chest would tighten and I would wait for the searing pain. For the fear to consume me and whisper songs of my death.

But the faint light of our room would swim into view and I would float back to the present.

I fought to control my Gift, to subdue its power so as to not wake Aedin, but I could feel his waiting hand on my back. Rubbing and caressing until I drifted back to sleep. Every day, I waited for my mouth to betray me and tell him of what I'd seen.

But my mind was stronger, and the secret remained hidden.

I'd become accustomed to my heightened senses with the Gift, even though it proved occasionally difficult to tune out the buzzing in my head. In brief moments in between trainings or silence, I would flip through the sounds, words, and people who passed through the halls of the Haven. I sometimes found it difficult to fall asleep with the abounding distractions. But with the daily grind of training, my body would eventually win and cast me into the merciful void of sleep.

Aedin was still followed by guards, but it felt more ceremonial than intentional. Following our normal routine, we exited the residence one morning to find Selena and Ophelia lounging against the wall, chatting gaily.

Selena looked at us with a knowing smile. "A bit later than usual," she commented with raised eyebrows.

Aedin was stoic, but I blushed in response. "Yes…" I said slowly, "But we're ready now."

A surge of desire rose again in my chest as I remembered the feeling of his body pinning me to the bed. Selena's sharp green eyes were laughing, as if she knew exactly where I was in my mind.

Ophelia shot her comrade a knowing look as they fell into line ahead of us. Aedin gently held my hand and pressed my knuckles to his lips, and I knew he was thinking the same.

The scent of herbs and lavender wafted through the air as we exited through the courtyard. The sun was already high in the sky, mercilessly emitting its heat and light—I shielded my eyes. The courtyard wasn't as crowded as I'd expected for the late morning. Some wardens passed, other Gifted seeking counsel, but for the most part it was empty. We followed the trail along the cliffs—Farist resting idyllically in the valley.

When we reached the guards' quarters, a small group of guards was already present, stretching and chatting quietly. Selena was prompt to pick up her sword, and I didn't miss her eager expression as she turned to face my husband.

Ophelia held out a blade to me. "Would you like to spar?"

"Yes, until Rowyn arrives," I agreed, taking the handle. I twisted it nervously in my hand, remembering the merciless strikes I'd observed her making the other day.

She stepped forward to address me with her blade, and I swung to meet it in the air. My memory had n't failed me—Ophelia was lithe and strong. Her feet were light as we traded blows, her amber eyes bright and quick to perceive my feints. At the end of one round, I was already sweating.

"Again," I said, rubbing my sore thigh where the flat of her blade had hit. The wins I'd garnered against Rowyn amounted to little against her power.

Ophelia eyed me with a knowing grin and held out her sword.

We sparred for nearly an hour, and by the end I was exhausted. Drinking eagerly from a jug of water, I felt in the vicinity for Rowyn's presence, surprised he hadn't appeared. It was unlike him to be late, especially when he'd preached time and time again the importance of training.

A small tug appeared at the back of my mind, as if some primal instinct knew my search. He was outside—far away but by the cliffs.

"I'm done." I held out a hand to Ophelia as I put away my sword.

She frowned at me. "You need to practice more—your reactions are slow."

I shot her an exasperated look—she was beginning to sound like Aedin. "Yes, I know. I'm going to take a walk and look for Rowyn."

Ophelia folded her arms and shrugged, tucking a brown lock behind her ear and turning to watch pairs of sparring guards, including Aedin and Selena. The latter had become stronger since they'd begun training together. Aedin had poured most of his time into her, as she had been the guard most eager to accept his teachings from the beginning. I jealously eyed her lightning-fast reactions and powerful hits. My husband was thoroughly enjoying himself—he had found a worthy opponent.

Shrugging away from them, I eased into the hall and left the quarters, grateful for the fresh air on my face. The field stretched out like an endless tapestry. I listened for the echo of Rowyn's Gift and it pointed along the same path I'd taken the week prior when I'd encountered the Prophet.

The grass was still verdant and thick from the occasional summer storms. Small flowers of yellow, purple, and white dotted the scene. The world around me hummed with life—it was enough to make me almost not miss Lailan. Almost.

Their faces flashed before my open eyes again—Mary, Tieren, Marks, William… Andrea and Catherine… Ephraim. I wondered if they knew we were alive. If *they* were even still in this world. They wouldn't have hurt Ephraim and my father, would they? And yet Ephraim had been alive when Aedin had seen him in his Dream. At least that was a consoling thought.

As long as we were alive, I knew Tours would keep Ephraim alive. His life was a mere bargaining chip that could easily be used as leverage against us. My stomach twisted as I realized that my mind had come to naturally navigate this new reality of threats. The threat of death and torture, and the ever delicate balance of dominance and strength against our enemies.

The Gift would not be enough. I realized this with the feeling of a stone descending in my stomach. Our Gifts—the pure Gifts of Iselleden—would not be enough unless we had something else. What would it be? The success of this war would not be defeating the Rhidge—although it had to be done—but healing centuries of division and reintroducing the Gift into the common vernacular of the Empire. How was that possible?

The thought was interrupted by the insistent tug of Rowyn's presence. I looked up at the slope of cliffs, realizing my feet had taken me farther than I'd intended. The sharp scent of the ocean invaded my nostrils as I squinted against the bright sky.

A familiar spark of red hair marred the sky. And a blonde and tanned figure. Celion.

They were ahead on the path, their hands intertwined and their steps light and casual. My feet ground to a halt as I watched, suddenly realizing that I was intruding on an intimate moment. I looked away abruptly, seeing Celion's smiling profile lean in to meet Rowyn's face. A tenderness in their eyes.

Chastising myself and turning on my heel, I hurried back down the trail, hoping they were too far away to have noticed me.

I felt awkward—Rowyn had never said anything to me. But why should he? I was nothing more than a foreigner he was forced to train—a tool for shaping. Our afternoon with Rea was the one personal glimpse he had shared. There was little I knew about the man that was supposed to guide and prepare me for the greatest trial in my life. The thought was suddenly terrifying.

Ducking my head with guilt the entire way back, I was thankful when I finally reached the cool interior of the guards' quarters.

I ignored the surprised glance from Ophelia. "That was fast," she commented.

I shrugged, picking up a dagger. "Let's continue."

She quickly pushed away any doubts and picked up her own dagger, effortlessly resuming from where we'd left off.

Aedin and Selena were still at it—practicing the spinning final kill move that I'd seen Aedin perform with his guards.

Some time later, Rowyn and Celion entered the quarters. The tenderness was gone and replaced with the professional coolness I'd come to expect.

"You were late," Rowyn addressed me tartly, folding his arms.

I put away the dagger, looking at him apologetically. "I'm sorry—we slept in."

He ignored my excuse. "Raine says she'll have a decision for the Council by this afternoon. We should leave to make it in time."

"Yes," I agreed, wiping my sweaty palms on my pants. I nodded at Aedin, who looked reluctant to stay. This decision could change our lives. But Selena engaged him in another bout and he dutifully continued to train.

Chapter Sixteen

ROWYN AND I descended onto the path in silence. I shot him a sidelong glance, wondering if he suspected anything. His tanned face was tight and cross, no doubt thinking of the upcoming decision. Entirely unlike the easy, pleasant expression I'd seen earlier with Celion—a completely different man. He ignored me as we neared the growing stone structure of the Council Tower.

I finally found the courage to speak. "I saw you… earlier."

"Hm?" Rowyn looked distractedly at me. "What do you mean?"

"With… Celion."

Rowyn didn't respond. The furrows in his brow seemed to grow deeper as his eyes shifted to his feet.

"Why didn't you tell me?" I asked.

"Why is it relevant?" he shot back.

I struggled to find words. "We spend… so much time together. I thought that you would tell me."

"Is it relevant to the prophecy?"

"No, but—"

"Then why would I need to *share* my personal life with you?"

"I just thought—"

"Well you thought wrong." Rowyn's green eyes were slitted and sharp. I turned away from his gaze.

"I'm sorry I said anything," I snapped quietly.

We continued in silence. I tried to focus on the expanse of beauty in front of me, but it felt stale. Rowyn was fuming, and I found it hard to concentrate with his power pressing into the space between us. The leaves of grass whispered as the summer wind rolled through the field.

Passing through the courtyard and under the kaleidoscope of lights, we entered the Council Room to a buzz of conversation. The palpable energy hit me like a wave. I stopped in my tracks, swallowing my fear as all eyes turned towards me.

Rowyn gruffly left my side, exchanging low words with Josiah and helping him up the steps to the dais. Each Council member followed in turn, awkwardly avoiding my gaze. Perhaps they were reluctant to be the bearers of bad news. Or relieved to not see Aedin at my side.

Raine was already seated on her throne, examining her nails as she patiently waited for the chatter to die down. When everyone was seated, I took my spot in the center, feeling ominous as we repeated the exercise yet again. At least Aedin wouldn't be tortured this time.

Silence overcame the room and I held my breath. Raine looked up.

"We have come to a final decision regarding the execution of the prophecy." Her voice was soft yet resolute. "I believe it is in the best interest of Iselleden and in accordance to the will of Fate that we send a force of soldiers to the Empire—"

Rowyn exhaled audibly, a hand rubbing his face.

"—that will be *trained* for combat with the sword and the Gift. This force will include the Council guards, Ciaran Aedin, and any civilians who wish to contribute their lives to the cause. Ciaran Aedin will assist in training and recruiting those capable and willing to fight. Gwyneth Aedin and Rowyn, son of Reynolds, will share joint leadership on this mission."

My eyes snapped again to Rowyn—his arms were resting upon his knees as he glared at the white stone of his throne.

"Of course..." Raine paused, meeting the eyes of everyone in the room. "I understand that this decision will bring pain and suffering to some, so if any are unwilling to contribute to the mission… let them remain here." Her emerald gaze rested upon her brother.

No one spoke. I summoned my courage and opened my mouth. "Raine—thank you for your direction and wisdom. Although your decision may bring pain to some, I hope that our combined strengths will lead to a victory against the Empire—"

Rowyn stood abruptly and descended his dais, cutting off my words. Shocked stares followed his footsteps as he strode out of the Council Room. Raine looked at me pointedly. Muttering a curse under my breath, I followed him out the doors, blinking in the bright sunlight.

When we were outside, I raised my voice at his slumping form. "Rowyn—*stop*!"

"No!" His face was red as he turned on his heel. "*You* don't get to tell me what to do."

"Yes I do." I ground my teeth, fixing my stance. "Just as you have every right to tell *me* what to do. You heard Raine—"

He shook his head. "No—no. She is mistaken. This is *not* the will of Fate—"

"How do you even know?" I cried, throwing up my hands. "The Prophet didn't tell you *how* we would complete the prophecy. He only told you what will happen—"

"We can't defeat the Empire by going straight into the lion's mouth!" Rowyn sputtered. "It's madness!"

"We can make a plan." I tried to lower my voice as passers-by were beginning to stare. "Like Aedin said, we can go to Lailan —"

"The Rh—*They* will kill us," he hissed, his green eyes lit with a dangerous fire. "Do *not* think it will be easy."

"Don't tell *me* about what's easy or not." I could feel my anger beginning to rise again. "You know what I Dreamed!"

Rowyn's fists were tight and coiled at his side, as if he wanted to strike something—or me. "You *should* die." His words were scathing. "*You* were the one that the prophecy spoke of. This is *your* burden to bear."

"Yes, this *is* my burden," I exclaimed. "But to do it alone—to *die* on this mission alone—will not help to save Iselleden." My voice became low and rough. Tears of frustration begin to prick in my eyes. "I'm sorry, Rowyn. I'm *sorry* you have to do this with me."

He winced at my words, the flush in his cheeks gradually receding.

"I'm sorry you have to leave your home," I continued. "I'm sorry that you have to leave the island that you *love* and have devoted your *life* to protecting, and travel to the gates of hell… I'm sorry that this prophecy has made you do things you never wanted to do—to spill blood and spurn everything you ever knew. I'm sorry…" I stopped and swallowed, watching his hands loosen in defeated acceptance.

Taking a step towards him, I placed a hand on his arm. I could the power beneath his skin vibrate—slow and steady—as I looked up to meet his eyes. His tanned brow was lowered and guarded; his emerald eyes misting.

"I know you don't trust me," I whispered. "But we *have* to trust something. We have to trust each other."

His voice was strained and low. "It… doesn't seem right."

"There *is* no right decision. There's just… worse and less worse. But we have to come together to make it work. We will find a solution… together."

Rowyn begrudgingly patted my hand before brushing it off. It was the most acknowledging touch he'd given me so far.

He pushed back his long red hair with a sigh, looking irritably at the Council Tower. "We…" His chest heaved a sigh. "We'll need to make a plan… together."

I bit back a smile, folding my arms. "Yes… Yes we will."

Something caught his eye over my shoulder. I turned to see Aedin and Celion entering the courtyard, watching us expectantly. Celion's bright blue eyes were fixed unwaveringly on his partner.

Rowyn gave another heavy sigh and brushed back his hair. "I need a drink."

"Nothing sounds better," I agreed.

Chapter Seventeen

ANDREA'S HANDS WERE red and aching.

She gritted her teeth and dug again into the water, swishing around the clothes in the basin. Grabbing a dirty napkin, she rubbed it against the board, her forearms throbbing with the action. It had been over an hour since she'd started and there was still so much left to do.

Wiping the sweat from her forehead onto her shoulder sleeve, Andrea continued rubbing. Water splashed against the apron covering her gown, but she didn't notice. A gritted grin emerged on her face as she worked—it felt good to be dirty. It felt good to work.

The past weeks had shown Andrea what was possible when she put her mind to something—she was capable and strong. She spent most days at the orphanage, primarily helping out with laundry or cleaning as she had not yet summoned the courage (or comfort) to entertain the children.

Once she gained a routine of appearing more regularly, she brought along Felicity. The dog, too, appreciated being among children and her master, rather than at home, alone, in the estate.

Andrea held up the sopping napkin, studying it in the afternoon light. It was still slightly discolored, but a couple more beatings would do the trick. She threw it back in the water and continued kneading.

The children were shrieking with delight in the playroom. Insects buzzed and hummed lazily in the humid air. Though annoying and distracting, she was grateful for the open door to their small backyard. She looked up with satisfaction at the line of clean linens swaying in the breeze—like trophies collecting on a shelf. She had done that.

"Good work," Philippa muttered briskly, bringing a basket of freshly soiled laundry from around the corner.

Andrea groaned dramatically. "Does it ever stop?"

"No." Philippa eyed her with amusement as Andrea bent again to her task. "You *are* allowed to take breaks, you know."

"Are you offering me some rest?" Andrea shot her a playful smile. "What a benevolent master."

Philippa allowed the corners of her mouth to twitch into a smile. "You're the only one driving yourself. Do what you like." She set the basket on the ground and left again for the playroom.

Andrea held up the napkin again and was satisfied to see it was somewhat white. She rinsed it in the water, wrung out the cloth with her hands, and tossed it on the pile of clean, damp linens.

Her shoulders and arms were aching—she hadn't realized it until that moment. Stretching her neck to the side, she picked up the clean pile and exited to the backyard. The muscles in her arms had grown and strengthened with labor, though her back felt continually sore. She winced as she bent to grab a linen, clipping it to the line alongside the others.

They fluttered in the humid air—rows and rows of evidence of hard work.

"I don't see why it makes a difference," a voice grumbled from the back of the yard. "They're just apples."

"They're *green*—she wanted red," came a clipped retort.

"But those were more expensive!"

"She's going to string you up by your fingernails."

Andrea watched as two young men emerged from the maze of fluttering linens, their argument stopping as soon as they noticed her. They were opposites—one was tall and thin; the other was short and strong. One wore a casual grin with ease; the other was tight-lipped and sour.

They both wore plain, homespun linen clothes and watched Andrea warily, until the tall one spoke, his thin face a jumble full of sharp corners. "You're still here."

The short one hit him in the arm, continuing into the house with a scowl.

"I am." Andrea raised her chin challengingly. "And why are *you* here?"

"I *live* here," he replied indignantly, his hazel eyes narrowing with humor.

Andrea looked him up and down—though he must have been several years younger than herself, he somehow held muscle and grace on his lanky frame. "*You're* not a child," she objected.

"No, but I am an orphan." He grinned cheekily and held up the bag of apples. "I've got to be getting these inside. Lovely to see you, Andrea."

Andrea frowned, clutching a damp linen. "How do you know my name?"

He shrugged casually. "Philippa told us about you—there aren't many ladies who choose to spend their days in the laundry room."

"I'm not that type of lady," Andrea scoffed, clipping the linen on the line.

"No, you're not," he said with a bittersweet grin, turning to go.

"What's your name?" Andrea asked.

He hesitated. "It's… Tieren," he admitted quietly.

"Tieren," Andrea repeated with a graceful curtsy. "Lovely to meet you."

Tieren gave a short laugh accompanied by an elegant bow and continued inside with the apples.

When Andrea was finished hanging the clean linen, she returned inside and eyed the newly soiled towels with something like regret. It was growing late and she should return to the estate before Liam.

Untying her apron, Andrea hung it on the peg and looked around her feet. Felicity was nowhere in sight. Grumbling under her breath, Andrea reluctantly entered the playroom, wincing at the wall of cheerful noise.

Felicity sat obediently in front of a gleeful child, eying the ball in her hand with eagerness. She barked insistently and the girl threw the ball across the room. Felicity scrambled after it, picking up the thing in her small mouth and returning to the child with a wagging tail held proudly aloft.

Andrea gently kneeled beside the child, holding out her hand. "May I try?"

The girl looked at her with large, blue eyes, wiping her nose. She silently handed her the ball as Felicity pranced impatiently.

Andrea bounced the ball across the room—Felicity jumped several times to catch it. The girl giggled as Felicity finally caught the ball in a triumphant leap and returned it to Andrea.

"Well done!" Andrea cheered, patting her dog on her head. Felicity barked in anticipation. "What's your name?" she asked the girl gently, satisfied to see a smile on her solemn face.

"Tabitha," she whispered, watching Andrea with those wide, blue eyes. She wiped her nose again—Andrea cringed.

"This is my dog, Felicity." Andrea held out a graceful hand. "She seems to like you. Do you like her?"

"Yes," Tabitha said with a growing smile. "She's so soft."

"Yes, she is." Andrea reached out a hand to pet her, but Felicity evaded her, barking insistently at the ball in her hand.

Andrea rolled her eyes. "It seems she has a singular focus." She handed the ball to the girl. "Why don't you give it one last toss before we have to leave?"

Tabitha threw the ball with her skinny arm, letting it bounce like Andrea had. They giggled as Felicity sprang again into the air, growling as she stalked the ball. They cheered when she finally caught it.

When Felicity returned, Andrea gently grabbed the ball from her mouth and handed it to Tabitha. "Would you mind holding on to this until we return tomorrow?"

"Yes!" Tabitha cheered, watching Andrea with shy grin. Andrea couldn't resist a smile as she gathered Felicity in her arms and exited into the hall.

Philippa was blocking the way, guiding a child by the hand to the bathroom. Andrea waited patiently behind as she opened the door and instructed them what to do.

She turned to Andrea, eying her with surprise. "You stayed late today."

"There was a lot to do." Andrea struggled to brush back an errant curl with Felicity in her arms. "But I'll be back tomorrow to finish that load," she added quickly.

Philippa shook her head. "You're under no obligation to be here, but we appreciate the help regardless."

"Is there anything else I can do?" Andrea shifted, making way for another child passing through. "Does the orphanage need money? I heard Tieren saying that the red apples were more expensive… I would be happy to donate some of our food, or give some gold…"

She caught the sudden shift in Philippa's expression—wary and stern. "Tieren?" Philippa repeated.

"Yes, the tall, young man," Andrea said impatiently. "I heard him and another in the backyard saying that they bought green apples because red were more expensive. If you want red, I'm happy to provide them."

"We can make ends meet," Philippa replied. "You should go." She held open the front door expectantly.

"Very well." Andrea looked at her in surprise. "See you… tomorrow then."

Philippa shut the door in her face in response.

———

Andrea and Felicity took the carriage back to the Spence estate. When they arrived, Andrea groaned at the sight of two other carriages already parked in the dirt—Liam was home. And he'd brought company.

"We have to be quiet," Andrea hissed under her breath.

Felicity licked her lips in response, understanding in her large brown eyes.

Carrying Felicity, Andrea crept through the entry hall. Voices echoed from the balcony as servants fluttered through the rooms, preparing for dinner. Thankfully, Andrea made it to her room without being seen. She set down Felicity, tore off her dirty gown, and turned on the bath.

Andrea grimaced at her reflection—her honey-brown curls were more of a mass of frizz than elegant spirals. She thought of the man with hazel eyes with a blush—had she looked like this *all* day? Perhaps she would be washing her hair after all this evening.

Felicity waited patiently as Andrea bathed her body and hair in the tub, painted her face, and attempted to dry her hair into its usual coherent ringlets. She wasn't successful.

Cursing the heat and lack of time, Andrea shrugged into a semi-sheer, pink gown. It was one that Liam had mentioned he liked—perhaps it would distract him from her unruly hair. She shifted the fabric to cover her nipples and pulled down the tight sheath that hugged her hips. A layer of tulle floated over her legs, reaching down to the ground. She eyed the ensemble in the mirror, watching the curves of her body with satisfaction— although her marriage had ruined many things about her life, at least it hadn't ruined her figure.

"Let's go to battle," Andrea muttered to Felicity as she barked in response. "And *yes*, dinner as well," she added impatiently.

They walked through the open-air halls, enjoying the slightly less hot evening breeze as it moved through the house. Massaging her aching forearms, Andrea wondered if tomorrow she should take a day off.

No, she corrected the thought—there was too much work to do at the orphanage. Philippa was clearly overwhelmed and needed help with the children.

Despite how smelly and messy they were, they obviously needed her. She was desperately wanted.

She followed the voices to the balcony, where Liam sat with a glass of thick, amber liquid, smiling at a larger man in silk.

Andrea internally winced—she'd never liked Renalt Cabot. And she liked him even less now that he was Lord of Lailan.

"Dee," Liam cooed, lifting his glass in her direction.

Andrea hated that name. She had gently reminded him several times before that her name was Andrea, but he obviously didn't listen.

"My lord." Andrea curtsied with a simper directed at Cabot, accepting a well-earned glass of wine from a servant.

"Madame Spence." Cabot's eyes raked over her body with satisfaction. "You're looking lovely this evening."

She murmured thanks, taking her place next to Liam and accepting a polite peck on the cheek. The breeze cooled the sweat on the back of her neck, although her thighs stuck together under the tight fabric.

Liam wasn't unattractive, but nor was he the most attractive man she'd ever laid eyes on. His brown eyes were dulled and glassy from the alcohol, and his brown hair was stuck to the sweat on his forehead. Andrea had begun to notice of late that his tanned face was beginning to lose its sharpness from their life of luxury. She wondered if all men became like Cabot when they were older—fat, obnoxious, and presumptuous.

Andrea desperately hoped that Liam would not succumb to this natural progression but feared the worst.

"Where were you?" Liam eyed her face as Andrea self-consciously brushed back her hair. "I thought you would be here when I returned."

"I was at Catherine's with some other ladies," she lied easily with a breezy laugh. "We got a bit carried away—Felicity found a friend and they were playing in the yard."

Felicity had disappeared into the kitchen in search of a well-earned meal. Andrea's stomach grumbled at the thought of food —she had hardly eaten anything since breakfast.

"Did you not you have three or four dogs?" Cabot squinted at Andrea. "I remembered hearing you were quite the breeder."

"I had two—Roger passed away unfortunately," Andrea said, wincing at the memory. "He was quite a lovely soul. I was hoping to keep one of the puppies that Felicity bore earlier this year, but we found them all homes."

"Those dogs"—Liam shook his head with a chuckle—"have the best life."

"We have quite a good life," Andrea purred, putting on her best face.

Cabot saluted her husband with a sly smile. "Only because I pay Liam so well."

Her husband grinned in response, raising his glass. "The lordship of Lailan has never been better."

The way they said the words made Andrea's stomach turn. "What constitutes this pleasure, my lord? Why grace us with your presence?" she asked archly.

"We had a successful day at the port." Cabot shifted in his chair, motioning to a servant to refill his glass. "Liam was, er—very helpful."

"I'm glad to hear that." Andrea looked to her husband as he slid his gaze to the darkening sprawl of Tahuna. "Why was it successful?"

"We switched back to the fertilizer from Cachelle—it has saved us quite a lot," Liam said quickly.

Andrea's brow furrowed. "I thought it was more expensive to import fertilizer all the way from Cachelle."

"It can be costly," Liam said evasively. "And it was, considering Lord Aedin's previous import fee. But we removed that, and now the benefits certainly outweigh the expense."

"What benefits?"

"Well," Liam stuttered. "It's said to work well and we get certain… benefits from working with Welm Charles' brother-in-law. You know Welm—he's an old friend of the family."

"Yes," Andrea said impatiently. "I know Welm, but importing all the way from Cachelle when we have perfectly good fertilizer here doesn't sound cost-effective."

"Oh, it's quite complex," Cabot drawled, sipping his wine. "You wouldn't understand."

"Would I not?" Andrea retorted, unable to hide her annoyance.

Liam looked embarrassed at her frustration and said quickly, "He's giving us certain benefits for working with him."

"Like... bribes?"

"No, no." Cabot brushed off the word with a wave of his hand. "They're more like... discounts for working exclusively with him. Discounts that help to subsidize our... economy."

Andrea looked between the two men as the realization dawned on her. The lordship of Lailan had returned to how it always had been—corrupt.

"Do these benefits appear on the island's profit statements?" Andrea asked quietly.

"Dee." Liam forced a laugh as Andrea gritted her teeth. "Does that matter?"

She wasn't sure how far she should push this.

She looked across to Cabot, snugly ensconced in his chair like a king, watching her expectantly as he sipped his white wine. *Her* white wine, to be exact. The barrels she had ordered.

She watched the blush from the alcohol spread across her husband's neck.

She saw their gilded estate on the coast—built from Liam's family's success and his comfortable position as accountant for the Lord of Lailan.

She thought of the orphans at the port—of Philippa's dreary clothes and the loads of dirty laundry awaiting her return.

If she kept her mouth shut, she would have a greater chance of getting some gold from Liam later that evening. Perhaps an advance on her allowance for next month. Or make up some excuse about needing more dresses for upcoming events.

Now was not the time.

Andrea deflated and took a large sip of her wine. "Not at all," she responded carelessly, putting a hand on her husband's arm. "Whatever you think is best."

Liam ate it up. She watched his eyes rove to the bare skin of her chest, the outline of nipples underneath her dress, and waited for the spark. The recognition and appreciation of her beauty. Perhaps he would finally bed her tonight when he wasn't drunk.

Instead, his gaze continued to the servant standing by the door as he finished his drink with a satisfied sound and raised his glass for another.

Andrea gritted her teeth to prevent a sigh from escaping. "Will you be dining with us tonight, my lord?"

"No, but thank you." Cabot lifted his weight out of the chair, finishing his wine and setting down his glass. "I must be returning to the villa."

The thought of that man living in the villa made Andrea cringe. The place of beauty where Gwen and her husband had lived in peace, until—

"Of course." Liam bowed politely as Andrea kneeled into a curtsy. "Thank you for stopping by."

"Thank you for the wine." Cabot exited the balcony, gesturing to a servant for the carriage.

As soon as his footsteps echoed out of the house, Felicity came trotting around the corner with her usual smile. Andrea narrowed her eyes at her dog—it was as if she'd known that Cabot was an undesirable companion. Traitor.

"Shall we?" Liam gestured towards the dining room.

"Of course." Andrea finished her wine in a gulp and they sat for dinner.

The meal progressed with little conversation. Liam continued to drink, but Andrea declined the subsequent glasses of wine. There was something about Cabot's presence—and the revelation that her husband was assisting him in his financial schemes—that was unsettling. It might have been legal, as long as the king was aware. But was he? Was it worth writing to the palace? Or spreading the word?

The thought suddenly appeared—would *she* be at risk if Lord Cabot were to be removed and Liam found guilty? Like Gwen?

Andrea picked at her food, her appetite gone.

"Are you not hungry?" Liam looked at her plate with a frown.

"I had some food at Catherine's." Andrea gave a quick smile.

He grunted and returned to his duck, slicing through the meat with a single cut.

"Francesca is hosting a party in several weeks," Andrea began haltingly, keeping her voice casual. "I was hoping I could get an advance on my allowance to purchase a new dress."

Liam nodded distantly in response. "Yes, of course."

"Thank you." Andrea adjusted her utensils so that they were aligned on the table.

She looked around the dining room—they were alone. It was so rare that it was just the two of them—without any distractions or staff. Maybe now was the time to talk—to broach that subject that had been weighing on her shoulders since their marriage.

"Why do you not… want me?" Andrea asked suddenly.

Liam met her eyes with confusion. "Whatever do you mean?"

"I mean…" Andrea shifted uncomfortably, glancing again around the room to ensure that the servants were gone. "Why do you not bed me… that often?"

Liam considered this as if the thought had never occurred to him. "We… have intercourse," he said haltingly, his plain oval face scrunching in confusion.

"Hardly." Andrea fought to keep the malice out of her voice. "I just mean… I would prefer if we did it… more often."

It was like pulling teeth. She had never dreamed that she would even be having this conversation with her husband. She remembered her previous words to Gwen, what felt like a lifetime ago. *I would hope my husband would ravage me in bed— kissing me softly every night—*

Was she just naïve? Or had she set unrealistically high expectations?

Her husband paused and put down his fork, eying her with sudden humor. "Is it because Catherine is pregnant? Are you jealous?"

"No!" Andrea said quickly—maybe too quickly. "I simply wish for us to—to *enjoy* each other more."

At her words, Liam's expression darkened. "You are not enjoying me?"

"I mean, I enjoy you as a person, yes," she lied. "But I would like to have some… some… more romance." Andrea cringed as she said the word aloud.

"Romance," Liam repeated dully, raising his brows and taking a swig of his drink. "I am not romantic enough for you."

"I simply think *we* should try harder—"

"Is providing for your lifestyle not enough?" Liam spat. "All of your dresses and parties and *dogs*."

Perhaps she was digging herself deeper into a hole. She said quickly, hoping he wouldn't retract his advance on her allowance, "No, Liam, you misunderstand me—"

"I fuck you whenever I want to," Liam growled as Andrea blanched at the language. There was a dangerous glint in his eyes—she stiffened.

"Yes," she agreed automatically, watching the low liquid in his glass. "Yes, you do. But I just think if we put more effort into —"

"Do you want me to fuck you right now?" Liam demanded challengingly, pushing back his chair. "Because I will."

She suddenly became aware of how small she was—her body stiffened at the threat. Andrea glanced immediately to Felicity; she was curled up on her bed in the corner, warily watching the scene.

"Hm?" Liam eyed her expectantly.

A servant came around the corner. Liam pointed his finger at their form and snarled, "Out." They retreated with a quick bow, and they were left alone.

Andrea felt as though her heart might explode out of her chest. Her fingers gripped the arms of the chair. "Not like this," she said quietly, watching her husband's belligerent gaze.

"Well you can't have it both ways, Dee," he chortled darkly and stood. "Stand up."

"No." She placed her weight in her chair.

"Stand up."

"*No.*"

"Andrea." He grabbed her arm as she threw her weight into her seat.

"Let me go!"

"*Stand up.*"

"No!"

Andrea ignored the pain of his tight grip on her skin, gritting her teeth and sinking lower. She could hear Felicity gather herself from her bed with a whine.

Liam pulled both her arms with his weight as she was catapulted out of the chair, gripping the table. The plates jolted with the sudden impact.

Andrea turned to face him, her arms free. "Not like this," she hissed, pointing a finger.

Liam pushed down her hand and pressed his face against hers in an aggressive embrace. The stink of rum and the heavy weight of his lips crashing down on hers was too much to bear. She squirmed, pushing against his heavy weight. "Liam—stop it!"

"You wanted me and now you don't," Liam sneered, pushing her hips against the table. "Make up your mind!"

"Not like this!" she protested, her voice threatening to break.

Felicity's bark was insistent and accusing.

"Shut up!" her husband snarled at the small dog, but Felicity was undeterred.

"Don't say that to her!"

"She's a *dog.*"

"She's more than a dog."

"This is ridiculous." Liam muttered, grabbing the tulle of her dress and pushing it up.

"Stop it!" Andrea slapped away his hands, fighting it down, praying the tulle wouldn't rip. He grabbed the fabric and pulled hard—Andrea winced as she heard the threads of it break apart and she continued to beat off his attempts.

"No!" She managed to say before suddenly his hands stopped.

Liam looked down at the mess of tulle, his hands frozen mid-air. She saw the inner workings of his mind begin to whir as his eyes focused with a frown. His mouth opened and closed again, but he was silent.

She wondered if he was having a heart attack. Or maybe a sudden change of heart? Felicity's sharp barks ceased as she sat down with a whine.

But her body wouldn't sag with relief with his so close. Andrea shifted out from between the table and his form as her blood ran cold—he didn't move.

Liam was frozen in place like a statute—his fingers twitching and eyes wild as he watched her shaking form.

A tall, dark silhouette stood on the balcony, shrouded in the blackness of the night.

Cursing, Andrea grabbed a knife from the table and held it out in front as the shadow stood on the balcony. Should she call for help? Liam remained frozen, watching the figure as his face became red with fury.

"Who are you?" Andrea demanded, the knife unwavering in her grasp. "Show yourself!"

The form was still, their face shadowed. Liam struggled in his frozen state, his body aching to release itself from the hold. In another second, he was free.

"What in hell!" he bellowed as Andrea stepped away from his anger, brandishing the knife now at her husband.

A glass came whizzing out of the liquor cabinet and collided with Liam's head.

She stared in shock as the glass struck his skull and his eyes went dark. Liam collapsed on the floor, his large body slumping into stillness.

The thud resounded through the dining room—Felicity delicately sniffed the body and looked up at her in confirmation. He was out.

Andrea's head whipped to the balcony, but the shadow had disappeared. They were alone.

Suddenly shaking, she replaced the knife on the table and stepped over her husband's silent form. She gathered Felicity in her arms and rang for the servant.

When they arrived, she explained that Liam had had too much to drink and needed to be put to bed. It took three manservants to gather the body and ungracefully drag him into their room.

There was a cut on the side of his head from the impact of the glass. Andrea winced as she watched them stitch up the wound and decided it would be best to sleep in the guest bedroom that evening.

Shrugging off her dress and exchanging it for a nightgown, Andrea placed a tentative finger on her husband's throat. There was still a pulse of life.

Unsure as to whether she was disappointed or relieved, Andrea heaved a sigh. She pushed back her curls with resolve and rummaged through his purse, pulling out five gold coins. Andrea slipped them into her drawer of fineries, then she and Felicity padded out of the room and closed the door.

Chapter Eighteen

WE SHOULDERED INTO opposite tables in the open-air patio of a pub in the village. The sign above the door proclaimed the establishment to be called the Wheatsheaf and it swung precariously as we entered. Inside, the bar was warm, dark even in the midday, and stank pleasantly of beer. It was a comforting smell—one from my childhood, I realized as we shouldered up to the bar and placed our orders—the richly bitter and sour fermentation that sank into the floorboards and painted walls.

I'd tried to contain my surprise when Rowyn didn't protest at Aedin joining us to leave the Haven. Perhaps he felt that he and Celion were enough to guard the populace if my husband decided to attack. Or perhaps he didn't care at this point and thought we were all doomed to die regardless.

It was midday and (as Rowyn informed us) the usual farming crowds had not yet left the fields, so we had the patio to ourselves. Celion set down four tankards of ale, the generous pours sloshing unceremoniously onto the table. We'd informed him and Aedin of the Council's decision as we'd descended the hill and perhaps Celion felt the larger pours were more fitting for the mood.

Aedin took one, stretching his long legs out to the side and watching the canopy of trees dance in the wind. Since we'd left the Haven, he seemed quieter than usual, as if hesitant to push his luck with Rowyn's newfound generosity.

Nevertheless, I held up my mug and met Rowyn and Celion's eyes. "Here's to victory."

Rowyn said nothing and tipped the drink back in his mouth. Celion muttered, "Cheers," in response and echoed the movement.

It wasn't the cheeriest start to our mission, but it was a start.

After several deep pulls of ale, Rowyn eased from his tight posture and looked around at us. "When do we start asking for volunteers to join the slaughter?" he drawled.

I opened my mouth to retort, but Aedin spoke first. "Tonight… tomorrow… The earlier the better."

Celion watched Aedin with his bright blue eyes. "And you'll be able to train them? All of them?"

"I'll do my best," Aedin answered noncommittally, fingering his ring. "Considering we'll be fighting alongside them, our lives will depend on their performance."

"We should set an age threshold," Celion mused. "No younger than forty." I was surprised he was facing this more willingly than his partner.

"Forty?" I raised my eyebrows. "Isn't that a bit old?"

"*Our* people live healthily and well into their hundreds," Rowyn said possessively. "Forty is too young for warfare by our standards."

Aedin raised his eyebrows but didn't comment.

"So I'm just a newborn then?" I responded tartly.

"Yes," Rowyn agreed wholeheartedly.

I frowned at him. "How old are you then?"

"Sixty-six," he said proudly.

That age would have crippled most men in the Empire with bad knees and a full gut. Rowyn looked to be at least twenty years younger and in the same peak of health as Aedin.

"And you?" I gestured with my mug towards Celion.

"Fifty-one," he offered with a shrug.

"How long have you and Rowyn been together?" I directed my question at Celion, daring to push my luck with his good humor.

Ever since we'd descended into Farist, our fates clarified by Raine and the Council, he'd been… softer. With less glaring at us and more empathetic glances at his partner. As if our presence was no longer an inconvenience but a necessity. Maybe he saw Aedin's work with the guards or my efforts with Rowyn as proof of our intentions. Proof of our commitment to see this through, wherever it may lead us.

Regardless, Celion's blue eyes blinked from mine to Rowyn, who inclined his head in acceptance. "When I was Called to join the guards, about eight years ago. We met and have been… inseparable since."

Rowyn fiddled with the handle on his mug as he spoke. When he stopped, Rowyn reached over and squeezed Celion's knee. His voice was rough, his aggressive posturing gone. "Celion is my truest companion and holds my deepest affection… As Captain of the Guard, I'd never intended to bring another into the burdens of my life and my position. But I knew—as soon as I saw him for the first time—that I couldn't pass up the opportunity. The opportunity… to love."

His words punched me in the gut as he lifted his emerald eyes. I held his stare. "You must know…"

"Yes," Aedin answered hoarsely for us. "Yes, we do."

And it was true. I felt his hand wander along the bench until it met mine.

Rowyn acknowledged his words with the tilting of his head. "But our main priority is the protection of this island that *we* love… I have told few, as we never wanted our feelings for each other to stand in conflict to our duties."

"As we are to complete this mission together and fight alongside each other… I'm glad you've shared your life with us," I admitted.

He gave a low laugh, drinking from his mug. "I'd hoped you would be gone by now. I didn't imagine it would take this long… nor be this complicated."

Celion matched his reluctant expression. "It has been difficult… for all of us," he clarified. "But with the inevitability of it all, we should begin preparations for recruitment and the attack."

"Very well," I said slowly, waiting for Rowyn to interject. He remained silent. "I suppose the first thing we have to agree on is *where* to go. Aedin has suggested Lailan—as we're familiar with the island and there are many Gifted already there who may aide us."

"Why wouldn't we go to Radiance?" Rowyn looked at Aedin. "Isn't that where the king and R—" He paused with a wince, and forced out the word. "Where the Rhidge reside?"

"They're protected behind a large palace of stone." Aedin rubbed his chin. "It would be far more difficult to launch an offensive attack where they can easily defend."

"Lailan is also the easternmost island in the Empire," I pointed out. "That makes it the easiest for travel with minimal detection."

"Do I understand that we will essentially be *invading* the island?" Celion's tanned brow furrowed.

Aedin and I exchanged glances. It sounded appalling, invading our home. "Technically, yes," I said hesitantly. "I suppose we would."

Celion considered this. "Why not then claim the territory for Iselleden?"

"Our goal is not to expand the boundaries of Iselleden," Rowyn said quickly.

"Yes, but they don't know that, do they?" Celion looked at us.

"No," I said slowly, understanding his meaning. "They don't."

Aedin furrowed his brow. "But we want to draw out the Rhidge to Lailan, not to colonize and create subjects."

"Yes, and this *will*," I added quickly, meeting Celion's eyes with warmth. "If we act like it's an offensive attack to claim the territory, then Tours will have to play his strongest hand."

"What if he doesn't?" Rowyn asked. "What if part of the Rhidge is left on Radiance?"

"Then we follow with an attack on Radiance."

"I don't think it'll be possible to search and kill out every single Rhidge in the Empire on all the seven islands," Aedin said, leaning forward in his seat. "That's not the point. The point is to depose the regime—the centuries of subjugation of the Gifted. If we kill a large portion of the Rhidge, that *will* help, but our primary goal is Tours."

"And this will force Tours to come to Lailan," I added.

"I hope." Aedin gave me a bitter smile, taking a swig of ale.

"And then what happens when we arrive?" Rowyn asked.

We became quiet—listening to the sounds of the wind passing through the trees overhead.

"Perhaps we root out any existing Rhidge and assassinate them," Aedin offered.

"Should we not offer them a chance to repent?" Celion asked hopefully, cringing at the word "assassinate."

Aedin shot him a dark look as the tree branches shifted cheerfully in the breeze. "They would be better off dead."

"Yes." Rowyn nodded in confirmation. "They have corrupted the Gift."

"But *we* might offer them a chance at life," I said, surprised that I was agreeing with Celion once again. Perhaps his presence was the perfect balance to our group. "Wouldn't it give *you* an opportunity to practice the teachings of Fate? Love, kindness, all that stuff?"

"I don't think our mercy extends *that* far…" Rowyn muttered.

"It would be unwise," Aedin said with finality. "It often takes months or *years* to reverse the years of brainwashing by the Rhidge. They could easily kill one of us in the meantime."

"We can cross that bridge when we get there," I said diplomatically. "But we should come up with a concrete plan for when we arrive."

We spent the rest of the afternoon tossing ideas back and forth. When and how to arrive on Lailan and potential obstacles that might arise from our presence. And how to even begin outfitting the available ships for war. There were so many factors to consider.

Rowyn went back for another round, and by the bottom of the second tankard, my fingers were beginning to tingle. Even Rowyn's face loosened into a lopsided grin as Celion's arm rested gently on his shoulders.

When the farming crowd started to descend—and our stomachs were beginning to protest with hunger—Aedin and I left Rowyn and Celion to their friends and trekked back up the road to the Haven. My calves ached in protest, but I was grateful for Aedin's hand every step of the way.

Chapter Nineteen

"CELION IS EXACTLY what we need," Aedin said quietly as we closed the door to our room. The tray with our dinner had appeared on the table, and we eagerly sat on the couch to eat.

"I know," I agreed, tearing off a piece of bread.

"I didn't expect him to be more open to this than Rowyn. It will be good to have him on our side." He nodded to me. "Especially since he agrees with you."

"Well I also happen to agree with him." I paused to swallow a slice of meat. "Why shouldn't we give the Rhidge the opportunity to repent?"

Aedin loosed a sigh, lowering his brow. "It's not that simple…"

"Is it not?" I challenged.

"You… you can't just reverse years of brainwashing in a single hour or day," he said slowly. "It takes time… it took *me* time."

"So we just slaughter them?" I snapped.

"They're not innocent, Gwen." Aedin looked at me carefully. "They're trained *assassins* who pose a threat to our very existence."

I thoughtfully chewed another slice of meat, considering his words. It was true—saving the life of one could very well end our own. But… "Everyone should be given a choice," I protested quietly.

"In an ideal world… yes," he admitted, carefully cutting an apple. "But we don't live in an ideal world."

"But what if one of them is like you?" I watched as he deftly sliced into the flesh of the fruit. "What if they have the capacity to change… to live?"

Aedin bit into a slice of apple, his eyes on the darkening hills outside the window. "I just don't think we'll have the time to make that decision. Death happens quickly—often when you're not prepared. This war may be slow and ugly, but a targeted killing, an assassination, is quick and quiet." He paused, his words floating gloomily through the space between us. "But we don't have to make that decision now."

"No," I agreed, turning back to my food. "We don't."

Aedin wiped the juice on his pants and turned to face me. His palms were open as he watched me carefully. "But you say the word," he breathed. "You tell me to save someone's life, and I will do it. I promise you that."

I delicately placed my food back on the tray, holding his stare. "Are you sure?" I challenged. I knew this wasn't a light thing to promise.

A moment's hesitation, then, "Yes, I will save anyone that you deem worth saving." His throat bobbed as his lips fixed into a grim line, and I knew he meant it.

I eyed the smooth lines of his throat, a surge of desire rushing through my veins. "Then I will hold you to it."

Aedin's lips tugged upwards as he watched my eyes trace over his broad shoulders, to the slim line of his waist, and the long lean muscles of his curled legs. Leaning forward, he kissed me neatly on the lips. The bright taste of apple lingered just outside my mouth. "Good."

Pulling his body on top of mine, I quickly forgot our dinner. The callouses on his hands were rough against my thighs as he tugged off my pants. My fingers trembled with anticipation as I pulled loose the tie of his and pushed them down. The Gifted fabric slid off easily, as if it knew what we wanted.

I spread my legs to welcome him, nearly falling off the couch with a laugh. "Wait!" I clutched at the cushion and shifted my hips back. Aedin chuckled against my neck.

His hands were bracing against the arm of the sofa as he adjusted his legs to allow me room. "This is the hardest thing we've done all day," he murmured wryly, planting kisses along my jaw.

"Mm," I agreed, unable to come up with a witty response. My mind was stuck in the haze of desire, body arching, ready to receive him.

We moved together like the waves upon the ocean. Undulating, peaking, rising, and falling. I didn't last long. And when I came, he joined me. A flow of lightness washed through my body, and my ears began to tingle. My toes tightened, flexed, and stretched.

Aedin pulled off his shirt and mine, gathered me in his arms, and carried me to the bed. I snuggled into the crook of his shoulder—tired, aching, and satisfied.

The summer air from the open window tickled my back and cooled our heated bodies. A pleasant humming settled between us as his hands made long strokes up and down my skin. Whether it was from the Gift or the act of making love, I didn't care. I fell asleep next to my best friend and partner underneath the stars just beginning to rise and sparkle in the sky.

———

An insistent and clamoring knocking echoed through the room.

I started, opening my eyes to an unfamiliar darkness. It must have been hours later—I blinked away the fog of sleep.

A dagger glittered in Aedin's hand and he rose, naked and tall, from the bed.

In the haze of my mind, I was torn between confusion from the intrusion and amazement at how Aedin had illicitly procured a knife. The knocking continued erratically as Aedin let out a low curse and pulled on his pants. Celion's voice was muffled from behind the door.

I threw a sheet over my body and rose in the rumpled blankets. Aedin—still muttering dark curses under his breath—opened the door. The dagger was carefully held behind his back as he allowed Celion's face to emerge in the crack of the doorway.

"Aedin—Gwen," he gasped before my husband could say anything. "Come—quick."

"What?" Aedin demanded sharply. "What is it?"

Celion's eyes were bright with panic, his blonde hair messy from sleep as if he'd just been awakened as well. "It's them—they're here."

At his words, a thick oil eased into the recesses of my stomach. My hands nearly dropped the sheet covering my chest.

"A boat—there's a boat heading towards the island."

Chapter Twenty

HIS HEAD HIT the stone wall with a sickening thud.

Jon gasped in pain as Bela stood over him, her sword gleaming in the dim light of the room. It was in want of blood.

His legs weren't cooperating. Since returning to the Rhidge, the dismal conditions had begun to wear on Jon's body. Lack of sleep, daylight, and decent meals had made him unwilling to fight. Gingerly, he stood and shook off the fuzziness from the blow. It was the third one in the past thirty minutes. The training wasn't going well.

Seated in the corner of the small room, Tours crossed his legs with a look of displeasure. He thoughtfully straightened his mustache, watching Bela's fingers tighten around the handle of her sword.

Her face was sharp and unyielding—a mask of iron. Eying Jon with a steady gaze.

Waiting for the signal.

"Again," Tours called softly.

Her sword rose up and swept down in a graceful arch. Jon was able to parry the blow but with little success. He fought to maintain his grip, his actions slow and clumsy as Bela attacked again and again.

She was hardly giving her full effort. Tours wasn't sure if he was pleased at Bela's clear strength or disappointed in his trainee's response. Gone was the fervor, the anger, the fury he had so admired in Jon. He was a hollow shell—an echo of past glory.

A crackle of the Gift hit Bela's shoulder—the first blow Jon had actually managed to land so far. She barred her teeth in a hiss, swinging out a leg in a kick that hit his groin. Jon groaned and buckled over.

"Play nice," Tours growled, unable to restrain the smile that tugged at his lips. Bela stood back obediently, glaring at her master.

Jon coughed out a string of foul words that echoed in the small room. Tours clicked his tongue, coming to his feet and folding his arms across his chest. "Now, now, Jon. We don't use that language here."

"You can go to hell," Jon spat, casting a scowl at Bela's retreated stance.

Tours grinned. "But aren't we already here?"

Jon didn't respond. He wiped his brow, streaking a line of blood and dirt on his forehead and wincing as the salty sweat intermingled with the fresh cut. It wasn't deep, but it wasn't shallow either.

Tours knew he'd had far worse. So many years ago, he had inflicted it upon Jon himself.

"Why, Jon?" Tours leaned against the wall. "What do we need to do? Your performance is quite disappointing."

"Kill me."

There were circles under Jon's eyes—the bright blue fire had faded to a dull, watery color. He faced Tours with a serious set of his jaw, unapologetic in his words. "That's what you need to do—just kill me."

"Your cynicism is unappreciated," Tours said tartly. "Why not just *try*?"

"You're wasting your time, Tours," Jon snarled. "I've been here before. I know what you want, and I won't give it to you. You won't let me leave, you're wasting food on this body." He waved his hand at the lines of bone and muscle, devoid of fat. "Just. Kill. Me."

Tours shook his head, pensively examining the dried blood on his gloves. "But I can't, you see. Because I might *need* you."

Another string of curses exited his mouth. Bela shot out her hand, and a wave of power crashed into Jon's head. He rocked back at the unexpected blow, clutching his nose as blood began to seep through his fingers. A red fury descended into his cheeks as he threw out a fist and returned the gesture.

Bela batted away his attempts with a vague smile. Hardly moving an inch.

"See!" Tours cajoled with energy. "That's what we need. Give me *that!*"

Jon shook his head, gripping the bridge of his nose and spitting on the floor. The spittle and blood sprayed across the already filthy stones.

"Well." Tours pushed off the wall. "This has been enjoyable, but I'll leave you two to sort this out. Be good, Jon."

Ignoring Tours, Jon quietly watched Bela—clenching his jaw and dropping his hand as he contemplated her. He twisted the sword methodically, a smoldering hate beginning to burn in his eyes.

Yes—that was what Tours wanted.

Tours opened the door to the sounds of ringing steel and closed it to the silence of the hallway. He lit a flame in his palm, following the path upwards from the depths and back towards the palace.

There were never enough hours in the day to complete what he wanted, but he still made time to enter the Rhidge. If not every day, then several times a week at least.

It was a job he wasn't ready to give up; even with Bela as the new director, delegating most of the daily chores and training inductees. Granted, it would still take time until she was accustomed to her new duties. But Tours found it hard to relinquish the tightly held control he'd maintained for so long. It was personal—the Rhidge had made him into the man he now was.

Through his own long years of learning—the years of pain, hours of fear, and minutes of torture—to even now as the leader of its ranks. He and his contemporaries had helped to craft the Rhidge into a cunning machine built for domination. And to give it up after all these years? Not even the kingship could steal him away.

By superseding the king, Tours had already changed the course of history. Perhaps there were other directions he could guide the Empire.

Exchanging his bloodied gloves for his doublet and the diamond chain, Tours brushed back his hair and instinctively felt outside. The coast was clear. He pulled open the door and blinked at the sudden light.

Murmurs of conversation floated from down the hall. Tours entered his chambers; ignoring the crowd of bowing courtiers, he gestured a hand towards Daniel. The Lord of Radiance looked smug at being singled out, straightened, and followed Tours.

When they were alone in his private chambers, Tours shut the door. "My lord," he purred, pouring two glasses of wine.

"Your Majesty." Daniel accepted the glass with a gracious nod. In recent days, he'd had his brown hair cut and had taken to wearing it fashionably slicked back, in a similar style to Tours'.

"We need to talk about Kellen," Tours began darkly.

"Ah, yes," Daniel said delicately, sipping his wine. "Still been putting up a fight?"

"He coordinated the *unsuccessful* assassination attempt."

"You're sure?" Daniel looked surprised.

"You would question me?" Tours replied irritably.

Daniel recovered quickly. "No—of course not."

"I need to set up a meeting with the advisors in front of the entire palace—so we can make an example of him."

"Certainly." Daniel straightened with responsibility. "When?"

"This afternoon."

Daniel hesitated—Tours could see the wheels of his mind spinning, wondering whether it was even possible to wrangle everyone later that same day. But he didn't protest. Instead, he asked, "How do you intend to make an example of him?" His brown eyes were bright with anticipation.

Tours sipped his wine delicately. "I have some options I am still considering," he offered evenly. "You will arrange this now."

Daniel saw that was his cue to leave. He bowed low, regretfully set down his unfinished wine, and exited the room.

———

Daniel was able to execute as Tours had wished.

Later that day, the advisors were assembled in a semicircle in the great room. Unlike their more habitual advisor meetings, which were held in the king's private rooms, this room was reserved for public spectacles, official proclamations, and contained the more impressive—though uncomfortable—throne. It sat empty before the crowd of people gathered to watch the events unfold. Light from the afternoon sun warmed the gray stones as the courtiers mingled with glasses of wine.

Ephraim sat awkwardly to the side of the throne, his parchments laid before him and quill in the inkwell. When the trumpets announced the arrival of the king, he shifted uncomfortably at the sight of Tours ascending the dais. No matter where he looked, Ephraim always felt that Tours had one eye on him. It wasn't a pleasant feeling.

Tours sat gracefully on the throne, flanked by a tall woman in black and the Lord of Radiance. Daniel eyed the woman with cautious respect, giving her distance as he took his position next to the throne. The woman stared out at the crowd, her face unfeeling and blank.

The banners from the seven islands streamed down from the ceiling, unmoving in the still air. Tours gazed out at the crowd with excitement bubbling in his chest.

This was the moment—he would change the course of history.

"Kellen." Tours beckoned to the advisor with a wave of his hand.

Kellen ducked his graying head and obediently stepped forward. The eyes of the advisors shifted between them as Kellen kneeled before the throne. Greymont cleared his throat and unconsciously took a step back.

"Your Majesty."

"Rise," Tours commanded, and it was obeyed.

Standing before his king for ten long, agonizing seconds, Kellen looked as if he wished he were anywhere else. Tours stroked his mustache, relishing in the pause, staring down at Kellen with his predatory gaze.

Before the room began to mutter or whisper, Tours began, "It brings me great displeasure to announce that the assassination attempt on the life of your king was conducted by one of our own—our dear Kellen."

"Your Majesty," Kellen interrupted, looking astounded. "I did not—"

"It is quite an egregious action, especially when one has recently succeeded to the throne. However, I anticipate we can use this as a good *learning* opportunity for everyone."

Kellen's face went pale as he sputtered again, "Your Majesty —it is *not* so and I have only—"

Tours motioned to the woman at his left and she stepped forward. The blade at her hip gleamed bright as she held out her hand towards Kellen.

His protests were cut off. The advisor's form went still—his lips struggling to gasp for air. There was a sudden hush across the crowd as Ephraim's stomach knotted in fear. At the impossibility of the action.

Tours sat, watching Kellen with easy satisfaction. A soft, strangled gurgling echoed through the hall. The woman's hand was straight and unyielding—Kellen's knees hit the stone.

"Bela, that's good for now," Tours crooned, and the woman dropped her hand, mute frustration on her face. Hungering for blood.

Tours unfurled himself from the throne, watching Kellen's slumped, gasping form with pleasure. The crowd moved and murmured uneasily. Slowly, Tours prowled down the steps, just above his advisor's floundering body.

"There are some people in this world who are given a rare… *gift*," Tours' voice bellowed across the room. "Since the creation of the Empire, we have harnessed this power, creating a secret group of trained assassins who are trained solely to protect the king and the interests of the Empire. They are called the Rhidge."

The words caused stirs and mutters in the crowd.

Ephraim's quill was paused against the paper as his mind tripped over the new information—should he be recording this?

Tours' icy eyes were burning with relish. He waited patiently for the sounds to quieten. "*Now*," he continued, "I felt it was time to share this information with you all because the seven islands of the Empire face a threat. The threat of an *eighth* island in the east, who seeks to destroy our way of life.

"The inhabitants of this island all possess this magical Gift. However, they wish to destroy *you*—those without the Gift—as they believe in the purity of Gifted blood. We *cannot* let that happen." Tours straightened, his voice booming against the stones. "We will *not* stand for the killing of our people and we— the Rhidge—will defend even the weakest among us."

Through the echoing of Tours' words, Daniel's eyes met Ephraim's. They exchanged wordless surprise. It brought Ephraim some distant satisfaction knowing that even Daniel had been kept in the dark about this. That he also held that trace of fear in his brow. In the back of the crowd, Ephraim spied Hollyn's face—pale and gaping like the rest.

Kellen moaned on the ground and Tours shot out his hand— the advisor's head collided suddenly with the stone.

"But we will *not* stand for insubordination," Tours hissed. His eyes were a raging, blue fire. "We *must* be strong."

Tours held out his hand, and the gasping and clawing resumed. Kellen's face was becoming a sickly pale shade of blue. Bela was impassive, almost envious, as she watched, along with the terrified crowd, the struggling man on the ground.

The other advisors were shifting uneasily, grimacing at the sight of their own. They knew what was coming, it was plainly written on their king's face.

It was over fairly soon. Tours closed his hand in a fist and the air was shut out from Kellen's lungs. Clean and quick. No need to unnecessarily further terrify his people.

Kellen's body became limp and unresponsive.

Tours stepped back, his boots echoing against the silence of the hall, ignoring the stunned faces in the crowd. He waved his hand at Bela. "I give to you the Director of the Rhidge. She will command our force and respond to any threats from the eighth island."

Bela's black hair swung as she lifted her chin and gazed out at the crowd. Hungry and still.

"Send word to the lords notifying them of this threat." Tours motioned to Ephraim. "Our Lord of Radiance will leave at once for Lailan to help secure the eastern border."

Daniel's throat bobbled as he protested weakly, "Your Majesty…"

The quill met paper and a sudden scratching echoed through the deathly silence; Ephraim scrawling furiously to keep up. His heartbeat echoed in his ears—magical powers, an eighth island —it was madness…

"My lord, it is imperative that you assist Lord Cabot in bolstering his guards. Bela will go with you to help facilitate this transition," Tours added silkily, gazing fondly at the woman. "She is quite… capable."

Daniel swallowed nervously when he met the vacant eyes of the Rhidge. "Yes… Your Majesty."

"You will leave tomorrow."

The Lord of Radiance bowed stiffly in response.

"As for you…" Tours gazed out on his advisors with grim determination. "I expect you to take this lesson to heart. The power of the Rhidge cannot be defeated. We know, we see, we *hear* everything… I am king, and I intend to keep it that way."

Greymont stepped forward, easing his large body into a bow. "Your Majesty," he murmured as the others followed suit.

Tours allowed a smug smile, sauntering back to his throne. "I understand this is a shock," he admitted to the still hall, taking the seat. "But understand that our *power* has kept you safe all these years… and will continue to lead the Empire into stability and glory."

From his extended palms over the arms of the throne grew a pair of tall, spiraling flames. Rich blues, greens, golds, and blood red twirled together in harmony. Rising and heating the air without burning skin. Scanning the crowd, Ephraim felt the fear, awe and shock as one by one they knelt before the throne. Kneeling before the power that was unmistakable and unconquerable.

The fear that cut into Ephraim's gut was unlike anything he had experienced. He hastily rose from his chair and descended into a bow, avoiding the prying gaze of Bela. Daniel's mouth was set into a grim line, his hands fingering the folds of his pants. By the tight set of his lips and anxious scanning of the floor, Ephraim knew he also felt the same.

———

Kellen's body was removed and Tours exited to his rooms, beckoning the Lord of Radiance to, for the second time that day, follow.

Ephraim trailed behind, clutching his parchments and satchel with a mild panic. Tours could see the wheels spinning in his head, struggling to understand it all. It would take the feeble-minded some time. He had to be patient.

Bela stalked the party. Unused to the formal halls of the palace —warily eying each corner with skepticism. Longing for the dark dungeons of the Rhidge below.

"Please understand, Your Majesty, that I did not wish to be insubordinate…" Daniel's words stumbled. He left a generous several feet between himself and Tours, hesitant to be too close.

"Lord Terrace," Tours purred, "I understand that there will be *many* things that you are uncomfortable with, but I trust your loyalty. Your training in combat and willingness to serve will prove invaluable on this mission."

"How long will I be away?"

Their feet were hushed against the carpet as they entered the private rooms. Ephraim hesitated at the door but continued through.

"As long as it takes…" Tours trailed off, eying his historian. "My dear Mr. Doyle, you will excuse us."

His feet stopped in his tracks. Ephraim mumbled something in thanks and backed through the door.

Bela watched him leave with a faint sneer.

"Sit down." Tours pointed Daniel towards a pair of quilted chairs, pouring two glasses of wine. "Bela?" He looked at her, holding up the decanter in question.

She shook her head grimly, one hand on the dagger at her belt.

"I understand how uncomfortable this is for you," Tours murmured gently. "You may go."

"Your Majesty," she whispered with a swift bow and exited the room. Daniel didn't try to conceal the sigh of relief as she left.

"Yes, I know." Tours smirked at his expression. "You'll get used to it."

"Will I?" Daniel sipped his wine with a grimace. "It's been… quite a day."

"It's about to get more interesting," Tours announced slowly. "They were found."

Daniel frowned. "Who?"

"Gwyneth and Lord Aedin."

Daniel's face immediately paled. "What?" he breathed. "Where?"

"On a small eastern spit of land outside Lailan," Tours said breezily. "But we think they have since fled to the eighth island."

Tours watched the expressions move across Daniel's face—excitement, regret, fear, and… yes, there it was. The desire for revenge.

"But," he sputtered, "what does this have to do with—"

"Lailan? As the easternmost island in the Empire, it serves as a crucial base if we are to launch any attack on the eighth island in the future. If they also seek to return to the Empire for any reason, Lailan is the most likely first step." Tours sipped his wine with a thoughtful smile. "And I should like you to be there… when they return."

"Yes." Daniel's fist tightened around the stem of his wine glass. "I should like to be as well."

"And please take the historian."

"Ephr—Mr. Doyle?"

"Yes, and have Bela keep an eye on him. He could be useful."

"Of course, Your Majesty."

———

Just outside the door, her feet muted on the thick carpet, Hollyn stood still as the words sank into her chest.

They were alive.

———

Hours later, Ephraim winced as he read the words on the page. It was an urgent dispatch from the Lord of Radiance ordering him to depart for Lailan on the next boat. He hardly had time to pack. It was madness—all of it.

Crumbling up the parchment and throwing it on the floor, he drew a fresh piece and set out his ink and quills. He had to write to his father, to let him know about his departure. And the news of the Rhidge, and the eighth island… He hoped it wouldn't give him a heart attack. Or sound like Ephraim was out of his mind.

It was too much to understand. People with magic—this *gift*— had been living among them this entire time. And Tours…

He grabbed his quill and held it poised against the parchment, the words running through his mind again and again, revising and rewriting in his head.

Father, I have been called to Lailan on urgent business…
Father, I want you to know something that happened in the palace today…
Father, I hope you are well. The weather here is nice…

Frustrated, he set down his quill and rubbed his face.
The door creaked open. Hollyn slipped into the room.
"Well," he began dully. "I have some news…"
"Ephraim," she whispered, quietly shutting the door. "You *need* to listen to me."
His stomach dropped at the expression on her face. "What?"
Hollyn licked her lips, drawing up a chair next to his and taking his hand. She breathed in then out, her trembling red mouth moving as if she didn't know where to begin. "I… heard something…"
"Yes," he said with exasperation, unsurprised that the news had already spread. "I'm going to Lailan—"
"That's not it." She squeezed his hand. "Although… it's part of it. I-I heard Lord Tou—the king and Lord Terrace speaking… just now. They found your sister. Gwen is alive."
A hollow ringing echoed in Ephraim's ears, and he felt suddenly light-headed. "What?"
The words came rushing out of her mouth in a hushed whisper, her green eyes shining. "The king said he found Gwen and Lord Aedin—on a small island outside of Lailan. They must have escaped by boat that night you were there. And now he thinks that they're… on the eighth island."
He had become accustomed to living with a gaping, hollow hole in his chest for some time. Now, it was suddenly filled with a great, burning hope.
Alive—his sister was alive.
"But… why would he lie?"
Hollyn shook her blonde curls. "I know, it doesn't make sense," she hissed. "Unless… did your sister have this… power?"
"Gwen?" Ephraim huffed a laugh. "Magical? Certainly not."

"Then why would they have fled? And to that island? Or maybe Lord Aedin has the—the Gift and brought her along…" Hollyn's voice trailed off as she struggled to come up with answers. "I know it doesn't make sense—any of it. But there has to be a reason why they're there. And why you're being sent to Lailan. The king wants you there in case they return."

"He thinks they'll return?" Ephraim's voice became sharp. "To Lailan?"

Hollyn nodded. "He said you might be… useful. And that that horrid woman would keep an eye on you."

Ephraim's stomach dropped as the realization hit him. "I'm to be bait…" he whispered. "Bait for my sister."

"I don't think they're in contact with them," Hollyn protested. "How could they use you if they don't know when she'll return."

"That's the thing, isn't it," Ephraim's voice was thick. "It's *when*… not *if*… He's sure she'll come back… and with Lord Aedin."

Hollyn pressed her lips together in pain, before she continued, "He—the king—also mentioned that they may launch an attack on the island from Lailan."

Rubbing his face, Ephraim suddenly felt a sickness swell in his stomach. He didn't like conflict. Nor did he like being used to further the nefarious interests of others. He preferred the steady rhythm of a peaceful life. He wasn't adventurous—not like Gwen…

Uttering a low curse, Ephraim pinched the bridge of his nose. "Will you come with me?" he asked quietly.

"*Me?*" Hollyn repeated dubiously. "To Lailan?"

"Yes."

"I don't… think I'm allowed to."

"Why not?"

"I-I'm needed here." Hollyn waved her hands around the room. "I have a job. I have to manage the king's household. My father wanted me to work for the king…"

Ephraim grabbed both of her hands and looked her in the eyes. "What if we get married?"

"*Married*?"

"Yes!"

An astonished laugh bubbled in her chest. "Are you proposing to me?"

"What if I am?" Ephraim challenged, gripping her hands. He watched her face—the face he loved. The freckles dotting her nose, those small red lips, intelligent green eyes, and her wondrous curls…

He saw her hesitation and his heart sank.

"Well…" she said slowly.

"I know it's a lot," Ephraim admitted. "But I've been considering this for some time. It's not just to have you there, with me. It's that I can't bear to part with you, Hollyn. Ever since…" He swallowed. "Well, you know. Your kindness has filled the void in my heart, and your love has made me stronger. I want you in my life and I want you as my partner—to face this. Together."

Her face softened. "Ephraim," she murmured. "Are you sure?"

"Never been more sure in my life." And it was the truth.

Ephraim lifted her hands to his mouth and kissed them. "If you agree, I'll write to your father straightaway and ask his permission… Though we don't have much time to wait for a response."

A lively grin spread across Hollyn's face. "We're a bit improper, aren't we?"

"Well, you've already had me in your bed *more* than once—"

She cut off his words with a playful laugh and a proper kiss. The sickness Ephraim had felt earlier melted into a thick, resounding joy.

"I suppose I will have you." Hollyn caressed his beard as he kissed the tip of her nose. "But I have one condition."

"Anything."

"I need a job on Lailan. I can't just sit idly by and suffer in that infamous heat."

"Ah." A wry grin tugged at his lips. "Well, I've already thought of that."

"Have you?" Hollyn eyed him skeptically. "What is it?"

"It's a job for the both of us."

"Oh?"

A grim determination steeled his features. It was inevitable, wasn't it? He couldn't just sit idly by if there was a chance to help. It would be uncomfortable and perhaps even endanger his life. But he had to try.

"We're going to find my sister."

Chapter Twenty-One

THE NIGHT PRESSED against my chest with an unfamiliar dread. Not even the stars overhead offered comfort.

We rushed to the western cliffs overlooking the harbor. Rowyn and the entire troop of guards were already there. The moon lit the thin, dusty trail that descended from the hills to the beach and the ocean—a blanket of silver steel on the horizon.

There was a small ripple of a black shape moving through the metal—a boat.

Rowyn was stoic, staring at the small ship as a man about to meet his destiny. His brow was a hard, edged line and he didn't even both to acknowledge our arrival. The casual familiarity that we'd won earlier was now gone.

My heart beat wildly in my chest. "When did you first see it?" I asked, fingering the dagger at my belt.

"Several hours ago," Rowyn muttered. "It's so small it almost escaped our notice."

Celion moved to stand next to his partner, crossing his broad, tanned arms across his chest. "It's hardly a ship—"

"More like a dingy," Selena finished for him, appearing at my shoulder. "There can't be more than five or six aboard."

I realized they couldn't see that far in the distance—even with the Gift. I focused my power and trained my eyes on the speck. The scene enlarged and I traced a familiar hull and sail.

My blood ran cold. "Aedin..."

"What?" His voice was sharp at my tone.

"It's our boat."

My husband squinted into the distance and asked, "Do you see anyone?"

"Yes." My mouth went dry as I recognized a still and silent form lying inside. "Rebecca."

Rowyn shot us a questioning look as Aedin stiffened. "Are you sure?" he demanded.

Even in the distance, there was no mistaking the homespun shirt and pants, her long, athletic brown limbs, and the large swollen belly. I swallowed, remembering the last time we'd spoken. At the fortress, when we'd been attacked—when her husband, Jon, had betrayed us to the Rhidge.

"I'm sure," I whispered.

"Who is Rebecca?" Rowyn looked annoyed at having to ask.

Aedin and I exchanged looks. A silent conversation passed between us until he lowered his chin—just the slightest— indicating me to answer. "She's... an old friend," I admitted slowly.

"Is she Rhidge?"

We paused. I saw Aedin instinctively touch his dagger. If Rowyn or Celion had noticed it, they hadn't raised the issue. There were far more pressing concerns at present. "No," I offered the half-lie.

"How is it your boat?" Celion asked quietly.

"We used that vessel to flee Lailan and come to the fortress... We left it there when you brought us here."

"She was at the fortress that night?" Rowyn asked sharply. "I thought the inhabitants of that spit of land *were* Rhidge."

"They're not," I insisted. It was the partial truth. "They were fleeing from the Rhidge, just like us. Let Aedin and I be the ones that she first sees when the boat reaches the shore."

Celion's face tightened in anticipation as Rowyn cursed lowly. "Iselleden is becoming a harbor for fugitives," he muttered darkly.

"Isn't that what you want?" I spat. "Iselleden has always been a refuge for the Gifted."

Rowyn's face darkened. "We've maintained our ways for centuries since after the great wars—"

"Now is not the time." Celion shot out an arm and a warning look at us both. "The boat is growing closer."

Selena's face was white in the moonlight. "I will help—in case... of anything."

"We will *all* go together," Rowyn grumbled. "You and Aedin will be the first she sees... but we won't be far." He threw a glare in my direction.

I would have rolled my eyes if the situation hadn't been so dire. Aedin's face had tightened and I could almost read his thoughts. Jon and Rebecca had betrayed us to the Rhidge. They had given us up in an attempt to save their own lives. The fact that Rebecca had let me escape meant little to him—the damage had already been done.

"Let's go," I ordered and descended down the path. Aedin followed, mute and silent in the dark.

We followed the trail as it plunged swiftly through switchbacks carved into the hills. The echo of the waves crashing on the rocky shore was the only sound—no one dared to speak. I looked behind at one point to make sure the guards were still there—their uniforms were russet, black, and blue in the night, blending seamlessly into the rocks.

Training my eyes again, I watched the boat's progress—it would be here within an hour or so. The tide was strong and pulling the vessel to shore even as the sails hung limp in the still air. It was in a poor state, and I marveled at the fact that she'd made it even this far.

I shot Aedin a questioning look as our feet finally reached even ground and the guards disappeared into the backdrop of the bone-white cliffs. He ignored my gaze, fixing his eyes on the boat as it drifted closer and closer to shore.

"Aedin," I hissed. "You have to give her a chance."

His grip tightened on his dagger. "They betrayed us, Gwen," he responded simply. "I don't think we should pretend otherwise."

"She could have killed me at the fortress," I protested lowly. "She let me go."

"She could have been sent by Tours."

"We *don't* know that."

"And you know otherwise?" he demanded, raising an eyebrow.

"I think we should allow her to speak for herself," I murmured, thankful that the crashing waves covered our drifting voices.

Aedin's lips flattened in response, his strong profile sharp against the silver sea. I reached out to grab his hand as he reluctantly loosened his hold on the dagger and let his fingers entwine in mine.

We waited as the boat drew closer and closer.

When it reached the line of waves, I dropped Aedin's hand and moved closer to the break. My boots were quickly soaked in the cold, dark water. I held a breath as the vessel rose up with the ocean and down with the whitewash, jerking unsteadily. It wasn't being navigated—she was unconscious.

My breath caught in my throat at the sight of her limp form against the hull. I hadn't even considered the possibility—was she dead? A shot of grief shocked my chest along with the sudden frigid water. If it were the case, I would miss her. She had been kind to us… even though.

We went into the waves—the cold tightening my skin and seizing my muscles as we fought to grab the creaking, battered wood. It groaned at the force of the ocean—I summoned my power to ease it further ashore, and we dragged it along the rocks. When the boat was safely ashore, Aedin let go of the wood and pulled out his dagger.

We peered inside. Water dangerously lined the bottom. Rebecca was sprawled out along the length, her dark hair wet and tangled, round face void of any emotion or pain.

With one hand, I reached inside to gently place my hand along her neck. The skin was warm under my touch and pulsed with life.

Relieved, I looked up at Aedin. His face was grave, his body coiled and ready to pounce.

"Rebecca," I called. "Rebecca!"

There was no response.

I traced the curves of her face and grabbed her limp hand, counting to ten and then tried again. "Rebecca!"

Nothing.

Perhaps she was too tired, too dehydrated, or unconscious from a blow to the head. Perhaps she was drugged—just like we had been. Maybe she *had* been sent by Tours and was planning an attack.

Thoughts barraged my mind, swirling and spinning stories until my throat tightened with anxiety. It was all speculation. We only knew what was on the surface—what was shown or spoken. Unless…

I caressed her cheek, closing my eyes and focusing my Gift. It was an intuitive motion. A soft humming alighted along my fingertips as I searched the body below. There was pain and fear, and a heavy exhaustion vibrated just underneath the surface of her skin. Softly and gently, I pulled back the layers, reaching further below, until I could feel a slight stirring in the consciousness.

Rebecca, I called again.

Her eyes flew open.

I withdrew my hand and mind as I heard a gasping, gurgling noise. Rebecca rolled onto her side, coughing and struggling for air. At the sound, I could nearly feel the thick tension of anxiety resonating from the guards in the distance. They were aware— and waiting.

"Rebecca," I repeated softly. "You're here… you're safe."

I wasn't sure if she heard me or not. Her broad hands gripped her stomach and she eased herself into a seat. Head hanging limply, she struggled to breathe.

In one fluid motion, Aedin leaped into the boat and brandished his dagger at her limp form. "Who sent you?" he hissed, eyes flashing dangerously.

"Aedin!" I snapped. "Stop it!"

Rebecca stiffened, her hand reflexively coming up to reveal a dagger of her own.

The blade was shaking as she pointed it towards Aedin, her brown eyes pleading. "Don't..." she said quietly.

"Give me *one* good reason," he snarled, "why I shouldn't slit your throat right now."

Fury and power and grace pulsed through the night air, biting at my skin. His eyes were alight with rage.

"Aedin!" I reprimanded lowly, casting a panicked look at the guards in the distance. "Please—she's not here to kill us..."

Neither of them moved their blades—their eyes locked in a stare. Aedin's dagger was steady and waiting.

"I..." Rebecca's voice was small and weak. "I'm sorry, Aedin."

Something flickered in my husband's expression, though his hand was firm and unyielding.

"It was terrible... what we did." Rebecca licked her dry lips. "Inexcusable. And it was a mistake... I'm sorry."

"Where is Jon?" Aedin asked quietly.

Despair flashed across her face. "He was taken by the Rhidge —the night of the attack."

If Aedin was saddened by this news, he didn't show it. "Why weren't you caught?"

"W-When I saw the Gifted from the eighth island arrive and take you both, I stole your boat and left the shore. I sailed into the distance, away from the fortress and the Rhidge's ship, only returning to shore when I saw them leave. I... I didn't know what to do, I tried to survive on my own, but finally I decided to take the chance and follow..."

Her words faltered as she looked around, suddenly aware of her surroundings. "Is this it?" she breathed.

"You are on the island of Iselleden," I pronounced quietly. "The last harbor of the Gifted."

"Iselleden," she repeated the foreign word in her mouth. Her hand dropped the dagger, her body easing from its defense. "I…"

"You're safe now, Rebecca." I paused, looking meaningfully at Aedin's coiled body. "We *all* are."

Aedin grabbed Rebecca's dagger and sheathed his own. Reluctantly, he eased into a standing position and held out his hand. Rebecca took it, gingerly rising as the beached vessel rocked unsteadily on the rocks. As they stepped out of the boat, a line of guards appeared, baring the path in front of us. I wondered if they'd heard our confrontation.

Rowyn stepped forward, eying Rebecca with caution. "I am Rowyn, Captain of the Guard on Iselleden," he announced with pride, one hand resting on the sword at his hip. "You are… welcome here but must remain under guard at all times."

Celion watched Aedin's wary expression, his face coiling in concern. "Why did you attack her?"

Aedin shot me a significant look as I sighed. The truth would come out anyway. "Rebecca *was* Rhidge—she and her husband betrayed us to Tours when we were at the fortress."

My words sent a ripple of flashing blades through the night. Swords were drawn, and Rowyn's diplomatic expression melted with a growl.

"*But*"—I raised my voice—"she regrets their decision and is here to seek refuge… and help us."

"Where is her husband?" Rowyn demanded.

"He was taken… by the Rhidge."

Celion cursed underneath his breath. Rowyn looked wildly at me. "How could you?" he spat. "Do you want to betray us all?"

"She needs help." I gestured towards her limp, exhausted body. "She's also with child."

"She's a *spy*," he hissed. Aedin gave an approving look.

"I am no spy," Rebecca spoke roughly, hugging her arms across her chest. "I am here to serve you and Iselleden. I hold no love for the Empire or the Rhidge."

"She saved me—the night of the attack." I looked meaningfully at Rowyn. "She could have easily killed me before you found me."

Rowyn's lips were tight as he regarded her sopping-wet dress and swollen stomach. Perhaps considering her threat level, given the circumstances and story. "Ciaran Aedin," he said finally. "Will you take responsibility for this *Rhidge* and ensure that she will not harm any Iselleden life?"

Despite the desperate situation, I suppressed a grim smile. After all this time—Rowyn finally trusted Aedin. At least to a certain extent.

My husband touched the handle of his blade with a grave inclination of his head. "I will."

Rowyn turned to me, his emerald eyes flashing in the moonlight. "And?"

"*Yes*, of course I will," I growled. "Now can we please get her food and a warm bath?"

"Your lives depend on it." Rowyn pointed his sword in my direction before turning on his heel and making his way up the path. "Selena, Ophelia—you take the back," he barked.

I turned to Rebecca. "Can you manage?" Fatigue weighed heavily on her shoulders.

"Yes… I think so…" She took small, unsteady steps as we followed the guards up the path. Aedin quickly placed himself in between myself and her. No doubt in case she tried to kill me. I shook my head but didn't protest, and in this manner we slowly and painfully made our way back up the path.

―――

The journey back to the Haven took twice as long. When we reached the white stone walls, they were bathed in the colors of early morning. Golden and warm, Rebecca watched the building with silent wonder as we entered into the depths of the halls.

Rowyn deposited her in a room not far from ours. It held a single bed, bathing area, and a small fireplace. Austere and unadorned. Rebecca collapsed wordlessly on the bed as Rowyn muttered something about bringing food.

I eyed the pain creasing her brow with concern. "Are you worried about the baby?"

Instinctively, she placed a hand on her stomach. "No… I still feel it… I'll be fine."

"You can feel it?"

The ghost of a smile traced her full lips. "It's like a tiny spark of life inside of you… smoldering and growing with each passing month… It should arrive soon."

"We'll be here to help." I sat on the bed with her, gripping her hand reassuringly. Aedin positioned himself against the wall, stiff and unyielding, watching us with a guarded expression.

"Do you need anything other than food? I expect Rowyn will bring some soon."

"No, thank you… Thank you for all you've done." Her grip was tight as she met my eyes. "I mean it."

"I know," I said quietly, looking at Aedin. His pants had finally dried on the walk back, but we both looked a mess. "We'll leave you then."

"Thanks…" Rebecca's words trailed off as her eyes began to close and her mouth slackened. Deep breaths filled the room and we exited quietly.

Selena and Ophelia stood outside the door, eying us warily.

"Call me if *anything* happens," Aedin ordered, looking at Selena. She straightened with responsibility—Aedin eyed her with stern satisfaction.

We went back to our room and shut the door. I released a heavy breath that had been building in my chest the past few hours. My body was aching and filthy—I longed to strip off my clothes and dive into a hot bath.

"What did you do on the shore?" Aedin gripped my hand before I began to pull off my shirt.

"What?" I frowned at the rude interruption. Catching a whiff of our unbathed bodies, I wrinkled my nose.

"When Rebecca was unconscious, you put your hand on her and I felt a pulse of your power. What did you do?"

"I don't know," I replied honestly. "It was instinctive."

Aedin's eyes scanned my face, my body. "Since you touched the Prophet's cloak, you've been changed… like your power has shifted…"

"What are you trying to say?"

"I'm just… thinking out loud." Aedin ran a hand through his hair, looking away. "I wonder… could you do the same to me?"

"Are you serious?" I eyed him dubiously.

"Yes." His familiar mahogany eyes held my stare. "Do… whatever you did… to me. We need to know the extent of your Gift."

"I'm not sure if I can even do it again."

"Try."

I obeyed, lightly running my thumb over the hand that held mine and pulled forth my power. It was easier when I closed my eyes, so I did so and focused on the feeling of his skin. The warm flesh, sinews of muscle, and hard bones in his hand. Pulsating and calm, his heart beat life throughout his body. I followed the trail of veins from his hand, to his chest, to his heart.

Then to the mind. I peered over the edge of a black abyss.

Aedin's hand flinched in my grasp.

A small boy sat huddled at the bottom of the great darkness. Fanged shadows and harrowing shapes swirled hauntingly. Calling, crowing, mocking. I watched as he batted them away, fighting with every ounce of his feeble strength. I could help. I began to descend into the center—

"No!"

The choked word was a world away. At its sound, my eyes flew open. Aedin pulled away his hand, staring at me in horror.

I didn't move, terrified by what I'd seen. "Ciaran…" I breathed.

The Gift was thick and flowing through my blood. I heard his heart rate decelerate, but the fear still rang in his eyes. "You can't see…"

"You told me to," I objected quietly.

"But I didn't…" I knew what he meant as he avoided my gaze. "What did you see with Rebecca?"

"Just darkness—she was unconscious, and I pulled away as soon as I felt her wake."

Aedin nodded brusquely, turning away. I stood awkwardly, unsure of what to say.

The sight of the small, defenseless boy still haunted my waking eyes. Terrified, hungry, and alone to face the demons at his door.

Chapter Twenty-Two

REBECCA SLEPT THE entire day and through that night.

I wondered how long she'd floated alone on the boat in the great emptiness of the sea. Perhaps she'd fallen unconscious from thirst or hunger or exhaustion. Regardless, I knew whatever elements she'd faced were only a small portion of the greater pain in her heart.

I couldn't imagine the pain of betrayal—if Aedin had hurt our friends in order to save me. Would he have done the same? In a way, I understood Jon. And yet every part of my being hated him for bringing the Rhidge to the fortress. But Rebecca had known the entire time…

I blinked open my eyes in the gray of the morning and watched Aedin as he dozed beside me. My harbor and my refuge, yet just as fearful as I. Perhaps Rebecca's presence was a reminder of everything we'd escaped. A not-so-distant past now clawing its way back into the present.

Unsettled by this thought, I slowly eased myself out of bed and crept out of the room. I found Celion and Ophelia at her door—they nodded in greeting.

"How is she?" I whispered to Celion.

"Quiet." He shrugged. "We haven't heard anything."

"Is she still asleep?"

"I'm not sure." Celion exchanged a look with Ophelia. "Do you plan to go inside?"

"Yes," I replied as if it was obvious.

"I'll go with you," Celion stated.

"That's not necessary."

"I insist." His bright blue eyes narrowed and I understood it was a lost battle. Perhaps it was a direct order from Rowyn.

Ophelia opened the door and we ducked into the small room. At the sound of our footsteps, Rebecca's eyes fluttered open. Cautious, but calm.

"Yes?" she croaked.

"How are you?" I murmured, going over to sit on the side of her bed.

Celion inhaled sharply as I touched her side, his body tensing, ready to react.

"My head still hurts." She winced, sitting up and rubbing her temple. "But it's better than sleeping in that damn boat... Do you have any water?"

I looked at Celion, who eyed the empty jug. Reluctantly, he picked up the thing and opened the door, enough to hand it to Ophelia, and then shut it again.

Releasing a terse sigh, I said to Rebecca, "Please don't be offended."

She emitted a shaky smile. "I'm not. I understand."

"Rebecca," I began quietly. "We need to know... when you first escaped the Rhidge... was that planned by Tours?"

"No... I was telling the truth." She licked her parched lips. "That was my Dream of the future, and Jon and I *did* escape on our own. We lived in peace for some time... until they found us. Only several months before you and Aedin came to the fortress. Tours said it was because he Dreamed of the present and saw where we were."

The Dreams. I sighed, watching Celion's grim expression as he stood by the door.

"That was when we first saw the boats," he added quietly. "Several months ago. We saw them in the distance, circling the fortress."

"And Tours threatened you."

"You can't understand…" Rebecca's voice became thick. "To have believed that we escaped the nightmare of our past, only to have it flung back into our faces… Of course he threatened us. He threatened to bring us back to the Rhidge unless we told him if Aedin ever escaped. Returning to that place would've been worse than death…

"And when he left, Jon and I argued for days. I wanted to leave for the eighth island—for Is…"

"Iselleden," Celion finished for her.

"Yes, Iselleden." She pronounced the unfamiliar name carefully. "Even though it was a risk, I thought it was worth the chance. Jon was unwilling and afraid, and at that point, we weren't even sure if you and Aedin would ever arrive. Tours never told us that Aedin had married, but he alluded to the possibility of danger, saying that Aedin was unstable and might flee. And we believed him—we were there from the beginning.

"And so we stayed and waited until you and Aedin appeared… and then we were forced to make the decision. I disagreed with Jon, and I urged him to fight *with* you and Aedin that night the Rhidge attacked. But he would not… he obeyed Tours… he wanted to protect me—protect *us*." She grabbed her stomach possessively as tears leaked from the corners of her eyes.

I offered my hand and she grasped it with an iron grip.

"I'm so sorry…" she whispered. "Aedin must hate us… *I* hate myself…"

"He doesn't forgive easily," I admitted with a tight smile. "But I forgive you."

"When I was lying there… in the boat… in moments of pain, I hated Jon," Rebecca whispered, wiping away the wetness on her cheeks. "I hated that he sold Aedin to Tours—Aedin! Of all people… After Aedin had trusted him for so many years and helped *us* when we fled to Lailan. It was so cruel… I wanted to believe that Jon was better than that… But maybe I was wrong."

I didn't know what to say, so I settled for, "I'm sorry you've had to endure this, Rebecca."

"Don't feel pity for me." Her brown eyes were hollow and pained. "I made my choice—I stayed with Jon when I could have left. I wanted to believe it would end differently… but it didn't."

Mutely, I nodded and watched as she released my hand and brushed back her dark hair. She stared at the bed linen, one hand on her stomach.

Celion cleared his throat. "How long will you stay?"

A flicker of a smile crossed her face. "How long will you give me?"

"As long as you need," I replied for Celion, shooting him a threatening look.

"I meant that she could help." Celion looked at me significantly.

Rebecca watched us and asked cautiously, "Help with what?"

We exchanged glances—Celion gracefully inclined his head. I turned back to Rebecca and said, "Quite a lot has happened since we last saw you."

———

I told Rebecca everything. It took some time, even with the pause when Ophelia returned with a filled jug of water and a new tray of food. Rebecca ate slowly and remained silent as I spoke, only venturing to speak when I was finished.

"So you plan to invade Lailan," she said carefully, looking back and forth between Celion and me.

"Yes."

She considered this, pressing her lips together. "When do we leave?"

"As soon as we gather enough," Celion responded, folding his arms. His stiff posture had melted into a casual slouch against the wall. "We have no idea how many will join us, and we want to make sure they're properly trained. Which is where you could be of use."

A dark smile flitted across her face. "You want a Rhidge training your Gifted?"

"It's the only way we can prepare them," Celion admitted reluctantly.

"Very well." She pushed away her empty tray of food. "But my child may be born soon… I won't be able to do much combat until after the birth."

"Aedin will be working with you—you can do this together."

Celion looked to me. "Does he know this?"

"No," I admitted. "But… I'll tell him."

Rebecca gave me a careful look. "I'll help until you tell me otherwise."

I fixed a smile and patted her hand. "Then I should be getting back…"

"Thank you, Gwen," Rebecca whispered. "I truly appreciate it… I do."

"I know," I said, rising and making for the door. "Oh." I gestured towards Celion. "They'll be following you around the Haven but ask them to give you a tour outside. This island is… beautiful."

"If I feel up to it later, I certainly will." Rebecca rubbed her stomach. "But right now, a nap sounds perfect."

I left her with a smile.

When I returned to our rooms, Aedin was already up, lounging in bed with a book. He looked at me accusingly. "You went to see Rebecca."

"Yes," I said simply, joining him under the covers. "Don't you want to know what we discussed?"

He grunted in response, flicking a page of his book.

"She'll be helping you train the recruits to bring to Lailan."

Aedin's lips fixed into a thin line as he glared at the book. "You know *we* accepted responsibility for her."

"Yes, I know."

"Then shouldn't we be at least somewhat cautious? She could turn against us, just like Jon."

"Aedin, she told me about her Dreams and what happened in the Rhidge. They did escape, and were only found by Tours later —"

"How did Tours know they were at the fortress?" he demanded.

"Tours saw that in a Dream only after we were married. They didn't know until he came unannounced and threatened them."

I saw the fight in his eyes—he set down his book with a heavy sigh. "I don't know what to think," he protested lowly. "I want to believe that she's telling the truth—I really do. But I can't let myself be blinded by my desire to see what I want."

I bit my lip. "I understand your point. But we can't treat all of our friends with suspicion."

"She's not my friend," Aedin clarified quickly. "Jon was my friend."

"Well she's *my* friend," I countered. "And I hope you'll give her a chance to prove herself."

"Didn't I?" Aedin arched a brow with an innocent expression. "When I didn't kill her as soon as she arrived?"

I hit his arm as he playfully pulled me into his chest. "You know what I mean," I growled against his skin.

"I do." He placed a kiss on the top of my head. "And I admire your loyalty and persistence to believe in the goodness of people. But give *me* time, because… it's harder for me."

The memory of the small boy frightened by swirling ghosts swam into my vision. I swallowed, gently pushing away and said, "I understand."

He saw my expression and broke from my stare, uncomfortable. Clearing his throat, he ran a hand through his hair. "It's too bad the Prophet can't clarify this for us," he said lightly.

"Yes," I said casually, running my fingers up his arm, as the thought ran like a flash of lightning through my head—the Prophet.

———

Aedin left to train the guards with Rowyn as Celion began preparations for the boat. I told them I would join later, distracted and haunted by a nagging thought all morning. The

Prophet. The infuriating and nauseating cloak of colors. There had to be a way to get more clarity. Not just on Rebecca, but on our mission and the fate of the Empire.

The ambiguity of our last meeting continued to prey on my thoughts, along with the frail words of prophecy he'd spoken to Rowyn originally. Those simple words that had started a wildfire chain of events.

I hiked up the path along the back of the Haven, along the cliffs where the seagulls soared and dove fearlessly into the ocean. The wind whipped the hair from my braid as I crouched into a crawl, terrified at the sight of the drop below. This was where I'd found them last time and I wondered if I could find them here again.

There was a flat part up top—it was far, but I could see it from my position. Taking deep breaths and ignoring the sight of the ocean striking against the rocks, I continued to climb. The thought flittered through my mind with casual morbidity—I wondered if anyone would find my body if I fell.

Forcing away my doubts, I summoned all of the courage in my body and pushed myself up the hill.

A late afternoon rainstorm was gathering on the distant horizon. When I reached the flat area, I stood with bent knees, bracing against the frigid wind. The Haven was like a silver pool of water against the bright green of the hills. And further out— Farist was a collection of speckled dots against the vast valley and surrounding mountains.

Perhaps I was crazy to think this would work.

I summoned my power, pulling forth the Gift as I felt the familiar thickening of my blood and adrenaline spike my heart. The sparse blades of grass stood erect, responding to my call. The palms of my hands vibrated with warmth. Darkening clouds passed over the ocean.

This had to work. I closed my eyes and counted to ten. I focused on my breath—each inhale and exhale—and when I reached ten, I opened my eyes.

I was alone.

The Gift was pulsating through my veins, making it hard to ignore. I reached out my power and felt through the sky and the land—searching for that familiar tug of a presence. There was nothing, save for some birds and the distant people below. I felt Raine on the path along the Haven, and Aedin, Rowyn, and Celion in the guards' quarters.

Frustrated, I made a fist and shot forth a blast of air into the rock. Particles flew from the impact and tumbled down the cliff. The tempest was gathering closer and I knew I was going to get caught. I sat down with my back against the rock, facing the sea and watching the clouds stream towards me.

Raine was right—I couldn't call the Prophet. Although I'd touched the cloak and my powers had grown, they were insignificant compared to the great overarching will of Fate. Whatever that was.

I recalled Mary's story all those months ago—how the fire and the water arched over the sea to create the first beings. Imbued with the life of Fate itself. I lit a flame in my palm, relishing in the warmth as the first drops of rain sprayed against my cheeks. I winced as the sharp droplets hit my eyelids, nose, and neck.

The fire danced in my palm—the greens, blues, reds, and golds merrily ascending into the sky as the clouds darkened. Thunder rumbled in the distance as the wind and rain lashed at my face, grabbing at my clothes. I shivered, eying the distant path as the dirt quickly softened with the moisture. It would soon be a long, slick river of mud and I would be stuck.

A sudden flash of lightning sparked the flat earth.

I jumped to my feet as a cloak of swirling colors emerged from the bolt of light.

Prophet.

I spoke the word in my head, holding out the flame in my hand.

The cowl tilted its head, as if in recognition.

You are here.

The words were no longer lilting, soft and warm, like summer. They rumbled like the rocks, storm clouds, and thunder through my head. I steeled myself, stepping forward with my open palm.

Tell me what will happen, I demanded. *You are the incarnation of Fate—you know the future.*

The roar of the wind howled through my ears, but I heard the response clearly.

You are the matr *of a new time.*

"No!" I cried aloud, unable to contain my frustration. "I have called *you* to tell us what to do."

You have been given the Dreams—you know what to do.

The maddening, swirling colors were bright even under the darkening sky. I forced myself to focus on the inky blackness of the cowl and the gleaming opalescent eyes within.

You will tell me.

I reached forward and extended a hand. The fabric whipped wildly with the wind, just outside my reach. I wouldn't fall into the void again, I wouldn't—

As I touched the cloak, the blackness overwhelmed my senses. Gone was the rain, the wind, and the thunder. I returned to the haze of numbness, the world of darkness. My heartbeat and the sounds of my breath were mute. I briefly wondered if I'd fallen off the cliff.

No, I was alive. And I was in control. Remembering my power, I pulled out my hand—the flame danced in my palm, casting light in the darkness.

A thing glittered and hovered just in front of me—throwing shards of light as my flame drew closer. Like thousands of diamonds. The eyes were black and blank. I started, stepping back in fear. It was a form with the suggestion of a body, but entirely unlike a human form.

A thrumming of power echoed just beyond my outstretched hand. My Gift hummed in response, as if drawing closer to the source of all the power in the world.

You are the matr *of a new time.*

The words were whispered, caressing my mind.

Time had stopped. I didn't know if I stood there for seconds or hours, staring, drinking in the flickering shade. I wanted to touch it—wanted to worship its power, feel the endlessness. It was more than a thing, a figure, a person. I knew, in that instance, what it was.

It was the incarnation of Fate itself.

Fear and fascination fled as I reached my hand out towards the form.

It shot into a tower of flames.

I blinked as the blackness fled and thunder roared through my ears. The world came back to life. The storm had gone, leaving puddles of water in the dirt. The sun was shining and bright in my eyes.

I was alone again. A cruel echo of weight and materiality thudded in my chest. Space and time were fixed, no longer infinite; contained by the earth that held us.

Wiping away the water from my face, I saw the cloak lying in the wet earth. Void of any color, the fabric was gray and dull and lifeless. I retracted the flame in my palm and kneeled to pick it up.

When my fingers were inches away, I felt it. The same tug of power. The intoxicating breath of the Gift, wafting from the fabric in waves of desire. Promises of power.

Gingerly, I touched the cloth and gave in to the desire. The waves washed through me, gentle and humming until the rhythm grew faster and faster and my mind was spinning.

Ephraim squinted in the sun—sails towered above his head. A young woman stood at his side. His face was a mask of determination, etched with pain and fury.

Aedin held a heavy body in his arms, a large hulking mass of a man, bloodied and broken. Behind him was a wall of greenery and limestone arcades.

Tieren stood on a darkened balcony. On his face was an expression of terror and grim resignation as he watched a scene unfold.

Blood covered Celion's hands, splattered over his face as his sword sliced through a dark-clad body.

Andrea stood in the dirt, sweat staining her brow, surrounded by a maze of white linens, like birds fluttering in the breeze.

Tours sat on the throne, watching with grim satisfaction as a woman tortured a helpless man. His blue eyes were bright, waiting, as they shifted in an instant to mine—

With a cry, I pulled back my hands—a burning sensation in my palms.

"Gwen!" a voice called from just below.

Blood splattered the mud beneath my body. I kneeled shaking in the wet, sticky earth. A cough from my lungs sprayed more red in the dirt. My mind was aching and light; a headache throbbed in my temple.

I heard her call my name again as she climbed up the hill. Raine emerged onto the flat, the colors of her dress obscured by mud; dirt smeared across her beautiful face and long strawberry locks.

Her eyes were wide and fearful.

I had never seen fear in her expression before.

"What happened?" she demanded, looking back and forth between myself and the cloak.

I wasn't sure what exactly had happened, but I said weakly nonetheless, "I… the Prophet."

Her lips were set into a grim line as she kneeled in the dirt alongside me, cautiously easing away from the cloak. So she felt it too.

Another bubble in my chest—I coughed it out, wincing as more blood stained the earth. I wiped my mouth with my sleeve, shuddering at the sight of the red on the fabric. Gripping a nearby rock, I tried to steady myself, feeling as though I might fall off the cliff.

"What do you need?" Raine asked quietly.

I shook my head. "I-I need to get down," I whispered, afraid that if I spoke too loudly, it would inspire another bloody cough.

She eased towards me to grab my body until she stopped. Her eyes were on my hands.

Following her gaze, I saw the skin of my palms had become smooth and silver, spiraling with a multitude of colors in a kaleidoscopic haze. I felt another swell of nausea in my gut—my hands started to quiver. The colors began to spin as I felt my Gift pulse and throb with an ache for release. I wiped my hands on my filthy pants, backing away from the cloak, fear leaping in my throat.

I looked again—it was still there.

"What happened?" Raine murmured, her eyes fixed on my glowing palms. Wetness spread on my cheeks as tears ran down them, obscuring my vision. Another cry—or cough—bubbled in my chest.

"I touched the cloak," I managed to get out before my body doubled over and I released another round of unpleasant hacks.

Raine winced as the spittle reached some of her dress. Her hand hesitated over my body, before it gradually ran up and down my back in an awkwardly comforting motion. As if it was a foreign gesture.

We were silent as the cool wind shifted back to warmth and the crying gulls resumed their course. My body gradually stopped its shaking, the power withdrawing back again into my blood. I flexed my palms, fearful to look again. But the smooth skin had retreated its dizzying shades and had faded into a dull silver burn.

"I have read…" Raine began slowly, carelessly sitting in the mud beside me. "In some books of old, I have read that the Prophet was once a man. A man chosen by Fate to serve as the incarnation of that very power. And that when he was chosen, he gave up his… mortal body to *embody* the power of the Gift."

Her words hung in the space between us. I shifted against the rock, shutting my eyes and remembering the sparkling form in the black abyss.

"Is that all that's left?" Raine's voice was soft. I fluttered open my eyes to see her gazing at the cloak lying innocently on the ground.

"I burned them," I said hollowly, clearing my throat. "I burned the Prophet when I demanded that they tell me…"

Raine's expression was horrified. "But…" She struggled for words. "But the Prophet isn't mortal—they can't be killed…" Her eyes fell again to the cloak.

"Don't touch it." I licked my dry lips, wincing as I tasted the metallic ring of blood. "I… I saw things when I did, and then…" I flexed my palms, wincing at the memory of the burning.

I saw the desire in her eyes, the battle in those emerald irises as her hand inched towards the cloak. Waves of the Gift begin to drift again from the fabric, urging me to touch it. And despite my fear and rising nausea, I wanted to. I wanted to give in to it again—to see the multitude of scenes I'd glimpsed play out again and again.

Like the universe unfolding beneath my gaze.

Like time was irrelevant and I held the key to understanding.

The colors in my palm began to swirl once again.

Raine's hand hovered above the cloak as sweat collected on her brow, her red-blonde locks just hovering above the fabric. As if she felt the same rush of desire. The eager wanting. The dulcet call of power.

She clenched her jaw and put her hand on the cloak.

I waited with bated breath.

Raine gathered the cloak tenderly in her arms as if it were a mere garment and stood. She held out a hand to me—her palms were plain and creased.

"Let's go," she said gently.

I didn't move. "How?" my voice rasped. "How can you touch it?"

She eyed me carefully—almost tenderly. Without the familiar condescension or anger I'd become used to. "I've fought many battles through the years. *Many* battles… I've wanted power and sought knowledge. But this…" Raine gestured to the limp fabric in her hand. "This is not what I want. This has the ability to remove our humanity—to relinquish the chains on this earth."

I flinched at her words, unable to break her stare. "What do you mean?"

"The form of the Prophet may be gone, but their power is not. What if you hadn't let go?" She gestured to my palms and the blood on the earth. "What if you obeyed the call and gave in to the power? Would the life have left your body only to be replaced entirely by the Gift? Like the Prophet before you?"

You are the matr *of a new time.*

I swallowed. I'd been so close.

"Is that what *you* want?" Raine challenged, knowing the answer.

"No," I whispered. "I want to remain here."

"Good." She extended her hand again. "Then let me help you."

I grabbed her hand and stood. With one hand on my back and the other holding the cloak, she supported me as we slowly walked, slid, and crawled down the mountain.

Chapter Twenty-Three

ANDREA'S ARMS BORE angry red marks.

Like a pair of battle wounds, she eyed them with a grim, reluctant pride. They were evidence of the realization she'd suspected for some time. Her marriage to Liam was crumbling. And yet there was no way out.

She dunked the dirty laundry in the basin of water, wincing as the warm soapy liquid hit the tender flesh. Rubbing the cloths against the board, she began to grind, forcing her muscles to work harder than ever and ignore the pain.

Despite Tabitha's urgings to play fetch, Felicity had remained at Andrea's side all that morning. Watching her with her large brown eyes and a sympathetic tilt in her long brown ears. They both hadn't slept well last night. Whether it was from fear that Liam would wake or the mysterious intruder on the balcony, Andrea wasn't sure.

But there were things she couldn't explain, which terrified her even further.

Liam's frozen form. The glass that had collided with his head. She didn't see how any of it was possible.

And yet, the improbability of it all had saved her from being further attacked.

Attacked by her own husband.

Andrea bitterly wondered whether it was time to finally release the ideals of marriage. It wasn't what she'd expected—maybe this was just a mistake. Maybe she should write to her father and ask him to negotiate a divorce or run away or—

"Andrea," Philippa's curt voice rang out. There was a new load of laundry in her hands.

"Hello," she echoed dully, her hands wringing out the clean fabric. She'd left the ruby ring in her pocket and was grateful not to see it on her hand.

"What's the matter?" Philippa dropped the basket and stood akimbo, watching her with keen dark eyes.

"Didn't sleep." Andrea shrugged and tossed the fabric onto the pile of clean ones.

The woman stared. "Your arms…"

Andrea flushed, even in the heat, and looked away. "It's nothing."

Empathy flooded Philippa's quiet face—an emotion Andrea wasn't used to seeing in her sharp eyes. Her voice was low and short. "Did he hurt you?"

"No—no," Andrea lied and pulled a dirty towel from the pile, dunking it in the water. "It's fine. Honestly."

She didn't like how she was beginning to lie on a regular basis.

"If you ever… need anything—" Philippa began haltingly.

"Yes, thank you," Andrea cut her off. "Oh! And I almost forgot." She dried her hands on her apron and pulled out the gold pieces from her pocket, handing them to Philippa. "Here."

But Philippa didn't smile at the gold; nor did she move to take it. "Andrea—"

"Take it—I insist." Andrea held out the gold with raised brows. "It's for your smelly children."

The woman didn't react to her humor. Wordlessly, she accepted the coins and gently tucked them into her pockets. "Tabitha was asking about you this morning," she said quietly.

Andrea grinned at the thought of the innocent, blue-eyed girl. "Tell her we'll be in later."

Philippa gracefully inclined her head and left.

Sweat was already beginning to collect on her neck in the humid air. Andrea continued to dunk, rub, wring, and slap. When the pile of clean laundry had grown as large as she was able to carry, she gathered it in her arms and headed to the backyard.

The towels from the day before were swaying in the gently breeze. Andrea grabbed an empty basket and began feeling the linens—taking down the ones that were mostly dry. Some were still damp from the humid night air. They would have to wait another day.

When there was enough space on the line, Andrea began clipping up the clean, damp laundry as Felicity sat on the dirt, sniffing at a line of ants.

"Felicity!" a small voice cried as Tabitha came hurtling out of the house. She gripped a small blue ball and wore a large uninhibited grin.

"I see you've come prepared to play," Andrea said archly.

In response, Tabitha held the ball in front of Felicity's face. The line of ants was immediately forgotten as Felicity focused on the toy. She barked twice with an eager smile on her face.

Tabitha threw the ball in the dirt, giggling as Felicity jumped up to grab it mid-air.

"That was a good one!" Andrea cried with laughter. A weight suddenly lifted from her chest at the sight of the scene. Felicity returned the ball, and Tabitha threw it again with delight.

"Is there a famous dog around here somewhere?" a young man's voice echoed from behind a fluttering fabric. Andrea's heart skipped a beat in recognition.

Tieren popped his head around a hanging linen, making a face at Tabitha as she shrieked with laughter.

"Tieren—watch this!" Tabitha demanded, her skinny arm throwing the ball again as Felicity leaped in the air with the awkward grace of a newborn fawn.

"She caught it!" Tieren cheered. "That is one talented dog." He eyed Andrea with a wry grin.

She rolled her eyes but was unable to keep the smile from twitching at her lips as she clipped another towel to the line.

Tabitha grabbed the ball from Felicity's mouth, holding it teasingly aloft as Felicity barked her annoyance and insistence.

"You look tired," Tieren observed, watching Andrea's face.

"Thank you for the compliment," Andrea joked, turning away from his hazel eyes. They were persistent and watching.

"Are you alright?" he asked quietly, his words almost obscured by Tabitha's shrieking laughter.

Andrea winced at the high-pitched sound. "Yes, I'm fine." She put on an easy smile. "You look quite tired yourself."

It was somewhat of a lie—he was in the health of his youth—but Andrea could discern some rings beneath his eyes.

Tieren shifted uncomfortably. "I was out last night."

"Night out on the town?" Andrea raised her eyebrows suggestively.

"Something like that," he mumbled evasively, bending to grab a damp cloth.

"You don't have to," Andrea protested, putting out a hand.

He ignored her and clipped it to the line with a shrug. "I have nothing better to do at the moment."

"No more shopping for Philippa?"

He straightened a crease in the linen. "Not today. Just waiting for William to return."

"Was that your friend the other day?"

"Yes."

"The one with the sour face?"

Tieren's lips twitched. "That's the one."

They worked in silence, pausing occasionally to cheer with Tabitha as Felicity caught a particularly good throw. Together, the work passed quicker than Andrea had anticipated. The afternoon sun beat down on her neck, but she didn't mind. When they'd completed the entire basket and moved down to the end of the yard, Andrea looked back on their work with satisfaction.

"Well done," she sighed, both to herself and Tieren.

"And here I thought I would relax with Tabs this afternoon." Tieren ruffled the child's thin, pale hair as she looked up at him with a scrunched face.

"Felicity is tired," she stated.

The ball was still on the ground. Felicity sat panting in the heat, happy but exhausted, her brown-and-white fur covered in dust and leaves. Andrea winced—she would certainly need a bath and a brush later.

"You've definitely tired her out," Andrea chided. "Shall we go inside and have something to drink?"

Tabitha didn't respond. She was staring at the ball on the ground, her brow furrowed in concentration.

It rolled towards Felicity.

Felicity stared at the ball with a frown as Andrea blinked in surprise.

The ball inched closer, gently rolling along the dirt until it touched Felicity's paw. She leaped back with a growl.

"What…?" Andrea rubbed her face. Perhaps she *was* exhausted.

"Tabs." Tieren put a hand on the child. "*No.*" His tanned face paled as he took the girl's shoulders in his hands.

Tabitha looked up at him with confusion. "But you do it."

Andrea's heart leaped in her throat as she watched Tieren's eyes reluctantly meet hers. Her stomach dropped. "What?" she repeated, staring at him in horror.

"Andrea—"

But she'd already gathered Felicity in her arms, dropping her in the empty basket, and headed inside. Her heart pounded like a hammer, recalling how her husband's hands had frozen as they'd grabbed her. How the glass had hit Liam's head the night before. The dark shape on the balcony.

The things she couldn't explain.

———

They slept in separate rooms. It was better that way.

Since the incident with Liam, Andrea and Felicity had taken up residence in the guest bedroom. It was smaller, a little less grand, but Andrea wasn't bothered. She'd moved most of her dresses and fineries into the smaller wardrobe and kept the windows open to cool the jungle-facing room. It didn't have the luxury of a coastal breeze like the former. Most nights, Andrea couldn't even bear to touch Felicity's warm body as she lay sweating and tossing in the heat.

Her husband didn't seem to mind. Liam continued to spend most evenings with Cabot or at the port, only returning home to pass out when he'd had enough to drink. They never spoke of the incident—or perhaps Liam didn't remember. An invisible line now divided them, separating their lives into two distinct spheres. Neither of them ventured to cross this line, nor disturb the fragile peace that had ensued.

In the late hours of the night, when she lay sleepless and miserable in the heat, Andrea wondered what drove him to excess. Perhaps it was the pressure to continue building the wealth of the family name. Or his younger brother, Alexander, who'd left Lailan for an illustrious position on Tente—a fact that Liam's parents continued to champion at dinner parties to whomever would listen.

Perhaps he felt insignificant and desperate to please. And that's why Andrea's plea had angered him. Her disappointment in their relationship embodied the fact that he'd fallen short of another person's expectations. Yet it did not excuse the violence of his actions.

And so she remained distant.

Andrea waved away the servant as he poured a glass of wine for Catherine, rejecting the offer. She didn't want any. They sat on the balcony—sweating and silent—watching Felicity as she stood at the railing, staring intently at the birds below.

Catherine eyed her friend peculiarly. "Are you well?"

"Hm?" Andrea looked away from Felicity to meet Catherine's soft brown eyes. "Yes, very well," she said quickly.

"I have to admit, I was rather surprised to receive your invitation. You've gone quiet ever since I gave you the address of that orphanage." Catherine squinted at her. "Did you ever end up going?"

"Yes," she replied, folding her hands in her lap. "I did."

Catherine waited for her to elaborate. When she didn't, she asked, "Well? How was it?"

"It was… nice," she offered. "I was able to help some."

"Some?"

"I stopped going."

"Why?"

Andrea shrugged, swatting at a buzzing insect. "I just want to do something else…"

Catherine touched her stomach with an expression of concern. "Did you not like it?"

"No!" Andrea said quickly. "No, I did like it…. I just… wanted a break."

Only in the past week had strange reports begin to trickle from Radiance. She heard them repeated by the servants through the halls, whispered at luncheons, and cried loudly on the streets. They spoke of an incident involving the new king in the throne room; displaying a terrifying ability and unveiling the reality of an external threat. Something that could threaten their peaceful existence and disturb the ancient balance of power. Andrea wasn't sure what to believe—she was skeptical of most gossip she encountered, no matter how enticing. Yet this… Something had shifted since that day at the orphanage.

She thought of the ball that had moved of its own accord, just as the glass had hit Liam's head. And Tieren's face—anxious and fearful—his hands gripping Tabitha's shoulder.

It was terrifying—the possibility that something else existed in the world that was outside of her understanding. Outside of her control. *Magic.* She said the word to herself and shivered.

"Madame." A manservant bowed in front of her, extending a folded piece of paper. "This came for you."

Andrea thanked him, took the paper, and unfolded it. Her stomach sank as she read the words on the parchment.

"What is it?" Catherine demanded, eying her warily.

"Liam," Andrea grumbled, crumbling the paper and tossing it on the table. "Apparently Lord Cabot has decided to invite his *inner* circle over for dinner."

Catherine frowned. "That sounds lovely, doesn't it?"

"I suppose," Andrea admitted, irritably flicking at the paper. "I just don't want to go *there*…"

"Where?"

"The villa."

"Oh." Catherine's face fell as they went silent, both remembering the last time they'd been at the villa of the Lord of Lailan. The reception had begun pleasantly enough—full of wine, laughter, and distractions—until Gwen had disappeared. And they'd only received word of their friend's death the next morning.

"That was a horrible evening," Andrea vocalized their thoughts with a grimace. With the regretful curve of her lips, Catherine affirmed the statement.

Felicity had decided that she was done with the birds and came to Andrea's feet, looking up at her with a whine.

"You're lazy." Andrea rolled her eyes, affectionately scooping up the dog and placing Felicity on her lap. Her weight was comforting. Andrea thoughtfully stroked the fine hairs on her head, admiring her long brown ears and the white slope of her sweet nose.

Felicity licked her lips and gazed up at Andrea—and she knew the feeling was mutual.

Catherine sipped her wine delicately. "What time do you have to leave?"

Andrea shrugged at the horizon. "I should probably start getting ready in an hour or so." She glanced at her friend. "How are you? And Joshua?"

"Oh good." Catherine gave her ever-cheerful smile. "We're just preparing for this little one."

A smile tugged at Andrea's lips. "You'll be an excellent mother, Catherine."

"You think so?" her friend asked anxiously. "I've done as much as possible to prepare—I just hope I do everything right."

"Women have been raising children for hundreds of years." Andrea arched an eyebrow. "I'm sure your care will be at least better than half of them."

Catherine thoughtfully rubbed her swollen stomach. "I do hope so. It is quite a task—to raise a child."

"You're stronger than you think," Andrea said gently. "And Joshua will be an excellent father… A little overbearing, if you ask me…"

Catherine gave a tinkling laugh—the sound lifted Andrea's spirits.

"He might be even more nervous than *I* am. If that's even possible."

"I'm not sure it is." Andrea gave a teasing grin. "Your nerves are quite renowned in Lailan."

———

Hours later, Andrea was bathed, groomed, and ready for the evening. She reluctantly said goodbye to Felicity, watching her obedient, small form through the window of the carriage. The dog sat by the servant in the entryway, whining and thumping her tail.

Andrea had asked the staff to feed her an excellent dinner of lamb and chicken. She hoped they didn't overcook the meat and made it just as she liked.

It was the golden hour. The sunlight sank into the jungle of thick, waxy leaves as the carriage rumbled down the main road. Vines hung from the trees, covered in thick moss and spotted with bright flowers. Lailan was beautiful—Andrea had rarely wanted to go anywhere else. And despite the difficulties of her situation, she couldn't imagine ever leaving the island she loved.

She flexed her hands, feeling the moisture sink into her skin. Beads of sweat had already begun to form on the back of her neck. Smoothing her dark blue dress, Andrea suddenly thought of Ephraim Doyle. The handsome, tall man with the jovial smile. They'd chatted together on that night—a drunken amicable chat that had little memorable content but much heart. She wondered if he was back in Radiance and how he was faring after the incident. The loss of a friend was painful enough—she couldn't even imagine the loss of a dear sister.

It was an automatic reaction as the carriage passed through the familiar gates—the tightening of her throat and the skipping of her heart. The villa looked just as she remembered. The grand, arching palms and the wide fountain in the courtyard of gravel. The massive, warm stucco walls that extended into the distance, illuminated by the golden light of the sun. Her heart soared as she took in the beauty, then sank as she remembered what had happened.

Other carriages were already parked on the gravel. Descending at the front, Andrea accepted a glass of wine from a waiting server and wandered into the halls. The whitewashed walls had been redecorated with massive paintings, ornamental swords, and portraits crowded alongside the existing tapestries.

It was garish and tasteless. Andrea grimaced, sipping her wine.

Voices echoed from the garden atrium. Stepping beneath the limestone arcade, Andrea entered the courtyard and stopped in her tracks.

Massive chunks of stone were missing from the roof and hall of the eastern wing. As if a great animal had descended from the sky and taken a large bite but left the rest intact. Or an explosion had ricocheted from the roof and split the stones. The cracked floors were swept and clean, but part of the hall was open to the sky, and the great arches stopped suddenly in space.

"Terrible, isn't it?"

Andrea blinked; Liam's voice drifted to her side. She collected herself, wondering how long she'd stood staring at the wreckage.

"It's horrible," she admitted quietly, sadness washing through her body. She gripped her wine glass like a crutch. "What happened?"

"Nobody's sure. Cabot thinks it was destroyed intentionally by Aedin's men, as a sign of protest after his death." Liam paused to sip his rum and licked his lips. "It's going to cost him a fortune to repair it. He's been arguing with architects ever since he got here."

Andrea wasn't sure if she believed Cabot's account. "Whatever it was… It's a tragedy." A sharp orange sunset bit into the damaged stones, bleeding along the graying forms.

Liam exhaled—the sound was too loud for the solemn moment. "Well, thank you for coming. The other men's wives are here and I thought…"

"Yes, of course," Andrea finished for him. It was her marital duty. She was just a placeholder for the evening. It wasn't like he wanted her there.

Liam finished his rum with a satisfied sound and sauntered off to find a servant. Andrea forced herself to look away from the devastating destruction. The ruin of a thing that had been so beautiful.

She found the other wives—they were collected on the balcony and dressed in their best for an evening with the Lord of Lailan. Andrea was thankful for the wine; it helped to remove the painful edge from the event. It was almost like before— cheerfully chatting amongst the beautiful and rich of Lailan. For a moment, she almost felt part of it again. Confident, easy, and self-assured. Like she belonged.

But then she would see a couch she remembered sitting in— laughing together with Gwen. Or gaze out at the view and taste the same wine she'd ordered from Tente. The barrel that had been intended for *her* and was now being enjoyed by Lord Cabot.

The sharp knife would twist in her stomach. Nothing was the same. She was not the same.

They sat for dinner at the long mahogany table under sparkling chandeliers. Cabot was dressed in the ceremonial doublet of his lordship—the stitched silver vines glittering under the candlelight, ascending up his gut. The thick, pale blue stone of Lailan hung around his neck. It shook and swung as he gestured with his body, preaching loudly about some deal they'd struck with Acedes that would help bring even more money into his pocket.

Andrea ate little and chatted with forced gaiety with her table partners. Liam was thoroughly enjoying himself and likely on his fifth glass of rum. The blush of alcohol had become a permanent stain on his cheeks, descending into the collar of his doublet. Andrea wondered if it would ever come off.

When the last course was taken away, they all stood, and the men gathered along the sofas in the sitting room. Andrea followed the ladies into the atrium—the halls were lit with hanging lamps that swayed in the island breeze. Shadows danced off the wreckage, the warped shapes cavorting along the walls. Clutching her wine, she looked up at the canopy of trees and could see the glimmer of some stars.

As they seated themselves along a collection of chairs and descended into the routine gossip, Andrea desperately wished she could leave. She couldn't bear to spend any longer amongst the ruins—not here. She felt stifled and depressed, being here and pretending like everything was normal. Like her life was something it wasn't.

Mumbling an excuse about needing fresh air, Andrea picked her way across the atrium and exited the courtyard, wandering down the arcade. She followed the turn of the hall as it led to a circular dirt path and then the greater garden beyond. The moon dimly lit the flowers, bushes, and trees as she strolled through the path towards the outer edges of the property.

It was quiet here—the kind of quiet she needed. Their voices faded with the distance, muffled by the nightly chorus of crickets and frogs. Here, there was no need for conversation, no need to impress or flatter. Outside of those ruined walls tainted with the blood of her friend, she was herself, she *knew* herself and found comfort in the world. In the dirt. In the silence.

A low stone wall extended around the garden, pushing away the edge of the jungle. The wild bramble of leaves and trunks felt oddly comforting. A soft breeze moved the humid air as the sounds from the party floated through the garden. The port of Tahuna and the dark sea beyond were just visible beyond the terrace of the garden.

She took a sip of her wine, savoring the bright taste on her tongue. Through the glass, a dark shape flitted through the garden and into the trees.

Andrea swallowed, frowning at the part of the garden where she'd seen the movement. Maybe it had been an animal. Nonetheless, she instinctively froze, straining her ears for any unusual sounds.

A hand wrapped around her mouth, and a voice breathed in her ear, "*Please* don't scream."

Andrea shot out her elbow—it collided with something hard. Whoever it was swore lowly as she twisted out of their grasp, brandishing the wine glass at the dark form. She squinted in the dim moonlight at the familiar dark curls and tall, lanky form.

"Tieren?" she whispered.

Tieren coughed in response, clutching his stomach. "*Keep your voice down,*" he hissed.

"*What are you doing here?*" Andrea responded in the same tone. "And why did you have to *scare* me like that? Gods above!"

"I'm sorry." He did look sorry—he brushed back his curls, collecting himself. "I didn't mean to scare you."

Andrea took several breaths to slow her heart rate, gesturing with her glass at the villa. "What in the gods' names are you doing *here*?"

He shifted self-consciously. "Just going for a walk…"

Andrea hoped he could see her glare in the moonlight. "Oh really?"

"No," Tieren admitted sheepishly, looking back at the wall of jungle behind the wall. "But I should stay hidden."

"Hiding from your lord?" Andrea asked archly.

Tieren's expression became fierce. "He's not my lord."

"Yes he is."

"No he's not."

"Well he's *lord*, whether we like him or not," Andrea muttered, before looking at him accusingly. "What *are* you doing here?"

"Spying." Tieren stood tall and proud, staring down at her with satisfaction.

"Spying," she repeated skeptically.

"Yes."

"On Cabot?"

"Cabot, among others."

Andrea was dumbfounded. "Why?"

"You know." Tieren looked at her pointedly.

Andrea held her breath. "I was right," she breathed, remembering the conversation between Cabot and Liam. "Wait." She stopped. "How do *you* know?"

He shrugged casually, seeming satisfied with himself. "We know things."

"*We?*"

"William and I. We keep tabs on Cabot and his cronies."

"You mean my husband," Andrea corrected bitterly. "Wait—where's William?"

Tieren gestured back towards the wall of trees. "Here."

A dark figure materialized, sitting on the wall and scowling at them from beneath an arching tree.

"The one with the sour face," Andrea recalled softly with a smile.

"That's the one." Tieren grinned.

Her heart leaped as he held her gaze. He looked at her—really *looked* at her—and saw her.

Andrea swallowed, forcing herself to not look away. The thought suddenly clicked into place. "You were there. That night on the balcony… That was you."

There was a crack in his smile as he remembered. "Yes," he murmured. "I was there."

"Why?"

"We followed Cabot to your house. William left, but I stayed and saw… what happened."

A blush rose in her cheeks as she realized the truth: he had seen one of the worst moments of her life. She looked away, unable to form words.

"I'm glad I stayed," Tieren continued in a whisper, his hands tightening into fists. "I would have killed him if he'd…"

She didn't want to think about what would have happened if he hadn't. "*How?*" Andrea formed the one word she'd been pondering for the past week. "How is it possible?"

Tieren didn't feign confusion or shy away from the question, but he struggled with the words. "I have... a Gift. A kind of power... So does William, and Mar—Philippa... and some of the orphans..."

"Tieren." William's growl echoed from the darkness as he unfurled himself from his seat.

Tieren looked back reluctantly at his friend, then he hesitated. "You can't tell anyone this." His voice was low and insistent.

"You *do* have magic."

"It's not—it's something different," he protested, distracted. "Look, just please don't tell anyone."

"Why would I?" Andrea looked at him in amazement. "People would think I was insane!"

A smile tugged at the corners of his lips. Then suddenly he grew serious. "I want you to know something—"

"*Tieren*," William hissed. Andrea could just see his permanent scowl from the cover of darkness.

"Aedin and Gwen are alive. As far as we know, they escaped —"

"What?" Andrea's mouth was dry.

"I saw you—in a dream—you were here. We were all here."

There was a pang in her chest—a sudden hope. And fear. "*What?*" she repeated.

"Look." He held up his hands. "It's a lot to digest, I know, but please come back to the orphanage and we'll explain everything."

William moved like a predator—silently weaving through the plants with power and ease. "Tieren, they're looking for her," he muttered, just close enough for them to hear. He looked at Andrea pointedly. "*You* have to go."

"No!" She pointed at William's chest. "You tell me what's going on!"

"You have to leave," he snarled. Though a full head shorter than Tieren, his small form rippled with muscle, and green eyes glinted dangerously in the darkness.

"Please—come to the orphanage. We'll talk," Tieren said quickly, shooting a look over her shoulder. "You do have to go."

As soon as the words left his mouth, Andrea heard the voice of her husband echoing through the darkness.

She gritted her teeth and faced Tieren with resolve. "You *will* tell me."

"I promise." He held up his hands defensively, edging back into the darkness. "I hope to… see you soon."

A scathing cough sounded from the trees. Even in the darkness, she could see the blush that stained Tieren's cheeks. Andrea couldn't resist a grin—he *liked* her.

"I look forward to it," she agreed, smoothing her voice and meeting his eyes. "Goodnight."

Tieren gave a crooked grin and then disappeared.

In the thin moonlight, Andrea made her way back to the villa, calling out to her husband when she grew near.

"Where were you hiding?" He frowned at her, his brown eyes glassy and dull. "I was going to head home—"

"Yes," she agreed quickly. "I just wanted a walk. It is time to leave."

As they passed through the halls, she looked up at the great ruin of the arches with not despair or fear but hope as the thought flashed into her mind.

Gwen was alive.

They were alive.

Chapter Twenty-Four

RAINE AND I agreed that the cloak should remain with her. Even as we climbed down the mountain, I could still feel its call. It was so close—just on the other side of her body. If I would just reach out my hand—

She shifted her body between us, giving my shoulder a squeeze.

The path down the mountain was long and arduous. I slipped several times, wincing as the rocks and earth cut into my back. My hands were filthy—the silver palms concealed under a thick layer of dirt and errant grass, like the rest of my body. When we reached the open field of grass and saw the guards' quarters in sight, I nearly sighed with relief.

Raine was silent, pensive the entire journey down, but as we watched the white buildings emerge, she asked suddenly, "What will you say?"

I turned to her in question but then realized what she meant. The last time I'd had an encounter with the Prophet, I'd lied to Aedin. I couldn't bear to tell him what had happened, what I'd seen. But now—I grimaced down at my palms—there would be no hiding it. I couldn't lie to him again.

"The truth," I answered quietly.

The late afternoon sun beat down on us—I squinted at the sight of the familiar figures leaving the guards' quarters. I hadn't realized how long I'd been gone.

When we reached the path that looped down towards the quarters, Aedin saw us instantly. His head turned and he leaped into a dead sprint, leaving Selena and Celion gaping in the distance.

Raine eased away from me, the cloak in her grip, as she watched Aedin warily. Wondering if he would have the same reaction I did. She didn't give it a chance—she ignored Selena and Celion and strode ahead of them, towards the Haven, alone. The cloak dangling from her grasp, her face an iron mask.

Without her supporting grip, I nearly stumbled down the path until Aedin caught me in his arms.

I was unable to hide. His face paled as he eyed the mess of blood, dirt, and sweat on me. "What…?"

I gripped his arms with shaking hands, my strength suddenly fleeing as I realized what I'd done. I'd called the Prophet, dismantled him, and nearly died in the process. Or worse— ascended to an altered state. Disembodied, cloaked in swirling colors and nothingness. Not entirely human, yet chained to this earth.

Perhaps it was the expression on my face that betrayed my inner thoughts. Aedin didn't say a word. He gently gathered me in his arms and carried me to the Haven. Holding my body close to his chest, as if I were a child.

When we arrived at our room, he gently placed me on the couch. I stared up at the ceiling, the sound of running water echoing from the bathroom. Seconds later, my husband's familiar dark eyes appeared above me. I pushed back my hair, wincing at the cracking sound of caked mud.

"You look terrible," Aedin muttered.

I managed a flickering smile, struggling to sit and pull off my clothes.

"Here." He pulled off my shirt, grimacing at the sight of the bruises on my back, and helped me wriggle out of my pants.

With one hand under my shoulder, he guided me to the bathroom and eased my body into the tub.

Instantly the water turned brown, the dirt settling to the bottom, the top of the water becoming a thin film of gray. I dunked my head, scratching at my scalp as I felt my hair become soft again.

The warm water freed my body from its rigid and painful state. I relaxed in the tub, almost moaning with relief, and scratched at every inch of dirt that covered my legs and arms.

Aedin sat pensively on the counter of the sink, his arms folded across the flickering colors of his tunic, watching me carefully. The fabric suddenly reminded me of a dimmer version of the Prophet's cloak—I looked away quickly.

"Aren't you going to chastise me?" I asked hollowly, rubbing at a patch of dirt on my arm. "For endangering myself?"

He rubbed his chin with a wry expression. "Gwen, I learned a long time ago that you'll do whatever you think is right, despite what *I* think you should do."

I was suddenly conscious of the dirt leaving my palms—they glowed silver under the dirtying water. I didn't respond.

"I've come to terms with it," he continued with a short, reluctant laugh. "And I've accepted it—"

"Aedin, I saw my death," I said quietly.

My words echoed against the tile in the small room. Aedin's face became blank—an impassive mask. He opened his mouth to speak, but no words came out.

"The first time I saw the Prophet—when I touched the cloak—I saw my death. I Dreamed of the future and saw myself bleeding to death on the floor of the villa in Lailan."

His dark eyes avoided my face—Aedin was staring at the veins in the tiled floor. The interlocking geometry of white shapes. My breath became loud in my ears.

"Are you sure?" he rasped.

"Yes."

I had no control over the future, and what I saw was unavoidable. But the pain in my husband's face was enough to make me summon an apology. Or say something to ease his suffering. "I'm sorry," I whispered.

"Don't." He winced as my words stung. "*Don't* apologize."

I continued, "I'm sorry I lied to you earlier and was reluctant to tell you. I was afraid… of how you might act."

The sound of water dropping from my face into the tub echoed hollowly. I grabbed some soap and scrubbed at my cheeks, hoping to remove any smears of blood.

"If we return to Lailan"—I could see the cogs slowly turning as he verbalized his thoughts—"then you'll die."

"I'll die regardless," I pointed out wryly. "This could be years in the future—"

"The moment we set foot in that villa, the likelihood it happens that day is just as high," Aedin countered lowly.

"True."

I realized this was the cleanest I would be unless I drew a fresh tub of water. Wringing out my tangled hair, I wrapped a towel around my body and stepped out of the tub, then pulled the plug and watched the muddied water slowly swirl into the drain.

Aedin followed me into the bedroom as I pulled a fresh set of pants and shirt from the wardrobe. His lips were set into a thin line—fixed and firm. "And where were you today?" he asked.

Pulling on the shirt and pants, I was conscious of my hands and kept them in loose fists. Tugging down my shirt with a sigh, I finally faced him, holding his stare. "With everything that's happened, I wanted clarity on our position, so I decided to call the Prophet… and I succeeded."

Aedin stood before me, his body tensing in anticipation, his eyes roving over the residual dirt in my hair and fresh bruises on my skin.

"I climbed up a mountain on the back side of the Haven, overlooking the cliffs, where I encountered them the last time. A thunderstorm came from across the ocean and I was caught in the rain. The Prophet… came to me as lightning hit the earth. I demanded that they tell me what will happen, but they kept repeating the same thing as last time. I touched the cloak and fell into darkness, but this time I lit a flame in the darkness and…"

Aedin's voice was dull. "And?"

I licked my lips. "I saw a shining body. And as I held out my hand, the flames engulfed the body and burned it… When I awoke, the Prophet's cloak was lying on the ground and the storm had passed. I—I touched the cloak and gave in to its power…"

I slowly unfurled my hands before him. The smooth skin of my palms shimmered in the early evening light—reflecting dimly in his mahogany eyes. I was thankful the colors were duller than before, although the sight, even to my eyes, was still shocking.

My husband froze, his own hands clenching and unclenching automatically in response. He took a cautious step forward, then another, his eyes locked on my skin.

Gently, very gently, Aedin touched my palms, tracing a finger over the burned skin. A rainbow line of color followed his touch —reds, oranges, blues, golds, and greens—before fading into the muffled, glowing silver. Amazement and fear flickered across his brow.

"When I touched the cloak, I saw… things. Glimpses of moments—whether past, present, or future I'm not sure. I could have stayed longer, but thankfully Raine found me and called my name… I pulled back in fear—I saw the cloak had burned my palms and I coughed up blood…"

My husband's warm hands wrapped mine in his grasp. He folded the palms shut, staring at the glimmers of silver beneath my fingers.

"Raine said that the Prophet was once a person, but the power of the Gift consumed them and they became… a kind of vessel for Fate. They chose to give up their mortal body to the Gift. I don't know if they're still alive—or part of this world—but if I'd held on long enough, I wonder…"

"You would have become the Prophet?" Aedin's dark eyes traced my face, flickers of fear fanning across his face.

"I think the blood would have left my body… only to be replaced entirely by the Gift."

Shutting his eyes in a wince, Aedin lifted my hands to his mouth and pressed my knuckles to his lips. We stood in stillness as the sounds of the road and echoing birds drifted through the room. The Gift pulsed faintly through my veins as I heard the passing conversations in the hall. I shut them out.

"Do you want that?" he demanded in a whisper. Aedin's eyes fluttered open to stare into mine. "Do you *want* to be the Prophet?"

"The call is… strong," I admitted, remembering the waves of power from the cloak. "But no, I… I want to remain myself… I want to remain here."

"This cloak…" I saw the struggle in his face—the struggle to comprehend and digest. "Can you control the visions?"

"I don't know," I answered honestly, flexing my fingers in his gentle grasp. "And I'm fearful to try again. But Raine was able to touch it without giving in to the power. So it might be possible to… harness it somehow."

"But the risk…" Aedin finished with a sigh, his hands contracting around mine.

Slowly, I leaned my forehead against his, breathing in his familiar scent. "The risk is great."

"What did you see this time?" His expression was guarded.

I told him the visions in as much detail as I was able to remember. The memory of Tours' bright blue eyes meeting mine sent a shiver down my spine. As if he'd known—but that was impossible. And the others… my heart ached at the memory of my brother. The bright sails underneath a clear blue sky. There was a hope I would see him again.

You are the matr *of a new time.*

Chapter Twenty-Five

WE SETTLED INTO a routine that consisted of training and hesitant camaraderie. For the first time, Aedin was no longer the distrusted outcast—Rebecca had taken his place. Aedin's gaze was ever on her as she recovered and began to join us in our daily activities. With her due date drawing nearer, she was slow and often tired, refraining from fighting but offering instruction and any other wisdom she could in combat.

Rowyn and Celion were cautious and often conferred with Aedin in low tones, asking repeatedly for confirmation of her loyalty. Rebecca watched this with a slightly amused expression, ignoring their whispers, and continuing with the tasks at hand. I realized we had quite a road ahead of us if we were ever going to succeed at this mission together.

Since Celion and Rowyn had spread the word regarding the new plan, we'd received an influx of interest from those in Farist and the outlying towns. We turned away almost half—some were too young or unskilled—but those who were able and willing were asked to stay and trained by Aedin, Celion, and Rebecca.

As word began to spread, we had our desired number of a hundred within two weeks. A small, yet strong army of Gifted who were being trained for the battle of their life.

Raine oversaw the outfitting of the ships. She would often spend long hours at the port, building and directing whenever possible. The other members of the Council would join her, bringing laborers and helping wherever they could be useful.

For the first time since we'd arrived at Iselleden, it felt that we'd found our place. I felt that the harmony we'd hoped for was finally falling into place. Even if it meant ultimately leaving it.

Aedin appeared to be himself, though still cautious around Rebecca during their training sessions. He never spoke to her about what happened with Jon, and I assumed she didn't dare to broach the subject either. I hoped that time would heal the wound between them—perhaps it was the only salve that could.

While Rowyn, Aedin, and Celion worked with the guards and recruits, I spent more time with Raine. Since ruling in my favor that day in the Council, she'd become an unlikely ally. She considered my opinions, unafraid to voice her own, and together we spent long hours at the ships or overseeing food and supply preparations for our journey.

One afternoon, she handed me a small vial with a wordless smile.

"What's this?" I frowned at the thing in my hands.

"Drink it." She shrugged. "It helps to prevent any… unwanted children."

I stared at her in amazement. "You mean…"

"It's a recipe that's been finely tuned for generations." She gave me a coy smile. "I heard you might need it."

My face flushed at the realization that she—or someone—had heard Aedin and I having sex, but I couldn't resist the laugh that bubbled in my chest. "I suppose I was more surprised that you… need it."

"Why?" Raine purred demurely. "Because I'm an unmarried woman in power?"

I gave her hand a gentle squeeze in thanks as we continued down the path to the Haven.

When we arrived at the outer courtyard, we nearly ran into Celion as he rushed out of the halls. "There you are!" he hissed at me, his eyes wide.

"What is it?"

Gesturing wildly, he beckoned us back into the halls. "Come —she's giving birth!"

"Gods above," I cursed, quickening our pace through the winding halls and into Rebecca's room.

The room was warm—a fire was lit. Selena sat on the edge of the bed, gripping Rebecca's hand with a terrified expression.

"How long?" Raine asked her, coming over to where Rebecca lay.

Her forehead was beaded with sweat, and her breathing was labored. I bit my lip, suddenly nervous. What if it all went wrong? I'd heard horrible stories about childbirth and it had never felt like an enterprise I'd wanted to undertake.

"Several hours, I think," Selena whispered. "Celion was with her when her water broke."

The only man in the room made a face and ran his hands through his hair. "What do we do?"

"Go get fresh water and towels," Raine commanded without missing a beat. "Now."

Celion looked slightly relieved to have orders. "Yes." He nodded distractedly. "Yes—I'll be back."

"Thank the gods," Rebecca moaned as soon as the door closed. "His hovering—" Her words were cut off as she gritted her teeth and closed her eyes.

Even Selena didn't suppress a grin. I placed a hand on Rebecca's forearm; her fingers tightened around the sheets of the bed.

I was uncomfortable at Rebecca's pain, and my inability to do anything about it. I looked at Raine with a pleading expression. "Can you give me something to do?"

Raine nodded at the door. "When Celion returns, heat up half of the fresh water and soak the towels in it. The other half will be in case she needs it for drinking."

The contraction passed. Rebecca blinked open her eyes and scanned my face, a faint smile on her lips. "Don't tell me *you're* afraid?"

I gritted my teeth. "I'd rather face a Rhidge than watch you endure this pain."

"Well, not to worry." Rebecca patted my hand. "It's my first time as well." Her teasing smile didn't comfort me at all.

Raine stood with authority and gestured to her patient. "Let's me examine you then. It's not my first time."

Rebecca obeyed Raine's prodding examination, wincing through another round of contractions as a low growl echoed through her throat. My hands were clasped together so tightly that my knuckles shone white.

A low knock echoed through the room as Celion ducked his head in through the doorway. I stood up to grab the towels and a large bucket of water—it sloshed awkwardly against my arms.

"Anything else?" he asked Raine, avoiding the sight on the bed.

"You're relieved of your duties."

Relief washed over his face before he shut the door.

I bent to my task—pouring half of the bucket into a pitcher and notching the handle to the spit above the fire. Rebecca's groans slowly turned into grunts of effort and pain.

"Do you need help?" Selena's small voice asked.

She buzzed in the corner, her feet unsure of their steps and her hands fluttering at her sides. Torn between hovering over my tasks and the bed, Selena's face had turned white. She was a soldier, not a midwife. I jerked my chin at Selena and told Raine, "Give *her* something to do."

"You can leave." Raine gave her a generous nod.

Selena sighed audibly in relief, her hands finally relaxing on the handle of her blade. She muttered something under her breath as she left the room and shut the door.

"So there were… three," Rebecca bit out, her jaw tight. Her eyes glimmered with humor, watching me methodically go through my tasks.

I offered her a playful glare, wringing out a towel.

And then we waited. And waited. And I soon grew impatient. It was all I could do to keep the fire going, the water hot. And yet my frustration was only an ounce of what Rebecca was experiencing, I understood that well. Her body seemed to be content with its current rhythm and hardly willing to speed up. Hours passed, and I was ready to call for a temporary reprieve, when her contractions quickened. And then it happened all at once.

We were thrown into action.

Raine's orders were hurled like a commander on a battlefield. "Push… *Push.*" Positioned in between Rebecca's legs, her long hair braided down her back, she was unwavering and fearless.

And Rebecca… I couldn't look at what was happening so focused on her face. On gripping her hand and wiping the sweat from her forehead. On shouting encouragements as I could feel the energy in the room escalate.

Rebecca's lips were taut, and a feral growl of pain and release erupted in a single moment. Raine grabbed at something and pulled it forward, her voice easing to a murmur. My head felt light and my ears rang, suddenly devoid of the shouting. In its stead came gurgled crying from a small, ruddy infant that was being cleaned in Raine's arms.

"Gwen—more towels," she ordered without looking up.

I leaped into action, dropping Rebecca's hand to obey. She sagged in relief, tears escaping from the corner of her eyes.

"It's a boy," Raine murmured to Rebecca. "A beautiful boy."

"Thank you…" she whispered to the ceiling. "Thank you…"

The small room was filled with noises from the infant. I handed Raine the towels, watching her gently clean the writhing, wailing form. Such strong lungs for such a small thing. I grimaced and cleaned up the bed as best I could, replacing the soiled linens with clean ones.

When Raine handed the infant to his mother, I eyed the weary set of her mouth and said, "You can rest… I'll stay with her."

Raine pushed back a stray lock of hair. "You don't mind?" I heard the relief in each syllable.

"No, not at all." I situated myself in a chair, showing her my resolution to stay. It was the least I could do, being the least helpful one in the room up until that point.

Raine flashed me a gentle expression as she gathered the soiled linens and towels in her arms and exited the room.

In her arms, Rebecca held her son. I watched her nurse him, whispering softly and holding him so, so gently in her arms. As if he would break.

The fire was warm on my back. The chirping of birds filled the absence of chaos. My eyelids became heavy and I struggled to stay awake as a peaceful haze descended on the room. As if pain and blood had never touched the air.

Chapter Twenty-Six

THE SAILS WERE puffed and shone bright against the crisp blue sky. A sharp bite of salty air hit Ephraim's face with every wave they crested. It was the feeling of adventure—true adventure. For as much as he resented change in his life, this wasn't so bad. He was on a ship with his wife, on a journey to save his sister.

Beside him, Hollyn gripped the railing with gritted determination, her skin slightly pale in the bright sun. The last time she'd been on a boat was when she'd arrived at Radiance— over three years ago. With her knees bent and stomach tight, she stared at the horizon with a grim expression.

"Alright?" Ephraim asked casually, patting her hand.

Hollyn gritted her teeth. "Just fine."

He chuckled under his breath as she loosened her grip just enough to swat his chest.

They watched the whitecaps dance among the deep cerulean blue. The green and copper hills of Radiance were receding into the distance. Sailors were busily moving about the deck— adjusting sails, tightening ropes, manning the massive wheel on the upper deck. As their crisp, purple-and-white uniforms moved quickly, there was a single form in black that stood motionless amidst the dance.

Bela caught his gaze. Ephraim blushed and looked away.

"I hate that woman," he muttered under his breath.

Hollyn didn't respond. She understood who he meant. Her hand gingerly moved to grasp his, and he knew she felt the same.

"Well aren't we just enjoying our honeymoon?" a low voice drawled beside them.

Aside from Bela, Daniel's presence was the only other downside to this trip. It was unfortunate that they had to suffer his company for the three-day journey—a very unromantic voyage, although Ephraim had at least secured them a decent private room.

"My lord." Ephraim acknowledged Daniel with a terse nod.

Daniel took a swig from the flask at his hip. His hair was ruffled by the wind and his eyes were bloodshot, as if he hadn't sleep in the past several nights. Slumped against the railing, Daniel clutched the flask like a lifeline. Ephraim wondered if he had finally felt the weight of his position and the task set before him.

"Lailan," he muttered. "That damned heat nearly killed me last time."

"Yes, my lord," Ephraim said lightly, refusing to let the bitter words spill from his lips. There was little he could say that he really felt. Like *I hate you for what you said about my sister* and *You lied to me letting me think she was dead* or *You're just an ass who's only a pawn in Tours' game.*

Instead, Ephraim tightened his lips and stared into the waves.

Hollyn eyed Daniel with faint humor. "Should you be drinking so early, my lord? The waves will only grow stronger."

"You look like you could use a sip," Daniel drawled in return, eying her clenched form.

Hollyn shook her head and looked away. Her blonde curls were escaping the low bun at her neck and whirling about her face like a halo of light. But Ephraim's attention was drawn elsewhere by Daniel's next words.

"Look at us." Daniel emitted a short laugh. "We've escaped the clutches of Berge, risen above our fathers' stations, and are living a life envied by others."

Ephraim wasn't sure how to respond. If he had to admit it, he missed the perpetual chill of Berge. The furs, the dark taverns, and the misty mountains continually shrouded in a veil of white.

And although he was proud to have achieved a higher ranking than his father, he knew it wasn't his doing at all. Lord Aedin had given him the position. If anyone should be proud of themselves, it was his sister.

"At least I don't deceive myself with lies," Ephraim muttered.

Daniel looked as though he would respond. His lips twisted, and Ephraim could see a retort rising to them.

But then the flask rose to his lips and he took a swig of whatever was inside.

"My lord." That horrid woman appeared at Daniel's side. Ephraim automatically flinched at the sudden black shape against the bright blue sky.

"Yes?"

"We need to talk." Bela's lips hardly moved, and the words were spoken just above a whisper. Ephraim looked away as her sharp, pitiless eyes flickered to his, then back to Daniel.

Daniel pushed away from the railing with reluctance. "Of course."

He followed Bela like a child being taken to school. They crossed the deck and ducked into the stairs below.

"Good riddance," Hollyn said, watching them go. "Perhaps the Lord of Radiance is finally atoning for his foul mouth."

Ephraim couldn't stifle the chuckle that rose in his throat. He coughed and met his wife's eyes, which were shining with affection. "He's had it coming for a long time," he admitted.

Hollyn intertwined her fingers with his, turning her gaze again to the sea. "Did he love her?"

"Who?" Ephraim frowned at her question.

"Gwen. Did Lord Terrace love her?"

It was still strange to hear him referred to as such. Ephraim ran a hand through his hair in an attempt to soften the mass of tangles from the wind. It didn't help. "I think he did," he admitted softly. "I think *they* were in love… But it all changed when she married Lord Aedin."

Hollyn nodded quietly. "That must have been hard on him."

"Whose side are you on?" Ephraim gently jostled her shoulder as a smile flickered on her lips.

"I mean it," she protested. "That must have been hard. It's probably all show, you know."

"His callousness?" Ephraim said tartly.

"His *act*." Hollyn lowered her voice as a sailor passed. "He's probably still hurt that Gwen chose Aedin over him."

"It doesn't sound like it."

"Of course it doesn't." Hollyn rolled her eyes, as if it was obvious. "But look at him—returning to the place where he was renounced by his childhood best friend *and* grappling with the possibility of his previously dead ex-fiancée returning with her husband?"

Ephraim furrowed his brow. "That is… a lot," he admitted.

Hollyn rolled her eyes. "Men. Unable to balance the slightest emotional dichotomy."

"I'll have you know that I've been told before that I am *very* emotionally capable." Ephraim wrapped his arms around her shoulders as she giggled and kissed his cheek.

"You're better than most, I'll admit." Hollyn laughed. "But there's still room for growth."

Ephraim didn't deny it. "You must be feeling better," he noticed.

"A bit." Hollyn took a large gulp of air. "But not enough for food… for now."

"Just let me know what you need." Ephraim placed his cheek against hers and fell silent, pondering over her words.

———

Four days later, they reached Lailan.

The sharp peaks covered with twisted and tangled trees, vines, and leaves were cast in the golden light of the morning.

Ephraim rose with the sun and watched the land emerge from the small window in their room. It took his breath away.

After that night, he'd told himself that no one could ever force him to return to this place. And yet—with the now slim possibility of his sister being alive—here he was. There was no turning back. If she was alive—*if*—then he had to ensure that she succeeded. Even if he was bait.

A soft groan echoed from the tangled sheets of the bed. Ephraim slid back under the covers, next to Hollyn's warmth. "Yes?" He placed a line of kisses along her neck as her eyes fluttered open.

"Are we there yet?" she rasped, her voice thick from sleep.

"We should be docking soon."

"Mm." Hollyn twisted her body, pressing her heat against his chest. "It's already hot," she complained.

Ephraim couldn't resist a smile as he ran his hand up and down her back. "It is."

Her mouth found his, and Ephraim ignored the thin layer of perspiration on his brow as his heart melted.

Later, they met Daniel on the top deck. As the ship crawled into the harbor of Tahuna, Ephraim watched the terraced houses above the port rise along with the sharp cliffs set into the mountains. His eyes traced the familiar warm shades of stucco, rooftop gardens, and winding streets that wove through the mass of houses.

Among the fresh, warm breeze was the scent of flowers and salt.

The villa stood to the right—nearly obscured by the terraces of gardens and trees. Even while squinting through the sunlight, he could hardly make out any sign of life on the balcony. He wondered if Lord Cabot had a family or wife, and if they were enjoying the cool halls, the murmuring of fountains through the buzz of insects, the peace that existed within that place.

It felt sacrilegious to think of anyone else there but his sister. She'd been so happy.

He felt Hollyn's hand tuck itself in the crook of his forearm and was thankful for her touch.

The anchor was cast, and the rowboats were raised and secured for loading. Daniel watched them ready the boats, grimacing under the sharp sun. He bore the dark doublet stitched with silver vines, and the thick blood-red stone hung heavy around his neck. Ephraim slowly filed behind him as a queue began to form, leaving ample space between them.

Waving away an insect fluttering in front of his face, Ephraim flinched at the sudden black form that emerged from the lower deck. Bela—towing something else behind her…

An enormous man winced and blinked in the bright morning sunlight. His face was pale, bloodied, and bruised. The crisp and clean black uniform looked alien on his dirtied skin and hung loosely about his shoulders, his mouth nearly obscured by a thick reddish beard.

Ephraim intuitively took a step back, even as he saw the chains around his wrist and the irons latched to his ankles. Everything about him clawed at Ephraim's instincts to run—to hide. He felt so incredibly small as the black forms drew closer and closer.

The entire deck seemed to give an awkward pause as Bela and another Rhidge led the prisoner towards the boat. Daniel paused with the flask halfway to his mouth, regarding the trio with hesitation. The prisoner's eyes were clouded and nearly closed, as if he might fall asleep standing. He swayed dangerously—Bela gave a sharp tug on the chain at his hands and his eyes fluttered open again to attention.

"Move," she hissed at the Lord of Radiance. Daniel cowered at the tight expression on Bela's face with an unfamiliar look in his eyes—fear.

He obeyed, stepping aside and clumsily corking the flask and slipping it inside his doublet.

The other man entered the boat first—Bela handed him the prisoner's chains—and he tugged the prisoner towards him. The tall form stumbled, just barely catching himself with his chained hands, as Bela nearly pushed him inside the vessel, following shortly behind. She signaled to the nearest sailor and they grabbed the ropes, yanking them into the air, and down into the water.

"At least there's another one," Daniel grumbled under his breath as the boat disappeared from view. An echoing splash sounded before the orders were called to begin rowing.

Ephraim ignored him, exchanging looks with Hollyn. Her face was white—she shook her blonde curls as if to brush off the terrible sight of the prisoner.

Daniel stepped forward to climb into the second boat and they followed obediently. "Who d'you think that was?" Ephraim muttered to Hollyn.

"I have no idea," she whispered, glancing back at the waiting queue. Hollyn shifted uncomfortably. "But whoever he is, they're afraid of him."

"Why do you think that?" Ephraim frowned at her.

"Aside from the chains, he was drugged." Hollyn blinked. "Didn't you see?"

Ephraim recalled his drunken steps as they carefully stepped into the waiting boat with Daniel. "Yes," he admitted quietly. "I guess you're right."

Ten others joined them in the boat. The Lord of Radiance was seated at the bow, shielding his eyes as the boat was hoisted into the air and down into the water. In the distance, they could see the three huddled black forms amidst the cerulean bay—two sailors awkwardly manning the oars.

The journey was fairly quick and painless. When they arrived at the dock, Lord Cabot was already there, flanked by two men and smirking broadly at the sight of their boat.

The black forms were nowhere in sight.

"My Lord Terrace," he announced loudly, sketching a bow as Daniel straightened his doublet.

"Lord Cabot." Daniel gave him a tight smile in return, shaking his hand and regally accepting the bows from the other two men.

"Have you met my accountant? Liam Spence—he keeps me honest. And this is Welm Charles, a good friend and ally."

The two men murmured their respects with ready smiles as Daniel gestured towards Ephraim and Hollyn. "And you remember Ephraim Doyle, the king's historian. And… his new wife, Hollyn Doyle."

"Ah, yes." Cabot's eyebrows rose as he scanned Ephraim's face. "Doyle, is it? I was sorry to hear about your sister."

Ephraim twisted his lips to prevent a sharp retort. "Thank you, my lord," he said.

"Well then." Cabot clasped his meaty hands together, looking at Daniel "I have prepared an afternoon banquet in your honor —"

"Perhaps it could wait an hour or so. I should prefer to go over the accounts with you first," Daniel interrupted with a wave of his hand.

Cabot's smile froze. "But you must be exhausted from your travels…"

"I insist."

Ephraim was surprised to see the look on Daniel's face—a sharp resolve that could cut through glass. A clarity he hadn't seen for days.

Cabot must have seen it as well. He gestured reluctantly towards his carriage. "Very well." And they continued along the dock.

"Do you need me, my lord?" Ephraim began hesitantly.

"No." Daniel turned back with a short expression. "We'll see you at the villa for the banquet."

Ephraim nodded, slightly relieved to watch them go, wiping away a line of sweat with his sleeve. The ramshackle houses and terraces rose before them, a tangled mass of stucco and stone. People and animals wove between them, shouting, braying, and calling to one another. The cacophony of sound and dirt in the port was so at odds with the pristine jungle and polished houses that lay just outside.

Through the humid air, Hollyn's fingers found his. They had work to do.

Chapter Twenty-Seven

THERE WAS A soft knock on the door.

I awoke with a start, my head and back aching from sleeping in the hard chair. The fire was out—the ashes sat motionless in the hearth, clinging to the clumps of charred wood. Rebecca was asleep; her body was curled around a small bundle from which I could hear soft whispers of breath.

Struggling to my feet, I pulled open the door. Aedin stood in the doorway, his shoulders hunched as his eyes immediately scanned the room. "Is it…?"

"Yes. He's here."

I held up a finger to my lips and stepped aside to let him enter. He moved quietly, his eyes absorbing the scene. I'd tried to clean up as best as I could, but there were still dirtied sheets bundled in the corner and some traces of blood or bodily fluids on the bed. Even after opening the windows to invite in the breeze, the sharp tang of blood remained. But it didn't seem to matter—Rebecca was still asleep on the sheets, the small body swaddled just beside her.

"How is she?" Aedin whispered.

"Alive," I replied in the same tone. "Exhausted. Everything you would expect…"

He nodded wordlessly, taking several steps closer to the bed. Some motherly instinct must have kicked in, as Rebecca's eyes fluttered open and her hands tightened around the bundle.

She licked her lips and whispered, "Aedin."

My husband gave a rueful smile. "You're a mother."

Her lips tugged upwards before she frowned and rubbed her face. "Is there any water…?"

The nearby jug was light and empty. "I'll get some more."

I shot a quick glance back at the pair before I exited the door. Aedin had taken a seat cross-legged on the floor, next to her bed. Curled on her side, Rebecca was cradling her child and staring down at my husband without any fear or animosity, something like kindness in her eyes.

And in his expression was a tenderness, an offering of forgiveness.

I shut the door.

———

Whatever happened between Aedin and Rebecca was ultimately the best outcome I could've hoped for. When I'd returned with the water, I hadn't dared to open the door, hearing the soft voices and gentle laughter that echoed from within. I'd placed the jug outside and crept quietly back to our rooms, opting for a long, hot bath.

Only when I was clean and sitting in bed, trying to decide whether I should give myself some rest or seek out Rowyn for an update, did Aedin return.

He unclipped his belt, placing the sheathed dagger at his bedside and looked at me accusingly. "Rebecca was very thirsty, you know."

I smiled innocently. "I thought the water could wait for a little while longer."

Aedin leaned forward in reply to press his lips against my cheek.

"Did she name him?"

"Zaccheus—or Zac for short."

"How sweet."

"She…" he began haltingly, looking down at his twisted fingers. "Apologized."

Something leaped in my chest—a fragile hope—as I saw the look on his face. Rebecca had apologized for betraying us to the Rhidge and I supposed he had finally accepted that apology.

"So you're friends again…?" I ventured gently.

"Friends," Aedin said with a short laugh. "I suppose that's what we *were*, and I expect that's the direction we're heading in."

It was a good enough answer.

We rested well that night, curling together on our sides and letting our bodies relax and our breath become light. When the morning sun hit my eyelids, I squeezed them shut, burrowing my face in the pillow, and continued to sleep for a little longer.

But the day was calling us with responsibilities and tasks unfulfilled. And when I finally eased myself from the bed, Rowyn was waiting for me in the hall, his arms crossed over his chest.

"Finally." He rolled his eyes. "I thought you would sleep forever."

I cuffed him on the arm. "*You* didn't witness a birth yesterday."

"I can only imagine," he growled with a wince. "But… I don't want to."

"Wise choice."

We fell into step down the hall, making our way into the bright courtyard and along the path to the guards' quarters.

"Where are we with the army?"

For once, Rowyn didn't wince at my choice of words. "Combat training is coming along, but it's slow going. They'll have to rely on their power more than I'd hoped. And now with Rebecca out…"

"Only for a week or so," I reassured him. "Barring any ailments of course. She told me she hoped to be back soon."

"Still." He fixed his jaw. "We don't know what we'll face when we arrive on Lailan. It could be a massacre…"

"Always the optimist."

"I'm just being practical," he grumbled. "Preparing for the worst-case scenario."

A fly buzzed in my ear and I brushed it away. Just outside of the guards' quarters, a large swath of field had been cleared in preparation for training. The grass was mowed, and tents were erected to keep the food and drink cool while our soldiers trained under the hot sun. It was Aedin's idea—to prepare them for the heat the only way we could. By exposing them to the brunt of the sun on a summer's midday, we would get them accustomed to the sweat and blinding heat of Lailan.

Our home.

Home. I said the word in my mind with resolve. We had to make this work—it was the only way. We couldn't be hunted all our lives and allow the Rhidge to win. We would choose bravery over fear, and hope over despair.

It was incredible to think that almost a year ago, I'd never even known of the Gift—never even met Aedin—and now I was placing my life on the line to defend it.

The soldiers were sweating with practice swords in hand— swinging at each other as Celion called out exercises. His voice was slightly hoarse, and beads of sweat collected on his tanned brow.

"How long?" I asked Rowyn as we drew closer. The white tents billowed like sails in the afternoon breeze.

"Several weeks."

It felt like forever, and yet I knew it wasn't long enough to prepare them for what they would face. "It won't be enough."

"It has to be." Rowyn brushed back a stray crimson lock. "Every day we scout the horizon, waiting for sails to appear. We need to stay on the offensive rather than be taken by surprise."

He was right. I nodded quietly, listening to the thwack of the wooden swords as they connected again and again. We settled under the shade of a tent, just behind Celion as he shouted instructions. The men and women sweated in their uniforms; the same Gifted fabric flickered a bright gold and silver under the summer sun. They looked like a geometric formation of stars, dancing around the clearing, sparkling and oblivious to the potential brutality of their combat.

After some time, Celion called for a break. The soldiers dropped their weapons, heading for the water tent, chattering amongst themselves, wiping the sweat from their necks and faces.

Celion raised his eyebrows at us, reaching for a jug of water. "Don't say it."

"Say what?" A smile flickered at the corners of Rowyn's lips.

"That we need more time." Celion took a large gulp and let out a satisfied sound.

"We agreed that we need to leave within three weeks at the latest," I told him, looking at Rowyn for agreement—he nodded.

"Or sooner," Celion grumbled. "They're anxious for some action." He jerked his head towards the troops milling about the water tent.

"We'll give them the fight of their lives." Rowyn grasped his partner's shoulder, gripping it tight.

Celion bent his lips towards Rowyn's knuckles, then twisted his face. "I'd feel better if Raine was coming."

"What?" I frowned.

Celion gestured towards the Haven with his jug. "She told us this morning before practice. I thought you knew?"

I didn't. "No," I replied hollowly. "I just assumed she would…"

"Who else will defend Iselleden should we fail?" Rowyn's grin didn't reach his eyes.

Who else indeed? And yet since coming to Iselleden, my affection had only grown for Raine, and I felt unusually slighted by her choice. I would have felt more confident going into battle with her at my side. But she was the leader of her people and it was her choice, wasn't it?

After the break, the soldiers picked up the swords again, and Rowyn led them through some drills. I picked up a sword and joined them, in part to unite in the camaraderie but also to distract myself from Raine's decision. Aedin joined us later and we broke up into smaller groups, allowing for more flexibility of combat instead of the rigid drills.

We sparred until late in the afternoon, when my fighting arm and legs had grown sore though my spirits were high. I clapped hands with my opponent, not missing Aedin's satisfied look that I had yet again quickly disarmed my adversary.

When the early evening set in, we meandered back to the Haven, chatting and laughing among ourselves. As the white stone buildings grew taller, so did the red speck standing straight along the cliffs overlooking Farist. Raine.

Her head turned and her emerald eyes met mine. I lengthened my strides, going to her side and leaving the group as they continued into the halls. The sky was a light gray with remnants of blue—the chirping of crickets just emerging from the grass.

"You're staying," I said without preamble.

Raine nodded wordlessly, turning her sharp chin to the town.

"Are you sure?"

"Why wouldn't I be?" she asked, lazily arching a brow.

I smiled to myself. "I'd hoped you would join us."

"I will admit," she began haltingly, "that… part of me does desire to leave Iselleden. To see new worlds, experience new things. But the other part knows—deep in my bones—that I should remain here." Her full red lips stretched into a grin as her eyes appraised me. "Such is the irony of life—the last thing my brother ever wanted to do was leave and yet he must."

"And he will fight alongside us," I agreed. "Thought I wish it were you."

I felt Raine's fingers snake into mine—she gripped my hand tightly. "*You are the* matr *of a new time*," she whispered. "You do not need me or anyone. Your path is lain before you—I have confidence that you will follow it in stride."

I wrapped my hands around hers as we stood along the cliffs, watching the sky sink into a deeper gray as the sun left the world.

Chapter Twenty-Eight

THE SHIPS AND army were ready. All that was left to do was for us to leave.

There wasn't much for us to pack. My only personal possessions on Iselleden were the boots that Aedin had given me back on Lailan and the black cloth of the Rhidge. The slightly torn uniform had been cleaned and sat folded in the same pile since the day I'd arrived. I didn't plan to take it back—I didn't need it. The Gifted fabric was a more comfortable and durable substitute. It was the new uniform I would wear proudly into battle and beyond.

Aedin scratched at his beard, frowning at himself in the mirror as he fingered his knife. "Should I shave?"

I laughed at the unexpected question. "Why does it matter?"

"It might be uncomfortable on Lailan… and it's not necessarily the custom for the lords in the Empire."

Wrapping my arms around his waist, I met his eyes in the mirror. "*Are* you still a lord?"

Aedin made a face, running his finger perpendicular along the knife's edge, without cutting the skin. "If we're going to pull this off, I suppose we'll have to claim the island for our own."

We. I swallowed, grimacing at the memory of tight dresses and tea parties. "We'll have to do things a little differently…"

As if reading my mind, Aedin chuckled low, dropping the knife and squeezing my hands. "You don't want to be a lady?"

"Not *that* type of lady," I grumbled, pressing my face into his shirt. "I can't go back to that role… It never fit me anyway."

"No," Aedin agreed. "It didn't."

I swatted his side, removing my embrace. His laughter echoed through the bathroom and I couldn't resist a giggle. "It was *so* hard!" I protested.

"Yes—I'm sure," Aedin agreed quickly.

"Oh stuff it." I wriggled away as he attempted to gather me into his arms. "Listen—*we* will claim the island for our own"—I pointed a finger at him—"and I will rule beside you."

Aedin's arms fell to his sides as his good humor paused. He cocked his head. "Yes, you will."

"Good." I folded my arms across my chest.

"What do you want to do?"

"What do you mean?"

"If we take over the island, what then? How do you want to govern? What changes would you make to Lailan?"

The thought hadn't occurred to me—what we would do if we were to succeed. The steps to success themselves seemed impossible—I hadn't dared to hope or plan that far into the future. I said the only thing I *had* considered, remembering those early long-ago days in the Empire's history. "I think the islands should become autonomous states—that each lord and lady should rule their own as countries and there should no longer be an Empire."

Aedin considered this with a tilt of his head. "That's a solid start, perhaps even beneficial for some of the current lords."

"You agree?"

"I do, and I think it would help to strengthen our position and case to the other lords and ladies."

"Good." I stepped forward to envelop him again in my embrace. "And as for the particulars of Lailan, I'll have to give it some more thought."

"Mm." Aedin bent his head to brush his lips against my ear. "I'm inclined to give you all of the control… just so I don't have to sit through those tiresome meetings."

A low noise echoed in my chest as I cleared my throat. "I can certainly take control…"

"Can you now?" Aedin's hands gripped my hips, and my heart leaped in my chest.

I placed a line of kisses along his neck as a low growl slipped through his lips. "Let me show you," I whispered.

———

The morning we were set to leave, we woke to a gray sky tinged with the beginnings of blue. It was a long, solemn walk to the harbor. The army snaked along the path through the wet grass, murmuring and chatting softly in the early hours. As the hours passed and the sun began to rise, the voices grew louder and even some smiles began to broaden.

Aedin's mouth was grimly set and he spoke little as we walked. Rowyn and Celion, too, were quiet, exchanging wordless looks every now and then. I was eager to finally draw closer to the unavoidable task but anxious as I heard the echoes of casual laughter and chatter from the army behind us. They didn't know—they couldn't know—what awaited us in the Empire. They had never lived in fear or secrecy, never been persecuted, beaten, or broken.

I decided to hold my tongue and let them enjoy their last hours on Iselleden, knowing that some of them may never return.

A low gurgle echoed behind me. I turned to see Rebecca grinning at Zac as he shifted and frowned in her arms. She adjusted the swaddling cloths, catching my eye with a smile. "I think he's ready for an adventure."

"Are you?" I asked pointedly.

Rebecca shrugged, turning her gaze again to her child. "I'm always ready for whatever life throws at me."

"You don't have to return," I gave her the option again. "You can stay here… live in peace."

Rebecca swallowed, shaking her head. "I can't do that…"

And I understood. It was because of Jon. Even after everything he'd done, there was still the possibility of saving him. Their story was unfinished, and she intended to see it through.

As the morning continued to lighten, people from Farist climbed up the hill and joined our walk, tossing flowers on the path and murmuring words of encouragement. I spied a red-haired woman, flanked by three children, holding out a handmade bouquet of wildflowers to Rowyn. Rea—I recognized her from my first days in Iselleden. Her brother stepped out of line to embrace them, saying something I couldn't hear as I passed.

Celion and I shared a sympathetic glance.

I looked back. Rowyn hadn't moved—he clutched Rea as she stroked his head and whispered into his ear. I turned away from the uncomfortable sight and focused on the ship just ahead.

Its sails were full with the morning wind, the vessel straining against its anchors. Smaller boats moved back and forth from the shore to the belly, hoisting up last-minute supplies. A group of cloaks sparkled softly against the horizon, standing at the intersection of the path—the Council. Raine stood among them, her shoulders straight and proud. Her eyes scanned the mass of people, and she lifted her chin ever so slightly. There was no sign of fear or anxiety on her face, only a familiar and stern resolve.

We paused as we reached them and I went to Raine, embracing her. Her body was stiff, even as she awkwardly patted my back and allowed me several more seconds holding her.

"Fate be with you," she said as we pulled away.

"And with you."

Raine nodded to my husband. Aedin stretched out his hand and they clasped arms—it was as much intimacy as I could expect after what we'd endured.

We said our goodbyes, exchanging kind words, hopeful smiles, and shaking hands. Aedin, Rebecca, and I began to head down the path to the beach, leaving Rowyn, Celion, and the rest of the army to linger a bit longer. Although I was eager to be on our way, I didn't want to press them. Instead, we waited on the beach, watching as Rowyn and Celion slowly began their descent, hand in hand. When they'd reached the shore, we jumped into the boats and paddled to the ship.

A fierce gust of wind hit my face along with the spray of seawater. There was only the tang of salt and the empty arching sky.

It felt like I was going home.

Chapter Twenty-Nine

A SUDDEN JOLT from the waves woke Rowyn from sleep.

It was bright—the yellow light of morning seared through the small window in their cabin. He was grateful that the seasickness had finally passed. The first day on the ship had been the most painful, but after several days, Rowyn had become accustomed to the rhythmic rocking and odd swings from their journey. Their journey to the land he had always feared. The Empire.

Celion's body shifted beside him, his golden hair bright against the clean linen of the pillow. He looked up at him with a smile that was so tender and sweet, it nearly broke his heart.

Rowyn bent his head to press their lips together. It was a beautiful thing to appreciate and savor amidst the uncertainty and fear. They rested peacefully in the quiet of the morning, feeling worlds away from the muted footsteps above deck and the duties that would soon draw their attention. For the moment, it was just them. It was all he'd ever wanted—and Rowyn was content.

"You're doing the late shift tonight?" Celion's voice was thick from sleep. He yawned, pressing his face into the crook of Rowyn's arm.

"Yes." Rowyn couldn't suppress a grin at the muffled grunt in response. "Are you feeling better?"

"A bit." Celion turned his head, his blue eyes looking up at Rowyn once more. "I think the worst has passed…"

"You need to eat something—I'll get you some food from the galley." Rowyn moved to shift out of bed, but Celion's arm tightened around his waist.

"Not yet," he protested. "It's too early."

Rowyn didn't disagree. He settled back down, stroking the long arm draped over his torso and admiring the flecks of gray beginning to dot Celion's golden hair. It had been so long since they'd first met. Almost eight years. During a time when Rowyn had willingly consigned himself to a life of a solitude—a life solely dedicated to his island and duties.

Until Celion.

With his arrival had come the hope of companionship, then the spring of a growing love. Rowyn hadn't known how lonely he'd become, until he grew accustomed to Celion's presence. He eagerly awaited their long walks and conversations, the rare moments when they could be alone. And the nights they spent together.

It was a meeting of two souls—both committed to the protection and perpetuation of a life they loved. Until recently.

The revelation of the prophecy had changed many things. It had thrown Iselleden into terror, grappling with the sudden threat of bloodshed. And since the arrival of Gwen and Aedin, Rowyn had felt that his life had been turned on its head.

But it had also spurred a sudden urgency to love. To be with the one man who truly saw and knew him. It was an unspoken feeling—the inevitability of change, the fear of being torn apart. And as much as Rowyn resented bringing Celion into this mess, he knew it was impossible to exclude him. Celion was a balm to his fears, a strong weight to counter his anxiety. As if they existed solely to complement each other and endure this journey —together.

Rowyn pressed his lips to the top of his head, feeling the arm tighten around his waist. It wouldn't hurt to spend a couple more minutes alone. Once he left that room, the duties for the day would hound his steps and require his every thought. Until then…

Celion's warm body crawled atop his chest, meeting Rowyn's eyes with their familiar warmth. Rowyn smiled and let himself forget about the prophecy—forget that they were headed into the mouths of wolves. To the last place in this world he'd ever wanted to go. Just for now.

Until it was finally time to face the dawning day.

Rowyn rose from the bed, dressed, and grabbed an apple from the galley on his way to the top deck, savoring the sweetness on his tongue. Ascending the stairs, he winced at the sudden brightness. The sun was beginning its path through the sky. Faint clouds dotted the horizon in the direction of their course.

The deck was a flurry of activity. Aedin stood amidst the chaos, directing orders to their new army. His dark clothing was stark against the Gifted uniforms surrounding him.

Rowyn found Gwen manning the ship's wheel on the quarterdeck. Those blue-gray eyes that had haunted his dreams were now soft and familiar. They watched him as he leaped up the stairs.

"You slept in," she murmured.

He ignored her comment, craning his neck to study the compass. "On course?"

"So far." Gwen studied the arrow and shifted the giant wheel slightly to the right.

The high, arching sails were full, the ropes taut to support the weight of the wind. Rowyn tucked an errant lock of hair behind his ear, studying the maze of people below, and the black spot in between them.

"He changed," Rowyn commented lowly.

Gwen shrugged. "He wanted to wear it. And besides, your uniform is starting to lose its luster." She gestured towards Rowyn's shirt. The kaleidoscope of colors had faded into a haze of perpetual gray, only interrupted by occasional sparks of silver or gold. He frowned—he hadn't noticed it until now.

"Aedin is more comfortable in that anyway," Gwen continued. "If it comes to combat…"

They both fell silent, suddenly aware of the impending reality. Combat sounded too formal a word. Rowyn wished she would call it what it was—brutality, bloodshed, attack, or even a massacre. The very real possibility that they would lose their lives.

At least it would be fighting for a worthy cause.

Gwen flexed her hands from the wheel, closing her fingers over the burned skin of her palms. They were no longer swirling with color—just like the fabric and everything else they'd brought from Iselleden. It faded, as if the colors had only been a dream.

"How are you?"

Her voice broke through his thoughts. Rowyn blinked, suddenly focusing as Gwen scanned his face.

"As good as can be expected," he responded coldly, then sighed. "I'm terrified that we're leading so many good people to slaughter."

Slaughter. That was it. That was the best description of what this was.

Gwen didn't wince or shy away from his words. "There will be bloodshed—we knew that. But they are trained. We have Aedin, Rebecca, and the combined strength of a hundred Gifted. We know what to do."

The strength in her voice was enough to slightly lift his spirits. He spied the other Rhidge curled in the corner of the deck, rocking the small child in her arms. As if she was a mother, not a trained assassin.

"How is *she*?" Rowyn asked quietly.

Gwen followed his gaze. "Rebecca's doing the best she can given the reality of her situation. Just as we all are…"

"You don't think she'll—"

"No." Gwen cut him off with a sharp gaze. "She isn't daft."

"But if they were to use Jon against us…"

"It could happen, but it's just as likely Jon could be dead. Tours may have killed him by now. We don't know."

"You haven't seen anything?"

"Not concerning Jon, no."

Rowyn left it at that. He watched Celion's golden form emerge from the belly of the ship and straighten on the deck. He exchanged words with Aedin before joining a group of men and women, pulling one of the sails and hooking the line to the peg.

"I think you'll like Lailan."

"Why is that?" Rowyn gave a humorless smile as Gwen eyed him coyly.

"The variety of plants, trees, and natural life… The warm air and expansive sea… You're lucky we're not going to Berge."

"Is Berge in the north?"

"Yes—it was the island of my youth. Full of rocks, ice, and emptiness."

"A quiet, cold island sounds quite lovely at the moment."

Gwen smirked. "It is, until it isn't. It gets old pretty quickly."

They shared a smile. Rowyn scanned the horizon, saying half to himself, "It's empty."

A frown faintly creased her brow. "Every hour I wait for sails to appear, but they never do."

It was something he also feared. Rowyn inclined his head almost imperceptibly. "They're not far."

"And yet—for now—we're alone." Gwen placed a tie on the wheel, holding it in place. She flexed her hands and stepped away from the wheel.

"For now," Rowyn agreed.

Chapter Thirty

AS THE DAYS trickled by, the feeling became more and more apparent. A shift in the wind—the sharp salty breeze making way for something softer, warmer, and sweeter.

The familiar smell of home.

It sank into my skin—the moist air, the hint of flowers and fresh rainwater on the tails of the wind. I'd longed for this moment for months; to return to the place where we'd lived, grown, and fallen in love. And yet I knew we would be returning to a place that was no longer our own.

Fear of the unknown gripped both of our hearts, but I suspected it ran deeper for Aedin. In our brief moments of rest, I saw him staring keenly at the horizon, the dagger spinning mindlessly in his hand. As if waiting for a ship to appear, to challenge our arrival.

But none came.

And slowly, the dark form of earth rose from the sea. It was still distant but close enough to view. The final rays from the setting sun cast a golden hue over the mass of tropical jungle, deepening the shadows of craggy rocks along the cliffs. A hush fell over the boat as our world was thrust into darkness and we navigated by the thin light of the moon. We docked far enough away to watch the shore, without daring to draw closer.

Rowyn and Celion stood at the railing, staring somberly in the direction of Lailan, the dark water lapping quietly in the night.

I grabbed Rebecca's hand, giving it a squeeze as she tore her eyes away from the sight.

"I never thought I would return," she mused quietly, stroking Zac's head.

"Nor did I," I admitted.

The sound of a dagger being sheathed echoed through the silence on deck.

Aedin appeared at my side. "Let's go."

I looked at him dubiously. "Now?"

"Yes." His arms were crossed, his fingers tight on his arms. "Our first journey ashore should be under the cover of night."

Rowyn and Celion turned to watch Aedin skeptically. "Shouldn't we wait until we've watched the shore for another day?" I challenged.

"We're in a large ship, docked off the western shore. Though all the activity is in the east, our presence will not go unnoticed in the morning. I would rather go ashore now before we risk attracting the wrong type of attention."

The words poured out of his mouth in a rush. I waited until he was finished and had taken a breath. There was a frantic, uneasy glint in his eyes—Rebecca shifted away automatically.

"Listen…" I pulled him aside, turning our heads from the crowd on deck. "I know you're afraid—"

"I'm not afraid," Aedin said quickly, forcing a posture of casualness.

"But we can't be impulsive about this."

"We need to go before it's too late."

"Who will watch the ship?"

"Rebecca and Celion."

"Why me?" Celion protested glumly, hearing our whispered conversation. Rebecca was unperturbed, watching Aedin with a knowing gaze.

I scanned his face, feeling the inevitable direction of this conversation before I asked quietly, "And where will we go?"

"There's a trail through the jungle that leads to the main road, and then to the villa. It should only take a few hours if we move quickly. We would be back at sunrise."

I now saw that the past hours when he'd been standing alone at the railing, he'd been mulling through the options; sorting and picking them apart. Aedin was eager to breach the unavoidable, to run headfirst into this nightmare, but it wasn't without thought.

I turned to Rowyn. "What do you think?"

Rowyn shifted his emerald eyes to my husband and then again to the shore. "We should go before the morning."

"Then we'll go," I stated. "But we won't unnecessarily engage in combat." I directed my last words at Aedin.

He touched the handle of his dagger in agreement. I caught Rebecca's eye, and she offered a slight smile as I suppressed an exasperated sigh.

"Then we're to just stay here?" Celion opened his arms in question. The other Gifted behind him murmured their agreement.

"We need someone to protect the boat. You know how to sail, Rebecca knows how to fight—you'll be fine." I shot him a glare that he easily returned.

Rowyn laid a hand on Celion's arm and said, "I'll return, I promise."

Celion reluctantly deflated his posture. "You better," he muttered, grabbing his hand and kissing it.

"Stay sharp." Rebecca looked at me in warning, shifting the child in her arms. "If it comes to killing, don't hesitate."

Her voice was low and insistent—her words sank into the pit in my stomach. "It won't come to that," I said firmly.

Rebecca didn't respond as her eyes slid from mine to Aedin's. She hoisted her child higher on her shoulder, revealing the sharp dagger buckled at her side. Even with a child in her arms, she was a deadly weapon.

In acknowledgement, I grabbed my belt and buckled the dagger to my waist. I didn't want to think about it—about the possibility of bloodshed. It felt too soon, even though we'd been preparing for this moment for months. Were we ready to begin the assault on our home? Was I?

Rowyn, Aedin, and I descended into a rowboat with a small sail and began to paddle ashore. We alternated using our Gifts to puff the sails and provide a smoother ride ashore. Still—it took us about an hour of rowing and gliding through the waves. Aedin and Rowyn were quiet—the only sound was the thin whip of waves against the wooden hull as we slid through the water.

The familiar beads of sweat began to dot the back of my neck. Home indeed.

As the shore drew closer, I recognized the familiar curve of jungle and jumble of boulders along the shore. This was the place where we'd fled, nearly a year ago.

Aedin and I exchanged knowing looks; he rowed a final pull and we let the waves carry our boat to the shore.

We jumped over the edge and sank into the sand, pulling the vessel ashore. Through the labor, I continually looked over my shoulder, scanning the deep bramble of trees and vegetation for any hidden movements. But there were none. The waves crashed, some animals echoed in the dark, but we were utterly alone.

Setting the boat by a large boulder outside the long grip of the tide, Rowyn finally straightened and looked around. The dark night glittered with stars. I felt the Gift ricochet through the air as he and Aedin projected their powers—probing and sensing for any hidden threats. Seeming satisfied, they exchanged nods, and Aedin began hiking up the beach to the line of trees.

It was a miserable business. The fearful joy from being home soon shifted into annoyance and grim resolution. My boots were soggy, my pants chafed, and I had forgotten about the heat. Even in the middle of the night, I longed to tear off my clothes and dive into the ocean.

The air in the jungle was thick. Branches hung just above our heads in a tangled maze, obscuring the light from the stars. I lit a small flame in my palm, picking my way through the mess of roots, fallen leaves, and mud. It was hardly a trail—more like a vague route that meandered further and further uphill. It wasn't long before my lungs ached with effort; I could even hear Aedin's breath from up front.

Aedin held a plant so it didn't whip back into my face. I pushed against the stem, doing the same for Rowyn. He muttered a low thanks, slapping a bug that had landed on his forearm.

"You said I would like this place," he grumbled as we continued to climb.

"You will," I corrected. "Just… not now."

Aedin shushed us, and we were quiet.

My calves were aching by the time we reached the top. We came upon a large tree with moss and vines draped over its branches, obscuring tiny lights in the distance. The main road.

We paused to suck in air as Aedin passed around a leather skin of water. I brushed back the sweat-drenched hair from my forehead and wiped my hands on my pants. Checking that the dagger was still buckled to my belt, I met Aedin's gaze with a knowing look. His knees were bent and his hands were ready— as if ready to spring into action at any moment.

"Why are we going to the villa?" Rowyn asked quietly.

Aedin took back the leather skin and secured the top. "We'll use it as the primary base to secure the island. It's the place we know best. We'll scout it tonight and then bring the full force tomorrow night."

Rowyn nodded, seeming satisfied with the answer, as I quietly wondered who was now lord. And if they would put up a fight.

We continued through the jungle, parallel to the main road, hiking through the roots and trees under the cover of darkness. Few carriages passed given the late hour, and I was grateful we were at least finished with the climb. I nearly tripped over a root when Aedin's hand shot out to grab my arm.

"Thank you," I muttered, cursing at the ground.

I was thankful he didn't let go of my hand.

In the dark of the night, it was hard to distinguish where we were exactly. Until we rounded a bend and Aedin suddenly stopped. A familiar broad iron gate stood silently in the distance. I couldn't resist the relief that washed through my body at the sight. Perhaps a part of me had thought that our home had been destroyed or ceased to exist at all. But it was here—it was still here.

There was a sudden crack of a breaking twig.

In one swift motion, Rowyn drew his sword, facing the direction of the noise. My breath caught in my throat as I summoned my power, pulling from the adrenaline shooting through my blood.

But Aedin peered into the thickness of the jungle and held out his hand. "Wait…"

And then I felt a familiar presence. But it was impossible—

Tieren and William appeared through the trees, moving slowly to remain as quiet as possible. I covered my mouth to prevent any sound from escaping as I saw Aedin's expression melt.

At the sight of our reactions, Rowyn lowered his sword but did not sheathe the blade.

When they were close, I nearly tackled Tieren in a tight squeeze. His long arms wrapped around my body as I stifled the cry of relief bubbling in my chest. Underneath my grip, his frame felt larger, more muscular than when we'd parted. I pulled away, looking up into his familiar hazel eyes and crooked grin.

"Is it possible that you've grown taller?" I whispered, and he choked back a laugh.

"Of course not, my lady." Even his voice was lower. I squeezed his arms and embraced William's short, thick frame.

"Tieren… William," Aedin breathed in a voice drenched with relief. He hugged each in turn—joy expanded in my chest at the sight.

Tieren was unable to contain his excitement. "We knew you'd come!"

I shook my head in disbelief. "We thought you were dead… What are *you* doing here?"

Tieren straightened with pride. "We've been spying on Cabot in preparation for your return."

"Cabot... of course," Aedin uttered the word like a curse. William grumbled in agreement, folding his arms across his chest in disapproval.

"Our return?" I repeated. "How...?"

Tieren explained, "I Dreamed of the future. I saw us in the villa... with others as well." His gaze shifted to Rowyn as the latter straightened under his gaze.

"My name is Rowyn. I am Captain of the Guard on Iselleden."

"Iselleden," William repeated quietly.

"You're here to help us, right? Are we taking back the villa?" Tieren asked eagerly, scanning our faces.

Rowyn shifted with a frown. "That wasn't the plan for tonight..."

"Our plan was to scout the area and determine how best to proceed," I clarified quickly. "The rest of our army is floating just off the coast."

"Army?" Tieren whispered, his eyes growing wide.

I was satisfied to hear Rowyn repeat the word with relish. "Yes, our *army* of Gifted. We are unafraid and will no longer hide. It's time your world knew of the existence of our power."

There was a brief silence as Tieren and William exchanged pained looks. "Well, actually... Tours has already done that." The words left Tieren's mouth with a visible wince.

"What?" Aedin's voice was sharp.

"He brought the Rhidge to light," William clarified in a whisper. "They no longer hide themselves... or their power."

My blood ran cold at his words. "But... how?"

"He used his Gift to kill one of his advisors—in front of everyone! And announced the existence of an eighth island," Tieren said in a rush, the words pouring from his mouth.

Aedin grimaced, tightening the grip on his dagger.

"The Rhidge walk about in broad daylight—some are here, in Tahuna. Most have remained in the palace or been deployed to the other islands."

"How many?" Aedin asked grimly.

William answered, "Ten or so on Lailan. Bela arrived last week with several others, as well as…" His eyes shifted to me in the pause. "My lady, your brother is here with his wife. And Daniel Terrace has been sent to oversee Cabot."

I wanted to chastise him for using my former title, but the words were caught in my throat from the surprise of it all. "Ephraim is here? And *married*?"

"Hollyn Litany," Tieren finished lightly. "She seems lovely."

Aedin swore under his breath.

I didn't feel I needed to repeat the other name. The past was nipping at our heels more quickly than we'd anticipated. This was getting out of hand.

"We need to act soon," I said to Aedin. "Or else we'll be caught here in daylight."

"Let's take back the villa now," Tieren hissed with a grin. A budding smile even flickered at the corners of William's lips in anticipation.

Rowyn straightened his stance, giving me a nod. "We've come this far."

My husband didn't say a word, but I saw the expression on his face. The tight eagerness that wound his body; the power that wafted from his shoulders in waves. He wanted it. Badly.

There was no deterring him from doing what he did best.

"Let's do it," I said quietly. "Let's take back our home."

Chapter Thirty-One

THE STEEL GATES shone silver in the moonlight.

We emerged through the jungle and crept across the road, our footsteps muted with the Gift. A thrumming of power surrounded the space between our bodies in anticipation of the attack. As I trailed Aedin's crouched form, my heart felt it might vacate my chest.

Thanks to Tieren and William's scouting, we knew the guards' exact positions and weren't surprised to see their slouching forms just beyond the steel bars.

A naked dagger was in my right hand. The skin of my left palm began to swirl and gleam with the shimmering of a thousand rainbows. As if Iselleden was here—its power just stirring beneath my skin.

We skirted to the right, leaping over the low stone wall that extended around the perimeter. By the time our feet touched the ground on the other side, the soft crackle of fallen leaves against the gravel had alerted the guards. I saw them stiffen in the distance and exchange soft words.

Aedin didn't hesitate.

He ran to the closest one, hitting him with a sudden blast of power and knocking him back.

I hastened forward, doing the same to the other before he could rush to help his fallen comrade. A grunt echoed through the night as he fell back against the gravel, then scrambled to his feet. He uttered a low curse, drawing his sword with a slick sound.

The sound of my husband's dagger plunging into the body of the other guard was a thick, resolute thump, followed by a sharp exhalation of air.

Raising my own dagger, I parried the attack, sweeping through the movements of the dance I'd been taught. The distinct ring of metal reverberated through the gurgle of the fountains. I heard Tieren, William, and Rowyn continue across the gravel and into the halls of the villa.

I shot another gust of air, hoping to knock him out. The guard growled, his thick skull rocking back, but his feet held firm. His hands reached out to steady his balance.

There was an opening, so I took it.

I sliced my dagger across the naked skin of his throat.

Something thick and wet sprayed across my knuckles and face. A horrid gurgling gushed from the body—a look of unrestrained shock on the face. The feet stumbled and then the body fell to the ground, the mass of flesh, blood, skin, and armor crashing loudly against the gravel.

Aedin watched me carefully from the still body of the other guard, a small throwing knife ready in his hand. Ready just in case.

In case I didn't take the opening.

In case I couldn't do it.

But I did.

And as my body was vibrating with adrenaline, I had little time to consider what I'd done. How all these months had been preparing me for that one moment—so that I wouldn't fail.

Aedin tucked the knife back into his sleeve and gestured towards the villa with a tilt of his head. There was no emotion on his face.

Wiping the blood from my hands onto my pants, I readjusted my grip on the dagger and followed him inside.

The smooth stones beneath my feet were just as I'd remembered. But when my eyes traced the rest of the scene and rose up towards the night sky, I stared in horror at the gaping hole in the villa arches. It was as if the stone had been ripped apart, terribly slashed and torn.

Aedin gazed at the arches in silence, a tightness spreading across his lips and cheeks. The fountains echoed peacefully, hardly disguising the muttered protests of the men clustered beneath the atrium garden. Tieren, William, and Rowyn had mustered the other guards from their sleep and had bound their hands, placing them seated along the dirt path through the trees.

"What happened here?" I asked Tieren, gesturing to the broken limestone arcade.

"I'll fill you in later," Tieren murmured, finishing a tie on a grumbling guard.

We counted the guards—other than the two bodies in the front, the other ten were clustered on the ground and contained.

But Rowyn was restless, his eyes roving from the guards to the hall and back. "Are you sure there are no others? No Rhidge?" he asked us.

Tieren and William exchanged glances. "We can walk the perimeter if you want," Tieren offered. "But last we checked, they were scattered around Tahuna and the eastern shore. Where's…?"

"Revenge," William guessed quietly.

In the brief pause, Aedin had disappeared. But minutes later, I heard the noise of a thick body being dragged unceremoniously across the stones. Labored breathing and choked protests echoed through cries of pain. Then, from around a corner, came Aedin, tugging the bound feet of Cabot as the large man helplessly squirmed in his nightclothes.

Despite my dislike for the man, I couldn't help but pity him. His head knocked hard against the ground as Aedin pulled him from the stones to the dirt of the garden. With bleary eyes, he gazed up at us, stupefied.

"W-What in *hell*—?"

Aedin dropped his feet, unsheathing his dagger in one long, slick motion.

Cabot saw the expression in his eyes. "N-No," he began to stutter pitifully. "Pl-Please! Please!"

I held my breath. Rowyn was frowning at the man, as if attempting to summon emotions of regret or pity.

"I-I promise to do w-whatever you say," Cabot begged quickly. "I'll do whatever you want!"

William tugged on the last binding of Cabot's guards and came to stand over the blubbering man. There was an unforgiving emptiness in his eyes, and I pitied Cabot for being the subject of his attention. "You have embezzled profits from the island and put them in your own pockets."

I blinked—I'd hardly ever heard William speak so many words together in a row.

Cabot's frightened eyes turned to him. "Y-Yes, yes! I'm sorry!"

Aedin's dagger was steady as he watched his former guard.

"Are you?" William challenged, his hand on the hilt of his sword.

"Yes! I promise, I won't do it again—I'll do whatever you say," Cabot blubbered.

William's eyes were firm and glittering. The bound guards began to shift uncomfortably, half struggling against the bonds, half shying away from the pure disgust on William's face. I knew what he would do, even before it happened.

William's gaze flickered towards Aedin, as if waiting for a signal. In response, Aedin closed his eyes briefly; an acknowledgement. Giving him the right to proceed as he wished.

With relish, William drew his blade and plunged the point into Cabot's chest.

Cabot uttered a loud cry, and I cringed at the sudden sound. Rowyn stiffened as blood began to sputter from the gaping hole, and Aedin, Tieren, and William watched on in impassive silence.

The blade had sliced cleanly through the ribs and pierced the lungs. It was an undignified and slowly painful death as the blood rose to his lips and he choked, gasped, and bled into silence.

William wiped the blade on his black pants before efficiently re-sheathing the sword. He released a low sigh, looking up at the night sky, as if a weight had suddenly left his shoulders. As if he'd been waiting to do that for a long time.

"Will you kill us all then?" one of the guards on the ground drawled.

"No," Aedin responded quietly, also sheathing his blade. "There's been enough killing for one night. We will let you go, but under one condition."

He extended his palm; a spark sputtered, then a tall flame spiraled to life. They flinched at the sudden light, their bodies stiffening as one let out a sharp cry.

The flame illuminated the sharp ridges of my husband's face, casting shadows on the hollows of his cheeks. Blue, green, red, and gold, the colors spiraled endlessly, like the colors in my palms.

"Tomorrow you will board a ship and leave Lailan. War is coming to these shores, and we do not wish to end innocent lives. But should you stay and challenge us…" Aedin gestured with the flame, tilting his head towards me.

I flexed my palms, exposing the bright, swirling colors to the darkness of the night. Fear flickered across their faces as Tieren and William watched on in stunned silence.

"… my wife will ensure you pay for your disobedience," Aedin finished softly, closing his hand and extinguishing the flame. "Understood?"

The row of heads nodded in silence, their eyes fixed on the glowing skin.

The colors danced and spun madly across my palms. As if the spirit of Fate was delighted to finally reach these shores and end the centuries of bloodshed.

———

When the sky began to lighten into gray, Rowyn left the villa and, accompanied by William, began the long trek back to the western shore. I was grateful he wouldn't be alone. For one, it was a dubious route through the jungle. And another, the threat of the Rhidge was always present.

Cabot's guards had scattered into the night, exiting along the main road quietly. When the servants arose and realized what had happened, our presence was met with mingled relief and suspicion. Those who wished to stay and contribute were gladly welcomed, but many left. When all was sorted, Aedin, Tieren, myself, and six servants stayed to occupy the villa.

I wondered if the Rhidge knew by now and when they would come for us.

"I'll walk the border," Tieren offered when I expressed this concern. "See if there's any activity. And then… I have to go into Tahuna."

"Why?" Aedin asked.

Tieren was unable to conceal the smile that tugged at his lips. "You'll see."

I frowned at this secrecy. "What are you hiding?"

"I have a surprise," he confessed with a grin. "Don't make me reveal it. But don't worry… you won't be upset."

Aedin eyed him dubiously. "If you insist…"

Tieren smirked and sauntered off to the gardens.

It was surreal to walk with Aedin once again through the halls —to hear the chirping of the birds and the murmurs of the fountains. As if we'd never left. And yet so much had changed.

The garish weapons, portraits, and clutter that lined the halls extended even into our bedroom. Aedin muttered something about redecorating as I took down a portrait of Cabot from above the bed. It was freshly painted and cut a handsome figure of the portly man whose body now lay among the dead. Placing the canvas outside the room, I saw the blood on my hands had turned a dark, crusty brown.

I shivered and went to the bathroom, dunking my face and hands in the sink. Using a towel, I scrubbed at the crusted remains, just as I'd done to Aedin in Iselleden.

But now the blood was on my hands.

Gritting my teeth, I felt my skin become red and irritated. But I wasn't clean enough. I scrubbed harder, ignoring the creeping pain—

Warm hands grabbed my own. I started at the sudden intrusion. Aedin gently grabbed the cloth from my hands and put it aside.

I looked up into his familiar face—the eyes that I loved. They were filled with an aching sadness.

His hand reached out and cupped the side of my face. I closed my eyes and let myself sink into the feeling of his skin—warm and alive.

Aedin's voice rumbled lowly throughout the small room. "You are brave and you are strong." I squeezed shut my eyes as I felt the prickle of tears.

"You did what you had to do," he murmured. "And what you did is protect yourself and those you love."

I killed someone—I ended a life.

"You could have done far worse. It was quick and merciful."

Had I said those words aloud?

"I could have pushed him," I whispered hoarsely. "Or frozen his movements..."

"But you didn't. And you are stronger for it."

I didn't feel strong. I felt frightened—frightened of what I'd become. Frightened that I would be unable to recognize myself when I looked in the mirror or was among those I loved.

"You *are* strong."

Aedin wrapped his arms around me as something broke in my chest, releasing a rush of guilt, fear, and shame in one horrid stream of emotion. I let myself cry in his arms, even as we stood in the space we loved. Now stained by the blood we had spilled.

Chapter Thirty-Two

EPHRAIM WOKE TO the echoing of voices murmuring in the hall. The rocking of the ship had become habitual—he didn't stagger as he untangled himself from the sheets and rose to his feet. It was early in the morning, a thick layer of marine fog clung to their small window, obscuring the port.

Pressing his ear against the wood, he strained to identify the voices and words. The sounds were hurried and desperate.

Ephraim's heart pounded—he looked back at Hollyn's sleeping form. Gritting his teeth, he grasped the handle of the door and slowly—very slowly—pushed it down. There was no sound as he tightly gripped the handle and pulled open the door ever so slightly.

The words became distinct.

"*Here*?" Daniel's voice rasped. "In the villa?"

Bela replied in her low and withering tone. "We found them only early this morning. I've sent word to Radiance on the fastest ship."

"But how did they get here?"

"A large ship was spotted on the western shore—it has been emptied. We think it's from the eighth island."

A muttered curse or expression of disbelief.

"What are you going to do?"

"Wait for the signal."

"What signal?"

"The signal to attack."

"But that could take *days*. Gods above—where is Cabot?"

"Dead."

"*Dead?*"

"Are you questioning my authority?" came the scathing reply.

There was a moment of silence before Daniel replied. "So we'll just let them remain there? Unchallenged?"

"For now."

A short, frustrated pause, before, "What if we negotiate something—like a deal—?"

"The Rhidge doesn't make compromises."

"But we need to act quickly unless—"

"The king wants them alive," came the growled reply.

"Gods above…" The rest of Daniel's words were growled and muffled.

"I need to go ashore to monitor," Bela hissed. "You stay here with them. Keep everyone on the boat."

"No, we need to alert the public for their safety." Daniel's voice broke a higher note. "*I* was entrusted with this job, and *I* need to see it through."

A low scathing laugh bubbled through the Rhidge. "*Entrusted*? The king would never be so stupid as to trust *you*."

"Yes, he does—"

"You think you would stand a chance against them? In a fight?" There was a pause. "No, you're only a pawn for leverage. Like the rest of them."

There was no response from Daniel.

Ephraim shifted his weight back into the room, still clutching the door handle, and waited until the silence lasted longer than ten seconds. He didn't hear the retreating footsteps of that horrid woman. He only heard the depressing thump of Daniel's door as it closed.

Ever so slightly, Ephraim eased his tension on the door handle and let it click shut. His palms felt sweaty and, his heart began to race as he considered what he'd heard. This was their time. It was now.

"Hollyn," he whispered, rubbing her shoulder.

The mass of golden curls shifted in response as she turned her head to frown at him. "What?"

"We have to leave."

———

It didn't take them long to prepare. Once Ephraim had explained what he'd heard, they'd quickly and quietly dressed, exiting the room with only the clothes on their back.

The lower deck was empty. Feigning casualness, Ephraim and Hollyn walked hand in hand to the stairs and climbed above deck. The morning sun was beginning to pierce through the fog and already warming the air. They wove through the sailors as they tended to their duties—Ephraim was relieved to not see the signature dark uniform of the Rhidge. But they could be anywhere. He gripped Hollyn's hand tighter as they approached one of the smaller boats, suspended in the air.

A sailor stopped them, holding out his hand. "No one goes ashore."

"What? Why?" Ephraim furrowed his brow.

The man shrugged carelessly. "Orders are orders."

Hollyn straightened to her full height, looking down at the man. "Who ordered this?"

"The director." He jerked his chin at the small boat headed towards the port. Two black forms were visible even from that distance, sitting still while the sailors rowed.

Ephraim's stomach sank as he struggled to come up with the right words to say.

"Oh no, we were too late!" Hollyn sighed through her teeth, pointing at Ephraim's chest. "I told you we had to get up… You never listen to me!"

Ephraim wasn't sure how to respond. "Er… I'm sorry?"

She let out an exasperated sound. "Listen, my new *husband* decided to sleep in this morning and seems to have put us behind schedule. We were supposed to be on that boat—the director wanted Ephraim to record a meeting."

The sailor scratched his sunburned cheek. "What meeting?"

Hollyn looked expectantly at Ephraim; he swallowed and said the first thing that came to his mind, "Cabot's funeral… and deciding a successor."

The man's eyes widened. "So it's true? The lord is dead?"

Hollyn shook her head sadly as Ephraim replied, "Yes… So tragic."

"How did he die?" the man asked as he leaned in.

"Beheaded," Hollyn whispered, also leaning in with a knowing gaze. "And I heard it was by the previous lord of Lailan… Lord Aedin!"

The man took this news with excitement. "I heard whisperings…"

"Now you know." Hollyn smirked. "Would you mind helping us with the boat? We'll make it worth your while…" She reached into a hidden fold in her skirt and pulled out a silver coin.

It worked. The man eagerly nodded and began to loosen the boat.

As they paddled to shore, Hollyn continued to feed him false news, weaving ridiculous stories always grounded in a grain of truth. The sailor ate it up, his eyes shining as he stroked the paddles closer towards the port. When they reached the docks, Hollyn slipped him another coin and a generous smile. He helped her up, leaving Ephraim to balance and climb awkwardly onto the dock.

"Well," Ephraim muttered to her as they watched the sailor push away and head back towards the ship. "You continue to impress me."

Hollyn dipped her head demurely, gazing up at him from under her lashes. "I believe thanks are in order."

He gave a short laugh, leaning in for a kiss. "I'll thank you properly later."

"And I won't forget it." She raised her crown of golden hair and slipped an arm in his. Together, they weaved through the busy docks and made their way ashore.

Although they'd overcome the first obstacle of getting ashore, Ephraim wasn't at ease. From the corner of his eye, he continually checked for black shadows, darting his gaze back and forth and forcing nonchalance.

Donkeys brayed, people yelled, and the smell of rotten fish was heavy in the air. Hollyn wrinkled her nose as they weaved around a particularly disgusting pile of fish bones and guts. But even when they reached the earthen floor of Tahuna, the seawater mud and stones were a maze of refuse and litter baked by the morning sun. The fog had worn off, and Ephraim was beginning to feel beads of sweat accumulate under his collar.

"How do we get to the villa?" Hollyn looked up at the winding road and spread of houses along the terraces. "Is it a long walk?"

"I don't think we can walk," Ephraim muttered. "We might be better off hiring a carriage... if we can find any."

But the carriages that rattled past were all full. It became clear that they were unlikely to find any for hire in this area. Ephraim pulled Hollyn out of the path of a teetering cart laden with exotic fruit.

"Can we stop to ask for help?" Hollyn gently pulled his elbow. "There's a wine shop—look."

A festive yellow-and-red awning fluttered in the breeze. It wasn't the nicest establishment, but it would have to do.

"I suppose..." he admitted, but Ephraim's nerves were on edge. He felt like a fly trapped in a glass. They were too visible. They had to get out of here—badly—but he didn't know how. Every time he'd been to the villa, he'd been shuttled back and forth in a carriage. Was it even possible to make it on foot? And in this heat?

Hollyn wandered inside, calling out for the owner as Ephraim lingered on the patio, watching the crowds pass with trepidation. The Rhidge could be anywhere. They might already be watching him without him even knowing. This was a fool's errand—he should never have roped Hollyn into this. He would never forgive himself if she was killed—

A tall young man and woman emerged from a dirtied building on the opposite side of the street. The man bent down to whisper something in the woman's ear as she carefully watched the street, her hand gripping something within the folds of her skirt. Through the wave of passing merchants and carts, Ephraim locked eyes with the woman. Hers widened.

She said something to the young man and he followed her gaze. They were both watching him now. Ephraim's stomach flipped, and he racked his memory to recognize their faces. Had he seen them before? The woman looked more familiar than the man. But he couldn't place them…

They began to weave through the crowd towards him. Ephraim straightened and looked back—Hollyn was gesturing empathetically and exchanging cross words with the owner of the shop.

"Hollyn… Hollyn!" Ephraim tried to catch her attention. "*Hollyn!*"

She turned and, seeing the expression on Ephraim's face, immediately left the owner of the shop and came to his side. "What?"

But before he could explain, the young woman was only several feet away. "Ephraim?" she asked carefully, cocking her head. "Ephraim Doyle?"

Was this a trap? He'd never heard of Rhidge wearing normal clothes, but perhaps they were part of the gang. Sent by Bela to kill him and Hollyn…

"Who are you?" Ephraim asked, despite his fears, placing one hand on the knife at his belt. Not that it would do him any good against trained assassins.

The young woman placed a hand on her breast, as if attempting to assuage any doubts. "My name is Andrea Taylor. We met at the reception at the villa earlier this year."

Andrea Taylor—he did recognize the name. But her plain dress and dirtied apron hardly suggested that she would have been at the most fashionable event on the island.

Before he could even open his mouth, Andrea continued, "You need to come with us—we're heading to the villa right now. Lord Cabot has been killed, and your sister and Lord Aedin have returned."

Ephraim swallowed the budding joy in his throat. "How can I trust you?" he whispered.

"You can't," said the tall man, his hazel eyes narrowing. "But you have no other choice. Come with us—or risk getting caught."

Ephraim realized he was right. They'd made it this far, but it was unlikely they would succeed without help. "What's your name?" He nodded at the young man.

"Tieren." A small crooked smile flickered across his long face. "I was a guard for Lord Aedin and know your sister well."

"It's really true then…" Hollyn breathed. "They're alive?"

"Yes." Andrea looked up at Tieren as they exchanged small grins. "And they're here."

It was all Ephraim needed. "Let's go."

Chapter Thirty-Three

IT WAS JARRING to wake up in the same room I had hated, then loved, for so long. Sunlight streamed through the curtains as the faint chorus of birds sounded from the garden.

Aedin's dark form was resting in the chair by the door. In his hands spun a dagger, thoughtfully and softly. At the sounds of my movement, his gaze went to me, and the dagger stilled. Tiredness was etched in a hollow blue line under his dark eyes.

"How was your watch?" I asked quietly.

"Uneventful." His eyes flickered away as he continued spinning the blade, gazing out at the garden. The fountains gurgled, the early morning chirping of the birds sounded gaily, but nothing was the same.

I winced, stretching my limbs as my mind ached to fall back into the abyss of sleep. My watch had ended in the earliest hours of the night, but four hours wasn't enough to feel rested. I heard the echoes of servants moving through the halls, muttered laughter, and then something else—

Aedin saw the thought flicker through my mind, a soft grin tugging at his lips. "Tieren is back."

"Who else is here?" A breath caught in my throat. I pushed back the covers, rubbing my face.

"You should go see."

I was itching to know, but instead I walked to the garden doors and pulled Aedin's face into my chest, inhaling his familiar scent. A dark chuckle emitted into my shirt as he looked up at me. "Aren't you curious?"

"Of course!" I lovingly traced the teasing line of his mouth. "But I wanted to make sure you were okay."

Aedin's head burrowed again into my stomach, his arms wrapping tightly around my thighs. I felt the warmness of the sigh even through my shirt. "Yes, I'm fine." The muffled words were tired and short.

I ran my hands through his hair, massaging his scalp, as a low purr vibrated against my body. "Are you sure?"

"Now I am." Aedin didn't bother to look up.

"You need to rest," I whispered. "You can't carry us all."

In response, his hands gripped the backs of my thighs. Beads of sweat were already dotting my skin—I felt one roll down the curve of my spine.

Aedin didn't respond, and I didn't push it. There was so much left to do and so little time to digest. And yet he still hadn't healed from what had happened—the torture, the complete shift of his world, and the impending war… I remembered the small boy—sitting at the bottom of the vast abyss—haunted by swirling ghosts. We breathed together in the brief silence, appreciating the moment of calm.

"Go and see." He pushed me away, summoning that playful grin. "You won't be disappointed."

I rolled my eyes, bending down for a kiss. "You sound so confident."

"You can tell me I'm right later." He sheathed the dagger and unfurled himself from the chair.

Pulling on the belt with my sheathed sword, I exited to the hall with Aedin trailing behind. It didn't feel as though we were on the brink of war. The halls were peaceful, and the garden air hung heavy, perfumed with flowers, mist, and the fresh, rich earth. I followed the sounds of merry chatting to the sitting room, nearly running once I recognized the voices.

Mary, Tieren, and Andrea were sprawled comfortably on the couches. Our old steward was the first to notice me, her quick brown eyes flickering in recognition as she stood promptly from her perch on the edge of the cushion.

With the utmost grace, she dropped into a curtsy, murmuring, "My lady."

I gripped her small shoulders, a laugh bubbling in my chest, and pulled her into an embrace. She awkwardly patted my back, accepting the hug with a reluctant smile.

"Please don't call me that anymore," I begged as she narrowed her eyes at me.

"You are certainly still the Lady of Lailan—I don't see what's changed. Especially now that Cabot's dead," she grumbled.

We shared a wry grin as Andrea called out coyly, "You're still my lady as well."

"Oh stuff it." I pulled Andrea into my arms, her auburn curls tickling my cheeks. Her thin arms hugged me with an unfamiliar ferocity.

"How I've missed you," she whispered. I fought back the tears that pricked in my eyes.

I pulled back, looking her up and down. "You've changed." Her gown was simple—a light blue cotton that hugged her curves and held some stains and creases. It almost felt utilitarian. Entirely unlike the golds, creams, and pinks I was accustomed to seeing her wear.

She pushed back a stray curl, eying me with that familiar wicked grin. "And you as well."

I had never felt more comfortable in my loose shirt and pants, casually resting a hand on the hilt of my sword with pride. "But what are *you* doing here?"

Andrea casually tossed an arm around Tieren's waist. "Well, it's a long story…" He looked at her with a mixture of guilt and pride.

I laughed out loud at the expression on Tieren's face. "Then we must hear it!"

At the sound of footsteps, two more figures emerged from the halls. And at the sight of familiar brown eyes, my heart threatened to break free from my chest.

"Ephraim!" I cried, crossing the space between us in several long steps.

I heard my name breathless on his lips as I ran into an embrace. His hands gripped my hair, and something hard broke into my chest. A muffled, dry sob caught in my mouth as I held him. My brother was alive—and here.

"What are you doing here?" I demanded, brushing at the tears once again brimming in my eyes.

Ephraim shrugged helplessly and brushed back his brown hair. "Tours—er, the king—sent us here with Daniel. We've been offshore for about a week, waiting just in case..." He gestured towards us and I understood.

"But how did you get away?"

"I had some help..." Ephraim held out his hand gestured towards the woman standing nearby. Respectfully giving us the space and time we needed as siblings reunited. She offered a gentle smile and a small wave. "I'm Hollyn Litany... Doyle."

I recalled Tieren's words last night with a smile. "I've heard great things about you." I stepped forward to give her a quick hug. "It's wonderful to finally meet you."

"And you as well!" Hollyn grabbed Ephraim's hand, and I saw my brother watch her with a swell of love and respect.

Ephraim's gaze locked over my shoulder. "Lord Aedin..."

"Ephraim, please." Aedin stepped forward to clasp my brother's hand. "Aedin will do."

Hollyn stuttered through a curtsy, then abandoned the idea and offered a cordial hand as well. "Lovely to meet you."

Aedin grasped hers and then placed a hand on my shoulder. "We have a full house then."

I met his eyes, and through the unexpected joy, I saw the concern. Andrea, Ephraim, and Hollyn—they were unprepared for what would come. And now we were tasked with keeping them safe along with the rest of our army. It was a large burden to shoulder.

A small dark shadow darted through the room, situating himself at my side. "Gwen," William said quietly.

"Back already?" I blinked at him. "Where are the others?"

"They're on the trail." He folded his arms. "I ran ahead—we need to secure the villa."

My breath caught in my throat. "Are they here?"

A slight angling of his head. "They know. And they've been watching our path through the jungle."

"But no attacks?" Aedin frowned.

"No." William readied his stance. "It's… odd."

"How far out are the others?"

"Two—maybe three hours."

I nodded. "Good. When they get here, let me know. Go back and ensure they arrive safely."

William inclined his head as Tieren stepped forward. "I'll join him."

"Yes, please," I said quietly, watching Andrea let go of him reluctantly. "Be careful," I added for good measure.

"Always… my lady." Tieren gave me a teasing smile. His hazel eyes shifted to Andrea. "I'll be back."

"You better, be" she growled softly. They exchanged a soft look. Tieren grasped her fingers, kissing the tips before he ducked out of the room and into the hall.

"Well"—I shot Andrea a look of approval—"we have a lot to discuss."

"Yes," Ephraim added, stepping forward. "I heard Bela—the Director of the Rhidge—and Daniel talking this morning. They've only just notified the king and are waiting for a response before they… do anything."

Aedin looked concerned. "They're waiting?"

Ephraim swallowed before continuing, "She said he wants you"—he nodded to myself and Aedin—"both alive."

"They must know about the army," I said to Aedin. "The delay will give us some time to fortify the villa and prepare for battle."

"Battle?" Hollyn repeated warily.

"Yes." I touched the sword at my hip. "We have some time to prepare, but conflict is inevitable…"

Hollyn swallowed, exchanging a wary glance with Ephraim. A pit dropped in my stomach—I was responsible for them along with the lives of our army. Was it worth the risk? To have them here and in our lives?

Sensing the pause, Aedin offered casually, "Let's run through the defenses together—with everyone—once the army arrives. We'll ensure that this place remains secure."

I wasn't sure if it put my brother and his wife at ease, but Andrea straightened and nodded approvingly.

"I'll be able to assist but would prefer to defend those who are defenseless," Mary spoke softly.

I turned to her in question.

"My orphanage," she clarified. "In the port. We've managed to remain hidden, and I would prefer to keep it that way."

Aedin nodded. "Do whatever you must. But we would welcome your assistance of course."

Mary nodded demurely, curtsying in our direction. I shot her a disapproving look but she just stuck her nose in the air.

Andrea jerked her thumb at Mary. "I'd prefer to have her on our side. After seeing the explosion and all."

"Explosion?" I repeated dubiously.

"Yes." Andrea waved her hand in the direction of the hall. "It's hard to miss, isn't it?"

I looked at Mary in amazement. "*You* did that?"

The small, elderly woman brushed back a lock of graying hair. "Someone had to rescue the guards. I merely provided a… distraction for Tours and the Rhidge the morning after that party."

A soft chuckle echoed at my side—Aedin was beaming. "I bet he was surprised."

"It was a shame to ruin the arcade." Mary shrugged. "But at least worth their lives."

"It was worth it," I agreed, looking at Andrea.

My friend smiled sadly, nodding at me. "So it's true then… about the Gift."

I wasn't sure what Tieren had told her, but there was no denying it. "Yes, it's true."

"Wait, that… power that the king revealed?" Ephraim struggled to find the words. "You have it too?"

I took Aedin's hand. "I do. As do Aedin, Mary, Tieren, and William… and the others you'll meet."

"But why didn't you…?" His words faltered as I felt my heart swell in pity.

"I didn't know," I answered honestly. "And I'd only just found out before you and father arrived. At the time, it wasn't something I could share. But now… well, that doesn't seem to be an issue."

"He said that those on the eighth island seek to destroy us," Hollyn whispered, her blue eyes round. "To ruin our way of life… Is that true?"

Aedin caught my eye and I saw the frustration within his gaze. "It's a false narrative," my husband said softly, the inflection of his words laced with anger. "We have been there and seen the truth. Iselleden is the last refuge for the Gifted and under threat from the Rhidge and Empire. That's why we've returned—to remove that threat and return peace to all eight islands. Together."

The grip on my hand tightened. I smiled. "It seems we *do* have a lot of correcting to do."

Chapter Thirty-Four

THE ARMY'S ARRIVAL later in the afternoon kept us busy. Although the villa was grand and luxurious, it had never been suited for housing more than a dozen guests at a time. But now it would become a compound for a hundred. We began the laborious task of sectioning off sleeping quarters in the inner courtyard, laying down sheets and couch pillows to create makeshift beds for our coming guests.

We were only halfway finished when they arrived, Rowyn and Celion at the helm and Rebecca trailing behind, her child strapped to her chest. She shot Aedin a warning look and went immediately to him; they conferred in low voices as I juggled the onslaught of questions and directions. William and Tieren began assigning posts and guard schedules; Ephraim, Hollyn, and Andrea continued crafting beds from whatever we could find. The few servants were busy in the kitchen—I wondered how much food was in the cellars. And how long it would last.

I showed Rowyn and Celion to a guest room, offering to give them their own space as commanding offers. Celion nodded approvingly at the large bathtub, and I left to give them privacy. The other private rooms were allotted to Ephraim and Hollyn, Tieren and Andrea, and Rebecca. She cradled Zac with one hand as the other unstrapped the dagger at her waist and set it on the bed.

"You must be exhausted—let me pour you a bath," I offered.

A wry smile flickered at the corners of her mouth. "I am, but I need to walk the perimeter with Tieren. My shift begins in six hours."

"We can give you a night off—"

"No," she said emphatically, shaking her head. "I didn't come this far to be killed. Not now."

"You'll kill yourself if you don't rest," I pointed out.

Rebecca brushed off my rebuttal, placing her child gently on the bed and beginning to unwrap his soiled napkin. "I know my limits."

She did. So I didn't push it further.

We were all assigned schedules for guarding the exterior. William had allocated the primary spots that offered the fullest vantage points and Tieren had put together a time sheet for everyone, excluding the non-Gifted. Andrea looked offended as she browsed the list, searching for her name.

"It's a bit unfair, isn't it?" I heard her grumble to Tieren. "I know how to use a knife!"

"You've only started learning." Tieren's voice was stressed. "We can't risk you out there. There are other ways to help."

"What? More laundry?" she challenged with a scoff. "Might as well go back to the orphanage with Phil—I mean, Mary."

"You can be with me," I said, stepping forward and pulling her aside. "You can join me on my watch. I'll teach you what I know, and I would enjoy your company."

Tieren looked about to protest but wisely shut his mouth. "She can stay with me—" he began to retort, but Andrea held up a finger.

"Don't try to redeem yourself," she advised with a mock glare. "I think I'd prefer to be with Gwen rather than *you* anyway."

Tieren rolled his eyes. Andrea snickered, coming to my side. "That'll teach him."

"Anytime. Now let's assess those skills of yours…" I wrapped an arm around her waist as we walked down the hall to the gardens.

———

Four days passed in a steady rhythm of watches, meals, training, and camaraderie. It felt as though we were holding our breath—preparing for the inevitable plunge into the chaos of war. The villa's tranquil halls had been transformed into a flurry of activity. We began stockpiling food and venturing out only for necessities.

Aedin and I wrote letters to the most powerful families on the island, informing them of Cabot's death, the Rhidge, and our mission on the island. We also posted the letters publicly as signs in Tahuna, nailing them along the most trafficked routes. We felt the people had a right to know—they were not at fault for this war. A war that might destroy their property and claim their lives if they were caught in the crossfire. And we offered them a choice. Fight with us and for the independence of the island. Fight with us for economic rewards should we succeed. Join us should we need the numbers in an outright battle.

Even Andrea had written her own letter to her former husband and family. Despite the separation, she had hoped that they would understand the situation and respond to our plea for aide.

And so we waited. But no response came. Neither from the townspeople, nor from the families.

Day after day we saw ships leave the harbor. It felt as though the entire island was emptying itself, preparing for the eventual bloodshed.

Andrea swirled her glass of wine as we watched the largest ship sit idly in the harbor, the crest of the Empire on its flank. "The great calm before the storm."

"Perhaps that's what it is," I agreed glumly, taking a sip of wine.

The early evening crickets were beginning to emerge. Their chorus washed over me with a relief I hadn't felt in days. As the sun sank beneath the waterline of the horizon, purple, orange, and blue clouds danced along the sky. For all of the beauty

Iselleden had offered, I'd missed Lailan. There was nothing like home.

"What happened to Liam?" I thought of what Andrea had told me of her story.

She shrugged delicately, sipping her wine. "I left him."

"Well obviously, but you're still married."

"Marriage is only a social construct—that's it. It's simply a paper supported only by whatever the legal system can sustain." Andrea's lips were tight as she spoke. "Whether I'm still married or not hardly matters. I couldn't live with someone who treated me that way, who wouldn't allow me to become the fullest version of myself."

She flexed her empty left hand with a smile. "And a ring is just a ring—only a symbol. I sold it in Tahuna and gave Mary the money. I don't need it."

I grasped her hand. "I'm proud of you. Where is Liam now?"

Andrea snorted, gesturing out at the sea. "Perhaps he left on one of those boats. I hope he threw himself in the ocean and sank under the weight of the coins in his pocket."

"And Catherine?"

"Gone to Joshua's family on Avellian. She sent a note the morning they left. They'll stay until things… settle."

We grimly fell into silence.

"Another ship leaving?" Hollyn appeared at my shoulder, holding a glass of wine. Her blonde hair was tied back casually; she brushed at a wisp, taking a seat.

I followed her gaze to a small ship weaving along the western side of the coast. "It's going in the opposite direction." I frowned, watching the ship as it headed for the larger one.

My heart skipped a beat as I realized what it was. Training my sight and summoning my power, I focused on the boat as it cut through the water. It was a messenger ship. There were only a few men—I didn't recognize their faces, but I knew their purple doublets. I'd seen Ephraim in the same uniform.

I heard Andrea distantly mutter a curse as the small ship sidled up to the larger one. Anchors were drawn and ropes were thrown to secure them together. The men climbed up onto the deck of the larger ship and conferred with the sailors on board. Then they disappeared below deck.

"A messenger ship," I vocalized now what they knew. "Likely from Radiance."

Andrea furrowed her brow. "What does that mean?"

"They've received *some* direction from Tours." I took a deep sip of wine. "Although what that could be, I don't know. I didn't see him on board."

"You can see that far?" Hollyn's eyes widened.

Although they now knew of the existence of the Gift, I wasn't used to using the power in their presence. "Yes," I replied. "When needed."

"Can you read minds?" Andrea piped from my other side.

Rolling my eyes, I jostled her shoulder. She chortled and took a swig of her drink.

I felt my husband's presence before I heard his footsteps echo through the living room. His words floated in without preamble. "There's a ship—"

"We saw." I turned to him and explained what I'd seen. When I'd finished, he was quiet, pensively staring at the horizon.

"Tours is coming," he began quietly. "I know it."

"There's nothing we can do but wait."

"Are you sure no one else was on board?"

"No one that appeared significant—no Rhidge nor anyone I recognized."

We lapsed into silence as the darkness deepened. Small lights appeared on the large ship—they were likely beginning their dinner. It was odd to think that human rhythms like meals continued in times like these.

"Dinner is ready," Ephraim's voice called from inside. I heard the growing chatter of our other inhabitants and smelled the rich aroma of stew. My stomach grumbled in response.

"Let's eat for now." Andrea patted my hand, looking up at Aedin. "Might as well enjoy ourselves."

Aedin didn't protest. I felt his arm wrap around my waist as we made our way towards the crowd. The villa was full— perhaps as full as it had been during the night we'd left. I watched Ephraim chat with Selena. Andrea and Tieren were huddled together in a corner, exchanging soft gazes and tender touches. Hollyn was joking with Celion as Rowyn conferred casually with Ophelia. Something swelled in my chest; I looked up at Aedin and I saw in his eyes that he felt the same.

Pride. And joy.

He pressed his lips to the side of my head, forgetting the ships in the harbor and enjoying the vitality of the crowd.

Hours later, when we were satiated and exhausted, we stumbled back to our room. I crawled in between the sheets, my limbs aching and eager for rest. Aedin's breath was hot on the back of my neck as he held me in his arms. A cool breeze rolled through the room from the open garden doors, smelling of honeysuckle, salt, and fresh earth. It truly was as if we'd never left. I fell asleep quickly, my heart content and my mind finally quiet.

———

It was a late hour when I felt Aedin move from the bed. My eyes were crusted from sleep and unwilling to open—I rubbed at my face and cleared my throat. The distinct ring of steel was barely distinguishable from the gurgle of the fountains in the garden.

"What is it?" I croaked.

Aedin didn't respond. I sat up to see his readied stance— knees bent, arms loose—eyes scanning the garden.

"I felt something," he finally whispered, his words hardly audible.

My body froze as my ears strained to identify any sound. The shuffle of guards in the distance—the chorus of night-time insects—the sound of Aedin's breath—and then there it was.

Soft and calculated footsteps—hardly noticeable through the barrage.

A breath caught in my throat. Aedin's head cocked slightly to the side. He heard it too. The muscles in his wrist flexed in response.

Now I was fully awake. I slid out from under the covers, grabbing my knife.

Gripping his own dagger, Aedin stepped out of the garden doors, heading towards the entry hall. The limestone arcades were a pale blue in the moonlight. A balmy wind tickled my exposed skin. I shivered instinctively as we crept silently through the dirt, scanning the garden and looming halls for any sign.

We stepped onto the cool stones, pausing by an arch. The entry hall was quiet—the footsteps had stopped. It was then that I felt something was horribly wrong. A deep and cavernous fear had settled in my chest. How had I not noticed it before? I held my breath, tightening my grip on the knife as I scanned the empty hall.

It was there before I was able to react.

A flash of black flitted from the corner of my vision, appearing from behind an arch. A warning cry caught in my throat as I watched a man and a long thin sword rush soundlessly through the dark.

But Aedin was ready.

With one step and his dagger raised, he thrust himself towards the attacker, blocking the blow. The high note of metal sounded like an ocean of noise through the quiet. A blast of power emitted from the small man—Aedin hissed in response, the blow hitting its mark.

I held out my hand, throwing a wave of power in the direction of the attacker. The figure froze in response, struggling visibly against my net, but it held firm. It was then that I finally took a breath and realized what had felt like a full minute had only been several seconds long.

A low guttural sound echoed through the halls as the man twisted and strained against my power. "Stop," I commanded, straining to maintain control. Gritting my teeth, I focused everything on keeping my hold. My palms glowed dimly in the darkness, the colors dancing across the skin.

By now the noise of our combat had been heard—rushed footsteps echoed down the hall. William appeared—breathless—alongside Rebecca and Celion.

"Gods above," William whispered in panic, his skin paling even in the moonlight. "How did—?"

"It doesn't matter," Aedin cut him off, switching his dagger to his non-dominant hand and shooting me a sidelong glance. "You have him?"

"Yes." And I was sure of it, even as I looked into the man's eyes and saw that lethal predatory gleam. It was the same expression I'd seen on Tours' face what felt like a lifetime ago. The only difference was this man had slightly more angular features, void of any feeling, and dark hair clipped close to his scalp. He looked young. Perhaps my age or younger. But it didn't change the gnawing dread in my stomach as I met his gaze.

The gaze of a Rhidge.

"Is this…?" Celion took a step forward.

Rebecca put a hand out to stop Celion from coming any closer. "Don't," she ordered lowly. Her eyes were fixed on the man, unwavering and still.

He struggled again, the sword still clutched in his grasp. I ignored his efforts, lifting my chin and asking softly, "What's your name?"

There was no response. The man continued to scowl, the veins of his neck tightening as he struggled under my grasp.

"I asked your name," I repeated.

Aedin shot me a look. "It's not necessary." He took two long steps and held his dagger up to the man's neck. "Where is Tours?"

The man didn't flinch. His eyes shifted from mine to my husband's and a leering smile replaced the hate. "I know you," he said quietly.

The dagger in my husband's hand was still; his face had become a mask. "Where is Tours?" he repeated softly.

William eased anxiously closer to Aedin, as if ready to pounce at any moment. Just behind, Rebecca and Celion watched with bated breath.

A growling laugh caught in the man's throat. He coughed through his sneer. "You will not receive what you want."

Aedin blinked, shifting his knife ever closer to the man's neck. "Answer the question and you may live."

"My life is replaceable." His lips curled back. "I do not fear you *or* death."

My husband growled low, a matching smile flickering on his mouth as he whispered, "You should fear me over death."

He dropped the dagger and turned away, crossing his arms over his chest. "But if your life is truly meaningless, then let's finish this quickly and get on with it."

"Aedin…" I murmured with a frown, shooting him a look of concern. I didn't want to kill for the sake of killing.

Aedin caught my meaning and tilted his head in consideration. I saw the hesitation, the fight to follow his instincts. To not take any chances and kill without bothering to ask questions.

But we needed information, and I wanted to offer him a chance. A chance to redeem himself as Aedin and Rebecca had done. A chance to recover the humanity the Rhidge had beaten from him. It might be there—just under the surface.

The man blinked back at me, tilting his head in thought. I forced a mask of nonchalance, ignoring his wandering eyes as he scanned my face and glowing palms. A momentary pause, before he offered, "They call me Samael."

I was surprised that he'd complied but tried not to show it. "Samael," I echoed. "When did you last see Tours?"

The reply was prompt and efficient. "I last saw the king two days ago on Radiance."

"And where is he now?" Aedin asked again.

Samael sneered again, narrowing his eyes. "How should I know?"

"Who sent you here?" I demanded.

"The director," the man replied casually.

William spoke softly, touching the knife at his belt. "At which point did you enter the property?"

A cruel smile stretched across Samael's face. "A Rhidge never reveals his secrets."

William opened his mouth to retort, but I cut him off. "Where is the director?"

"Here and there," he said carelessly. "The island is small—she is everywhere."

I shivered, imaging her just at the edges of the property, waiting like a wolf at our door. "Secure the perimeter again," I ordered William. "Take Celion and whoever else you need."

Rebecca met my eyes and firmly planted her feet with a nod. I needed her here—just in case.

Celion's shoulders straightened with responsibility. He clapped William on the shoulder, and they eased away slowly, reluctant to turn their back on the Rhidge.

"You won't kill me, will you?" Samael's voice echoed thinly in the dark. "You are not a killer."

My heart shuddered at the sound, and I swallowed as I faced him again.

"I am," Rebecca snarled softly, drawing the sword from her belt.

"*You.*" Samael's eyes finally turned to Rebecca, noticing her for the first time. "You *are* indeed…" He cocked his head, as if remembering something. "You still wear his ring."

Rebecca's face paled in the darkness. "You shut your mouth!"

"He's here—don't you know?"

Aedin twirled the dagger in his grasp. "You're lying."

"I would never lie." Another cruel smile stretched his lips. "What reason do I have?"

Pain was etched on Rebecca's face. I wanted to wipe the smirk off the Rhidge's face, to press his face against the stones until his skin was bloodied and bruised. Jon was here—he could be telling the truth. And if so…

"You can see him if you wish," Samael crooned, his eyes burning into Rebecca. "You can return with me…"

"I would rather end my own life," Rebecca growled.

Aedin straightened at her side, warmth in his gaze as he watched her anger.

This had gone too far.

"Not too long ago, our friend made the wise decision to leave the Rhidge. To defend her friends against the growing darkness," I said carefully, watching Samael's expression as his eyes slid again to me. "She turned against hate and fear and instead chose to fight for peace and love."

A mirthless smile darted at the corners of his lips, but it was soon replaced with hunger and longing.

"Drop your weapons," I ordered softly. "And surrender to us. We will offer you life. You will never have to return to the Rhidge."

"Gwen," Aedin muttered under his breath in warning.

"Do you want to join us?" I asked, slowly removing the hold from my power.

Samael stood still and unmoving. The desperate writhing was gone.

I held my breath for a second before I asked again, "Do you want to join us?"

Aedin instinctively stepped closer, feeling my Gift withdraw. I could hear the thunderous echoes of his heartbeat and smell the fear on his skin. I knew he would prefer to kill, but I wanted to offer a choice at life. It was something that many in his position likely never received. But there should always be a choice.

The sword dropped from his hands and clattered to the floor. I started at the sudden sound.

Samael cast his eyes to the ground and kneeled at my feet. "You have spared my life," he said to the stones. He didn't look up, but his voice was heavy with gratitude. "I can never repay you."

Aedin and Rebecca exchanged a wordless look of confusion, but I had already bent down towards the Rhidge to help him up. "There is no debt. You are free."

In a sudden movement, a naked blade appeared in his hand. The steel was hard and passionless in the thin moonlight.

With a graceful arching movement, the silver point pierced through my shirt and into my skin and muscle, driven into my body with determined hate.

As the seconds slowed and the blood began to seep from my body, I became aware of the blade removing itself and being prepared for another strike.

In that moment a loud and shattered cry pierced the night—Samael's body was thrown against the stones with the heavy rage of my husband.

A thick nausea roiled in my stomach as I felt a wetness began to seep down my arm and chest. My body was limp; my head was light. I struggled to stand, finding my feet were unsteady. The world spun as strong hands held me up, and I heard my name echo drunkenly through the villa. In the dark of the night, I could feel the warm breeze and smell the distant flowers in the garden. And then I knew nothing.

Chapter Thirty-Five

STICKY WITH SWEAT from the humid air, the King of the Empire went above deck in search of a breeze.

Tours brushed away an errant drop of sweat, inhaling the sweet breeze of Lailan as the ship glided through the water. The peaks of jungle rose sharply out of the sea—dense and thick in contrast to the pure cerulean waves. Even the fastest ship wasn't fast enough; Tours watched the passing earth with bated breath. They were finally here—this was finally happening. He would end them.

The upper deck was busy with activity—some clad in the black of the Rhidge, others in the deep purple of the king. As the ship cut through the waves, Tours watched the distant vessel grow closer and closer.

He'd hardly slept the past several nights. His mind ran through scenarios at every waking second; guessing at and preparing for what might come. Assembling, identifying, and sorting through the information he knew, the information he guessed, and what he did not know.

Tours knew they had taken the villa. He knew about the army of Gifted from Iselleden and that Ephraim and his wife had managed to join his sister. He knew Rebecca was also likely among them—her disappearance from the fortress and subsequent silence told Tours that she had also sought out the eighth island. And she wasn't one to shy away from conflict, especially when her husband was involved.

But even for the little he did know, there was much unknown. He didn't know the strength or capacity of the foreigners' powers. He didn't know whether Gwen posed a threat or whether Aedin had grown soft. He didn't know their intent, their ultimate goal, or what they wished to accomplish. Thought it was quite easy to guess the origins of their discontent.

"Your Majesty," a voice broke through his thoughts.

Tours turned to see a Rhidge bow low before him. She squinted in the bright sun. "We'll be docking shortly. What are your orders?"

"You and him come with me." Tours jerked his chin at a tall man nearby. "The rest stay aboard until I've met with the director."

The girl bowed, her rust-blonde hair swinging just above her chin. "Yes, Your Majesty."

Tours turned his gaze back to the ocean, watching the tiny terraced houses grow larger with each passing second. The ship swung around the mouth of the port, staying outside the shallow harbor and providing a view of Tahuna as the port city loomed before them. But the port wasn't as busy as it usually was—nearly half of the boats and ships docked in its waters were gone. Tours frowned, his blue eyes scanning the crowded houses and the hills above. Along the edge of the mountains in the distance, he saw the tiny forms of the grander houses—then the villa.

"What have you done?" he murmured to himself as the ship gradually came to a stop.

Order were shouted, and the anchor was lowered. They parked themselves next to the sister ship in the deep harbor. Only a stone's throw away on the opposite deck stood the Bela and Daniel, both frowning in the sun.

A long walking plank was set across both vessels—Tours easily balanced on the length and strode across. The crowd on deck dropped into bows and curtsies. Ignoring them, Tours approached the director, his dark eyes glaring at the distant horizon.

"Where are all of the ships?" he asked quietly, with a coy smile. "Did you scare away my merchants?"

Bela didn't respond with words—she inclined her head to the side and they descended below deck. Daniel and the two other Rhidge trailed wordlessly behind.

When Tours was seated in the dining room with a glass of wine in hand, he nodded at Bela. "Let's have it."

Bela picked at her nails irritably. Her skin had grown more tan from the tropical sun—freckles dotted the bridge of her nose as it scrunched. "The merchants have left because Aedin and his wife sent a letter to all of the prominent families on Lailan alerting them of an impending war."

"War," Tours scoffed. "Isn't that a bit of an exaggeration?"

"They have an army." Bela looked at him meaningfully. "As do we."

Tours took a sip of wine with a satisfied sound. "And where are we with Gwyneth Aedin?"

"She was critically injured by the Rhidge you sent." Bela sounded hopeful. "Although we can't know her condition, she could easily die in the upcoming days. Aedin killed the Rhidge shortly after it happened."

The loss of one Rhidge was worth Aedin's pain. Tours could only imagine with relish Aedin's despair—how he wished he'd been there to see it. How the assassin ever managed to get that close, Tours didn't know. But he was impressed that he had.

"Good," he murmured, his eyes finally settling on the Lord of Radiance. Daniel didn't look well—his skin was unusually pale given the Lailan sun, and dark circles were etched under his eyes. He clutched his glass of wine with desperation, staring glumly into the liquid.

"My lord," Tours announced brightly. "How are you faring?"

Daniel's eyes fluttered to Tours. The bright spirit of revenge had been replaced by a hollow ache. "Fine," he muttered.

"I heard that Mr. Doyle and his wife escaped under your watch."

Daniel gritted his teeth. "I wasn't expressly told to *watch* them. Isn't that why you sent *her*?" He jerked his chin at Bela as she bared her teeth.

"Bela has been quite burdened with duties of her own," Tours replied lightly. "And now we hear that Mr. Doyle has rejoined his sister at the villa. It must be lovely to be reunited after all this time."

Daniel swirled his wine silently, his expression darkening.

"Well…" Tours set his hands on the table, shooting a look at Bela. "Since you have failed your only task, I believe we have no more use for you."

At this, Daniel looked up with surprise. "You sent me here—you said you wanted me to be here when they returned."

"You *are* here," Tours said silkily.

"I'm on a boat offshore—utterly useless—"

"Yes, you are," Tours growled.

Daniel fell silent, fuming at he stared at his king. "I can lead an offensive against the villa," he began quickly. "I know I can."

A low laugh echoed across the table as the Rhidge exchanged looks among each other. Even Tours was unable to suppress a smile.

"My dear boy." Tours shook his head with a grin. "You don't know what you're up against."

"Magical powers—the Gift—can't replace swordsmanship." Daniel puffed out his chest, staring down at the Rhidge. "I have a talent for combat. I served in Lord Tremer's guard."

Tours gently traced a finger across the lip of his glass. "It's not experience that you lack but a *thirst* for blood. A cloying darkness that blinds you to everything else."

Daniel clamped his mouth shut, realizing that words were useless. Sipping his wine with thin lips, he settled back in his chair with a glum expression.

Tours softened his voice. "We don't want you harmed or killed. This is a war of the Gifted, who possess extraordinary powers. Anyone without would easily be destroyed within a second."

Bela placed her hands flat on the table. Her cuticles were raw and red from being picked and peeled over and over. Her dark eyes watched Daniel with humor as she lowered her chin. "A second… or less," she whispered.

Ignoring her comment, Daniel pushed back from the table. "If you don't need me, then you'll excuse me." The chair scraped audibly against the floor, and Daniel exited the room, leaving his wine on the table.

When the door was shut, a cruel smile hardened Tours' mouth. "Oh to be young and desperate."

Bela's temporary good humor had fled. "We need to go ashore and pay him a visit."

"Ah, dear Jon?"

"Yes."

"Who else knows of his presence?"

"None."

"Good." Tours rose and the other Rhidge followed suit. "Let's go."

————

Tours swatted at a buzzing insect near his ear.

The chains clinked as the large man shifted in the opposite seat. Sweat and crusted blood were fused together on Jon's forehead—when he lifted his hand to brush it away, bits of the cracked brown audibly left his skin. The afternoon sun beat down on them as they sat in an open courtyard, the stucco walls baking in the heat.

Black figures littered the building—crouching on the roof or lingering in the shadow of a wall. Bela stood just behind her prisoner, a hand resting mindfully on the back of his chair. Just in case. Jon's light blue eyes watched Tours with a steady clarity he hadn't seen for weeks. The effects of flussidik had finally worn off.

"I'm glad you're feeling better," Tours began gently.

"Aside from this miserable heat," Jon muttered, crossing his arms and extending his long legs before him. "And the boredom. That doesn't help either."

Tours shrugged, picking a stray thread from his doublet. "Imprisonment doesn't have the same appeal as being a fugitive now, does it?"

A hoarse laugh choked in Jon's throat. He shook his head and looked away. "What do you want then?"

"So businesslike," Tours chided. "What if I wanted to chat?"

"I'm here—on Lailan"—Jon counted on his fingers— "removed from the ship and placed in a secret location under guard. You show up, which only means that things are happening and you finally have use for me."

Tours grinned, leaning forward and resting his arms on his knees. "That is my position *exactly*."

Jon lifted his shoulders casually. "I'm not stupid."

"No," Tours agreed. "But you are limited in your options, which means you'll have to make a choice."

As the words left Tours' mouth, Jon tensed. He didn't respond, waiting in bated silence.

The echoes of the outside world passing by were cruel reminders of the normality of life. Tours had requested this place exactly so that Jon was close and yet so far removed from his hope—freedom. Near the port but lost in the maze of buildings, the house was indistinguishable from those around it.

Tours listened to the sounds of chirping birds, yelling merchants, horses braying, and carriages passing before he began. "Aedin and Gwyneth are here on Lailan. They have killed Cabot and taken control of the villa along with some other Gifted from the eighth island. Among this rabble is your wife."

"You're lying," came the automatic response, a knee-jerk reaction to soothe the pain.

In response, Tours' mouth curved into a cruel, soft smile. "No, Jon," Tours said slowly. "I am not lying."

Jon stilled, holding his breath in expectation.

When Tours leaned back in his chair, appearing to leave it at that, Jon dared to ask, "Is there a child…?"

"Yes—she was seen with an infant. A boy."

Something cracked in Jon's blue eyes; a desperate sorrow that had been buried for months. His lips trembled as he forced an expression of nonchalance, staring fixedly at the stones beneath his feet.

"You have a son."

A hollow sob broke through his lips. Jon gritted his teeth to force it down.

Tours watched him struggle with a look of satisfaction. "Here is your choice. You can either stay here and wait out this war. You can rest here safely as we infiltrate the villa and kill everyone inside. Or…" Tours paused for dramatic affect. "You can aide us."

Jon struggled to form the words. "Why would I aide you?" he whispered.

"Because we can promise to spare Rebecca… or your son."

A sudden rage lit in his eyes. "You—" His words were cut off by the cacophony of chains moving as his feet planted firmly and he prepared to stand. Bela's hand snapped to his shoulder, pressing him down.

"Oh no, Jon.—" Tours didn't bother to move from his seat, crossing his feet casually. "I wouldn't."

Jon let out a loud curse, rubbing his face in his hands. The clanging metal reverberated through the courtyard.

Bela's hand didn't move from Jon's shoulder. In a jerking movement, he attempted to brush her off, and she looked at Tours for direction. He inclined his head slowly—the hand was removed.

Tours waited patiently in the ensuing silence, fingering the dagger at his belt. His quick blue eyes met Bela's. She frowned impatiently. Jon made no response—his large hands were covering his face. Tours wondered if he was crying. He didn't blame him—it was an impossible choice. Perhaps he wouldn't agree to help them at all—leaving their lives to Fate and the very, very slim chance of survival. But Tours knew Jon, and he knew he wouldn't be able to stand aside when he had the opportunity to fight.

"What will it be, Jon? Rebecca's life? Or your son's?"

Chapter Thirty-Six

THE FIRST THING I noticed when I regained consciousness was the pain. I'd never felt anything like it before. A searing, throbbing agony that gripped my shoulder—lighting a fire along the sinews of my hand and the muscles of my neck. As if the entire right side of my body had been burned with a merciless flame.

I lay there in the pain, letting it soak my body; unable to leave or tear myself away. The stab of it soon dulled, and my head became light. My body started to float, and nausea crept through me. I found my thoughts flitting from tasks undone to memories of Ephraim and my father, and soon I fell into the abyss.

And I was gone again.

The next time I woke, it was the warm air, not the pain, that I registered. There was someone near—I could feel their skin on mine—and for a second I believed I was still in Iselleden. The summer breeze and the smell of freshly cut grass was unmistakable.

I opened my eyes to Rowyn's gentle gaze. The dulled Gifted fabric shone a modest beige in the walls of my bedroom.

A sad smile stretched across his lips. "Hello," he said softly.

I frowned in response. "What...?" The words fell away as I twisted my body to search the room for clues as to what had happened. The pain came roaring back, seizing my body and wringing the inside of my flesh.

Rowyn's hands quickly pushed me back down onto the mattress. "No moving—please."

I didn't bother to lower my voice as I cursed loudly. Tears pricked at the corners of my eyes. A constant throbbing echoed under the skin of my shoulder and arm. It took all of my weak willpower to control the wild beating of my heart, to not panic or give in to the hurt.

"I'll give you some more," Rowyn murmured, removing one of his hands and gently grabbing a vial by the bedside. "Here," he commanded. "Open your mouth."

I obeyed, and he poured several drops of the liquid into my mouth. It was sour. I winced and made a face as I swallowed.

"Good." Rowyn replaced the vial and settled back in his chair. One hand remained over my shoulder, but I didn't dare to give a closer inspection.

I was lying in our bedroom in the villa. The birds were chirping, the fountains gurgled, and the balmy breeze teased the fabric of the curtains. A calming numbness began to lighten my head. "Am I dying?" I whispered.

Another smile—or a grimace—stretched across his face. "I hope not."

"How long have I been…?"

"Here?" Rowyn finished delicately for me. He shrugged, looking around the room. "Half the day or so. The attack was in the early hours of the morning—it's late afternoon at the moment."

I swallowed as he said the word "attack." I had been attacked. I remembered the face of the Rhidge, Samael, as he'd preyed on my naïve hope for change. When he'd demurely bent his head, I'd thought of Aedin, of Rebecca, and of the hundreds of others like them who had the potential to give up the darkness and wish for the light.

But I suppose for every one that could change, there were a dozen others that wouldn't. Perhaps even more. Many more that would have chosen to kill me.

I had been a fool to believe him—a blind and trusting fool. Tears of humiliation and anger, not pain, stung my eyes. I focused on the shifting colors in Rowyn's shirt, unable to meet his gaze, ashamed of what I had done. Beige, grey, a dulled silver—

"Aedin killed him," Rowyn continued carefully, watching my face. "Not long after the first strike. He tried for a second but didn't succeed. The weapon was laced with a poison common to the Rhidge—it delays the healing process and quickens death. Luckily, I brought some antidotes from Iselleden that have been somewhat effective."

I frowned up at him. "Somewhat?"

Rowyn grimaced. "When the blade struck your shoulder, it tore an artery that supplies blood to the rest of your body. There was… a lot of blood. If we hadn't acted fast, you likely would be dead."

I remembered that day on the mountain, when I'd seen my death in the Prophet's vision. The blood that had pooled on the stones and dripped down my arm. A lump rose in my throat as I gritted my teeth to hold back a sob.

"I was supposed to die," I mumbled. "I saw it in a Dream of the Future… on Iselleden. I was s-supposed to—"

My words were cut off through a jerking sob that rocked in my chest. Tears—hot and stinging—poured down my cheeks. Intuitively, I moved my hands to rub my face—and a spasm of pain echoed down my left arm. Frustrated, I grabbed at the sheets with my right hand, dabbing my face and ungracefully blowing my nose.

"You're going to live." Rowyn flexed his hand on my shoulder. "I won't let you die."

I realized he was knitting my skin back together, exactly how Aedin and Jon had taught me at the fortress. "Who taught you?"

"The previous captain taught me the basics, but it was primarily Raine who finished my education." Rowyn looked away in memory. "She taught me extensive combat medicine, believing it was necessary when others didn't… I guess she was right."

His sister did have a talent for being right. We exchanged brief smiles. I sniffed and rubbed my nose again with the sheet.

"Doesn't it exhaust you?" I asked quietly.

"A little," he admitted with a shrug. "But we've been taking turns—Rebecca, Aedin, and I."

"Where are they?"

Rowyn looked at the light outside. "It's almost dinner time, so likely helping with that. Or resting… it's been a long day."

I could only imagine. Guilt swelled in my stomach, thinking of the pain and fear I'd caused them by being so careless. And Aedin…

"I'm sorry," I said to Rowyn. "You're probably exhausted."

Rowyn brushed back his hair with one hand, keeping the other on my shoulder. "I am tired"—he stretched out his legs—"but what I feel doesn't matter. Thank Fate that you're alive."

I picked at the sheets with a dark expression. "Fate has nothing to do with it," I muttered.

"Hm?"

Gesturing to his hand, I asked, "If you left me here, would I survive? Without any attention at all?"

Rowyn twisted his lips and admitted, "It would take a miracle…"

"That's what I mean. Fate has nothing to do with it. It's not an obscure thing out there controlling us. It's you, it's me, it's…" I gestured around the room. "Everything."

Rowyn was silent, staring at the embroidery on the covers. In the distance, I could hear the sound of pots clanging and idle chatter. I tried to focus my Gift—to feel Aedin or someone I knew—but my senses were dulled by the medicine. All I felt was Rowyn and the soft vibration under his hand as he knitted me back together.

"Perhaps that's all Fate is," Rowyn said quietly. "It's our best intentions to do some good in this world."

We exchanged a solemn look as I heard the antechamber door open and then the bedroom door.

Aedin stood in the doorway, his shoulders hunched in defeat and his face etched with pain. There were no knives or daggers at his belt, no blood on his clothes—his skin was clean, as if he'd just bathed. The dark etchings under his eyes were even worse than I remembered.

He walked carefully over to my bedside and looked down.

At the sight of my husband, new tears stung in my eyes. "Aedin… I'm sorry…"

Rowyn didn't move his hand. He awkwardly shifted his chair to allow Aedin room.

My husband perched on the bed, placing a hand on my leg and fixing his lips. "Don't apologize," he said hoarsely. "I… I failed you."

The mahogany eyes that I loved locked onto mine; in them was a well of suffering and self-loathing.

I swallowed, unsure of my next words. "Aedin," I whispered. "It's not your fault—"

"I should have protected you," he continued, licking his lips. "I knew he was lying."

"It doesn't matter."

"But it does," Aedin insisted, his hand curved around my leg. "I should have acted, but I didn't. I remembered what you said… and I wanted to believe…"

I, too, remembered what I'd said when we were in Iselleden; when I'd asked him to spare a life of the Rhidge and he'd agreed. How deeply I'd wanted to believe I was right…

I smiled sadly at Aedin. "But you were right. It was a foolish hope… and I've learned my lesson."

Aedin didn't respond—his hand only tightened around my calf. The corners of his mouth twitched as if he was going to say something more, but instead he chose silence.

Rowyn lifted his hand and peered beneath. "This should do it…"

Aedin leaned forward to look as well. I saw him wince before he quickly forced indifference. "Yes," he agreed. "But I can continue."

Rowyn looked about to object, but seeing the steely determination in my husband's expression, he changed his mind. "I'll get dinner then."

Standing, Rowyn gently touched my fingers before leaving the room and closing the door.

Uncurling himself from his seat, Aedin stood and walked around to the opposite side of the bed. He quietly removed his boots and shifted onto the mattress, nestling into my side. Very carefully, he reached across my chest and placed a hand on my shoulder. The soft vibrations continued.

I had forgotten the comfort of having his body next to mine. It was as if the breath I'd been holding since we'd arrived was finally released. The tension from the pain relaxed into a muffled and quieted hurt. I dared to ask, "Is it bad?"

Aedin's breath was warm on my neck. I felt a smile flicker across his mouth as he replied, "It's not pretty."

"Let me see."

Aedin stilled but then obeyed, lifting his hand just enough so that I could see underneath. Just inside the shoulder, where the collarbone met the arm, there was an angry red mark. The skin was cratered, and though the surface was healed, underneath the thin tissue spread tiny rivulets of deep purple, red, and blue. A spider's web of veins and blood that stretched towards my neck and bicep.

"It's just inflamed," Aedin assured me. The sound of his voice was thin in my ears. "It will go away in time."

I turned away and Aedin's hand returned to my shoulder. The quiet pulsations continued.

"What are you doing?"

"Knitting together the muscles that were torn. Rowyn fixed the artery—which was the most important part—but the tissue may still take some time."

I nodded quietly and stared down the blanket at my hidden feet. Someone moved through the garden. Outside in the hall, I heard bright laughter and chatter. Life moved on, and I was lucky to be part of it.

"Did you get some rest?"

Aedin shook his head against my skin. "I was here since you… were brought in. I'd only gone to bathe and find something to eat when you woke up."

"Doesn't it make you tired?" I gestured to where his hand lay on my left shoulder.

Aedin was stubbornly silent, his hand unmoving.

I whispered my next words. "It's not your fault."

A flicker of pain flashed across his face. His mouth moved to make words to disagree, but nothing came out.

"What happened was no one's fault but my own. It was meant to be," I began slowly. "Despite what I saw, it didn't end with my death…" I added the caveat in my mind—*I hope.* There was always still a chance—and a very real one indeed.

"I don't care about what was or is meant to be," he said bitterly, his words partially muffed in my skin. "I denied my instincts and allowed it to happen. It's my fault."

"But it's not," I replied, frustration heating my face. "I am also responsible for my own life. I made the choice to believe him, and I chose wrong." A raw laugh bubbled in my throat. "Do you know how that feels? I feel so—so… stupid! I can only imagine what Rebecca thinks of me now."

"I could have saved you," Aedin continued, swallowing audibly as his words became choked. "I can't imagine not l-living without—"

Hot tears began to slide down the skin of my shoulder. My body froze at the realization—my stoic, aloof, and impenetrable husband was crying.

"Ciaran," I whispered in consolation, but it only made it worse. Choked sobs racked his body as he tightened his body to mine. I gently reached up to touch the wet skin of his cheeks and stroke his hair.

"You are enough. You have done your best for me and our situation since we first met. It's not your fault."

The sobs were exchanged for short, stuttered breaths that finally transformed into long exhalations. I felt him sniff and rub his face into the pillow with a low sound. "Sorry," Aedin muttered, wiping my wet shoulder with the sheet.

"Remember what you said?" I teased, touching his face as he lighting grabbed my hand, kissing my fingers.

We lay together in silence, our breaths in harmony as the light through the curtains turned a fading orange, then purple, then gray.

When the crickets came to sing, Aedin said, "The last time I cried—truly cried—I was just a boy in the Rhidge."

I didn't respond—merely turned my head slightly to press my lips to his.

"Of course, I cried out of fear and pain when I was first captured, but this was six or seven months in. It was after a particularly brutal day, and I remembered crying because at that point I truly understood that I was alone. My parents were dead and my life as I knew it was gone—forever changed. I cried from understanding—knowing that this nightmare had become my reality and that I was a prisoner. I was caught and would never get out."

As the sound of his words faded into space, I added, "But you did get out."

"Yes," he murmured against my skin and cleared his throat. "I did. I am now free."

I imagined that the giant hole of guilt and pain was gradually closing—getting smaller and smaller.

Aedin's hand lifted from my shoulder as he peered at the skin. "It seems to be healing…"

I gently grabbed his hand and placed it on my stomach. "Let's rest."

His hand obeyed, and I was glad he didn't argue. Aedin wrapped his arm around my waist, naturally as if we were sleeping, and shifted his pillow so that his head was close to mine. The smell of cooked food mingled with flowers from the garden wafted through the room. I nestled into the sheets and his body, ignoring the dull pain in my shoulder.

A soft and gentle kiss on the lips. "I love you," Aedin murmured against my skin.

Sleep was drawing me closer and closer to its chest. "I love you too," I mumbled as my body shifted to rest. A soft and encompassing nothingness descended on my mind. And soon, we fell asleep.

———

The sun woke me from sleep. It was bright through the thin curtains, already heating the parts of the floor it touched. I blinked away the sleep, crinkling my toes and fingers in a stretch. A twinge echoed through my left arm.

Frowning, I turned to examine the wound—the skin on my shoulder was more even, and the veins lighter and less inflamed. There was still some pain, but my mind was clear, and I felt as though I had rested for a week.

I flexed my left hand, gauging and familiarizing myself with the aching sensation. It was manageable—I would live.

The door was opened quietly—Rebecca poked her head through.

Her eyebrows raised in question and I turned to my husband's sleeping form. Aedin's head was heavy on the pillow, his eyelids shut and face in utter relaxation.

I smiled in welcome to Rebecca, and she carefully shut the door, going over to the chair at my bedside.

"How are you feeling?" she whispered, her warm hand automatically going to my wound.

I cleared my throat from sleep before responding, "Much better. Thank you for helping."

In response, Rebecca's hand again began to emit the now familiar healing vibrations. "I thought he would never sleep," she murmured, eying Aedin. His peaceful snores had subdued into long and slow breathing.

"I'm glad he did."

We exchanged knowing looks. Aedin's breath was still hot on my cheek, but I didn't dare to shift or turn away to wake him.

As we sat in silence, I remembered Samael's words that night. *He's here—don't you know?* My stomach sank—Jon could be here on Lailan. "How are you feeling?"

Rebecca understood what I meant; her dark brows knitted together. "I don't know what to believe," she said quietly. "I don't know what to feel…"

"Do you think it's possible?"

Her mouth twisted in a humorous grimace. "Anything is possible. And it *is* likely that Jon would be here. But…" Rebecca struggled to find the right words. "I don't know what I would do if I saw him again. I really don't."

I remembered the massive man with laughing blue eyes— they had been so cold and pitiless the night he'd betrayed us. I wished I could help her somehow, and I wasn't sure what to say. "Do you have to decide now?" I asked.

"Deciding a course of action before conflict makes it easier to act in the moment." Rebecca shrugged her broad shoulders and pushed back her hair. "Makes it less likely that I'll freeze in panic or do something I'll regret…"

Offering her a half-smile, I said, "I know you'll do the right thing."

Rebecca smiled sadly to herself, her eyes lingering on the pale curtains, lazily turning in the breeze. "That's the trouble, isn't it? What is the right thing? Do I condemn to death the father of my child for terrible actions he committed to protect his family? Or do I forgive and forget and hope that he can change?"

I didn't know either. I stared at the sheets in silence as Rebecca continued to work on my shoulder. The villa began to stir with the echoes of morning routines. A bird chirped cheerfully in the garden. I wondered where my brother, Hollyn, and Andrea were, and whether they knew what had happened. The thought hadn't crossed my mind until now.

"They were informed," Rebecca clarified when I asked. "But we're limiting access to this room until you're recovered."

"Limiting access?" I repeated skeptically.

Rebecca didn't miss a beat. "For security reasons."

I was about to insist my full confidence that my friends and brother were least likely to harm me when Rebecca gave a careful look. "We won't take any chances."

And so I shut my mouth and didn't protest.

Aedin blinked open his eyes and rubbed his face into the pillow with a low groan.

"Good morning," Rebecca called out cheerfully.

"Morning." His voice was thick from sleep as he glanced at me with bleary eyes. "How late did I sleep?"

"Late," I answered with a grin. "Seems like you needed it."

"I did." Aedin sat up and peered at my shoulder. "How is it?" he asked Rebecca.

Rebecca moved her hand briefly to show him. "Much better."

And she was right—even throughout our conversation, the redness had continued to decrease. My shoulder looked almost normal, save for an ugly scar where the blade had pierced my skin and bruising along the point.

Rebecca grimaced at me. "I'm afraid my skills are limited to function rather than aesthetics."

"I don't care," I replied lightly. "What's another battle wound?" I turned to Aedin who nodded quietly and pushed himself up from the bed.

"Where's Celion and Rowyn?" he asked Rebecca.

"It's Rowyn's watch"—Rebecca nodded to the front—"so he'll be at the gate."

"Good." Aedin opened the drawer on the bedside table and pulled out a dagger I hadn't known was there.

"Can I come?" I shifted under Rebecca's hand.

Aedin and Rebecca exchanged a look of hesitation. "You should rest…" Aedin fiddled with the blade in his hand.

"I'm better," I insisted, wriggling out from under Rebecca's grasp. She reluctantly dropped her hand. "And besides, my back is killing me. I need to stand."

Pushing back the covers, I set my feet on the ground and stood. The world swayed slightly—I gritted my teeth and reached for the chair.

"Easy." Rebecca grabbed my hand, guiding it to the back of the chair.

"Just a minute." I waited, ignoring my husband's pained expression as my mind cleared and I focused on the solid ground. "There. Let's go."

Aedin saw there was no deterring me, so he inclined his head in agreement.

"I need to check on Zac." Rebecca gave me an encouraging smile. "But I'm around if you need me again."

"Thank you." I gripped her hand before we left the room.

Aedin and I headed towards the front, weaving through the lingering Gifted as they chatted and rested in the open halls. I ignored their stares and their venerable whispers of *"Matr"* as we passed, lifting my chin and focusing on each step and breath.

After lying in bed for over a day, my feet were clumsy and my mind was slightly fuzzy. The warm breeze wafted through the shadows of the hall as we emerged into the bright sunlight of the entry courtyard. And then the heat hit us—baking the gravel beneath our boots and our exposed skin.

I spied Rowyn just near the gates, conferring with William, his scarlet hair fiery in the light. They looked up in surprise as we approached, a smile instantly spreading across Rowyn's face.

"You're alive," Rowyn teased when we came near. I punched his shoulder with my right arm in response.

"What's happened?" Aedin asked William. He didn't smile or grin—his forehead was wrinkled with concern as he squinted in the sunlight.

"A second ship from Radiance arrived late yesterday," he said quietly. "It docked next to the first, and Tours was spotted in Tahuna with other Rhidge. They're here."

Even in the heat of Lailan, those words sent chills down my spine.

Aedin's face steeled into a mask of iron. "What else?"

"Tours was seen leaving Tahuna for the boat late yesterday, so he's not staying ashore—making him a difficult target." William looked frustrated as he said the aside. "The Rhidge in Tahuna have increased but not to a significant amount, which makes me think that most of them remain on the ship."

"Waiting for their purpose," Rowyn mused, flicking away a bead of sweat.

"Exactly," Aedin grumbled under his breath. "No messengers? No communication attempts?"

"None." William shrugged. "And no further attempts to enter the property."

Aedin's hand twitched to his dagger in frustration. "I hate this waiting game."

"Me too," I agreed glumly, scanning the property. A line of Gifted stood proudly at the wall, spaced evenly every thirty feet. They watched our conversation in between eying the jungle and the world outside the villa.

It was then that I noticed that the usual rhythm of passing carriages had stopped. There were no ladies attempting to call, no merchants driving their merchandise from the fields to the port, no horses or livestock ambling down the road. The Lailan that I'd known was gone—vacated by the possibility of war. I wondered if the women I had called friends would even recognize me now—with my wounded shoulder, sparse uniform, and a sword at my hip. It felt natural to change even though much of the world remained the same.

"We'll watch the ships for any sign of activity," Rowyn continued. "If they move or send boats to shore, then we'll know."

"Good." Aedin looked at me with an arched brow. "Are you feeling up to a spar?"

I grinned in response. "Only with my right arm."

Chapter Thirty-Seven

THE SHIP MOVED later that night.

After spending the day regaining my strength with Aedin, I'd retired to the living room and settled into the chairs. A rotation of people passed through—sitting down and chatting in between tasks—and slowly the afternoon turned to evening.

Dinner was served, and Rowyn came for a final check, running his hand over the scar with a satisfied expression. The majority of the pain was gone, although some bruising remained. "You'll live," he stated confidently as Celion chuckled at his side.

"Good." I shot him a glare and tucked into my bowl of soup.

It was after dinner, when we'd begun to clean the dishes, that Selena noticed the other ship had disconnected from its sister.

"Its lights are out," she called us to the balcony. "Look."

It was hard to see under the thin light from the crescent moon, but she was right. The second ship—the one that had housed Tours and the Rhidge—had extinguished all of its lights and was moving away from the port.

"Where are they going?" Ephraim frowned at my side.

No one knew the answer.

We watched with bated breath as the ship grew smaller, seeming to fade into the darkness of the horizon. Even with my Gifted sight, it was difficult to distinguish its path. The late marine fog and inky blackness swallowed the vessel whole. Until—

"They're heading north," I said aloud. The sails had turned just before they disappeared completely.

"They're heading to another island?" Andrea wondered aloud.

"No—the eastern shore." Aedin pushed back from the railing with conviction. "They'll attack us from the opposite side."

Celion took a swig of wine. "Then I suppose it's time."

"It's time," Rebecca agreed, looking at me. "I'll remain to secure the villa while you're gone."

"Gone where?" I repeated stupidly.

Aedin gave me a sidelong look. "You wouldn't miss the battle, would you?"

"No!" I exclaimed quickly.

Ephraim grimaced, and Hollyn shouldered closer to his side. "But how do we know that this isn't some trick? What if they just come right back to the port? Or land on the northern side?"

"The northern side is riddled with rocks and cliffs," William answered. "It's impossible to get close to land even in a boat at night, let alone a ship."

"It could be a misdirect," Aedin mused. "But we have to watch the eastern shore regardless. Where is Tieren?" Aedin turned to Andrea.

"He's napping before his watch." Andrea saw the seriousness in his expression. "I'll go wake him."

"Please," Aedin added as she quickly set down her wine and exited the balcony.

When Tieren arrived, he and Aedin set off for a high point above the main road. Once they'd left, Rowyn, Celion, and I began the preparations for battle.

We distributed armor—the same light metal that I'd first seen Rowyn wear—and swords. The Gifted fabric—dull and beige since we arrived—began to gleam a light silver as a buzz of anticipation overcame the crowd. I felt it as well, the same hum of power that had haunted our time in Iselleden. My palms began to shimmer once more.

Ophelia helped to strap armor on a young woman, handing her a sword with a look of approval. Selena and Celion were conferring in a corner—dividing and assigning soldiers from a list of names.

Ephraim, Hollyn, and Andrea were quiet as they watched us organize in the courtyard. Andrea wore an expression of visible frustration on her face, crossing her arms and leaning against a column. I took the piece of armor that was handed to me, gingerly easing my bruised shoulder through the straps.

"Here," Andrea muttered, pushing off the column and holding up the strap so I could ease my arm through.

"Thanks." I winced as I slid it through. Flexing my left hand, I gingerly picked up a sword, weighing it in my palm. "At least it was the left," I mused under my breath, switching the sword back to my dominant hand.

"At least you can fight," Andrea retorted. "I hate being sidelined."

My first instinct was to reject her words, but I stopped my tongue and reconsidered. "You would be killed," I said to her lowly. "And I don't want you to die."

Andrea brushed back an errant curl, her gaze softening. "I know the stakes—"

"You don't." I sheathed the sword at my belt and crossed my arms. "Putting yourself in the crossfire for martyrdom's sake isn't heroic. It's stupid and careless. Don't let your death come so easily—fight to survive."

I held her gaze until her brown eyes flickered down to the stones at our feet. "I want to help," she offered quietly. "I want purpose."

"We have an entire villa that needs protecting." I gestured to the dagger at her belt. "Use that to defend it."

Andrea straightened with a coy smile. "Oh I will."

An easy grin spread across my lips, and at that moment I fervently wished that we could retire to the balcony—as we used to—with a bottle of wine in tow. "I'm glad you're here," I said, meaning every word.

"Of course you are." Andrea wrapped me in a tight embrace. "I'm your best friend and you are mine."

I laughed into the curve of her shoulder, inhaling her familiar perfume as the preparations for combat continued. Tears sparked in my eyes and I winced, pushing them down. When Andrea pulled away, she gestured to Ephraim and Hollyn with a jerk of her head. "I suppose I'll help them prepare the medical supplies."

"We'll definitely need it," I agreed, swallowing audibly.

Only when she turned away did I allow myself to brush at my eyes, dispelling any trace of sorrow. I prayed to whatever gods —or Fate—was listening to get this over with. I hated this tense anticipation—lingering in this limbo of uncertainty. I wanted to take a boat myself and climb aboard a ship full of Rhidge just to get this over with.

But instead the waiting continued. For hours.

I watched the moon cross the sky and arc through the constellation of stars. I wondered where Aedin was and whether the ship was docked or still drifting through the sea. Its sister ship remained anchored just outside the port, casting a soft glow in the distance.

I wondered if Daniel sat inside its depths—and if he knew what side he was on.

The crickets chirped unaware as the sounds of clanging metal echoed dimly through the halls. Selena gripped a sword with an expression of visible frustration, training lightly with another Gifted. I wondered if I should join—perhaps it was the distraction I needed from this tense anticipation.

I was still making up my mind when Rowyn called out my name, beckoning me to the front.

I went to him, attempting to quiet my mind as it ran through hundreds of scenarios regarding what he might say. We ducked into a quiet part of the entryway, where I saw Tieren. "Tell me," I commanded.

He was bent over, sucking in air as he gripped his waist with a pained expression. Rowyn wordlessly handed him a jug of water. Tieren eagerly grabbed it and drank—sweat poured down his thin face. After several seconds, he pulled the jug away, wiping his mouth with the back of his hand and attempting to slow his breath. "Sorry." He gasped through the words "I've just—ran from the eastern shore."

"Are they there?" Rowyn asked quietly.

"Yes." Tieren nodded jerkily. "They set anchor—they're preparing to invade from the cove."

My heart began to thud steadily in my chest. "Where's Aedin?"

"Hiding—waiting for them."

"Good." I turned to Rowyn. "Let's go."

"Yes," he agreed, his mouth tight with resolution. "It's time to fight."

Those were the sweetest words I'd ever heard leave his mouth.

Rowyn clapped me on the shoulder as he left us in the entryway, orders ringing through the villa halls.

———

We left the villa under the light of a thin moon. It didn't take us long to get to the eastern shore. The last time I'd fled there, I hadn't truly known the extent of my powers. I had been weak, afraid, and terrified of the ghosts at bay.

But now—now I was changed. Now I was ready and ran with the rest of the Gifted, our feet flying across the dirt, our breath coming easy, our bodies vibrating with a familiar and ancient energy.

The world was quiet, as if waiting for the crash of thunder and blood.

I ran beside Celion; his blonde hair was stuck to his forehead with sweat. His tight, golden jaw melted into a grin as he felt my eyes on him. "Yes?"

"I'm glad you changed your mind about us," I said quietly. "Thank you."

Celion looked amused. "You're thanking me? At a time like this?"

"You helped to change Rowyn's mind," I pointed out as we slowed to a walk along the main road, the dark tangle of jungle looming before us. "We wouldn't be here without you."

He was quiet for a moment, considering my words. "I tried to understand what it would be like, if our roles were reversed. If I had been rejected, hated, and unwillingly expelled from my home. I would have fought for my home as well. And so I suppose I understood… eventually."

My hand reached for his. He squeezed it, and I gave him a sad smile. As soon as we let go, we reached for our swords.

Just under the cover of the tangled branches, Aedin was waiting. Even in the dark, with my Gifted sight, I could see the thin layer of sweat already dotting his exposed skin. Gone was the dark uniform of the Rhidge and instead he wore the Gifted tunic once more—it shimmered and glowed as we drew closer. Underneath the airy fabric I saw the daggers strapped to his forearms and calves, and another broadsword tied across his back. He was like the angel of death—ready to bathe in the blood of the evil.

I went to him, placing a hand on his cheek as he inclined his head for a gentle kiss. "Ready?"

"Yes," he replied, and there was something in his eyes that agreed with his words—a solidness I hadn't seen before in his gaze. Strength and will without fear or hurt. I saw it in the peaceful arch of his brow and the wrinkled corners of his eyes. He was ready.

And so was I.

The deep thumping in my chest was steady and willing. It was an even beat that resounded throughout my body, distributing the blood from my heart and lighting it on fire. My fingers tingled as I gripped the sword.

"Lead on," Rowyn commanded.

Aedin ducked back into the jungle and led us on the path that curved and descended to the cove. Through the crowded trees, I caught glimpses of the black waves, light sand, and a ship shrouded in darkness. It was moored just outside the line of waves, bobbing innocently in the water.

The soft rustling of leaves only betrayed our presence. Among the nightly calls of animals, we weaved through the damp earth. When we finally reached the beach, the sky felt too expansive, and we remained along the protective shrouding of the trees. But they knew we were here—they had to know. Along the shadows, our tunics glittered a muted starlight, waving gently in the invisible breeze.

I held my breath and turned to Rowyn with a questioning gaze.

He opened his mouth to reply when a sudden wind rushed at our faces. It howled and roared with an ancient ferocity that sent chills down my spine. Instinctively, I lifted my sword in response, but the beach remained empty.

In the previously calm bay, waves were rocking the ship, lapping eagerly at the shore. They grew larger and larger with each passing second—the boat creaked in response, righting itself towards the shore. The waves and the boat grew higher and higher, water now rushing towards the jungle and licking our boots. My heart sank as I saw a humongous wall of water emerge from the pack—hungry and ready to break the boat on the shore.

Rowyn saw it too—his face paled as he shouted, "Back!"

But anything else he might have said was lost in the roar of the water as the massive ship catapulted itself towards us on the beach. I didn't have time to consider how it remained upright amongst the rushing tangle of waves, nor even try to count the dark shapes that littered its deck, clinging to the sails and railing —I ran to the right.

Focusing on the shape of his head, I followed Rowyn as he darted back through the trees, seeking higher ground. My boots slipped on a root—I reached out with my left arm to brace my fall, hissing in pain as my shoulder jolted with the impact. All around me flittered darts of pale moonlight—Gifted fleeing the advance.

The ship hit the shore with a sudden boom that shook my bones. A final burst of water rushed up the jungle path and then receded back. Waves continued to slosh around the bay, growing smaller and smaller as they returned to their normal state.

I peered through the branches—the ship was lying in the sand, slightly sloped to the right but entirely whole and undamaged. From its belly, small black flies began dropping, spreading out across the sand. The Rhidge.

"Rowyn!" I called, scanning the jungle wildly—our army was scattered, hardly visible among the tangle of branches and leaves.

Selena appeared at my shoulder, her thighs wet with ocean water. "I saw him go that way." She pointed with her sword, her face white "We need to get to the beach. We can't fight in here."

She was right. I saw the black shapes growing in number, beginning to make for the jungle. They just kept appearing and appearing—I heard the next words in my mind before I spoke.

"Attack—now!"

An instinctive and guttural cry echoed beside me as Selena, too, raised her dagger. Among the trees, I heard the cry answered—some muffled, others clear as day. It was the call to fight, the call to attack.

I let my feet guide me—stepping over roots and brush and sliding down the soaked path towards the beach. When my feet hit the sand and the expanse of a starry sky rose above my head, I didn't look. All my attention was reserved for the massive hulk of wood and the figures of the Rhidge strewn around its sides.

And the army at my side—the familiar pulse of the Gift as it rushed through my blood and lightened my steps. Feeling them behind me.

They were ready—their swords, daggers, or bare hands facing us. Men and women—their faces blank and unfeeling. The black of their uniforms seemed to absorb all the light of the moon. My long braid thumping against my back, I ran across the beach with a roar ripping my chest. I let it loose, the sound unfamiliar to my ears. It was a sound of hate and passion.

Legs already burning and my mind swimming with adrenaline, I hardly noticed Aedin as he appeared at my side. His long strides overtook mine, and he collided into the first body with a sudden thud and screech of metal. I reached out my hand, sending a blast of power towards the figures in front—some were thrown back, others remained standing, matching my power with their own.

But when the power was dropped and the swords were naked and waiting, all of my training snapped into place. I knew their moves—I recognized each slash of the sword and returned with the appropriate counter. Block, parry, twist, slice—I was almost surprised when my sword slashed across the stomach of my opponent and cut through fabric and skin. His young face creased in pain, and his body fell to the sand.

In the space of a heartbeat, I waited for the aching regret and pain, but there was none. My body and mind steeled themselves for the next attack.

Ignoring the pain in my left shoulder, I focused on the colors before me. Black meant attack, glittering white meant wait or turn away. Figures were tangled and twisted just like the jungle behind us. Jumbled together with arms and legs and steel and sand.

In the distance I saw Celion, his golden arm smeared with blood as he hacked through a fallen figure. Rowyn's scarlet hair was just behind, exchanging blows of the Gift in between slashes of his sword. His opponent flew with an unfamiliar speed, her thin blade sparkling with moonlight. A lump formed in my throat as I recognized the sharp features—it was her. The woman I'd seen with Tours all those months ago. She was here.

They weren't far. I sprinted towards them, ducking to avoid a rogue blade. A Rhidge appeared in my path, her eyes narrowing in recognition as she reached into her pocket. I threw up a wall of air before the first dagger connected with my stomach—it thudded into the sand. I hurled out my power, knocking her back several feet and reaching for my sword.

In an instant, she was standing before me, and then the next she wasn't. The graceful arc of a blade swept across her neck and severed the head from the body. I stepped away from the spouting blood as she fell to the ground.

Aedin's sword was in his right hand, a dagger twirling in his left. His face, arms, and torso were streaked with blood—he smeared more across his face as he tried to wipe his forehead of sweat. "Good?"

"Yes," I managed to gasp in reply before another black form was upon me. I met the blade as it swung towards my waist, clenching my jaw at the jarring impact from the blow. My wrists ached with the effort of keeping my sword light, aloft, and moving. A guttural cry ripped from my throat—I forced through the actions, ignoring the creeping fatigue. The metal pierced flesh, but I didn't wait to see; as soon as the body sank, I leaped into a run, leaving Aedin locked in his own battle. His sword was nearly invisible as it sliced cleanly and efficiently through the air—the Rhidge before him struggled to keep up. It was a graceful dance of death; an intuitive state of being.

I forced my eyes in front—stumbling and running through the sand and avoiding the chaos of battle.

Death was everywhere; it was unavoidable and without prejudice. The Gifted of Iselleden lay motionless on the beach, their blood clotting the sand, alongside the black figures of the Rhidge. Swords and daggers were scattered among them, the metal half hidden in the sand like waiting traps for the careless.

The hulking ship cast an eerie shadow on the beach—I wondered if there were any Rhidge still inside. I didn't feel any living thing, but then my power was drained. I was exhausted— not just from the pain of combat but from my barely recovered injury and the use of my Gift. I wished for something to revive me, but there was nothing that could. My will remained my only power.

And it would have to see me through—alive.

A ragged shout cut through the night.

In an instant, my eyes locked on Celion's face. He was just ahead. The body of a Rhidge fell in his wake as he leaped to attack Rowyn's opponent—the woman. But there was no fear on her face as she faced the incoming attack—even against both she parried their blows with ease, exchanging each sweep of the sword for a shot of the Gift. A grim smile emerged at the sound of Celion's grunts of rage.

A parry, an opposing block, and then a swift cut to his exposed shoulder. Celion cried out as he fell back from the fight, dropping his sword to grip his arm as blood began to seep through his fingers. But Rowyn continued, his features scrunched and impenetrable, meeting each swing of her sword with focused concentration.

She grinned, casting a shot of air towards Celion—he was thrown back further into the sand.

Rowyn growled, his actions growing slower with each bead of sweat that poured down his face. His blade was growing heavy —he missed an opening. My heart pounded, my stomach sinking at the sight of it. I forced my feet forward, fighting off an incoming attack as I continued to watch my friend. One second, Rowyn was swinging for an impossible reach, and the next, the woman's sword stuck solidly into his stomach.

I saw his knees buckle, then hit the sand. A scream caught in my throat. Blood spouted from the wound as she retrieved her blade and turned to face Celion with an unfeeling smile.

Celion scrambled to his feet with a bellow of fury, his body shaking with the effort. I knew she wouldn't waste any time before the next kill.

Fighting off my opponent, I sent a blast of power towards her —it hit. She turned to me with a look of surprise that quickly turned to recognition.

"You!" I screamed as I lunged across the sand, forcing out my hands for another blow. She nimbly sidestepped my power with a knowing smirk.

"It's over." She gestured towards the scene at my back. "But you haven't won." She sheathed the sword at her belt and turned to run.

I threw out every ounce of my remaining power—trying to freeze her movements or stop her—but she brushed it off. Her black uniform soon faded into the tangled brush, and she disappeared.

Celion kneeled again in the sand beside his partner as a sob ripped from his chest. "Rowyn!" he cried.

There was no answer—the wound had taken him quickly, and his eyes were vacant and glassy. Celion's tears dripped from his face, creating clear rivers down the caked blood on Rowyn's skin. Even I knew there was no power of the Gift that could bring him back to life. I kneeled alongside Celion in the cold, damp sand and watched the agony of a man who'd lost the love of his life.

Tears ran freely down my cheeks, uninhibited and unconfined. I realized the woman was right—we hadn't won. Even as the battle around us grew quiet, there were just as many Gifted who lay among the dead as the Rhidge.

I saw specks of black flee into the jungle—some Gifted ran after to hunt them down. In the distance, Aedin thudded his sword into a squirming body and looked across the bloodied sand to find me. He broke into a sprint, but his steps slowed when he saw the dead body beside us. Several feet away, he stopped and kneeled into a position of respect. "I'm sorry," he whispered to Celion.

Celion didn't answer—his hands rubbed at the sweat, blood, and tears on his face. Sniffing, he stared vacantly at the calm water of the bay, towards the invisible eastern shore of his home.

I gripped his wounded shoulder, ignoring the nauseatingly thick fluid as I knitted together his skin. My head began to grow light, and I had to stop after several minutes—I wiped away the blood and saw it would heal on its own.

"I will break Bela," Aedin swore under his breath. His eyes had finally torn away from Rowyn's body and met mine with a cold ferocity. It was a look he'd rarely allowed me to see—the glimpse of the killer beneath his skin. "I will kill her."

Although I hadn't known her name, I knew who he meant.

And I had no doubt that his word would become reality.

As the surviving Gifted regrouped around us, I reached out a careful hand to touch Rowyn's already cooling fingers. I leaned forward to kiss his skin, remembering the respect and loyalty of a man I'd grown to love. He'd gone against his closely guarded beliefs to help us—strangers—on a quest to defend our home and save our world. He'd fought desperately for what he loved, doing what was right, rather than what was comfortable.

Now it was my turn.

Chapter Thirty-Eight

AEDIN'S BODY HURT. All of it—from his wrists to his calves, everything ached with a tiredness that sat deep in his soul. Even the simple act of brushing his forearm against his face sent lines of pain through the muscles of his shoulder. It had been a long time since he'd fought directly with the Rhidge. He was still surprised he'd even survived the battle. Half of him had expected to die that night, but the gods had not chosen him.

They had chosen Rowyn instead.

As they trekked along the jungle path and back up the main road, Aedin remained vigilant, scanning the quiet road—barely lit by the coming dawn—for any shadows. They hadn't killed them all, and Aedin knew they would regroup again soon.

He wondered what they'd wanted—to demoralize them? They'd wiped out most of their army, leaving their ragged group of twenty to continue with their mission. If their aim had been to solely kill, then the surviving Rhidge wouldn't have fled into the jungle. Aedin made a mental note to send William into Tahuna (once he was recovered) to search for any outpost. They had better chances of infiltrating and eradicating rather than outright combat at this point.

Birds began to chirp at the rising sun. Aedin turned instinctively to scan the trailing group for his wife. There she was—at the back, guiding Celion with a gentle hand on his arm.

She felt his gaze and met it with her own; there was pain in the depths of those familiar blue-gray eyes. Aedin winced as he watched Celion stumble over a protruding root, his large boots careless and awkward. Gwen murmured something in his ear, tightening her grip on his arm.

Aedin turned back to the front, a sickening sensation in his stomach. He didn't want to dare imagine what it would be like —to lose a partner. He had almost been there—it had almost happened. The fearful emptiness gaping through the hole ripped in his heart. It was an unimaginable pain. But they had survived—for now.

"All I want to do," muttered Tieren at his side, "is eat the largest meal of my life, drink a barrel of wine, and sleep."

A smile flickered at the corners of Aedin's mouth. The boy looked exhausted—bloodied, bruised, and drained like the rest of them. Aedin ducked his head in assent. "If only."

William didn't smile. "Now is when we're most vulnerable," he growled, wincing as his boot hit a rock. "We need to stay vigilant."

Tieren opened his mouth to respond but his gaze was pulled to the villa gates. The iron was dark and gleaming with the morning mist. Just beyond, the courtyard of sand was empty, void of any presence, any noise, save for the tinkling of a distant fountain. Aedin released the dagger from his belt, a warning sounding in his mind. Where were the guards? Where was Rebecca?

William felt it too—he straightened, his hand on his sword, glowering at the still scene, just fifty yards away.

"Andrea," Tieren breathed, his body flinching as wild fears tore through his mind.

"No—wait," Aedin hissed.

Tieren obeyed, freezing with a look of discomfort.

Putting a hand on Tieren's shoulder, Aedin said, "I'll go first. Don't come until I call you."

Tieren agreed with short, jerky nods, reluctantly stepping back and pulling out his sword. The entire line came to a halt, clustering just outside the gates, along the side of the main road.

Ophelia fearfully scanned their expressions. "What is it? The Rhidge?"

"I don't know," Aedin murmured, sending out tendrils of power, careful to not tire himself too much.

Nothing responded.

Gwen appeared at his side, scanning his face. "What do you need?"

Aedin pulled her away from the group, careful to lower his voice. "Do you feel anything?"

Gwen followed his gaze to the villa gates, her expression darkening. "No… but wait." She paused. "I feel something… but I'm not sure…"

"Who?" Aedin pressed.

"Rebecca," she whispered. "And the others, but I don't know. I'm sorry, I've expended myself…"

Aedin placed an understanding hand on her back. "I know," he whispered, pressing his lips to her head, ignoring the smell of dirt and taste of sweat and blood. "Stay here to protect them."

Gwen nodded with a challenging look. "Call if you need help."

It was a warning, but Aedin took it to heart. He inclined his head and walked to the villa gates, stifling every urge to stay away. Something felt wrong. Very wrong.

The iron was cold to the touch. Opening and closing the gate, Aedin walked towards the front, careful to mute his footsteps on the gravel. A layer of marine fog clung to the leaves, wetting the limestone arcades as they appeared like ghosts from the mist. There should be people guarding the front, the sounds of cooking from the kitchen, or Gifted in the courtyard. But all was still. It didn't make sense—were they all dead? Aedin tightened the grip on his dagger, continuing to press outwards and feel for anyone—anything.

Until there it was.

An innate sense of dread sank into his stomach as everything clicked.

And he knew.

A familiar hulking form rose from the mist in the courtyard. Aedin stood tall, waiting for that voice, the voice he'd known all his life.

"You're smart to come alone," Jon called. "To not risk the lives of your friends… like I did."

Aedin was quiet as he waited for the inevitable, watching the massive form take shape and come closer. It was Jon, but a reduced version. The muscle that had lined his body had dissolved into skin and bones. Those jovial blue eyes were vacant and wide, bulging from a skull that was thinly covered in hair. Something like pity and regret echoed in Aedin's breast. It was him, but he wasn't here.

When he was only several steps away, Aedin held up his dagger, daring him to come closer.

The skin on Jon's skull tightened into a smile. "Afraid?"

"Where are they?" Aedin was relieved to hear his words came out steady.

Jon looked surprised, almost offended. "Do you think I would harm them?" He opened his hands as if showing the lack of weapons. But Aedin didn't believe he wasn't armed, nor capable of inflicting any hurt, not for one second.

"Where are they?"

In response, Jon tilted his head. "Alive. Likely hiding somewhere I haven't found yet."

Aedin's blade was anchored and motionless in the humid air. "Why are you here?"

"To help you." Jon took a step forward until the point of the blade was right on his chest, at the hard bone of his sternum. "I want to help."

Aedin scanned his face for any sign of the man he'd once known. He didn't know what to trust or what to believe, and fatigue weighed heavily on his shoulders. "You can't help," he said quietly.

"You may have survived the night," Jon whispered through cracked lips. "But you can't win this war. Tours is here—he wants to find a diplomatic solution."

The point of the blade pressed against his sternum, just enough to break skin. Jon blinked as a small drop of blood pooled at the point.

"We're not here for a diplomatic solution," Aedin warned. "We're here to end the Rhidge."

Something like hope flickered in Jon's eyes, until it was replaced by a cruel hardness. Jon laughed, a raw and aching laugh that echoed through the limestone arcades. His chest sagged and he bent his body, placing his hands on his knees.

Aedin dropped his blade, waiting as the cutting laughter faded into the morning mist.

Jon straightened and looked around, wiping his eyes with a painful grin. "You can't end the Rhidge. No one can destroy them."

"We will end them," Aedin repeated, his patience growing thin. "And you can run back to Tours and tell him exactly that."

"You don't understand—you've been gone too long." Jon's smile faded into a pained grimace. "They'll kill you. All of you."

Aedin waited until the last notes of his words had disappeared. "No," he replied quietly. "They won't."

"What makes you so sure? Hm?" Jon challenged, straightening his broad shoulders.

Aedin raised his dagger again but didn't take a step back.

"You lied about your Dream of the Future—didn't you? What have you seen?"

"What I've seen doesn't concern *you*," Aedin growled. "Leave here. Now."

Jon paused and looked around. "Not yet," he said under his breath, almost to himself.

Aedin's blood ran cold—he knew what he wanted. *Rebecca.* "You have no right to be here," he continued. "Leave now and I will spare your life."

"No." Jon turned from his blade and began to walk down the limestone arcade.

Throwing out his hands and the last reserves of his power, Aedin froze his movements. A terrible headache began to echo in his temple, and he gasped as Jon fought with every inch of his massive frame. Jon's power began to carefully lift the claws of air—one by one—until there was nothing restricting his movements. Aedin stumbled, gritting his teeth at the sluggishness of his actions.

There was little he could do, save call for help.

"Leave now, Jon!" Aedin shouted, raising his voice so it echoed through the halls.

Jon stopped, turning to him with a curious expression. "Are you tired?" A coy smile flitted at his lips. "How quaint. The interminable Aedin has grown soft."

A sharp retort rose in Aedin's throat until the sound of another voice echoed behind him. "Leave now, Jon."

Jon froze at the sight of Rebecca.

Soundless and powerful, her lithe form stepped around Aedin and stopped just ten paces away. In the crook of her arm was cradled a small child, hardly visible under the swaddling blankets. Her other hand held a long dagger, gleaming silver in the morning light.

Something broke in Jon, an unconscious sob that ripped gently from his chest. With uncertain steps, he staggered towards her. "Is he—?"

"You come any closer and I will cut your throat," she snarled.

Jon believed her—immediately he stopped. "Rebecca," he gasped, eyes pricking with tears.

"You do not belong here," Rebecca continued. "You do not have the right to come here and threaten us."

Jon rose a shaking, placating hand. "Rebecca, listen to me. Let's leave here together—"

"I don't have to listen to you," she said coldly.

"We can leave," Jon whispered, tears openly running down his unshaven cheeks. "You and I. Come with me. We'll be safe."

"I don't abandon my friends."

"You have to—" Jon fell silent at the sight of the others filing into the hall. One by one, the Gifted of Iselleden—their shining clothes ragged and torn—appeared alongside William and Tieren. They situated themselves along the open paths, barring any exit, faces bloodied and bruised. From their ranks came Gwen, placing herself solidly at Aedin's side.

Her presence was a comfort, a shining energy that filled Aedin with warmth. He gently closed his hand around hers, reveling in the feeling of her life, even among the pain in the villa.

Jon's vacant gaze slid from the remnants of their army, to Gwen at Aedin's side, and his wife and child. The tightness in his mouth trembled. "You're all going to die," he said hoarsely. "Tours wants a diplomatic solution—tomorrow at high noon. Meet him. Don't oppose him."

"Why should we believe you?" challenged Rebecca.

"Because *I*"—Jon beat a shaking hand against his chest— "don't want you to die. Come with me, Rebecca. *Please.*"

There was a pause as Rebecca stared at her husband and doubt began to claw its way into Aedin's mind. After the past months, after all they had endured, would Rebecca go with him? What if Aedin had been wrong to trust her? It was her choice in the end, but would she turn against them as well?

In the brief quiet, a soft cooing sound echoed from Rebecca's arms, and a small pink fist rose up from the blankets. At the sight of it, Jon's face melted again, and he took a step forward.

"No." Rebecca brandished her weapon, and Jon stopped again in his tracks. "Show me your arm."

Jon's face paled. "I am a prisoner without a choice—"

"Show me. Your arm."

Rebecca's husband was quiet, his lips quivering as he tried to summon the right words. After a moment, he bent down to grab a small blade tucked into his boot. With his left hand, he cut into the black fabric on his right arm, angrily ripping the hole wider.

Aedin prepared his stomach for the familiar sight. He tightened his grip on Gwen's hand, as if telling her silently to prepare as well. She had seen the healed scars but never one that was fresh and new.

When Jon exposed his shoulder, Aedin felt Gwen automatically flinch; he too steeled himself as the memories began flooding back. When his shoulder had also born the raw and ragged cut of the Rhidge.

The "R" was fresh—likely reopened only several days ago—yet the clear lines of blood had only begun to clot and crust.

Rebecca didn't shrink or shy away from the sight; she met it with clear understanding. Her dark eyes flashed through cycles of pain, pity, and rage. Jon's eyes never left her face; they were searching for recognition or understanding.

"I had no choice," Jon repeated quietly.

At the sound of his voice, Rebecca blinked and her face became a cold mask. "There is always choice."

She turned away from her husband, clutching Zac in her arms, walking towards Aedin and Gwen. Standing beside them with uneven breath, as if holding back invisible sobs, she lifted her chin.

Gwen placed a supporting hand on her shoulder, tightening her knuckles, and staring down the man she had also trusted.

"No," Jon whispered, the fabric on his arm hanging loosely. A thread had become untethered, unleashing a desperation. He staggered towards them, repeating the word over and over.

Gwen took a step forward, shielding Rebecca and Aedin with her body. "Stop," she commanded, holding out her palm.

At the sight of the colors twisting and whirling under her skin, Jon's eyes grew wide.

Out of the corner of his eye, Aedin saw Andrea, Ephraim, and Hollyn emerge, huddled together behind a column, watching with wide eyes. Defenseless—like sheep before wolves. Aedin forced his eyes forward, panic rising in his throat at the thought of Jon noticing. Should his eyes stray from Rebecca…

"You've changed," Jon said quietly to Gwen, his body crouching instinctively.

Gwen locked her spine, and the power swelled like a bubble of air. "Stay away from us," she snarled.

Something within Aedin felt relief at her strength—that she was able to face him, when he was not. Even battered, bloodied, and bruised, her power shone from within every pore and radiated through the hall.

Jon saw it too. Scanning the threat before him, his eyes darted to the exits, the Gifted, the guards, and then—

Aedin's blood ran cold as Jon moved before he could lift a finger. One second he was there, the next he'd grabbed Andrea and an instinctive yelp echoed along the arcades. Sweat beaded on her brow, Gwen raised her hand to freeze his movements, but there was already a knife at her friend's throat.

Andrea's eyes were wide with fear, her auburn hair pressed against his face as she stiffened under the touch of the knife. The point was aimed at her throat. Wildly she scanned the faces before her—Tieren fighting every instinct that roared at him to attack. Now.

"A life for a life," Jon snarled at Rebecca. "Come with me."

Or else. The threat was apparent. Rebecca paled, clutching the child in her arms.

Hands outstretched, Gwen carefully tracked the blade at her friend's throat. So helpless and exposed. A line of sweat trickled down Andrea's neck—her mouth began to tremble.

Aedin saw two ways forward. One was to force his already expended body into futile action—to trigger a potentially catastrophic chain of events that could leave Andrea dead. The other—

The thought was hardly formed in Aedin's mind as a blur of motion caught his attention. One second, Tieren was restrained, the next he was leaping towards the pair. And with Jon's gaze focused on his wife, he hardly saw the attack—

An invisible wind pushed away the blade and threw Andrea across the courtyard. In the newly opened space appeared Tieren, so small and thin against Jon's giant body. A flash of metal and Aedin saw the knife sink deep into Jon's stomach.

There was a sound as if all the breath had been released from Jon's body. His mouth fell open as he gasped and coughed for air. Gwen rushed to Andrea, pulling her up, her eyes scanning her body for any sign of hurt.

Rebecca's face was pale, her hands tightly gripping the bundle of cloth in her arms. She blinked once, then twice, and swallowed.

But she wasn't alone in her surprise. Tieren's face too held a look of astonishment that he'd even succeeded. As if he'd half expected to be the one with a blade stuck in his flesh.

Jon scrabbled for the knife—Tieren hadn't let go. Despite the surprise, his hands were steady with a grim resolution.

"Stop," Rebecca gasped. In a daze, she handed Zac to the nearest Gifted and rushed forward. Aedin followed.

Tieren obeyed and removed the blade with a sickening suctioning sound. He took a step back, then another, as Rebecca hurtled past, catching her husband as his knees sank to the floor. Jon groaned. Blood seeped through the hands gripping the wound.

Familiar blue eyes blinked up at Aedin and Rebecca. There was a tug and a stirring of a quiet power as Rebecca pushed aside Jon's hands and replaced them with her own. Healing him. Aedin paused.

"Help me get him to my room." Rebecca looked at Aedin. "Please."

Aedin shot a look at Gwen and Andrea, huddled together in the courtyard, then at Tieren. The blood dripped from his knife onto the flagstones.

There might have been a time when Aedin would have disagreed. When he would have chosen to let Jon die rather than offer him the chance to live. He had too much to atone for, given what he'd done to them. How he'd ruined Aedin's trust and memory. Ruined the lightness with the darkness of the Rhidge.

But looking at Rebecca's panicked efforts to save her husband, Aedin obliged. Despite the aching pains along nearly every inch of his body, Aedin gently bent down and gathered Jon into his arms. Cradling him—like Rebecca had cradled their child.

With slow steps, Aedin carried the mass of his former friend through the limestone halls.

Chapter Thirty-Nine

IN THE AFTERMATH of it all, I let my body overtake my mind and allowed myself to rest.

Curled in the bed—thoughts lazily spinning around and around—I considered what I'd seen. The blood and carnage on the night beach. Bela's blade slicing open my friend. Aedin carrying the hulk of Jon through the halls.

I'd seen that before—on Iselleden, when I'd last encountered the Prophet. Aedin and Jon. Although, I hadn't known it at the time. I wondered about the other scenes, whether they'd happened already or were yet to come.

Aedin's body was warm and slightly damp from the bath as he pressed himself against my back. Even through my exhaustion, I reached for the arm that was curled around my waist. Searched for the hand, entwining our fingers together. His breath was hot against the back of my neck, every inch of his body in need of comfort and assurance. I didn't protest—even as the warmth of Lailan began to dawn into the full heat of the day and the early morning chatter of the birds was traded for the cry of the gulls.

And so my body was pulled down into the abyss, and I slept.

I might had rested for hours until he found me. Or it could have been minutes. I wasn't sure.

But Tours' blue eyes blinked into my vision and everything in my body seized. I clenched my jaw, my arms and legs steeled in preparation for combat… or flight. Mouth dry, I realized I couldn't move. My body was stuck as I watched him stare right back—that keen and predatory gaze that was the basis of all my fears.

And then the rest of the scene melted into sharp relief, and I realized it was a Dream. A Dream of the present—the thought flashed through me like a bolt of lightning. It wasn't real, but it was. My body somewhat eased, realizing the threat wasn't immediately in front of me, although still entirely real.

Eyes watering, I blinked and shaded them against the full strength of the afternoon sun. The ship's deck was busy with sailors scurrying about, running through their daily tasks, flitting around and ignoring us. Or at least ignoring me. Some cast anxious gazes in Tours' direction as he stood at the railing, waiting for the boat that was being hoisted up. I saw the impatience written on his features, the gripping of his gloved hands on the wooden railing.

As soon as the boat was secured, Bela descended with feline grace, followed by several others. Their uniforms were torn, bloodied, littered with sand and soaked with ocean water. A mess. But Bela's head remained high, proudly bearing a cut on the high point of her cheek and ignoring the stares of the sailors and those who stopped in their tracks.

Her companions sank with exhaustion, only steeling their bodies as a low snarl slipped through Tours' lips.

"What happened?" Daniel's voice echoed from behind.

I whirled around to see him staring, with unrestrained horror, at the trio. His auburn hair was long—longer than I remembered —his face sallow and sad. Entirely unlike the confident, arrogant man I had known, and used to love.

Tours curled his lip. "Battle. That's what happened. Not that you'd know anything about it…"

Bela inclined her head as if in agreement but spoke lowly. "Where is he?"

"I sent him off early this morning." Tours waved a dismissive hand. "We should hear back soon."

"*Who?*" Daniel demanded, edging closer. As close as he dared to the group. All around them, the sailors had resumed their natural course, wary of Tours' wolfish eyes.

Finally, Tours deigned to turn his body to Daniel, crossing his arms with a look of pure dislike. "None of this concerns you."

"I am the Lord of Radiance," Daniel began in a weak and low voice. "People are fleeing the island. Cabot is *dead*. We need to find a resolution—"

Tours grabbed at the fabric of his silver doublet, pulling him closer with a hiss. "I haven't survived this long to be scolded by some *boy*"—Daniel winced at the word—"on the basics of combat. Now…" Tours shoved him away, straightening the front of his own doublet. "Go down below, drink yourself into a stupor, and leave us alone. We are in charge of this situation."

Something in Daniel's face crumbled as the words sank in. I couldn't help but feel some pity for him—to be left behind and abandoned. And then… there was a gleam in his eyes that I recognized. I'd seen it months before in Lailan—the day he'd challenged my husband (and sorely lost).

But then it was gone. Daniel's face was a careful mask as he forced his feet to move towards the stairs, weaving slowly through the learned efficiency of the sailors. Then he disappeared into the depths below.

Bela jerked her chin towards where Daniel had stood. "Careful," she advised Tours.

Tours raised his eyebrows in response, and Bela obediently shut her mouth.

"Tomorrow at noon," he growled low in response. "If Aedin doesn't show by then, we invade with the full strength of the Rhidge."

My heart stopped at the sound of my husband's name.

Slowly, my body began floating up and up—away from the deck of the ship burning under the afternoon sun. Until I was nothing more than a speck in the sky, like one of the gulls circling the port, hunting for crabs on the rocks. I saw the villa, saw the bloodied mess on the eastern shore, saw all of Lailan in a blink.

And then it was gone.

And Iselleden rose up before me.

Rolling, green hills flanked by soaring mountains topped with snow. The scent of freshly cut grass and summer wildflowers. I saw the Haven and the peaceful ambling of the Gifted, their tunics shining like fallen stars along the stones.

"Have you missed me?"

Her voice pulled me into the Council Tower—an abrupt and nauseating drop that made me fist my hands and grind my teeth. The ground stopped moving and I turned slowly to face Raine, her long bronzed arms holding a simple gray cloak in her grasp. My heart began to thud as I recognized the worn threads, the slow vibration of power like a scent swirling from the thing.

"What are you doing?" I whispered, ignoring her earlier question. "What… is this?"

Raine shrugged, an elegant gesture. "It called to me… and I answered."

It was an instinctive urge I fought—to grab the cloak and put it on. It was exactly how I remembered; it called to me, soft and hard, promising both lightness and darkness. Infinite power and precious mortality. My fingers itched to reach forward—it was just out of my grasp—

"I think you should know something," Raine's lilting voice continued, her emerald eyes catching the movement of my body.

Her words caught me off guard. "Know what?"

"That you will succeed."

A hoarse sound broke through my lips, something like a laugh. I thought of the carnage on the beach, the blood that had soaked my hands, the bruises on my body, and my nearly broken soul. And in a flash, I saw him. Scarlet hair streaming against the pale moonlit sand. Her cherished brother—the years they'd fought for Iselleden together. "Rowyn…" It took an extreme amount of effort to say his name aloud. "Rowyn died."

The look in her eyes nearly broke my heart. Grief and pain. "I know…" Raine held up the cloak again, the loose folds floating uselessly. "It… told me."

"Do you hate me?" There it was. The question I'd wanted answered every minute since it had happened. It was me who'd brought pain and bloodshed—just as Rowyn had predicted. I had ruined their lives.

A thoughtful grimace flickered across her lovely face. "Hate is a strong word," she mused.

I prepared myself for her verdict—despite what she said, hate seemed to be the most appropriate word for what I deserved.

"Rowyn didn't hate you," Raine continued, stroking the folds of the cloak in her arms. "He was frustrated and plagued by things he didn't understand, but he never hated you. Nor do I."

The bubble in my chest deflated a bit. I was thankful it didn't burst. "I…" The words faltered as they left my lips. "I saw Tours on the ship—they're preparing another attack unless Aedin surrenders tomorrow. There's been so much pain and death… I don't know how to stop it."

She narrowed her eyes and scanned my face. "You know what you must do."

"But I don't—"

"Yes." She cut me off with a sweeping motion of her hand. "You do."

I was about to protest again until something in the back of my mind began to tug. My attention narrowed on the cloak within her embrace. The sweet, dulcet call of power. In response, an edge of the fabric lifted and gently waved.

A step closer, and then another. And before any sensible warning could sound in my mind, I gently lifted a hand and placed it on top of the cloak. But this time—this time I would not be lost. I did not desire what it offered—I was in control.

It slowly unraveled, consciousness and knowledge weaving together possibilities and realities.

And when my glowing palm left the fabric and I was left unscathed, I suddenly did know.

———

I awoke with a start, my body shuddering as it came back to reality. Or simply the material realm. There was nothing to prevent me from claiming that the Dream and interaction with Raine wasn't a reality—it simply wasn't one based here.

The other side of the bed was empty. It must have been late afternoon. Birds flitted through the garden, the noise a cheerful façade to the darkness waiting in the villa. I pushed out of bed with a groan, rubbing at my shoulders as aches and pains twinged at the activation of every muscle. Even the bottoms of my feet were sore from running.

Where was Aedin?

I cast out my awareness, feeling for him. My power had returned, its arsenal almost back to its full potential. Yet my mind was still a bit slow and sluggish—like my body as I trudged out into the hall.

So few. There were so few Gifted left. They talked quietly in the makeshift camp in the courtyard and slept under the bright sunlight. Guilt rose in my stomach, nauseating and twisting. It was my fault they were here—it was my fault we were in this entire mess. Maybe we should have stayed on Iselleden. Maybe I should have given myself over to Tours months ago. Maybe I should have never left Berge—

The thoughts stopped when I pushed open the door to Rebecca's room and the metallic tang of blood hit my nostrils. Aedin leaned against the wall, his arms crossed, studying the barely coherent Jon on the bed. Rebecca sat on the edge of the mattress, her swift and healing hands not on his body but picking at the fine linen sheets, a crease etched into her brow.

I went to my husband, lightly touching his fingers as a reminder of his presence. How little had he slept? The dark circles beneath his eyes had returned. As if noticing my gaze, he dropped my hand to rub his face and sigh.

My gaze shot to Rebecca, questioning and silent.

She shook her head slowly. In response, a deep, cagey breath rose from Jon. I knew the sound—there was liquid in his lungs.

No amount of Gift or power could remove that. Only a miracle would save him.

But—I looked again at Rebecca as her fingers gently reached for Jon—did she want to save him?

A sputtered cough and hoarse inhalation of air. Rebecca made a soothing sound and brushed back Jon's hair. His eyes fluttered open, staring up at his wife with slow recognition, everything clicking into place. And then they turned to us, standing awkwardly in the corner. Waiting.

"A-Aedin…" a shuddering breath called. I saw my husband freeze, every muscle suddenly taut.

Aedin's eyes locked on Rebecca in question. Rebecca slowly brushed back Jon's hair, trying to distract him. But those blue eyes were fixed on my husband, suddenly lucid.

The word was whispered again through parched lips. "Aedin…"

I saw the fight in my husband's face and I knew the thoughts that were swirling around his head. The hate for Jon's betrayal and the guilt for not stopping Tieren's blade. What if this was a ploy to kill him? What if Jon wanted to apologize? What if this had been entirely orchestrated by Tours?

A shaking hand was laid on the bed and Aedin stepped forward—just out of reach. "Jon," he said quietly in response.

It was as if that was exactly what he'd wanted. Jon lifted his blue eyes to the ceiling, staring at the swirls of pale stucco. "Please…" The word was barely a whisper. "Kill me."

Aedin blinked as his words hit home. His lips twisted, opened, then closed; he didn't know what to say. He turned to Rebecca, but her eyes offered no assistance. At the sound of his plea, she had closed them in pain.

It was the end—the end of their story together.

Jon's lips parted again, but before he could say anything more, Aedin spoke quickly. "No… I won't." His hand immediately went to the dagger at his belt, and I heard the second unspoken part of that sentence. *I can't.*

He couldn't kill the man who'd given him spirit and hope through his darkest hour, the man he'd also saved from the

Rhidge. The man who'd taught him to fight and kill and dream of the impossible.

Yet also the same man who'd sold him out for the chance to survive and protect his wife. The man who'd turned against us in our hour of need.

Rebecca's fingers gently traced the scars and callouses on her husband's hand, as if trying to fix them in her memory. Silent tears pooled in her eyes and began to run down her cheeks.

"Aedin…" Jon breathed again. "I'm… sorry."

My husband's hand reached again for me—his grasp was tight and unyielding. I gripped back hard, swallowing back any traitorous tears that began to burn in my eyes.

"P-Please."

The word was uttered softly as Jon's blue eyes searched around the room again, unable to find him. I could hear his heartbeat stuttering and slowing; the heat of the room slowly pressing into his body, his lungs filling with blood. Speckles of red spittle dribbled onto his chin as he coughed.

The grip on my hand relaxed. I looked up to see the tightness on Aedin's features loosen as he unchained himself of that iron mask. Pity and despair flooded his eyes; I nearly cried at the sight of it. All the pent-up emotion from years and years of history finally released.

Aedin unsheathed his dagger.

He looked to Rebecca—a final questioning glance. Slowly, she inclined her head in a nod.

I stood back as Aedin leaned over the bed. His right hand rested gently on Jon's thinning blonde head; in his left was a shining blade poised just over Jon's heart.

The word was again uttered through shaking lips. "P-Please —"

Blue eyes met black.

Aedin plunged the dagger into Jon's chest.

A sudden gasp, an instinctive arching of the body, and then calm. Half filled with blood, Jon's mouth was slack and open. Vacant and unseeing blue eyes stared up at the ceiling. I remembered in a flash the day I'd first seen those keen, laughing eyes. Before I'd known what would come. When he'd trained me for hours and hours, knowing I was stronger than I claimed. And now…

Rebecca sat motionless on the edge of the bed, one hand still stroking her husband's skin. Tears poured down her chin, wetting the sheets as she stared at the face she'd loved for so many years.

Aedin removed his dagger, carefully wiping the excess blood on Jon's black uniform. His eyes flickered to Rebecca and then to me.

Rebecca reached up a sleeve to wipe her nose, making a low noise that sounded half like a sob and half like a sigh of release. "Thank you."

Straightening, Aedin sheathed the blade but didn't move from the bedside. "He would have done the same for me… Even after everything…"

Rebecca gave short, jerking nods, her lips pressed together so tightly they became a thin line. Her brown eyes flickered to mine, then back to Aedin. "Will you go?" she asked him.

"Yes." Aedin's eyes hadn't left the body. "There's been too much death. I'll meet Tours tomorrow to end it."

"What?" My voice was sharper than I'd intended.

Aedin turned finally to me, his eyes tearing away from the sight of Jon.

"I need to face him," Aedin explained. "No more lives should be forfeited—it should be mine or his."

"Aedin, that's what he wants." Rebecca's voice became strained and hoarse. "Let me go instead. I can face him. You and Gwen can escape—leave—"

"No." Aedin shook his head vigorously. "We can't back down. Not now. Not after all we've given."

"You said it yourself—there's been enough death."

"You have a child—a life to live for—"

You know what to do. The words echoed in my head.

"I'll go." I forced myself to say the words before I let fear take over. "I will face Tours alone."

A long gaping silence met my words. At first, Aedin started, his mouth twisting as if to come up with words—any words—to convince me otherwise. He shifted on his feet, crossing his arms and looking down at the floor with mute frustration, pain, and blatant fear.

Rebecca stared at me with her large brown eyes, considering and thoughtful.

"I'll go," I repeated quietly, pushing away from the wall and moving towards them. Towards the dead body of Jon that lay quietly on the bed. "Tours doesn't know the extent of my power. I can face him."

Aedin let out a small broken noise. "He's more powerful than you think."

"And what am I?" I challenged, feeling the renewed strength of my Gift flickering just below my skin.

"Yes, you are powerful," Aedin conceded. "But you're still young and untested."

I scoffed at his words, ignoring the considering nod that came from Rebecca. *Untested.*

I scowled, a fight rising in my chest. "I have been tested—I've seen the Prophet, have battled the Rhidge, and *survived.*"

My husband's dark mahogany eyes flickered. "It's not enough —Tours is capable of inflicting unimaginable pain. I can face him —I know him."

"But I have the power. You've said so yourself."

Frustration bloomed in his cheeks. "Gwen—please." The words were uttered softly, so softly. A last-ditch effort to sway me.

"I will go."

"I can't lose you."

"And what about me?" I replied sharply. "Have you ever considered that *I* can't lose *you* either?"

In the ensuing pause, the only sound was Rebecca rising from the bed and closing the door to the bathing room. The muted sound of running water drifted through the thick humid air. I forced my breath to calm, brushing back a stray line of sweat as I met Aedin's eyes. They burned.

"You've given so much," I began softly. "To me, to Lailan, to our friends… I know this is where my path leads me. Just… please. Trust me."

With a snort of frustration he turned away, rubbing his hand over his face—and then stopping, as if realizing it was the same hand that had ended Jon's life. He shuddered. "Trust… I trust you. But I don't trust *them*."

I stepped forward, grasping his hands in mine, staring at the face that had become so familiar and so tender. The man that had sacrificed over and over again to protect me. Those mahogany eyes brimmed with tenderness as I pressed our entwined hands against my chest.

"Trust that I know where to be," I whispered, leaning up to press my lips against his dark brow. "I love you."

"I love you." Something jumped in my chest as he said those words. "And although I fear for you…" Aedin looked away, searching for the right words. "I accept your choice."

"Good." A smile unfurled on my lips. "Because I promise you this: I will end them."

Chapter Forty

WE BURIED JON'S body in the terrace gardens overlooking Tahuna. The earth was rich and fragrant as Aedin's shovel bit down and removed each pound of dirt. In the afternoon sun, the birdsong was brief and the insects buzzed at our faces. I held Zac in my arms as he cooed and slept, warm and heavy and full of so much promise yet entirely unaware of the uncomfortable and painful reality around him.

Alongside Aedin, Rebecca also dug with a shovel, her muddied hands grabbing the handle in an iron grip.

Jon's body was wrapped in a sheet, bloodstains visible on the surface. When the hole was ready, they gently lowered him into the earth. And then we stood in silence, gazing down at the silent body, never to return to life.

Aedin looked to Rebecca in question, but her eyes were locked on her husband.

Silence—save for the warm fragrant breeze that rustled through the palm trees.

I thought of death and wondered if it too was silence. Was it void of light or feeling? Or rich and warm and full of promise as the gods claimed? I thought of the dead Gifted, lying alongside the Rhidge we'd killed. Rowyn. Where would their bodies go? Where were their souls?

Finally, Rebecca released a heavy breath and dug her shovel into the loose pile of earth. The white and bloodied sheet become speckled with dirt as Aedin joined in.

An hour later, we couldn't see him at all. And by the time the sun neared the horizon, that particular section of garden had returned to the same level. The pit was gone, although the freshly turned earth remained.

Wordlessly, Rebecca handed the shovel to Aedin and held out her hands to me. As I eased Zac back into her arms, her brown eyes lifted briefly to mine. "Thank you," she said roughly.

In response, I squeezed her shoulder before she went back inside.

―――

My body had finally recovered to the point where it matched my mind. Although bruises and scratches still littered my skin, my limbs felt long and lean. A tingling sensation—light vibrations—ran up my arm as I twisted a small dagger in my hand. The metal gleamed a burnished orange in the light of the early evening.

Surveying the selection of weapons neatly lined up on our bed, I wondered what would protect me the most. Aedin had taken it upon himself to unearth every hidden collection of knives, daggers, swords, and assorted weaponry he'd hidden throughout the villa. They sat neatly on the white sheets, the metal only slightly rusted from our absence.

"Here." Aedin appeared in the doorway, holding a tiny blade the size of my longest finger. "This could be useful." He gently placed the blade in a vacant space, tilting it with his pointer finger so that it stood evenly in line. It looked so small against the others—unusually fragile.

Andrea folded her arms across her chest, studying the selection. "Well, at least you'll have a considerable armor for your skin, although you won't be able to move much."

A smile tugged at Tieren's mouth as he placed a hand on her shoulder. "Whatever Gwen doesn't choose, you're welcome to take."

"And you'll teach me how to use it?" Andrea turned her head to knowingly meet his eyes.

"Yes," he agreed, unable to hide the slight tightness in his jaw. "I will." Perhaps he would never forget the sight of Andrea with a knife to her throat—I knew I wouldn't. That flash of fear was something that would take a very, very long time to be erased.

As if reading his thoughts, Andrea gently touched Tieren's chin and leaned in for a kiss.

William grimaced in the corner, tearing away his gaze from the uncomfortable sight and motioning towards the array of weapons. "You should take a sword"—he gestured towards one that was particularly sharp—"and then keep daggers handy in your sleeve and boots."

Aedin nodded his approval, before adding, "And another one attached to your side. This one is good." He lovingly touched the handle on a dagger I'd seen him wear numerous times in Lailan.

"What about those?" Andrea pointed to a small collection of gleaming steel—they were hollowed circles with sharp blades attached, glittering innocently on the sheets.

"Useless for her purposes." Aedin sighed with regret. "It's my fault—I never taught you those," he said to me.

"Are they the same as throwing daggers?" I was hesitant to reach out and touch the small things, eying the nearly invisible points on each end. They were sharp.

"Similar goal," Aedin conceded. "But not the same method. Not easy enough to learn in the time we have left." His gaze flitted out to the sunset as it bled through the translucent curtains.

We had little more than half a day before it would all end.

Jon hadn't specified where Tours had anticipated meeting and so Aedin had sent William into Tahuna. He'd made contact with Bela and clarified that it was to be the villa—or the villa gates, as Aedin had asked William to insist. At least then, we could try to hold the villa if things went awry and we'd have the force of the Gifted at our backs. I supposed the Rhidge would also stake out the property, ending the lives of everyone in it should we fail.

Should I fail.

My shoulders suddenly became heavy with the realization of my responsibility. What I had chosen. I swallowed back the fear that was burning in my throat.

"I'm not sure…" I said, hesitantly surveying the array. My finger strayed on the edge of a curved dagger—a prick of blood emerged from where it had pressed against the metal. I blinked at the sudden spark of pain.

Aedin, Tieren, and William began debating the merits and pitfalls of the choices before me as Andrea looked on, amused. Brushing back an auburn curl and moving to my side, she said, "What's the point of being Gifted if you still have to use these?" She waved her hand carelessly over the immaculate presentation of weaponry. "Seems like a waste."

"It's a precaution," I found myself saying, remembering how Aedin had replied the same thing to me all those months ago. "And a good backup in case things turn south."

Andrea snorted. "So a blade will protect you better than your power?"

I considered her words, my eyes still scanning the weapons for some sign—something that would call to me, tell me what to do. Only metal glimmered ominously on the clean, white sheets.

And in the space of a heartbeat, Tours' blue eyes—as frigid and cold as the glacial waters of Berge—flashed before my waking eyes. A heartbeat later and they were gone.

"It's called a Gift, right?" Andrea was saying. I only half heard the words as they exited her mouth. But they connected in my mind.

"I don't need a weapon," I said under my breath, withdrawing my hands and stepping away from the bed.

Even amidst their arguing, Aedin had heard my words. He stopped mid-sentence and turned to me. "What?"

"I don't need a weapon," I repeated louder, looking at them.

As if in answer to a silent call, my blood thickened and roiled, running richly through my veins. It called to me, signing the song I'd ignored for many, many years, until Aedin. Until now.

Matr.

My husband lowered his brows, scanning my face. "Are you sure?" he asked a bit hesitantly, almost regretfully as he lovingly stroked the blade of a knife.

"Yes." I smiled at the confusion written on William and Tieren's faces; the pure, knowing joy on Andrea's.

"I *am* the weapon."

———

The sun easily scorched my skin; it seared unapologetically through the fabric, heating my shoulders and flushing my face. I ignored the sweat beginning to form on the back of my neck and surveyed the gravel courtyard. No sign of shadows or darkness. Just pure, piercing late morning light as the sun shifted closer and closer to midday.

Celion's head was a crown of pale gold. Catching my eye, he nodded once in recognition, tightening the grip on the sheathed blade. Weariness lined his face. He'd arrived back at the villa late last night, covered in sand and grime. Before the questioning words had even left my mouth, he'd said, "It's done… I buried him… and the others in the sand."

I'd hugged him fiercely, feeling there was nothing else to be said. Rowyn's body would forever lie on Lailan—the place he'd resented and feared, yet had defended with his life.

They had all made sacrifices—every one of them. The remaining Gifted were littered around the courtyard, still and beautiful as statues, the fabric clothing their bodies shining dully in the sunlight. As if it was aching to beam with full force.

Alongside them stood Ephraim and Hollyn, both armed with a sword and long dagger respectively. My brother sent me an encouraging smile, one hand shielding his face from the sun, the other wrapped around his wife's. On his other side was Andrea and Tieren.

William and Rebecca stood guard just in front of the group, prepared to fling themselves forward as the first line of defense.

And at my shoulder, just a step behind, stood Aedin.

I didn't dare look at him, lest I let him see the anxiety that was bubbling in my chest, threatening to break. We wouldn't make it easy, I told myself, scanning again the courtyard, gates, and jungle beyond for the hundredth time. We would fight with every ounce of strength.

I continued repeating this to myself—over and over again— until the sun reached its arch in the middle of the sky.

The afternoon had soaked everything in light, but amidst the glaring white began to emerge small pockets of darkness. Slinking and creeping, they emerged from the dense vegetation of the forest. Men and women clad in an impenetrable black. The black of death, the black of the Rhidge.

In response, my breath caught in my throat. Aedin unsheathed his dagger and the faint ring of steel sounded in my right ear. I didn't need to look back; I knew what I would see in his eyes—a fervent determination and hunger for revenge.

A low humming began in my chest. My fingers ached to release the tension that was building inside. The Gift was roaring to life through my blood and soul, weaving its power into the very fire of my being. But I didn't let it take over—not yet.

I remained silent and still, watching the figures creep through the open gates and position themselves around the courtyard at the very edge of my vision. Silently, I counted—three, four… eight, nine… twelve—they continued to appear until I'd lost count somewhere near thirty. My stomach twisted in knots— they would soon outnumber us. Very soon.

We hadn't bothered to close the gates—the decorative iron was hardly useful in keeping them out. A tall man stalked through the opening, proud and graceful as a panther. His dark golden hair glinted in the sunlight, a thin crown of hammered gold resting upon his head.

The last time I'd seen Tours, I'd been frightened. I'd been a lamb, betrayed by my own frailty and weakness. I'd cowered and bent before I'd fled for my life, unable to hold my own in combat.

But now…

At the sight of me standing in front of the army, Tours lifted his mouth into his predatory grin. I wondered if he saw the girl that had cowered, the girl that had fled, the girl who had fumbled for control. Or perhaps he smiled at the sight of my husband—just beyond my shoulder and armed to the teeth— and me, standing alone, arms hanging at my sides.

Stopping only ten paces away, Tours casually crossed his arms. A perfunctory blade hung at his waist, but I knew there were other concealed weapons. The Rhidge around him settled into position, some with naked blades in hand, others crouched with bodies ready to fling themselves into a dance of death.

The woman—Bela—placed herself nearby under the shade of an arching palm. She surveyed the crowd with pleasure; a cat patiently watching a skittering mouse. Brushing away a fly, she tucked her short dark hair behind one ear and bent her knees, one hand on her blade.

"Gwyneth Aedin," Tours crooned, a coy smile playing on his lips. "I hoped we would meet again."

I kept my mouth shut, and in the ensuing quiet, only the babbling fountain and shuffling of feet could be heard.

"I have to admit"—Tours cocked his head, eyes sliding to my right—"that I'm a little disappointed to see your husband cowering at your shoulder."

Again, I didn't dare look back to see Aedin's reaction; I could feel the build of his anger and hate through the echoes of power. Instead I flexed my empty hands and raised my voice. "We've come here from Iselleden to end the Rhidge. To end the tyranny and abuse of the Gifted and reclaim each island as free, independent states."

Surprise flitted across Tours' face, but it was soon replaced with a fascinated humor. "And you expect to accomplish this all… how?"

"I'll start by killing you."

A rumble of dark laughter flitted through the Rhidge.

Tours swept a hand over his mustache, shaking his head with a smile. "You can kill me—you can kill a *king*—but it won't erase hundreds of years. An institution is greater than one man or woman. A mindset is more powerful than flesh or blood."

The skin of my palms began to glow as I loosened my hold— just a bit. "You're not wrong," I replied casually, opening my palms. "It will take time—perhaps a long time to repair the destruction you've wrought. But you do underestimate one thing."

Tours' eyes met mine with a coldness I'd forgotten. They were dark and deep and empty, and that absence struck a chord of fear deep inside me. But as his eyes turned to the cascade of colors on my palms, I saw something similar in his gaze that gave me strength. A twinge of doubt or fear. It was there.

"What is that?" he asked quietly.

"Me."

I let it loose. All of it.

All of the hate and fury and passion and love that was pouring through my veins, aching to get out. In a single motion, I thrust out my hands towards Tours, palms glittering like diamonds in unfiltered sunlight. I wanted to hurt him, to pin him to the ground and suffocate him for all the pain he'd caused my friends, Jon, Rebecca… and Aedin.

Tours threw up his hands just in time to deflect the blow, bracing his feet as they slid in the gravel. Blue eyes widened; he set his jaw, fighting against the pressure. The humor was gone now, replaced with surprise and thirst—a thirst for blood.

A knife was flung from behind my right shoulder towards Bela, sneering from under the palm—Aedin followed the blade and rushed forward. She jumped to attention, tearing away from the crackle and blasts of power from our fight, and pulled out her own blade. It met Aedin's with seconds to spare, the clang echoing through the courtyard.

Drawing back, I flung myself to the side, avoiding the last tendrils of Tours' power as it lashed out in a violent flash of dark violet. Regaining my feet, I stood tall.

His eyes assessed my hands, another cruel smile twisting his lips. "Interesting."

As soon as the word left his lips, I threw another thrust of air. This time, he was ready, meeting mine with equal force. Without direction, the Rhidge behind him were frozen in place, observing with an uneasy fascination.

The wall of air between us sparked, loud pops and blasts echoing in my ears. My hold on the ground began to slip, the gravel crunching loudly beneath my feet. Teeth gritted, I summoned my strength, pushing back, taking hope at the sweat that began to pour down his face. It was pure determination tinged with a breath of fear.

Tours' face became red, ruddy, and warped with a sudden panic. "Do—something!" he spat behind him at the frozen Rhidge. At the sound of the order, they jumped into action, prowling across the way.

Towards the Gifted, towards Celion, my brother, and friends.

I shot a panicked glance behind, wondering if my power would protect them; if it could shield them from the onslaught. But Rebecca caught my eye with a look—a look that I'd become familiar with. She was ready and she wanted blood.

Together with the Gifted, William and Rebecca rushed forward to meet the Rhidge. They steered clear of the spinning mass of hard air, errant wind whipping at their shining tunics. Tieren stayed behind me with Ephraim, Hollyn, and Andrea, weapons out and waiting to face any oncoming threat.

Aedin was locked in combat with Bela—their blades cutting effortlessly through the air, sweat pouring down their backs, feet light on the ground. They traded blow for blow, steel ringing on steel creating bright notes of clattering music.

I tore my eyes away to focus on Tours, blurry but visible through the cyclone wall that sparked a golden red, green, and blue. My heart beat wildly in my chest—driven by adrenaline and the wild threat at bay. Bits of dust and gravel tore at my ankles and stung my cheeks.

I willed my feet closer, setting my jaw as the power cut into my skin, sharp and biting. I had long since lost track of whether it was mine or his. Through the colored wall, Tours had grown pale, his face twisted in concentration. He took a step back.

All around us were the sounds of battle—the clanging of metal, stinging cries, wails of pain. I didn't dare let my eyes tear away for longer than a second, only briefly acknowledging the darting black-and-white uniforms as they flitted in and out of my vision. But then something behind Tours caught my notice. Another group gathered at the gates. Through the flying sparks and shuddering air, I saw a familiar face, auburn hair, and those eyes—

"Daniel," I whispered in utter shock.

The crowd at the gate rushed into the fray with their swords unleashed. Daniel swung at a man in black, meeting his blows with timed expertise. Hope rose in my chest as their blades met again and again.

Tours was watching my face, and at the sight of my expression, he turned to follow my gaze. With the lapse in attention, I pushed forward, summoning my last reserves, every ounce of energy that resided in my chest. A wild cry was ripped from my lips and echoed somewhere in my periphery.

With a final whip of air, the opposing force suddenly stopped and Tours' body was flung back. It slid against the gravel with a sickly sound.

In the vacancy of his power, I became distinctly aware of a faint ringing in my ears, a heavy pounding in my chest. As if I'd been flung off a cliff and was yet to hit the ground. In the melee of sound and blood and sweat, I didn't hesitate. I rushed forward and instinctively reached for the dagger at my belt that wasn't there.

Blood lined his mouth and Tours blinked, wincing at the sun and licking his lips. The golden crown lay just beyond his head, knocked off by the impact.

Thousands of colors danced along the skin of my palms. I pushed him back down, pinning him to the gravel, ignoring the line of sweat that dripped from my wrist down to the ground. His skull knocked back again with a sudden thud—this time he winced in pain.

The pulses of power from my hands echoed through my blood in time with my heart. One beat, two beats. It was endless, as steady and predictable as the blood coursing through my veins.

"You—can't," Tours spat the words through the pressure pinning him to the ground, a red grin edging at his mouth.

In answer, I increased the pressure—it flattened his tunic and twisted his head to the side.

My focus remained on him, even as the battle raged on and I heard the rhythmic strikes of my husband's sword. Seconds ticked by and I realized I was waiting, waiting for something. Waiting for a sign, for someone to tell me what to do, or for Aedin to plunge his dagger into Tours' chest. This was the moment for which I'd trained, for which I'd shed blood—mine and my husband's.

This was the moment I had waited for, and I no longer had to wait.

With a clean motion, I pulled forth another wind of power, the Gift that had been imbued to me through gods and Fate, and I snapped Tours' neck.

Chapter Forty-One

IT TOOK SOME minutes before the news spread through the chaos of combat. The news that the King of the Empire, the former Director of the Rhidge, was dead. Only after Aedin had disemboweled Bela, slicing his blade cleanly through her stomach, did he look over and see me standing above the still body.

I was oddly empty for a moment when I should have felt pure elation or satisfaction. We'd accomplished a significant part of what we'd set out to do, and yet… there was so much more to face.

Slowly, the motions of battle stopped. The Rhidge ceased, staring in surprise at the sight of their unconquerable king, who now lay covered in dust. Some continued to fight, pressing mercilessly against our forces and uttering cries of rage as they were killed. Others dropped their weapons and were guarded, placed along a shady area under the watchful eyes of Ophelia and Selena.

Aedin came to my side, his dark eyes scanning my face. A heaviness had spread through my body—one that sagged my shoulders and face. I wanted to cry, out of pure fatigue or joy I wasn't sure.

He saw it, as plain as day. Silently, Aedin wrapped his arms around my shoulders, pulling me into the broad warmth of his chest. Sweat and dust and the metallic tang of blood filled my nostrils. I released a shuddered sigh, my body easing into his arms.

I'd done it. It was finished.

"Is he dead?"

Reluctantly, I pulled away at the sound of my brother's voice. Ephraim peeked around Tieren's broad shoulders, his useless sword light in his grip. His brown eyes widened, taking in my sweaty and dirtied uniform and the motionless body on the ground.

"Yes." My voice was steadier than my body. As the Gift began to retreat back into my blood, it left my mind light-headed and my limbs unsteady. I was glad to not have a blade in my hand—I would have likely dropped it.

Hollyn and Andrea stepped around Tieren, cautiously surveying the diminishing chaos. "Gods above," Hollyn whispered, her face white. "So much… death."

In reply, Andrea tapped her foot against a nearby Rhidge's body. "We should check to make sure they're dead… just in case."

Tieren shot Andrea a look of pure love and admiration and bent to follow her instruction. Hollyn and Ephraim also obeyed, cautiously handling the bodies as they sought confirmation.

I followed Aedin's gaze, surveying the courtyard. The bloodied bodies, tangled limbs, and remaining few who scowled at the dirt from their captivity. And then—the group of men in the livery of the king. Aedin stiffened, placing a cautious hand on his sheathed dagger as their leader came towards us.

The crunch of gravel sounded loudly in the awkward pause and I locked eyes with the man I'd once loved. Daniel. His tanned face was flecked with blood and crinkled under the sun. There was an unfamiliar and serious set to his mouth, one I hadn't seen before.

"How?" I asked before he could open his mouth to speak.

Daniel exhaled, wiping his forehead with the dusty sleeve of his doublet. The words came out in a rush. "The king—Tours brought me here to watch over Ephraim and eventually help capture or hurt you a-and—" He stopped himself, shaking his head. "I was tired of being used, and I decided to do what was right."

The tightness in my chest eased as his brown eyes flickered. "I'm sorry," he said quietly. "For everything."

"Thank you." I gripped his arm, meeting his gaze. "We needed your help."

Daniel nodded at me, then at the ground, before he looked up again, this time at Aedin. "I'm sorry for how I acted… before."

Aedin dropped his hand from the hilt and outstretched it, a sign of peace. "You're forgiven."

They clasped hands, a grim smile touching both of their faces. When they released one another, Aedin gestured around the courtyard. "Will you stay and help?"

"Yes, of course." Daniel gestured to the other men, before adding with an anxious look at the cluster of Rhidge. "But what do you plan to do with them?"

As if on cue, Rebecca set down a Rhidge by the makeshift prison area and came over to us. Bright red splotches stained her hands and clothes. I ran my gaze over her body, reassuring myself that the blood wasn't hers.

At the sight of her, Daniel automatically tightened his shoulders, knowing instinctively what she was.

"We should kill them," Rebecca said without preamble, nodding at me. "We can't make the same mistake twice."

Aedin made a low noise in assent but looked to me. My stomach turned at the thought of more killing. "How many are left?"

"Fifteen—from those who are here." Rebecca turned to Daniel. "Where are the others?"

"I'm not sure…" He rubbed his chin in consideration. "I believe there were no others on our boat."

"There are Rhidge scattered among the other islands—I'm sure of it," Aedin added quickly. "The question now becomes how to deal with *them* and the greater politics at hand."

"We can hunt them down." Rebecca folded her arms casually. "It will take a while, but it would be better this way… A clean slate."

The idea of more blood being spilled didn't feel like a clean slate—the fresh start we needed. But… "We let them decide." I jerked my chin towards the group huddled on the ground, Selena and Ophelia towering menacingly over them. "We tell them of our plan and let them decide if they want to assist us or not."

I could see the words forming in Aedin and Rebecca's mouths, and so I added, "They've seen me kill Tours—Bela is dead. They have no leader. They need one."

Without waiting for an answer, I strode over to the group sitting in the shade. Some stared at the ground, others scanned the scene, but all of their eyes snapped to attention at the sound of my footsteps. They were young—all of them. Some hardly twenty years of age. Though exhausted, I let a little of the Gift shine through, my palms shimmering in response.

Selena and Ophelia stepped back a respectful distance, though still close enough to strike.

"You have been defeated. We have killed your king and your director, and many of you. I know the power of the Rhidge, and I know what you now face. I know you've been tortured, beaten, and brainwashed for many years of your life. I know it's not easy to give up… But you have a choice."

Aedin shifted to my side, his unmistakable warmth pressing gently against the back of my shoulder.

"We are building a new Empire. A place where the Gift is cherished, not outlawed, and valued, not distorted. Come help us build that place and learn to live again. We will not harm you, nor impede your free will, unless you harm us."

A faint breeze shifted through the gardens, carrying with it the fresh scent of jasmine and citrus. It blew away the harsh bite of blood and sweat, bringing the once loved peace I'd known. They must have smelled it too—they lifted their gazes to the limestone arcades and distant palms, suddenly seeing them for the first time.

A young girl stood on shaky legs, wiping her palms on her pants. Small freckles dotted her nose. "I will help," she said softly.

I watched her eyes and scanned her face for any sign of distrust. She had a solemn, soft gaze and met my eyes with clarity.

"Then come with me," Rebecca's voice echoed from behind. I turned to see her step forward with an outstretched hand.

The girl hesitated, and I saw the instinctive warnings that flashed through her face at the sight of that hand. But she took one step, then another, and grabbed Rebecca's hand.

Rebecca smiled in response as others stood as well, following her to the side until only a few remained seated in the dirt. I waited some heartbeats longer, watching their downcast eyes stare sullenly in the dirt. No light, no love—nothing but emptiness.

I looked to Selena and Ophelia. "As you wish," I said quietly and turned away. Aedin followed me into the villa and we didn't look back.

——

It took two months. Two long months filled with extended periods of waiting in between hours and hours of activity. Rebecca assisted William in helping the young Rhidge readapt to the normal routines of life. Helping them exit the panicked state of existence and shift into something more domestic and civil.

When they were ready, William left to seek out the Rhidge on other islands, taking many of the reformed Rhidge with him. He wished to offer those he found the same option, if possible, although, as he told me privately, he wouldn't hesitate otherwise. I didn't disagree.

Rebecca remained at the villa, helping to manage our next steps while her child continued to grow and grow. Hollyn was often with her, helping to watch Zac as he grew into a round cherub, fond of playing with dirt in the garden. She and

Ephraim were now expecting a child of their own and appreciated any possible practice beforehand.

With its owner having fled the island, Tieren and Andrea moved into the old Spence estate. They filled its halls with much laughter and even allowed some of the Gifted to stay as they prepared their next steps. Andrea continued to visit Mary and assist when needed, with Felicity always at her side.

The villa was a hub of activity—letters flew in and out of its doors daily. There was much to be decided, and it was too difficult to make decisions over the course of delayed letters so we decided to host a summit. Inside the villa's halls, we would bring together all of the lords and ladies and decide on a common rule of law. It was a lofty goal, we knew, and Aedin acknowledged it daily, but it was worth a shot.

Meanwhile, reports from the palace confirmed that the throne sat empty. For good measure, Aedin invited a select few of Tours' old advisors, hoping to extend a branch of peace to the powerful on Radiance.

As the days passed and we drew nearer to the summit, Celion grew more anxious to leave. I would find him wandering the garden terraces, staring out at the horizon with a habitual frown. It was starting to permanently line his forehead, I noted playfully one afternoon as I took a seat next to him on a bench.

The corners of his lips tugged upwards in a brief smile, but he sighed. "As soon as this is over, I'm leaving."

I'd anticipated this and knew I couldn't convince him to stay. "We'll miss you."

"And I you. But I miss my home. Even if it won't be the same…" He trailed off, the frown burrowing itself again in his forehead.

We sat staring at the sea, and I conjured up memories of Iselleden; the steep cliffs dotted with lush grass and wildflowers, the polished stone walls of the Haven. I wondered if I would ever see it again. Ever see Raine or feel that familiar breath of power. Though since Tours' death and the dismantling of the Rhidge, I'd begun to feel a similar pull even in Lailan.

Though slight, it brushed against my skin, calling even now as we sat on the terrace.

"We'll visit," I decided out loud. "No matter what's decided."

Celion crinkled his eyes. "They may hate us even more after what we did."

"They don't know the full story." And it was true. That was the purpose of the summit.

The morning of the meeting, I dressed myself in a simple blue gown. Thankfully, Madame Porter hadn't left, and I was able to have her fashion a few things just in time. It was a compromise between the restrictive dresses I'd once worn and the more utilitarian garb I'd become accustomed to. My Gifted tunic, which had regained most of its power since the bloodshed, hung quietly in the wardrobe, fluttering gently each time I opened its doors. I would wear it most days but thought it would be an unwanted distraction for today.

I styled my hair and exited the bathroom, stopping in my tracks as I saw Aedin shrug on his black doublet. The thick blue stone of Lailan hung around his neck—as bright as the sky above. He returned my surprised look with a wry smile, adjusting the sleeves in the mirror. "Are we back to our roles again?"

I went over to him, brushing off some dust on the shoulders. "Where did you store it?"

"I have my hiding places." He winked and pulled me gently into his arms. "You look lovely."

Aedin's hands ran up and down my back, sending a tingle down my spine. "Thank you." I placed a soft kiss on his mouth, relishing the taste, the clean smell, the feel of him. A stirring of joy sang through my heart. Our hands were washed of the blood we'd spilled to be here, in Lailan, in our home.

I arched a brow at him. "We have our new roles, remember?"

"Ah yes, you do all of the tiresome meetings and *I* just get to sit"—Aedin leaned in to nuzzle my neck, placing a small line of kisses there—"and eat, and drink, and train."

I pushed against him with a giggle. "*Your* perfect life is only possible if we work together."

Aedin leaned his forehead against mine, the playfulness subsiding into solemnity. "You deserve *your* perfect life as well… And we'll work together to achieve it."

I knew his word was good. And despite the obstacles and challenges that would arise, we would build together a life with value and worth.

Arm in arm, we left the room and exited into the halls. The ruined section of the arcade was only just beginning to be rebuilt, and the blue sky shone brightly through the gaps. Beneath my sandals, the worn stones were still cool from the night. Birds flitted from branch to branch in the garden, chirping loudly.

As we turned a corner, two figures bowed in our direction. The perfunctory address—"My lord, my lady"—echoed from their mouths. I raised an eyebrow at Ephraim and Daniel as they straightened in their finery. Daniel still wore his doublet and stone, though, he'd admitted to me privately, he would happily give it to another. I supposed that was what this meeting would decide.

"Is that really necessary?" I asked with a pained expression.

Ephraim gave me a dubious look. "You've retaken the lordship, haven't you?" he challenged.

"I'm your sister"—I gave him a light punch in the arm—"not a title."

Daniel gave Aedin a sympathetic grin. "I wouldn't want anyone else handling this crowd. They're inside the dining room and ready for you." He nodded to both of us with an encouraging gaze.

Aedin squeezed my arm. "Shall we?"

"Yes, I'm ready."

With Ephraim and Daniel trailing behind, we walked the length of the hall and entered the main room. A sea of eyes turned towards us—many wary, judging, and a few encouraging. Celion folded his hands, watching us with a quiet smile, his tunic flickering shades of gold and blue.

Beyond the table of men and women, just behind the glass windows was the great expanse of sea. White caps and sails dotted the horizon, nearly swallowed by the great cerulean abyss. A breeze of salty air wafted through the room along with a peaceful easing in my chest. I did not fear. This was my home.

From the Author

What a journey it has been. In 2021, I dusted off a story I had written over a decade ago and decided to give it another go. What resulted was a whirlwind of writing, editing, and an *enormous* learning curve into the world of self-publishing. Although I'm not planning to quit my "day job" (which I enjoy very much), it's a thrill knowing this story is out in the world and finally *finally* finished. Thank you for lending me your eyes and attention.

To my husband—my partner and love of my life—I am grateful for your continued support as I've endeavored to finish this project. I have always written—first and foremost—for myself and my love of writing, and I will continue to do so (as long as time allows!). You are such a joy and light in my life.

To my friends and family—you know who you are—thank you for your love and support.

To my readers—thank you for spending your precious hours with this book. Although Gwen and Aedin's story has ended, I have a few others stored in my brain that might finally see the light of my computer. Keep in touch via Instagram!

From the bottom of my heart—thank you.

A.G.K.
October 2022

Sign up for my mailing list and check out my website for
writing updates.
www.agkarine.com

Thank you for finishing *Tempest*
Liked what you read? Please leave a review on Amazon,
share on social media, or tell a friend. In this great world filled
with amazing literature, every bit counts and I am grateful for
your time.

This is the part where we stay in touch.

Follow me on Instagram for regular writing updates and all
things #bookstagram
@a.g.karine

www.ingramcontent.com/pod-product-compliance
Lightning Source LLC
Chambersburg PA
CBHW061054210726
48294CB00001B/147